LIFE BEGIN

IOANA PÂRVULESCU

LIFE BEGINS ON FRIDAY

Translated from the Romanian by Alistair Ian Blyth

First published in 2016 by
Istros Books
London, United Kingdom www.istrosbooks.com

First published as *Viaţa începe vineri*, Editura Humanitas, Romania, 2009

Cover design and typesetting: Davor Pukljak, www.frontispis.hr

ISBN: 978-1-908236-29-6

NATIONAL BOOK CENTRE   ROMANIAN CULTURAL INSTITUTE

Istros Books wishes to acknowledge the financial support
granted by the Romanian Cultural Institute

Co-funded by the
Creative Europe Programme
of the European Union

The European Commission support for the production of this publication does not constitute an endorsement of the contents which reflects the views only of the authors, and the Commission cannot be held responsible for any use which may be made of the information contained therein.

CONTENTS

FOREWORD

For a few years before 1900 the days were capacious. The people thrummed like telegraph wires. They were optimistic and believed, as never before and never again thereafter, in the power of science, in progress and the future. This is why the New Year was the most important time for them: the ever-renewed beginning of the *future*.

The texture of the world permitted every mad notion and often the mad notions became reality.

Romania was in Europe, and her capital was now a cosmopolitan city, which was making great efforts to become organized and civilised. In Bucharest, as every period document attests, you *never* had a chance to be bored, night or day.

Sensitive souls were fearful of unknown dangers. A man fended off electric light with his cane. A woman obstinately refused to let her son take her photograph, although she allowed her portrait to be painted. Neuroses were transformed into poetry; pain and opium went hand in hand. Tuberculosis, syphilis and dirt either killed or left deep wounds in body and soul. Evil had not vanished from the world, and ignoring it was not the best method of preparing for the future. There were people who fought it.

The newspapers had become aware of their own power and it was already possible to die for the written word. And already the written word betrayed them. Money was a problem, but not an end in itself, and there were plenty of people prepared to sacrifice all their money for the sake of a beautiful idea. Children were precocious in imitating grown-ups, grown-ups sometimes behaved like children, and curiosity about life was a joy that did not vanish at any age.

Before 1900, people believed that God desired their immortality, in the most palpable sense of the word. Nothing seemed impossible and

7

nor was it. Every utopia was permitted. And *playing with time* was always the most beautiful utopia. Apart from that, people were quite similar in every respect to those who came before them and those who came after them.

For a few years before 1900 the days were capacious and people dreamed of our world.
They dreamed of us.

CHARACTERS

Dan Crețu or Dan Kretzu, 43, a stranger found unconscious in a forest at the edge of Bucharest

The Margulis family:

    Leon, physician, 47

    Agatha, his wife, 42

    Iulia, their daughter, 21

    Jacques (Iacob), their son, 10

Nicu (Niculae Stanciu, Nicușor), 8, courier for *Universul* newspaper, the character who links all the other characters

Costache Boerescu, Chief of Public Security, deputy to the Prefect of Police, a friend of Leon and Agatha Margulis since their youth

General Ion Algiu, former Prefect of Police, friend of Costache Boerescu

Caton Lecca, current Prefect of Police

The Livezeanu family:

    Alexandru, aristocrat, homme à femmes

    Mihai (Mișu), studying Medicine in Paris

    Marioara, divorced, with three children, including twins Anica and Ștefan

    Maria and **Hristea**, parents of the above

Nicu's mother, mentally ill washerwoman

Staff of *Universul* **newspaper:**

    Old man Cercel, the porter

    Neculai Procopiu, 43, the longest-serving newspaperman at *Universul*

    The brothers Mirto: Peppin, translator, proof reader, optimist, endowed with an operatic singing voice, and **Pavel (Păvălucă)**, editor, introvert, pessimist, writing a novel

    The Director, Italian **Luigi Cazzavilan**

Petre, coachman of Inger the pastry maker

Dr Rosenberg, runs the House of Health establishment on Strada
Teilor (Lindens Street)

Mr and **Mrs Movileanu**, lawyer and his wife, resident on Strada Teilor

Epiharia, devout woman who frequents the Icoanei Church, preparing to become a nun

Fane, alias the Ringster, crook

Episodic characters

George Lahovary, newspaperman, director of the French-language
L'Indépendance Roumaine, slain in a duel at the age of 43 by
Nicu Filipescu (former Mayor of Bucharest, who ordered the
demolition of the Sărindar Church)

Metropolitan Ghenadie, involved in a scandal culminating in the
theft of a miracle-working icon

Dimitrie Gerota, physician, friend of Dr Margulis

Vasilica, Iulia's cousin

Marwan, photographer for *Universul*

Elena Turnescu, widow of an eminent surgeon, involved in charitable works

Signor Giuseppe, Italian neighbour of the Margulis family

Otto, ethnic German from Transylvania who has come to the capital
to work as a church painter

The wounded **young aristocrat** (Rareş-Ochiu-Zănoagă)

Coachmen: **Yevdoshka** (Russian Old Believer), **Budacu** and **Ilie** (in
the employ of the Police)

Toader, servant of the Livezeanu family

Margareta, one of Alexandru Livezeanu's mistresses

Pet animals

Liza, Costache's old dog, **Lord**, General Algiu's Borzoi hound,
Fira the cow, a fridge magnet, **Speckle**, Nicu's pigeon

Unconventional characters

Bucharest, Capital of Romania
Time

For what you want is that life, and this,
and another – you want them all.
MIGUEL DE UNAMUNO, July 1906

AN EVENTFUL DAY

1.

I like to read in the carriage. Mama takes me to task; Papa, who never forgets, not even *en famille*, that he is Dr Leon Margulis, primary physician with a surgery behind the National Theatre, says that I will ruin my eyes and give birth to near-sighted children. But I am obstinate and still bring a book with me. Back in their day they probably had the time to read and do lots of other things, but we youngsters have to dole out our hours with care. I could hardly wait to find out what Becky would get up to next in *Vanity Fair*. Although truth to tell, I think that I am more like that silly Amelia, and I shall end up loving some rascal all my life. Today I had no luck with my reading: firstly, because my hands were frozen; and then, no sooner did we climb into the carriage than Mama and Papa, chopping the subject as finely as our cook does the parsley, began to dissect the case of the unidentified man whom Petre found lying in the snow this morning, in a field near the Băneasa woods and lakes. He was taken to the Prefecture of Police and placed under arrest. Mama, who is up to date on absolutely everything, says he is a fugitive from the madhouse and that he must have been driven insane by too much learning. And here she gave me a minatory look: 'It is high time that Iulia decided on a decent man to marry.'

Papa examined the stranger at the request of Costache, our friend from the Police, and said that he was not a vagrant, despite his wearing unbelievably odd clothes. Perhaps he is a clown from the circus. He is otherwise clean and has no "physiological" flaws apart from the fact that he does sometimes talk in a garbled way. But if he is a madman, then he is a cultivated madman; he "couches his words nicely". But when Papa asked him whether he had tuberculosis, the man gave him a scornful look, as if infuriated, and answered cuttingly: 'You're a two-bit actor!' Papa replied, as gravely as he does whatever the situation: 'Sir, if you please, I am not an actor, but a physician!' He added that his lungs sounded a little congested, that he was very pale, but that he could not find any serious illness. The man calmed down and said that he would like to smoke. Papa, who is against the habit, nonetheless brought him some fine tobacco and rolling papers from Mr Costache's desk, but said that the man under arrest, after giving him a savage glance, quite simply turned his back on him. He is ill bred! They retained his valise for examination, and a silver box, like a safe, which indicates that he might be a money forger, but they released him after keeping him under arrest for only an hour, following a brief interrogation by Mr Costache. On finding himself free, he straightaway made himself scarce. But the best coachman in the police force was assigned to follow him unobtrusively.

'How old is he?' asked mother, her favourite question.

'He declares himself forty-three. Well, that would mean he was four years younger than me, but I say he's lying. I reckon he is no older than thirty or thirty-five. He says that he is a journalist and that he was born here. Dan Kretzu. What surprised me was that he was completely shaven. You see this only with actors who play the rôles of women. Hmm!' And here Papa stroked the thin blond tuft of his beard, as wispy as maize silk, the cause of a lifetime's suffering.

'We shall find out more tomorrow, at dinner, because I have invited Mr Costache.'

Papa noticed that my face was flushed and immediately put his hand to my forehead to see whether I had a temperature. As far as he is concerned, all things have solid, bodily causes. He will not hear of the soul. Although Mama continued to interrogate him for a while, I preferred to take off one glove, now that my hands had warmed up, and to return to Becky. What I like about her is that exactly like me she can speak French and English. What I do not like about her is that exactly like me she has green eyes. I would have liked hazel eyes, the same as Jacques, and blond hair, the same as Becky, but it would seem the factory did not have that model in stock twenty-one years ago, and so I must content myself with black hair. How is it that from the same parents, both with hazel eyes, one child can turn out the same as them, while the other has green or blue eyes? I wish to finish the book by New Year, and so I shall try to write in my diary more seldom. There are still twelve days and a few hours to go.

2.

The people of Bucharest were having a good day. It had snowed, there were still twelve days till the end of the year, and twelve hours till the end of the day. The whiteness, which stretched from one end of the city to the other, from the Cotroceni Palace to the Obor district, and from the Şerban Vodă Cemetery to the flower-beds on the Chaussée, and then onward, into the horizon, was melting in the afternoon sun. The icicles looked as if they were coated in oil and here and there were beginning to drip onto the heads of the passers-by. The streets were quite busy, as they always were on the days before Christmas. Looking up, lest he get wet, Nicu fell head first into the snow, and was as annoyed as when he woke up with his face pressed to the sheet.

'Looks like you've taken another tumble, young man!' said the boy loudly, shaking off his red commissary's cap. 'I've told you *time after time* to look where you step,' he grumbled in his small voice, but with the tone of a bad-tempered old man. Since the year before, when he started to attend school, that pedantic tone had stuck to his tongue and he could not rid himself of it. But he had been in the habit of talking to himself for as long as he could remember, because to his great misfortune and unlike other children, he had no siblings. He would have been happy to have even a sister, at a pinch.

He dusted the snow off his coat, cast a glance of vexation at the patch of ice on which he had slipped, and at a trot arrived under the clock with the mechanical soldier above the door of *L'Indépnedance Roumaine* newspaper offices. At twelve on the dot, the chimes began to sound. Nicu always tried to be in time to see the soldier. It was not easy, because he had to tell the time by the sun and the length of the shadows. This time the lad's attention was caught by something else. On the ground, right in front of him, was a splendid icicle, more than a metre long, perfect for a sword. He picked it up and stroked its slightly rippled surface, oblivious to the chill of the ice. Holding it in both hands, he lowered it to his hip, raised it, still in a two-handed grip, and with a roar made a swordsman's lunge at an unseen enemy. Unfortunately, the icicle, probably inured to the greater peace and quiet at the edge of the roof, struck where it ought not to: to a man in military uniform, holding a silver-handled cane; a gentleman of middling height who was just emerging through the door beneath the clock. He was the Prefect of Police's right-hand man: the Chief of Public Security, Costache

Boerescu, a man always in a hurry, his short legs rapidly scything the air. In that period he visited the Frenchmen's newspaper two or three times a day, ever since the director, Mr Lahovary, had been slain in a duel by "that pig-headed Filipescu," the director of the *Epoca* newspaper. And so the policeman was in the mood for anything but a duel, irritated as he was by the investigation, which was going nowhere, and by voices from the press, who were persecuting him ever more sorely. He could no longer stand newspapermen: when he did something good, they ignored him, but when he failed to solve some matter swiftly enough, they jumped on him and blackened his name using his own words, but truncating and turning them upside down. Whenever he had occasion and only men were present, he would cool off by calling the press a "painted whore." Otherwise, he lived alone, and the brothel at Stone Cross had special reduced rates for him, should he so desire. He had visited the establishment both as a policeman and as a customer.

The cursed child ran off before the policeman could grab him by the ear. He made a suicidal dash across the road, dodging the carriages and sleighs, in the direction of Sărindar, not before being cursed by a number of coachmen heading in a column towards the Capșa restaurant, then by those on the other side, on their way towards the Dâmbovița River; one after the other, they had to pull on their reins, lest they crash into each other. The lad looked behind him at the same instant that the copper waved his stick at him threateningly. Nicu then put the incident out of his mind and headed towards the Prefecture, a few minutes' walk away.

'You were almost done for there, young man. Mr Costache won't forget you, he never forgets anything, and he's as cunning as a snake, he is. You've been getting into nothing but scrapes today,' said the lad, addressing a large snow-laden bush that grew slantwise in a shady spot next to a wall. Some sparrows were hopping with abrupt, bullet-like movements from one branch to another, then lingering a little, touching the thick whiteness of the snow with their plump bellies, and scattering the flakes, before moving to another storey of the bush, as if it were a house. Nicu wondered why they moved around so much, since they did not seem to be following or looking for anything, unlike him. He had a precise goal, which loomed tall in front of him: the entrance of *Universul*, Bucharest's most read newspaper. Granted, the men from *Adevĕrul* said otherwise, but they said everything otherwise. He stepped forward, having swiftly shaken all the sparrows off the bush.

He entered by the door on the left. The doorman shook his hand as if he was a grown-up. Old man Cercel told him that he would have to wait: the parcels had not yet been brought from the "distribution bee-oo-row." Nicu sat down in his usual place. He was most satisfied. Conversations with old man Cercel were always instructive, because the doorman read the paper every day and kept him up to date with the news. Nicu asked him whether he had decided to play the big New Year's lottery; the jackpot was ten thousand lei. Six numbers had to be chosen, and the lad had asked to try his luck, without any claim on the prize (although the money would not have gone amiss), just so that he could lend a helping hand. Nicu knew that as far as he was concerned, his choice was nine and eight, because next year would be 1898, and the doorman would choose the remaining numbers, except that he would make his mind up one day, only to change it the next. Old man Cercel replied yet again that it was no joking matter and he would have to think carefully. From today's paper he had a news item even better than the one about Jack the Ripper, who had thitherto reigned supreme over the headlines.

The doorman picked up *Universul*, held it rather a long way from his eyes, and read slowly, syllabically: "Sundry items. From Bor-del-... Bor-der-and... Bor-der-land magazine. The planet Mars and the Martians." 'Hear that?' And then he read on, slipping in his own comments, as he always did: "The Martians do not eat meat, but use mam-moths as beasts of burden. Their horses are no larger than our ponies." As large as our ponies – what ponies? "Their oxen are smaller – in other words, we have larger oxen, and so where we are, if you're an ox, you're a big ox – and have just one horn. The Martians have very pen-et-rat-ive eyesight. They have learned how to fly, but only for short distances. They walk on water with the same ease as they do on land. War has been ab-ol-ished on Mars. The Government is the-o-crat-ic. They have twelve states. They have no private property." Then I'm not going to Mars. This is my country here, my private property, my house, my garden, my wife, my pigeons, and my plum trees,' said the doorman, folding up the newspaper thus ending all discussion, having been fully enlightened as to the Martians.'

Nicu did not agree. He was something of a Liberal. He knew very well that the Martians could fly and walk on water and that they rode mammoths, as he had seen the drawings in *Universul Ilustrat*. And so in that respect, the same as in many others, he could not share Cercel's opinion, although the old man's broad face and splayed nose, beneath which grew a shaving brush of a moustache, demanded respect.

Nicu said diplomatically: 'I for one would go, if it were possible! I'd go to have a look and if it wasn't any good, I'd come back straight away.'

'For the time being, run and deliver these papers!'

Probably annoyed at having been contradicted, the doorman rather brusquely took the newspapers from the hand of the man who signed himself Peppin Mirto. Mirto was employed as a translator and proof reader, and was recently given the responsibility of dispatching the Gazette to important clients, if it included important articles: Mayor Robescu; Petre Grădișteanu, the director of the National Theatre; the Royal Palace; Caton Lecca, the Prefect of Police; and the directors of the other newspapers, even those with which *Universul* was at war. Nicu ran errands for the paper, earning five lei a month, paid on the first of each month, plus tips, in addition to his usual wage as a commissary. He had to deliver parcels containing all kinds of small items, which were sold from the newspaper premises. The items were kept in untidy heaps in the administrative office downstairs and in the director's office upstairs, since the director himself was more likely to be found at home or at his club than on newspaper premises. Nicu worked for two hours a day at most, straight after school. He clandestinely hitched rides on the back of carriages and sometimes even the horse-drawn tram, when there was a lot of traffic and he could pass unnoticed. But it was rare that he had such luck.

'How are you, laddie?' asked Pepin Mirto, in his sonorous, operatic voice, and Nicu doffed his cap by way of greeting. He was about to tell him about his plans to go to Mars, but the man quite simply turned his back on him, shouting a 'Be on your way now!' that boomed as far as the courtyard. Why did people ask you questions if they did not wait for the answer? True, here at *Universul* you saw only men who were in twice as much of a hurry as Nicu's other acquaintances. They were like Martians, the lot of them, but without their good qualities! As he was leaving with the parcel tied up with string, he almost collided with a young man who had slipped lizard-like through the door and was asking old man Cercel how he could place a small ad. He was agitated and kept knocking his gloved hands together, jerking his head.

'Good day, young gentleman,' said the doorman, still in the same voice as when he had been spelling out the words in the newspaper.

'Good day, young gentleman,' Nicu seconded, but without doffing his cap this time.

Too agitated to reply to these greetings, the young man got straight to the point: 'Where can I place a small ad? A wallet has been lost and the owner...'

'With money in it?' the boy and the doorman both asked at the same time.

'Not, not with any money...'

'Any jewels?' asked Nicu, just as the doorman was asking: 'Any documents?'

'No, with a... with something else. And my owner, its owner I mean, is offering a handsome reward. We live not far away from the Icoanei Church, on Strada Teilor, the new houses, which they were working on all summer.'

And here he knocked his fists together once more.

'The second door on the right where it says: *Announcements*. This way, please.'

As the nervous young man with his lizard-like movements was walking away with the doorman, Nicu set off to his first address, the premises of the rival paper on Strada Sărindar, scanning the snow in front of him, just in case. He now had a goal to make him forget the tedium of his daily duties and the water dripping from the eaves. He was searching for a wallet in which there might be a diamond ring or maybe a ruby tiepin, like the one owned by Jacques' father, Dr Margulis. But if the man-lizard had been telling the truth, which was not at all certain, then there were no jewels. All of a sudden he had a bright idea: it must contain a lottery ticket, the very one that was going to win!

'That's it!' Nicu said to himself, rather proudly. He had rejoiced when the snow arrived, but now it annoyed him; a good job that it had started to melt. His grandmother, who believed in saints, like all women, had told him that there was a saint to allay every misfortune. He hoped that there was a saint of lost objects too, particularly those lost by other people.

'Let us hope, young man, that you will lay your hands on that *handsome reward*.'

*

After he had completed his final errand, Nicu ran home to change out of his red work-cap and put on his free-time cap; for when he wore the red one, people stopped him on the street and sent him off on errands all over the place. From somewhere near the neighbours' old walnut tree, a crow croaked bitterly a few times. Since there was nobody at home (who knows where his mother might be?), he was able to make his way to Strada Teilor, the place where his *investigation* must surely commence. It was worse than looking for a needle in a haystack, but he did not have anything better to do, as it was the Christmas holidays. In any case, school had been suspended for a month because of an outbreak of typhus, and so he had been quite well off from that point of view. Lessons had not recommenced until the eighth of December. Nicu had every faith in his luck, despite, or rather precisely because God had already punished him with a feeble-mined mother and no siblings, not even a sister, and so He owed him for the rest of his life. Prudently, he made the sign of the cross, as he always did when he thought he was speaking too familiarly about the Lord in Heaven, but it was a tiny one, more like he was scratching himself.

The boy knew the streets of Bucharest well and a large number of their residents knew Nicu well. He had even made friends with some of them, such as the Margulis family on Strada Fântânei. He was an errand boy on whom you could rely, very useful for urgent business that required discretion. Theirs was a dependable firm, his boss used to say, taking upon himself the merits of the five lads in his employ, who were individually responsible for any mistakes. He looked up and by the Central Girls School he saw a police carriage, as red as the cherries in the bottle from which his mother tippled. He once more fixed his eyes on the snow, which after melting in the afternoon, was now beginning to form a crust, like the skin on boiled milk. How was it that ice and the hot skin of boiled milk looked the same if you held them in your hand, and that both turned your skin red? Nicu walked with long strides and kept his eyes on the ground. It was then that he clapped eyes on the most unusual pair of footwear he had ever seen in the eight long (and hard) years since he had come into this world. They did not look like galoshes or overshoes or even the latest styles advertised in *Universul*. They were neither officers' boots nor peasants' bast shoes. There was not even a word for them; they were strange thingies, the likes of which had never been seen.

*

'They were strange little thingies, the likes of which you've never seen, I don't even know what to call them, brother dear, neither you nor I have ever seen the like,' recounted Nicu that evening, in Strada Fântânei.

He was dead tired, having been on his feet the whole day, walking through the snow; the driver had not let him board the horse-drawn tram without paying for a ticket, and he had not wanted to waste the fortune in his pocket: ten pennies from tips alone. But his account of how he bumped into the stranger's legs reinvigorated him. He felt that all of a sudden he had become an important person in the world. It was not every day that you saw wonderful things on the streets of Bucharest.

'What do you mean?' asked Jacques, overjoyed. For Jacques, the errand boy's tales, mostly embellished and exaggerated as they were, were the water of life. Nicu's homecoming had got him out of bed. 'What do you mean, thingies, I don't understand, explain!'

Jacques sat up straight in the deep armchair that all but enveloped him.

'Just listen,' answered Nicu, enveloped in the armchair alongside and twisting his head over the velvet armrest, 'just listen, you'll never believe it. They were coloured. Coloured!'

'Colou-r-r-ed?' marvelled Jacques, who rolled his r's like a Frenchman. Therre's no such thing. I've never seen footwear that wasn't black, or brown, or white, in summer.'

'And they didn't have buttons, or laces, or hooks. It was like they were glued to his feet. I look up and I see ugly black trousers, without any stripes, and then an ordinary overcoat, like a cast-off, like a second-hand bargain, it didn't fit in with the rest. And, ah, yes, just listen, for you'll never believe it: he was bare-headed!'

'Weren't you afrraid? I would have run away, I mean...' said the host and blushed slightly.

Nicu hastened to continue, as if he hadn't heard.

'Well, no, but his face was quite nice, like... like your sister's there,' said Nicu, pointing to above the sofa, where there was a small pastel portrait. 'I don't know why, but it bowled me over. I'll never forget it as long as I live. Whether he was an angel, whether he was a devil, I liked him a lot; I'll have you know. May you have a brother like him!'

Although Jacques was accustomed to the way Nicu spoke when he was excited – Nicu was in the habit of addressing himself in the second person – he thought that perhaps here he was referring to him, because he too wanted a brother. 'He asked me.'

At that moment the "quite nice" face from the portrait above the sofa looked in through the half-open door. The face was rosier in the cheeks than the one in the framed picture, however. Iulia Margulis, wearing a green velvet dress entered, carrying two plates, two silver knives and two red apples. The doctor had demanded that the children eat at least one piece of fruit a day, and in the cellar there was a shelf full of apples, placed a finger's width from each other lest one spread rot to the others.

'Wait, I want to hear it too! What did the stranger ask you?'

'Have you met him?' marvelled Nicu.

His eyebrows were peaked like the outline of a roof, rather than finely arching, like the Margulis siblings', and that made him look permanently surprised or perplexed.

'He said... erm... he said to me: "Just a moment, lad, please. I'm quite cold and I'm afraid to go home." 'Why?' says I. 'I think somebody's living there,' says he. 'I need a place to sleep. Any idea where?' That's what he said, I remember it very well: 'Any idea where?'

'You should have invited him here!'

'No, no, no, how could I do that? Nor could I have invited him to my place, because I didn't even know when my mother would be coming home. When she's angry, she scares everybody, although she doesn't do anybody any harm. Since we were near the Icoanei Church, I said to him, the same as Granny would have said: Go inside, bow to the miracle-working icon of the Mother of God, the one cased in silver, and you'll be granted a miracle. *I've already been granted one*, he said, mockingly. And instead of making the sign of the cross, he asked me whether I had a cigarette. 'I haven't taken up smoking yet,' says I. 'Then don't start!' says he.'

Nicu rose from the soft depths of the armchair, thrust his hand in his trouser pocket, and produced an object.

'And he gave you this, young man. Look at this!'

It was a toy that almost fit in the palm of his hand, a soft, snow-white cow with pink ears and a black patch over one eye, like a pirate. The cow's four legs were folded under it, like four hands neatly resting in a lap. Jacques took the object with infinite care, as if it might break, he gazed at it gravely and then solemnly handed it to his sister.

'Can I examine it?' asked Iulia. And without waiting for an answer, she lifted one of the legs. When she released it, the leg snapped back in place alongside the other three. The young lady did the same with the other legs, but all four quickly snapped back.

'Oh, Lord, it is almost alive!' marvelled Jacques, his eyes bulging.

'Alive or not, it's got no udder, I've looked,' mumbled the owner of the animal. 'Who's so stupid as to make a cow without an udder? I think the legs have got a spring or something. I've seen things like this among the Christmas toys in the newspaper. I'll show you, I've got the issue at home, I asked old man Cercel for one, and because it had toys in it, he gave me it.' Nicu stretched out his hand for his cow, retrieved it, and hid it rather abruptly in the depths of his pocket.

'Did the strranger seem sane to you?'

'Jacques means to say: was he in his right mind?'

'Oh, yes.' Nicu lowered his voice. 'Ever since my mother... ever since they kept her *there*, I can tell one of them from a mile off.... The doctor says that it's not right to call them madmen, they're just ill. Anyways, that gentleman was sound in the head, just like you or me. I waited till he went inside the church. When I looked behind me, the police carriage was slowly approaching, at a walk, I recognized it by the colour: like rotten cherries. It stopped a little way away, by the bell tower, and some guard dogs started barking at it. The cops were on his trail, but I don't know whether he realized... You don't like the cops. I wanted to turn back and tell him, but I didn't have time to spare, I was in a hurry, because I had... a job to do.'

'I shall leave you now, because the cook is waiting for me, we have to confer about dinner tomorrow, when Mr Costache will be coming as our guest,' said Iulia, casting Nicu a meaningful glance.

To reassure her, he looked at her serenely and with a smile of perfect innocence. The young woman swiftly left the room, but not before arranging the logs burning in the fireplace with two or three deft jabs of the poker. Nicu congratulated himself on not having delayed his visit to Jacques, as he had been tempted to do, knowing that the door was always open to him. And he decided not to pay a visit to Strada Fântânei the following evening, lest he come face to face with the policeman: it was too soon after the unfortunate accident... the duelling incident. But he said not a word about what had happened with the ice rapier or about the wallet: they were secrets. He could not tell Jacques everything, although he considered him his best friend, because he obeyed strict rules in life, rules laid down by the doctor, ever since Nicu had been left without a father and with a grandmother for a mother, and he could allow himself some liberties. He had only managed to examine an insignificant portion of Strada Teilor, alongside the new houses, before darkness fell. He kept telling himself that he and he alone would be the finger and that the handsome reward surely to be had from that lizard of a young man would crown his efforts.

3.

Four windows of the *Universul* offices were still lit. The newspaper-men did not have a fixed schedule, they came at will, depending on how much work they had on any given day, but as for leaving, they left only after they had completed their duties. On the first floor, the room farthest to the left, as you looked from the street at the baroque façade of the building, or to the right, as you climbed the stairs and looked towards Sărindar, was the office of Pavel – Peppin Mirto's brother – and Neculai Procopiu, the newspaper's most faithful editor: he had been there for thirteen years, that is, from the very beginning. People treated him as they might a director. The newspaper had steadily increased in importance and had been the first to have a morning edition, and so now it was the most widely read. In the beginning it had been all advertisements, which was how it had accumulated capital, but now it had a little of everything. It did not dabble much in politics; at the most, it published the bare facts. They had tried to do two editions, a *Morning Courier* and an *Evening Courier*, but it had not lasted long, because of distribution problems: the newspapers arrived at the same time, and the news items repeated each other. Procopiu and Pavel Mirto had taken responsibility for the issue and so the last of the other staff had left. It was they who liaised with the printing press, located in the same building and extending like a huge train carriage to the bottom of the yard.

A knock caused both to lift their heads simultaneously. Marwan the photographer entered. It was an event: you did not often see photo-graphs at *Universul*. There were daily illustrations, but of the drawn variety.

'What have you brought us?' Procopiu asked him directly and stood up to shake the photographer's hand.

'Nothing yet, but I photographed some scenes on the street such as you will never have seen before, on my honour. I waited for hours in the snow, camera at the ready, stalking my prey. And yesterday, I climbed out of the window above the entrance to the National Theatre, I think the roof must be at least fifteen metres high, taking my camera with me, to do a panorama. A good job I don't get dizzy, not so much for my sake as much as for the camera's sake, because it's an expensive model. I'll bring you the clichés, if you're interested, I'll give you them for the New Year issue, but for six lei apiece instead of four, because they're quality goods,' said Marwan, trying his luck.

He had a reputation as a bit of a skinflint.

'Mind you don't break them, like last time,' he added with justified sorrow, causing the two other men to glance sideways, one at the wall calendar with lady skaters from Canada, the other at the papers on the desk.

It was an embarrassing memory. Marwan had brought them a glass cliché showing the trial of Dr Bastaki, one of a kind, the printer had dropped it and the glass had cracked in two. They had had to summon one of the three artists from home, a specialist in portraits–none other than Marwan's rival–interrupting him as he was enjoying a late evening collation with some guests. The artist had joined the two fragments of glass and drawn the image from scratch: the courtroom, with Miss Elena Gorjan in the foreground, wearing a little hat with a feather atop her head, with her nose which, due to the artist's haste, came out a little too long and drooping, and with the face of a splendidly moustachioed guard behind her, the artist's own addition. He had not had time to draw the woman's lover, Dr Bastaki, who was a paterfamilias, or Mr Horia Rosetti, one of the lawyers for the defence, although they could be glimpsed in the cliché, but he had drawn Miss Gorjan previously, her prudish countenance having appeared in the newspaper once before. Marwan had lost his temper and left closing the door very firmly behind him: very firmly indeed. And so now the two editors were eager to placate him.

Marwan sat down in front of Pavel, on the chair with a velvet cushion reserved for important visitors. Pavel took off his round spectacles, which tired his eyes, offered him a cheroot and took one for himself. Mr Procopiu discreetly opened the window a crack, letting in a blast of cold air.

'What will we be reading in tomorrow's newspaper?' asked Marwen, with genuine interest in everything to do with the future.

He had become a photographer from a desire to have at least one foot in the door of the new times.

Unlike his brother, Peppin, who spoke in a loud, melodious voice – a fact appreciated by the director, Signor Luigi, an Italian who missed the beautiful voices of his native land – Pavel Mirto smoked heavily and spoke very softly, so that you had to prick up your ears to understand what he was saying.

'What will we be reading?' he whispered. 'The usual, a small fire on Calea Victoriei, in the chimney of the house of a certain Ciuflea.'

'What?'

'Ciuflea. Ciu-flea. It was quickly extinguished by the firemen from the station on Strada Cometei. Then a lost wallet, whose contents seem to be very, very valuable, because the reward is three times bigger than usual – I don't know what it might be, it's an unusually closely kept secret – then two fraudsters who have been swindling the gullible, like the notorious Andronic used to do, in other words, he takes all their money to multiply them in a 'machine'... and what else... a Turkish vessel sunk in the Black Sea. Ah, yes, that was the most important thing: it would seem that the Senate is finally going to propose a law against duelling.'

'I heard that the Princess sent a cable to Lahovary's mother, express-ing her condolences.'

'No,' editor-in-chief Procopiu corrected him, 'the mother of the deceased, Mrs Olympia Lahovary, is in Nice and the news was not sent to her immediately, the other son went there to break it to her gently, because she has a weak heart. Her Highness Princess Maria sent an immediate message to Mrs Lahovary, to the widow, as it were...'

And the editor sighed, for the sake of form: he was too much of a veteran newspaperman to be easily moved any more. Nevertheless, the slaying in a duel of a fellow newspaperman, one of Bucharest's best journalists, George Lahovary, whom he had seen not long before, had rocked the capital. What was more, it had come after the campaign that Lahovary's newspaper *L'Indépendance Roumaine* had waged all year against the present Constitution and after Lahovary had been attacked from every side. It certainly made you think... A good job that *Universul* was not political.

'Ah, and another thing,' continued Pavel Mirto in a barely audible voice, running his hand over his thick hair, 'a curiosity, a man who says that he is forty-three, but looks much younger, he doesn't even have a beard, this man was found half-dead in a field, he was rescued by Petre, the Inger coachman.

'Which Inger, the confectioner from Strada Carol?'

'Exactly,' and here Pavel cleared his throat, before reaching for his cup of coffee. 'It's not known what the stranger is up to; the police are intrigued. He has a locked case with him, or something of the sort, and nobody can be found to vouch for him.'

Marwan was hard of hearing and did not make much of it, but he did understand that it was a trifle, like a bearded woman or some other circus act.

They moved on to a fashionable subject: Roentgen's rays and how a surgeon from Germany had been able to see the stone in a man's gall bladder and in another man's liver, and how he had operated on the patients. 'To see a man on the inside is worthy of the front page.' Mr Procopiu had written an article on Roentgen's discovery, titling it 'The Miracle-working Ray.' He had been happy to be able to write about his favourite subject: science. Apparently, one November day, exactly two years ago, the diligent researcher had seen in his rather dark laboratory a greenish ray that seemed to be coming from some cardboard covered with barium. He gazed in wonder before extinguishing the cathode tube, whereupon the light from the cardboard also vanished. He turned on the tube and placed his hand, probably by accident, between the piece of cardboard and the cathode tube. On the cardboard appeared some delicate and very real bones. His own hand, as if photographed on the inside! The upheaval he felt in his soul cannot be imagined! And so Mr Roentgen was the first mortal in the universe to see himself on the inside without so much as scratching his skin.

On learning this, his colleague Pavel, who was artistic rather than scientific by bent, declared that hypnotism was as good as proven, since it was probably also transmitted by an invisible ray. And the man who signed himself Marwen told how the director himself, Signor Luigi Cazzavillan, had recounted a few days previously, when he met him at the club, that in Rome a venerable lady had been sitting in the salon when all of a sudden she had clearly seen her husband, who was away in Milan, appear in the doorway and call her by name, before vanishing as if in a puff of smoke. The lady had fainted and, as a cable later revealed, her husband had died suddenly in Milan that very moment. Pavel recounted in a whisper a matter that was all the rage, especially among the servants, concerning a house maid who had told her master about how she dreamed that a wounded Turk had buried some gold in the roots of a gooseberry tree in his yard, and when the man dug there, sure enough, he found the gold. The girl had gone back home with a dowry, she never had to work again, and her master became a rich man and had built himself a palatial home in a leafy suburb. And then there was the startling case in the Procopiu family: a sister who at the age of thirteen dreamed she married a miller and her best friend drowned in a mill race, and now she was Mrs Miller, and her friend had indeed drowned, but in the waters of a lake. What was even stranger was that Mr Miller was an engineer. Neculai Procopiu sighed with envy; his brother-in-law's profession had been his own dream.

'You would say that all the things that have been and will be are now too, in the present,' said Pavel softly.

Having heard but half of the phrase 'all the things that will be,' the photographer took his leave. No sooner had he left than to the surprise of the two editors there was another knock on the door, firm and polite, which was not like the knock of the lad from the printing press. They both lifted their eyes once again. Mr Costache Boerescu, the Chief of Public Security, entered. He did not like to shake hands or to sit around and chat, and so when he did so they knew he had an ulterior motive. This time he asked the two men in a hectoring voice to introduce a short announcement in the morning paper, right that instant, while maintaining the utmost discretion as to his identity. Pavel Mirto stood up and took the piece of paper down to the printing press.

'Ah, lest I forget, is your number two-nine-seven?' he asked Procopiu as he was leaving.

'The telephone number? 297, yes, but in the evening there is nobody to answer it. Didn't the girl at the switchboard tell you?'

An hour later, the proofs arrived, for a last quick look before the edition went to press. Mr Procopiu read the headlines in capital letters, and the beginnings of the news items, and the most important announcements: *PLANNED LAW AGAINST DUELLING. OTTOMAN BRIG WRECKED in the Black Sea. Events from the capital. A confidence trick à la Andronic... Legal news. Births and deaths. Deeply moved by the tragedy... H.R.H. Princess Maria. Wedding banns. FROM ITALY. FROM LONDON. ... Opera. Mrs Olympia Mărculescu and Mr... in* RIGOLETTO. 'A chamois leather wallet has been lost in the Teilor-Clemenței area. Please contact...' 'A white cat has been lost. Left hind leg amputated...' 'The man under arrest found yesterday unconscious and half-frozen near the Băneasa estate (by the lakes) has declared that his name is Dan I. Kretzu, he is a journalist and not a malefactor...' Neculai Procopiu's eyes fell on Costache's announcement, crammed rather incongruously between the advertisements for the Inger Confectionary Shop and the Romania Weaving Loom. He noticed that the brand name 'Romania' lacked quotation marks and added them with an indelible pencil, wetting the point on his tongue, in order to make it clear that it was not a loom that wove the beloved homeland, although that would not come amiss, every now and then. Because of the indelible pencil, the editor-in-chief's tongue was permanently purple. He carefully read the Police announcement: 'A young man who seems to be of good family, around twenty-two years of age, has been found shot and is in a serious condition in the Health Establishment of Dr Rosenberg. Anybody with information about this person or who has information about the circumstances of his wounding should contact the Prefecture of Police, in Calea Victoriei, No. 25.'

All these items would be perused at leisure and with thoroughness by those citizens of Bucharest who subscribed to *Universul* on the following day, 20 December 1897, according to the Julian calendar. The subscribers included Dr Margulis, who would read the paper before setting off to his surgery on Strada Sfântul Ionică, behind the National Theatre. And old man Cercel, who would then convey its contents, censored and commentated upon, to young Nicu. And Costache, over his second cup of coffee, which he always drank at work, and his boss, Prefect of Police Caton Lecca, sitting at the table at home, coddled by his large-boned wife. And Iulia Margulis, who was looking for ideas for Christmas presents. And Luigi Cazzavillan, the newspaper's director, who, together with the diplomats from the Italian Legation, had already celebrated New Year. And there were many others, countless others, whose names and occupations do not concern us here.

The last lit window on the first floor of *Universul*, the farthest to the left as you look from the street, was plunged into darkness at midnight. Mr Procopiu set off home on foot. He was rather depressed, perhaps because they had been talking about so many unusual things. And so he hastened his steps and, when he heard a muffled sound behind him, he almost broke into a run. Feeling a hand on his shoulder, he let out a cry.

4.

Perhaps all that was and will be is now, in the present. Perhaps what was is what once more will be. Before you ask me any questions, try to get used to my voice, the voice of a man sundered from a world he had come to know quite well, and plunged into an unknown and unintelligible world. Perhaps without knowing it, we live in this endless moment, in many worlds at once. Perhaps the voice that speaks to you now and which thrashes among the voices here like a fish in a fisherman's net – this voice that finds itself in the city and the country of its birth, more alone than the voice of any man imprisoned in a foreign land – speaks even now with beings which you have no way of seeing. Or perhaps I, the source of the voice, have already been extinguished, like the sun that has just now set, but you still hear me, there, in your world, where the sun is at its zenith, there in your warm room, or outside, in a green park, on a bench. Or perhaps precisely when you cannot hear me, when you are sleeping a dreamless sleep or when you are yelling at each other like madmen, or when you are bored to death, desperate for the time to pass, perhaps this will be when the essential things will take place here. Or perhaps I will never reach you, although that would not sadden me.

But look how I finally raise my voice to the heavens, and I pray for both you, those afar, and for myself, I pray here, to this silver icon, within whose casing can be seen with the naked eye the head of a woman and the smaller head of a child: I pray for your health, your welfare, and that you not be punished, as I am. I pray that you have an old age as beautiful and soothing as roses. I pray that, if you hear a man's voice, you will understand. I pray out loud: 'Thou, the Relentless, spare us, spare me, release me from this net in which I am tangled, that I might find a tear in the net and swim into the open sea.' I pray: 'Merciful one, have mercy.' One day, I am sure, I will come to you somehow and you will hear me again. I don't know why I am here, in a church, in front of an icon. I don't know why I am shut up here, in the frozen silver of a world that I did not wish for, just as you, whatever you might say, are from birth shut up as if in a prison, as if in a butterfly net or as if in a birdcage, in a world that you did not wish for, did not know, and have no way of controlling. You thrash around in vain. We are prisoners, condemned, each in his own world, each in his own solitude. Why can you not see me? I am fettered in the frozen silver of the icon of a world that perhaps no longer is. I try to see you there, from the picture frame of my present day, and if you fall silent for an instant, like the waters deep in a well, perhaps you will hear what I say to myself, because I speak for myself and only for myself. I am alone: I who do and I who judge. I am the one who speaks, I the one who is silent and listens: It is always different than we think, dear Dan. You have been cast from life to life.

When I opened my eyes, I saw wide blue sky and many trees clad in hoarfrost. Hundreds of pinpoints took flight at each gust of wind. The air clasped me. I was lying on my back. With a city-dweller's wonderment, I immersed my gaze in the sky. All of a sudden I heard a sound like water flowing from a tap. It came from nearby, to my right. I turned my head without raising it and I could not believe what I saw. There was no doubt about it: next to me a horse had released a gushing torrent of urine. Steam wafted around the jet. It seemed unending, and a round hollow had formed in the snow. The horse was harnessed to a sleigh laden with blocks of ice and a few logs.

There was complete silence, a petrified silence. All around was whiteness, sun, a silence such as I had never heard before, because even silence is audible. The beast thrust its muzzle into the bag hanging from its neck and began to chomp. Its tail was tied in a huge glossy knot.

'On your feet, lad, or else nightfall will catch ub with you here in the snow. Who can have left you here to berish, where there's not another berson as far as the eye can see?'

He was a swarthy man, with huge hands, in which he was holding an axe. I took fright. The valise was a few feet away and I struggled to get up, to go to it. I tottered. My legs were frozen.

'Can't you bick yourself ub? Some friends you've got, leaving you here bissed, to freeze in the snow, dressed like a scarecrow and without so much as a cab on your head.'

When you understand nothing, all you can do is keep silent. He was talking, but it was as if his mouth were full. The man tossed the axe into the sleigh, next to a pick and shovel. He untied the horse's nosebag and stretched out a horny red hand to me. Half his index finger was missing and it ended in a knot, like the neck of a pouch pinched with a drawstring.

'Jumb ub, I'll take you back to town and you'll bay me two lei and a cub of wine. Let's fetch that box of yours... Bull this sheebskin over your shoulders. Can you stand ub? I've been out cutting logs. I cut some ice, too, on the way, from the lake, but I had to sharben the bickaxe. I'm all of a sweat now.'

As he spoke, steam poured from his mouth. He grasped the reins, and the horse gave its rump a lively shake. The sleigh glided back along its own tracks, as though along rails. It left the forest in its wake, and before it spread the endless white sun-lit plain. Everything glistened with droplets, like the sea. And so there it was: I still had not managed to leave the country. What was happening? Where had everything vanished to? From whence had everything appeared?

Unlike myself, who found not a trace of an answer, the man at the reins found an answer to all questions; he knew everything. A burly man, with long moustaches that joined to curly, greying sideburns, he inspired both trust and fear in me. But the fear was less aggressive than the curiosity. We advanced, gliding slowly.

'What time is it?'

Here was my voice, for the first time, hoarse and muffled.

'How should I know? It's early! I was ub at the crack of dawn. Ain't you got a timebiece? Lose it at boker, did you, the same as your coat and cab? Take that there overcoat. I was going to give it as alms, in memory of my old ba, who bassed away last month.'

The coat had bone buttons. He handed me a bottle, which was almost full, and again I saw the crudely stitched stump of his forefinger: 'Have a swig, to warm yourself ub! If you're feeling beckish, there's bread in the knabsack.'

'I drank; it was plum brandy. But I could not eat; a dreadful disquiet held me by the throat. We passed some crows, stark against the white of the road. They did not take flight, but minded their own business, croaking, tracing patterns in the snow with their claws.

'Betre is my name,' said the man. 'My mother was from Russia.'

'Petre?'

'Yes, Betre. Betre!' he shouted, as if I were deaf.

He was expecting me to reciprocate. Bored of my silence, he broached me directly: 'What's the name of your family? Where're you from?'

'Bucharest, Creţu,' I answered unenthusiastically.

'A relative of Kretzu the abothecary – with the ginger moustaches? And who was it shaved your moustaches off?'

I made no reply. Nothing matched up with anything else. From time to time, Petre cast me increasingly wary glances. I could see he was making a great effort to think. Suddenly he pulled on the reins. I jolted forward as if pushed. He jumped down with a nimbleness that was evidence of long practice. We were in a copse; snow clung to the tree trunks like white moss. A body lay on the ground, on its back. I had not noticed it.

'Here's another now!' exclaimed Petre and went up to the form in the snow. 'What is with you, good beople?'

I climbed down, gingerly. My whole body was aching. On the ground was a blond young man, with a carefully trimmed beard and a wound below his shoulder. My eyes remained glued on his clothing: an elegant, seemingly brand-new suit, whose pieces I could not quite name, and tall, highly polished black boots. Beside him a hat had been cast aside, but there was nothing other than that. I saw he was breathing. There was no doubt that he was alive.

'It was the devil himself made me leave the house today, to get away from my wife's brattle, and now I've met the devil himself, God forgive me. What to do?'

He suddenly turned around and looked at me suspiciously.

'It wasn't you, was it?'

He bent his forefinger, as if pulling a trigger.

'I? God forbid! I don't know one end of a gun from another.'

'Come off it! You can't fool me. Where's your bistol?'

'What do you mean? I don't have a pistol,' I said, feeling like a bad actor in a good play.

'What are you jabbering on about?' Petre began to shout. 'I'll bunch you in the head, see if I don't!'

And he brandished his fists at me.

'I have never held a pistol in my life, understand that once and for all! I have never seen this... this boy in my life. He should be taken to hospital as a matter of urgency. I think he has fainted. I do not even know where I am. I do not recognize anything. I think I must have fainted myself. Maybe I fell. Maybe I was struck. I do not understand anything of this. Anything at all!'

Unfortunately my voice trembled. Petre gave me a strange look: 'You're not in your right mind! You're lunatic. You escabed from the madhouse, didn't you? I read in the newsbaber that they make you swallow quicksilver, so that your beard and your moustache fall out. You fell to fighting, like our Lahovary on Filibescu Street, tried to kill each other in a duel, with swords and bistols! The devil take me if I can understand what's wrong with such beople!'

For a time he trampled the snow with the toe of his boot, without taking his eyes off me: 'I'm taking you to the Bolice. Let them deal with you. Even though I've seen that there aren't too many cobbers around the blace at the weekend, we'll find one to lock you in a cell sure enough.'

Then he tried to heave the young man into the sleigh. He struggled with the body for a while and in the end yelled at me, releasing a white plume from his mouth, as if he were smoking: 'Why don't you help me? I can't lift him by myself!'

I grasped the blond young man by the shoulders, as instructed by Petre. He was heavy. Petre looked at me scornfully. We laid him on a plaid rug, on top of the logs. Petre tidied him up, as if he were arranging goods for display, put his hat on his head, rummaged in the inside pocket of his coat, whence he removed a deer-skin wallet, which he immediately concealed in his own pocket. All of a sudden I realized what had been niggling me ever since Petre said he intended to take me to the Police.

'What do you mean there are not many people there at the weekend? What day is it today? Isn't it Monday? Today was Monday!'

Petre did not deign to reply. He seemed clear in his mind. The horse was moving at a trot and the surroundings were innocent enough, and yet I was about to lose my mind. The trees arched whitely overhead, then the open road, the sun, again clumps of woodland and a lone bird fluttering without a care. We soon reached the main road, where many different tracks could be seen mingling together.

'It's Friday,' he condescended to say – seemingly mollified.

Having risen before dawn, after a night of restless sleep and exhausted by my own agitation, I think I then fell asleep.

'Just a hob, a skib and a jumb and we'll be there!'

My opening eyes were seized by the most astonishing scene I had ever beheld. The sun was high in the sky. The light suffused a bustling street: carriages to which were harnessed pairs of glossy horses, an ox cart creaking under a gigantic barrel, hansoms, irritable coachmen, one- and two-storey buildings in whose windows glinted the rays of the sun, shops with gaily painted signs. The people were seemingly all dressed in the same fashion, one matching the other. The ladies wore hats swathed in scarves tied beneath the chin; their waists were unnaturally slender and their heavy garments reached to the ground. The men all had bowler hats and canes. Two officers in braided uniforms saluted somebody in a carriage. A hubbub, a merry buzz, with clattering hooves muffled by the snow, coachmen's cries, and jingling harness bells. The snow on the road was sullied as if with ashes and churned by the horses' hooves, but the pavements were white.

I felt rested and joyful. It was as if I found myself in the world of a young and active God, having lived in an increasingly ruinous world that had lost its God or which had been lost by God. It was as if I were seeing, after many long years, a sky I no longer knew existed. It was as if I had been resurrected, after a living death. It was as if I were under a protective wing. A good feeling, one of love for all that I saw, tightened my throat. My heart was beating wildly and I felt the pain that had long ago inured me to the thought of death. Something had happened without my knowledge. I did not understand why, but my eyes filled with tears. Might I be dreaming? When you dream, however, you do not necessarily realize it is a dream, but when you are awake you know for sure. I did not need to pinch myself to be sure that all I was seeing was real. Reality has an unmistakable consistency. When you go to work in the morning, nobody has to tell you that you are not asleep or that you are alive. I was in a world that was alive and awake. It looked familiar to me. I knew that I knew it, but I did not know how I knew it. I knew it and yet I did not really know it. I asked myself where I had ended up. I did not ask myself how. I shall think about it when I feel able; for the time being, I am not able. Like never before, I felt the urge to look, to feast my eyes on the spectacle of everyday life. Petre said something to me. I did not hear him, because my eyes, which focused on the details as if through a huge magnifying glass, had replaced all my other senses. Suddenly, one image struck my retina like a hammer. It was a building I seemed to recognize: Bucharest's National Theatre, on Victory Avenue. In the plaza in front of the building small hansoms covered with tarpaulins stood in a row, and the snugly dressed coachmen were talking among themselves. Snow-laden trees marked the semi-circle of the plaza. So, I was on Victory Avenue. I had, in a way, come home and my parents' house must have been but a few steps away.

'Good God, where have you brought me?' I groaned.

'To the bolice station. I told you!' came the immediate reply from up on the box. 'Whether they'll send you back to the madhouse, that I can't say, but at least there'll be beople to take care of you. I couldn't leave you lying there, like him, who got shot with the bistol.'

Petre's harsh but not hostile voice brought me back to reality: to the new reality. I plunged back into the unruly city. To the left, on the blank lateral wall of a splendid building, beneath the oddly squashed outline of a roof whose chimneys were smoking, I saw an advertisement in capital letters: *L'INDÉPENDANCE ROUMAINE*. The letters U and M, which were below a chimney, were blackened with soot. Bells were ringing somewhere nearby. Then I heard, like an echo, the chimes of clock, of the sort that provides entertainment to those new to the city.

'They still haven't appointed a new director at *L'Endebandans*, to reblace Mr Lahovary,' said Petre, who was suddenly talkative. 'I read it yesterday in *Universul*. Whoever they bring in, the baber won't change its bolicy. True, they bretend they're not caught up in bolitics. But that's what they all say!'

The street advanced in time with our sleigh, strangely fast. We reached an intersection that I was seemingly seeing for the first time, we crossed it with difficulty, since sleighs and carriages were passing along the boulevard and were not prepared to wait, and then we turned right, coming to an immediate stop. We were plunged within the shadow of a wall. I recalled the unconscious young man and wondered whether he might have died in the meantime. I looked at him and he seemed to groan. There was something terribly childlike about his face, and his blond, longish hair covering part of his cheek.

An imposing, yellowish, two-storey building loomed before us, and above the entrance, beneath the coat of arms, was embedded a clock, whose hands showed half past two. And beneath the clock, large stone letters read: PREFECTURE OF THE CAPITAL'S POLICE.

5.

The woman was approaching the end of her Friday prayer, the longest of all the prayers of the days of the week. Epiharia was a model parishioner, for although she was not yet twenty-five, she came before the altar every day, and the priest praised her and cited her as an example to the lazy and slack. In secret, she wanted to become a nun. She knew the prayer almost by heart, and murmured it in a low voice, glancing at the little book she held only to check. *"And since it is so, multiply, O Lord, my labours, my temptations and my pains,"* said the woman, although at the same time she thought that this was not what she wished at all, "but also multiply and make abundant my patience, my strength, my contentment and my blessedness" – this was more like it – *in all the trials that might befall me..."* The door opened and an unknown man entered. Epiharia lowered her eyes to her little book: *"in all the trials that might befall me."* The man walked forward, looking around him, at the saints on the walls, painted, as the young woman said to herself, with priceless grace. *"For, I know that I am weak, unless Thou givest me strength; fearful, unless Thou makest me bold; blind, unless..."* Now she could see him and instead of praying, she allowed herself to be drawn by the sly sins of this world and watched as he went up to the altar. Without making the sign of the cross! *"Evil, unless Thou makest me good; lost, unless Thou seekest me."* The man too looked lost, his face was as handsome as an angel's and he was dressed like... like a beggar at the church gate. Where could he have left his hat? He wasn't holding it and nor had he hung it on the hooks above the chairs... *"With Thy abundant and divine power, and with the gift of Thy Holy Cross, to which I bow and which I glorify, now and forever and ever, Amen."* She had fluffed a few of the words, but she was no longer able to concentrate on her prayers. She watched from the corner of her eye as the stranger stood next to the icon of the Mother of God, brought there long ago, in the reign of Constantine Brâncoveanu, as a blessing to all those who crossed the threshold of the church. People came to pray to the icon, some of them in misfortune, some of them for health, some for wealth or for children, and they knelt, their eyes lowered, their pious lips barely touching the saint's silver casing. But see that man, standing up, looking her straight in the eye, and not for a moment or two, but for minutes on end. How can you look the Mother of God in the eye? What can he be thinking? No, it is not fitting to judge a man standing before the altar, maybe he is an unfortunate wretch, a man without means, God alone judges us, each and every one, wherever we might be. But it is as if some people, like this man, make you feel, I don't know, they make you feel spiritually straitened. *"Lord, Jesus Christ, have mercy upon us sinners, your servants"* – and here Epiharia made a broad, emphatic sign of the cross, her hand coming to rest on her left shoulder – *"Amen."* When her mind reached the word *sinners*, as if bidden, the man turned toward her. Taking fright, she averted her gaze and looked to the side, at the shield of St George, who for centuries had been slaying the same Dragon with the same spear.

'Good evening... erm, madam.'

'The Lord be with you!'

Epiharia had a round childlike face, white skin, and a dimple, also round, beneath her lower lip. Only a single lock of her hair was visible, as her headscarf covered her ears, and was wound beneath her chin and knotted at the nape of her neck. Her expression was serious. The man looked weary. His voice (praise God!) was devoid of hidden thoughts, a downcast voice, and so the woman once more felt her soul at peace.

'Where might a man without money or belongings spend the night? Might he do so here?'

'Only if you wish to spend the night with a saint,' said Epiharia, without thinking of anything bad, but then quickly made the sign of the cross because of the unseemly implication and begged God's forgiveness aloud for being rash and foolish.

Now the stranger was smiling. He was a different man!

'No, but I would like to find somewhere. I am... I am unwell. I am ill.'

For as long as he smiled he was as young as a cherub. Without the smile he was much older. You would have thought his voice was bleeding. He looked like a man who had fallen on hard times, as she had rightly divined, and so she had done well not to judge him.

'Shall I take you to our deacon? He lives two houses further down the street, over there, past that light-brown carriage, or rather the cherry-red carriage. Can you see it? But he has many children; he too is needy. If you can't find him, come back here to me – my name is Epiharia – and we'll think of something else.'

The stranger left, but no more than five minutes passed before he came back, making a gesture of helplessness. Nobody had answered his knock on the door. The woman had another solution: 'We have the key to the house where the painters from the Stork's Nest stay in summer.

In June they started repainting the band of murals with the saints below the roof, but they broke off in November. I can ask the priest for the key, he has it because some of them came here to our church, to do some painting, and they worked now here, now there...'

'That would be wonderful!'

'But you ought to know that there is a problem...'

Now the man looked older and a furrow formed between his eyebrows again.

'It's a summer-house and there is no stove, nor firewood, nor bedclothes. But you know that man is capable of great control. Simeon the Stylite lived for a great long time atop his pillar. And one day he invited St Theodosius to come see him. On top of the pillar, that is! I can give you a plaid rug, from the priest...'

Off she went, chubby and full of kindness. An hour must have elapsed before she returned. She found the man sitting in the choir stall, his eyes closed. She had brought a large key and explained, with great indulgence for the stranger's ignorance, how he should get to the house and what he should do to avoid freezing during the night. She placed in his arms a threadbare blanket and gave him a large chunk of bread from the priest, wrapped in a cloth. She also gave him an icon lamp, to shed light. She did not tell him that the priest had urged her in a low voice not to let herself be beguiled by all the city's ne'er-do-wells; that was of no concern to the stranger. The man thanked her and smiled with teeth as white as fresh snow, although he seemed quite unclear about what she was telling him. But the woman was quite certain that the Good Lord would guide his steps to the right place, as certain as she was that in every path through life it is fated that we should lose our way: for, she herself had once gone astray.

6.

A soundless voice that I alone hear, stronger than my poor tortured body and my poor terrified brain. I talk to myself in order to grow accustomed to myself, in order not to be so afraid of my fear and in order to be sure I have not lost my mind. I am afraid of them, of myself, of Him who plays with us. I am surrounded by beings that seem to be the fruit of a diseased imagination. But why do they not disappear? Why can I hear them? Why am I unable to use my mind in order to understand how my mind works and whence comes this fear? It is as if I were inhabited by a stranger, who knows many things about me, and who shapes me as he wills. Why do you fight with me? I am beaten in advance; you, or Thou, will have the power. I am defeated in advance. What satisfaction can you gain if you show me that you are more powerful? I know it as well as you do! Yes, you have won.

When something bad happens, you always await the next blow. I huddle up inside myself and wait.

The three-pronged key swiftly did its duty and thus I entered. It was pitch black and I waited for my eyes to grow accustomed. Then, by groping around, I explored the place. There was a plank bed, like in a mountain cabin: a long platform on which, I think, ten people could have slept, squeezed together. I could have done with ten people. The room was cluttered with things, as in a store, and I kept bumping into them, without seeing them. In one corner I came across some empty buckets and even managed to knock them over. You're not a chair; you're not a table. But there was a small window with a broken pane. I placed the rolled-up blanket on the so-called bed and I would have lain down that very instant, had I not been so cold. My whole body ached, from my head to my wet feet. A hot bath, some hot soup, some mulled wine with cinnamon, or at least a cup of tea. I had eaten the bread during the first steps I took, all of it. The icon lamp had gone out. I had to light it; I had to kindle a flame in that icy room. Might the church be unlocked? There must be at least one candle burning there. I went back outside and dragged myself to the church door. It was locked. The windows were high up and there was no question of my reaching them. Shouldn't the House of the Lord always be open, especially at night, and especially in winter? But no, it seems that we are not welcome all hours. When the Lord is not ready for guests, he knows how to stay aloof. Or maybe He too needs his hours of sleep. I went back, discouraged and more exhausted than ever. Yet again I had to wait for my eyes to grow accustomed to the pitch black. I was shut outside the world. I undid the string tying the blanket and out of it fell a little package, wrapped in paper. It was surely a gift from the woman, from Epiharia. I groped for a long time on the cold, dusty, filthy floor. The package must have been very small and light; it made not a sound when it fell. I found it only after I had scratched my hands on some jagged objects or splinters. I went to the threshold, where there was more light, and tore off the paper. Inside the paper she had wrapped a box of matches, with long, thick sticks, and a little crucifix. 'God is awake,' I said to myself. 'God be with you!' the woman had said. I would have to be careful not to waste the matches. I readied the icon lamp, closed the door, lest a gust of wind blow it out, rubbed my hands together for a long while, so that my fingers would not be numb, and then, groping like a blind man, took a match-stick, carefully scraping it over the knobbly sandpaper. The matchstick snapped. It was only after a number of attempts, with impatient hands, that I succeeded. A flame appeared and gently tilting the lamp I managed to light it, although I burned my fingers in the process. Yet I did not feel the burn; for there was a light, which soothed me. It was my lamp. I was able to see the objects around me: some paintbrushes, empty leather chests, which were old, their lining torn, stones of every size, ragged clothes, an empty, dirty bottle, a broom made of twigs, a hammer, nails, and things to which I could put no name. I used them nonetheless. I warmed my hands on the lamp, and then I gathered the stones to make a hearth, in which I placed the torn paper from the parcel – a piece of newspaper – and the lining torn from the suitcases. I spent a while snapping the twigs from the broom and made a fairly large heap. I did not waste any more of the matches, whose white phosphorus was now more precious than gold, but set fire to a paintbrush, which gave off a revolting, suffocating, unbearable reek of paint, but which burned well. I kindled quite a decent fire and the air lost a little of its chill, while the smoke poured out of the broken windowpane. I gathered all the rags off the floor and laid them on the plank bed, and then, in the overcoat Petre had given me and in the blanket Epiharia had given me, I lay down. I kept the icon lamp burning. Behind me, unintelligible, the longest day of my life faded away.

Yet I did not fall asleep straight away, despite my exhaustion; probably because I was thirsty. I could see fragments of the city, jumbled together. The road here had been a labyrinth. I knew roughly the direction to Strada Berzei (Stork Street), but it was as if I were no longer a native of Bucharest and the city was playing with me, tricking me at every turn. The horizons, the buildings were different. The few lights were street lamps, the distances were deceptive, and I had found no street signs. I regretted that I did not even know the churches, whose names I had not made an effort to remember, although the woman had told me them, and I saw only the roofs gleaming like nickel teeth. There were fewer and fewer people on the streets. I asked them the way, and some of them gave me directions, but after the first corner I lost my way. I was frightened by all kinds of unlit horse-drawn vehicles, from which came shouts and curses. After a time I had to admit to myself that I was completely lost. The darkness became thicker and thicker and it was getting colder and colder.

In the middle of the night I came across a man walking quickly down the street. I tried to catch up with him, and when I did, I tried to stop him, I touched him, but the man almost leapt out of his skin, looking behind him in terror. I picked his bowler hat up off the ground. It fit my head and was still warm from the head that had been wearing it. I put it on. I continued to walk at random and just as I thought I could not go farther from my goal and had abandoned my struggle with the labyrinth, a church loomed in front of me, with a band of saints painted under the roof. It was the Church known locally as "The Stork's Nest". Right next to it, the woman had told me, was the painters' house, where I would find my own nest.

I was woken by the bells. I had dreamed of Bucharest, while in a different Bucharest. My colleagues from the editorial office had appeared, they were laughing, although I was uncertain as to whether it was laughter or weeping. And there was somebody – a woman, who had been looking for me, a woman with an absent and ineffably sad mien, but I didn't know who it was. Just as I was shouting at the top of my voice: *here I am, here I am*, I heard the bells and I thought: 'The bells mean death.' With those words in my mind, I awoke. The bells I was hearing meant life. The fire had gone out. The passer's-by hat was inside a bucket – the hat I had picked up off the ground after I frightened its wearer in the middle of the night. The room was in complete disarray. Through the broken windowpane I could see snowflakes. It had started snowing. It was my first snowfall in this world; a world that was either real or the figment of a ghost-haunted mind. I knew I had to start all over again. But I was quite simply incapable of getting up. I waited for a miracle to happen. No, I was not in a nest, not at all. Rather, I was shipwrecked, except that on my desert island it was winter and I had salvaged nothing from the disaster. Even my luggage had been sequestered by the Police.

You were waiting for some miracle or other, dear Dan. You were waiting for your new life, looking out of the broken windowpane.

The Ringster coughed and hawked a thick glob of phlegm onto the stone floor, deliberately, so as to nauseate the foppish sergeant who was guarding him, who looked like a young man who had had a mollycoddled upbringing. He was there for the sake of form, since Fane had no means of escape: the doors were locked and bolted. Unlike ordinary men, who sleep from evening to morning and work from morning to evening, Fane did things the other way around. During the day he had caught a few hours of sleep, but he felt on top form: there was money to be had. He could smell money from a mile off, and that invigorated him. He had begun the night stretching from Friday evening to Saturday morning in a good mood. The sergeant, bored, attempted to make conversation, but Fane cut him short: 'Shut it, Jean, I've got work to do!' To make his life simpler, he had once explained, he called everybody Jean.

The sergeant's head started lolling, and finally his chin came to rest on his chest. Soon, he started snoring, and Fane avoided making any noise, since he had the fine movements of a wild animal, an instinct he had imbibed with his mother's milk. He was a handsome man; narrow in the hip, broad in the shoulder, with cunning eyes the colour of frost-nipped plums, long eyelashes and long moustaches, which left no woman indifferent. The silvery box did not look like it had much of a lock, just three numbered rollers, but the mechanism was more like a toy. Fane dialled the rollers, with his ear pressed to the mechanism, to hear how they tumbled. He always went by his sense of hearing, like a bat. At first, he was unable to make out anything clearly, but when he repeated the circuit again and again, and the first roller reached zero, it made a faint sound. He left it in that position and went on to the second roller, which also made a click on zero. He did not even bother with the third: he turned it to the same figure as the first two and heard a clearer click, which coincided with a hiccup from the sleeping sergeant. The sergeant opened his eyes, and Fane leaned over the box as if he were hard at work, covering it with his broad chest. The sergeant watched him for a while, and finally his eyelids drooped over his small eyes again.

The Ringster put the box down and opened it without making the slightest sound. On his face could be read boundless amazement. He carefully rummaged through all the compartments, put everything back, turned the rollers, and crept to the door, whistling softly for Păunescu, who was on duty. He asked to leave the room for a rest break

At dawn, in the office on the first floor, Costache was informed that the locked case was missing. Down below in the basement, Fane kicked up a fuss to cover his tracks: 'What have you done, Jean, if you can't even trust anybody in a police station,' he shouted. 'Who can you trust then? Idlers, layabouts, bunglers!' Then he went back to sleep, satisfied that he had a wonderful Saturday ahead of him.

COMMOTION

1.

Thank the Lord, my little brother was jollier this morning, on our walk. He was also delighted to espy little Nicu, the errand boy; his red cap always strikes the eye. The boy never stays still. Jacques, the dear thing, would have jumped down, had he been able. But our carriage was moving, and the wee imp was in front of where the Sărindar Monastery used to stand (it still pains my soul that they demolished it, it was Bucharest's cathedral, and people say dire things will come of it). And so as the horses sped past he called out to him, telling him to visit us as soon as possible, although he had seen him just last evening. I am not sure whether Nicu can have heard and I do not think he will come; I saw yesterday that he is afraid of Mr Costache. Jacques and myself go out daily for an hour, in the morning, along the embankment, to look at the seagulls – this is his main entertainment – while Papa reads *Universul*, which is *his* main entertainment. This morning he gave a start when under the heading of *Events from the Capital* he found an item about the topic of our conversation yesterday and even more so when he saw (dear Papa!) that he himself was mentioned, albeit in a brief parenthesis. When we returned, he twice read us the news item, lowering his voice for the parenthesis: "The man under arrest who was found unconscious yesterday almost frozen near Băneasa Forest (by the lakes) has declared that his name is Dan I. Kretzu, that he is a newspaperman and not a malefactor. He has provided no explanation as to what took place and despite the efforts of the Police, it has not been possible to find one person to confirm his identity. Since his state of health is less than desirable, he has been given medical attention. (Dr Leon Margul*ius*...' they spelled my name wrong, the idiots! '...was kind enough to examine him.) Investigations are in progress." I laughed when I heard that he was 'a newspaperman and not a malefactor.' I think such an explanation is welcome in this day and age. Papa shooed me away.

With the notebook I started yesterday I began a new life. My life therefore begins on Friday. I have reached Chapter 25 in my book, 'in which all the principal personages think fit to leave Brighton.' As for us, here in Bucharest, all the principal personages have arrived in town, where they will remain until at least New Year. At least so I hope.

Mr Costache will be furious: the newspaper item does not mention him even in parenthesis.

*

Late evening. Here I am writing again, rather than reading. When Safta took his stovepipe hat, Mr Costache pinched her on the – –, as he often does when he thinks nobody is watching. But then he saw me and cast me a strange look. We sat down to dinner rather upset, because dear Jacques was feeling out of sorts. He was sad that Nicu had not come. I tried to cheer him up and because he is a good child, he feigned that I had succeeded. He did not want to join us at the dinner table. He lay in bed instead, and I gave him the clock with the figurines, to wind it up to his heart's content. He likes the sweet and ineffably sad minuet of the male and the female figurines, which bow, join hands, spin, part, and join hands once more. Jacques says he would like to know how the story ends; it is like a fairy tale. It depends how long you turn the key: Sometimes it turns out well and the two remain hand in hand. But sometimes it ends badly, and the two porcelain figurines stand twisting to the side and looking into the distance. Jacques swears that the expressions on their faces alter when they look into the distance. Mama can barely control herself in such moments, but nor can Papa, and he is a doctor and a grown man. And so it did us good when our policeman arrived with news from around town. He filled our heads with the duel in which poor Lahovary was killed, with the charges of intentional murder brought against the men from *L'Indépendance Roumaine*, with political pressure, since there are many who wish to believe that the crime was hatched by former friends, now adversaries. He also told us something spicier – the Bastaki trial, Bastaki being the adulterous paterfamilias, whom Miss Gorjan attempted to kill with a revolver. Miss Gorjan was the daughter of General Gorja, being the woman he seduced. The jury felt sorry for her and acquitted her, and after that the courtroom erupted in a cry of 'Down with Bastaki!' But Mama impatiently asked our guest how it could be possible that they had still not been able to open the stranger's case.

'How is it possible, my dear Mrs Agatha,' Mr Costache replied with feigned astonishment, 'that you know everything before I do?'

He knew very well that the ladies of Bucharest and the Police employ servants as their morning, afternoon and evening newspapers. He acknowledged that indeed they had not managed to open the case or box or whatever it was. The mistake was his. Instead of immediately ordering it to be broken open with an axe, fearful lest they damage its contents, which might be who knows what valuable items, they had tried to crack the combination and then invited a professional thief to do so: a certain Fane the Ringster, who was being held under arrest. But now, as if part of an illusionist's number, the box had disappeared!

The stranger had been held in the same cell as Fane for an hour yesterday afternoon, but he is said not to have spoken a word, apart from complaining of the cold a few times. 'What's with you, Jean, somebody die?' The Ringster had apparently asked him.

It amused me to learn from Mr Costache that Fane called everybody Jean, 'to simplify his life'. Fane is certain that the stranger is some international burglar, he says that he knows all the thieves from Bucharest and the surrounding area by sight, and he knows how the ones from the rest of the country 'work.' And this is my opinion too: he must be some *chevalier d'industrie* wanted by the police commissioners of every country. Nevertheless, I sense, without my being able to explain why, that there is more to this than meets the eye, something mysterious, which causes me heart to beat very fast. I am curious even; it is like an episode from *Vanity Fair*. The gas lamp has almost burned out; better I go to bed.

There are two things in life of which you are never bored: looking at falling snowflakes and gazing at the flames in a fireplace. At dawn that Saturday, Mr Costache was able to do both of these at once. It had started to snow and for a while he had looked out of the window onto Victory Avenue. Now he was looking at the flames. He had finished his Turkish coffee, laced with French brandy, to help him forget his annoyance at the disappearance of the case, and he had glanced at the announcement in *Universul*, taking note, without surprise, that it had been placed between two stupid advertisements. What prestige could the Police preserve if its requests were placed next to an advertisement for a confectioner's? And it was not even a renowned confectioner's, like old man Fialkowski's, but one that was here today and gone tomorrow. Then he came across the news item about the man found in the snow: 'The man under arrest who was found unconscious yesterday almost frozen near Băneasa Forest (by the lakes) has declared that his name is Dan I. Kretzu, that he is a...' and observed two things: *primo*, that they had spelled his name with a K and a tz, although in his statement the man had written it with a normal C and a normal ț, and *secundo*, that he, Costache Boerescu, had been omitted from the news item. But these were trifles. And he looked into the fireplace once more, at the dancing tongues of flame, which soothed him, and then he went to the window again. No snowflake resembled any other, and, so Costache hoped, no fingerprint could resemble any other. Unfortunately, it had not yet been proven whether the patterns on a man's fingertips might alter over the course of his lifetime, but Costache was almost certain that within a few years the fact that they did not would be demonstrated scientifically. His superior arrogantly contradicted him and gave as an example trees, which, when sawn in two reveal their own print. But if you compare the rings of a young tree with those of an old tree, you will see that in the latter the distances between them are greater and increase with the years, and that the accidents of good and bad years change their outlines. The same must also apply to a man, the Prefect of Police concluded.

Costache did not get on with his superior, although he acknowledged that he was not a stupid man. The 22nd of November had been the anniversary of his arrival, the date when, full of complexes and affectations, he had taken up the post. His brother Ion, the Prefect of Bacău, had been mixed up in a scandal involving the torture of a prisoner, from which he had got off scot free, while some poor constable had been made the scapegoat. Costache still missed Colonel Mişu Capşa, who during the year he had held the post of Prefect had made things run smoothly. He had been a just commandant, he knew how to give orders without humiliating a man, and above all he feared nothing. Indeed, he had been a war hero, decorated at Plevna and Vidin. Even the lawyer Deşliu, although he had been with them for only one summer, in '94, had been better. And the best of all had been in '89: General Algiu, who had remained a friend and whom he still visited when he needed advice. The more recent ones, good and bad, magistrates and career soldiers, these he did not count: they had come only in order to have a stepping-stone to other positions and so that they could be saluted by the crowd when they followed the King in their own carriage during parades.

The present chief, Caton Lecca, was a politician, the most slippery of species. He thought he knew everything. He had also been a member of parliament and a senator, suspected of electoral fraud. He acted the cockerel in front of his thickset wife, but the cannier agents directly subordinate to Mr Costache used to call him, with a hidden meaning, Cato the Elder. As for Costache himself, they called him Taki the Great, a double-edged epithet, since their dear chief was rather short, although well built and possessed of handsome eyes with velvety depths, seemingly unsuited to his profession. Apart from that, there was constant ill feeling and backbiting among the agents, sergeants and constables of the Prefecture. The turkeys, that is, the sergeants, who had numbers on their caps, laughed at the goldfinches, that is, the constables, because of the green or red patches on their shoulders. And the goldfinches called the commissars and sub-commissars, that is, Costache's men, who had degrees in law and spoke French and German, coxcombs, bookmen and earwigs. Mr Costache heaved a sigh. Ultimately, the quarrels and the prefects flowed by like water, while he, like a rock, remained. But it was not easy to be a rock.

At the Bucharest Police, they had been taking fingerprints for almost three years, since before the arrival of Caton Lecca. They had first done so thanks to Dr Minovici, the oldest of the three physician brothers, who had experimented with 'dactylloscopy' on dozens of convicts. A year later, Costache had proposed that he himself take over the Judicial Identification Service, a department such as existed in other parts of the world to deal with the biggest malefactors, criminals, forgers and rapists. They had anthropometric records, with photographs and fingerprints. Costache had secretly conducted an experiment on Fane The Ringster: he had demanded that his fingerprints be taken the first time he was arrested. It was a real honour for a jewel thief like Fane, who had not understood what was happening and thought it was some kind of signature – which only went to shown his innate canniness – and all the while he had shouted at the top of his voice that he confessed to nothing and that he wouldn't sign anything. Now, on his second arrest, Fane shouted no longer.

He merely looked at Costache from under lowered eyebrows and said: 'What you want from me, Jean? Why do you keep forcing me to get me hands dirty? What you got up your sleeve? What you accusing me of? I work clean, so I do, I don't maim or kill! I just steal.'

Costache requested the old fingerprints from the archive and studied them for an hour under a magnifying glass with an ivory handle. He could swear they were identical. But he did not know whether the two years that had elapsed were sufficient to provide conclusive evidence. We shall see in ten years whether they're like tree rings or not! At home, he had dipped his own fingers in violet ink, but nothing clear had resulted on paper. Then he got the idea of using wax. He dripped some wax from a candle and straight away pressed his the tip of his right index finger into it. He would have to wait a few years before repeating the exercise. Yesterday, he had had the fingerprints of the foreign-looking gentleman taken, the rather curious man Petre had brought in, and not only had he not been at all surprised, but he had seemed to know what it was all about. Only one conclusion could be drawn: he was an international crook, perhaps from New York, where, as he had seen in a photograph in the newspaper, criminal files were kept in a room whose walls were covered from top to bottom in hundreds of little drawers. It was Costache's ambition to have a similar room in Bucharest. He would have to keep this Dan Crețu under close surveillance, to see whether he had accomplices. Sooner or later he would give himself away.

Setting aside the snowflakes and his plans for reform, he went back into his office, rolled a cigarette, lit it, inhaled the aromatic smoke with great pleasure, and pressed a bell. A strident buzz was heard. When the balding head of the sergeant appeared in the doorway, he asked that Petre be brought in. Petre, known as Rusu, the coachman of the Inger family, knew the man who had been found almost frozen. Costache again recollected the advertisement for the cake shop adjacent to his announcement, but he swatted the thought away, like a fly.

'I've called you here to tell me all about the hijinks of yesterday.'

The coachman twisted his cap in his hands, and his cut finger seemed to throb. He answered determinedly: 'The man's from the madhouse, your worship. I think he shot that blond lad, but he don't want to admit it. He kebt shouting: I recognize nothing! I recognize nothing!'

'But why was that? After all, nobody was accusing him of anything, like the police...'

'I accused him, like the bolice, I did! And he goes: I don't know how to shoot a gun – imagine that! – and that I take him to the hosbital quick, lest he die, I ain't got no gun, he says, I don't know where I am, I don't understand nothing, *I recognize nothing*, berhabs something hit me on the head! He's guilty, your worship! But what about the blond boyar, didn't he die?'

Costache regarded the cake shop owner's coachman carefully: 'Why do you wish to know?'

Petre fidgeted and answered to the effect that it was a Christian sort of question. Costache changed his tone and threatened that if he were hiding anything from the police he would be in big trouble, and from the frightened expression on Petre's face he drew the conclusion that he had not told him everything. He did not think it was anything important: perhaps he had taken a ring from the man's finger or something of the sort, but sooner or later it would be revealed.

'What was he doing when you found him? Was he awake?'

'He was lying on his side and goggling at the horse, which was taking a biss, bardon my language, as if he'd never seen a horse bissing in his life. I found him just as I was about to go back to town. He could hardly sit ub. I was afraid he might fall off the box. I thought he was blind drunk.'

It did not seem that the coachman had anything else worthwhile to tell. He sent him away, first giving him an order to pass on to the confectioner, since on Christmas Eve he was invited to the house of both the Margulis family and the Livezeanu family (he had not yet decided which invitation to accept). He had not been hoping for very much from the coachman and he had not been mistaken. He rang the bell once more, calling the slow-witted old man back from the door and feeling sorry for him. He discovered that the coachman who had been assigned to follow the man named Crețu was in the building and he demanded to see him straight away. He received a report on all the details of the previous night, the man's crazy journey around the streets, his encounter with Nicu outside the Central Girls' School, his visit to the Icoanei Church, lasting one hour and twenty minutes, his knocking on the locked door of the deacon, something about a plump woman (named Epiharia) who presumably knew more, his departure holding a blanket, and the hours and hours he had gone round in a circle, at random, as if he were trying to make fun of those following him and had irked the trusty coachman more than he cared to say. He had tugged on the reins dozens of times, until the horse was dizzy. And then there was his chasing after a passer-by on Brezoianu Street, and finally, at the very end, his taking refuge inside a hovel next to the Church of St Stephen, also known as the Stork's Nest. At this point, the Police coachman had cheated: between midnight and the first cock's crow, he had gone home to bed, sure that the man was not capable of taking one more step, because, unexpectedly for a man of his status, he had not taken a single cab or coach ride during all his lunatic roaming.

'I'll bet you anything he's a madman. We ought to ask Mărcuța, and Dr Șuțu on Plantelor Street, and Dr Marinescu, at the Pantelimon Hospital.'

'Bravo, well said, Budac. I shall ask you to go there right away. I want an answer by this afternoon. And before anything else, go to the Hospice in Teilor to see how the young man who was shot is doing. If he is conscious, *come back immediately*. It is extremely important that I talk to him.'

Rather than clicking his heels and saying: 'Yes, sir!' the Police's best coachman soundlessly moved his lips. He knew very well that at Dr Rosenberg's Hospice, patients without any name or papers were taken in, many of them in a serious condition. The City Hall paid an annual fee to the Hospice for this service, and likewise to Dr Șuțu's establishment on Plantelor Street, where persons with no means of subsistence were treated. And on top of this, his wife was expecting him at home, as he had to slaughter the pig. It was the Feast of St Ignatius, after all. You can tell the chief's a bachelor! He thought to himself. Why had he got it into his head to make a suggestion like that, when he knew the chiefs' working method: if you're the one who comes up with an idea, then you're the one who acts on it? He ought to be charier with his words. But he promised himself that he would go home first and then visit every madhouse in the city. That vagrant was a menace. Since Petre brought him in yesterday, things had been going badly for everyone. He was like a curse.

'Who relieved you?' asked Costache.

'I sent Ilie, 'cause he's got a fast cab. But if it were up to me, two legs would be just as good. You don't need four wheels to follow him.'

'All right, never mind. See you don't stop off at home first! There's plenty of time for the pig this afternoon!' called the chief after the coachman, confirming his reputation as a mind reader.

Costache then ordered that Nicu should be sent straight to his office as soon as he returned from *Universul*, with further instructions that the lad should not be left to come of his own free will but detained as a matter of urgency. He went back to the window: a fresh layer of snow had fallen and the city looked unwontedly jolly that Saturday morning. But it was obvious that the coachman had cursed him, because the sergeant now entered bringing the unbelievable news that the stranger's chest had not been recovered, despite half of those on duty being responsible for finding it. After warder Păunescu took Fane back to the cell, the sergeant in the room with the safe had dozed off, but the door was locked and the box, likewise locked, was within. Quite simply, nobody had seen anything; nobody knew anything. They were all questioned. The sergeant was given a good hiding, Păunescu was likewise beaten black and blue, but there was something fishy going on, and nothing could be discovered. Now Fane was being questioned. Throughout this description, Costache's face remained inscrutable, and the sergeant quickly left the office, making himself scarce.

At around one o'clock they brought in Nicu, at a trot, flanked by two soldiers. The lad was swivelling his eyes every which way, but when he saw that there was no escape, he looked Costache straight in the eye, with a kind of scrutinizing mistrust. He held his thin lips clenched in a straight line, like a man who had just had to swallow an undeserved reproach, but controlled himself with dignity. Costache disguised his sudden good mood. The lad was holding his cap by the visor in his left hand and shifting his weight from one foot to the other, leaving splashes of water and mud on the wooden floor. The cop signalled the other two to leave the room.

'Are you left-handed?'

Costache had as keen an eye for details as did Dr Margulis, except that the cop had an eye for every single thing, whereas the doctor had an eye only for the symptoms of disease. The policeman knew by instinct when there was something untoward, as surely as the doctor knew when he had a stomach-ache. By instinct, Nicu lied to them both.

He unclenched his lips and determinedly said: 'No, sir, I'm not! I'm right-handed.'

'Sit down over here. Are you hungry?'

'No!'

'Just as well. Tell me to the last detail what you talked about with the stranger you met yesterday in front of the Icoanei Church.'

Nicu sighed and unbuttoned his tunic: so this was what it was all about. Not the accident with the icicles or the wallet, which he would not have like to come to the attention of the Police, because then he would not have received the reward. And nor could it be some roguery on his mother's part. It was the first time he had spoken to Costache and at close quarters he looked less frightening than he did from a distance. He recounted what he could remember, starting with the nicest part, about the toy cow, and finally he gave his own opinion.

He chose his words with care: 'I'm not certain of it, but he may be a Martian. I don't know whether you've heard of them,' he added. 'It was in yesterday's paper. You are sure he's not Jack, the Ripper, I mean?'

'Why?' asked Costache, rather confused by the 'you are sure?' not knowing that Nicu talked to himself in the second person when he was flustered. The Prefect had indeed discounted the hypothesis about Jack from the outset. Every police force and every newspaper in Europe were in ferment because of the murderer.

'Because he's a good man: I've seen him. He looks a bit like Miss Iulia. You would think that they were brother and sister.'

Costache's expression was inscrutable.

'Where's the toy he gave you? I want to see it!'

'At home,' said Nicu, resisting the urge to touch his pocket. He shrugged regretfully, as if to reinforce what he was saying.

In a sudden rage, Costache asked himself aloud what kind of subalterns he had and how they had gone about searching the stranger. Who knows what else they had missed? Even the case had vanished. Nicu waited for him to vent his fury; he was accustomed to the highly-strung, what with his mother, but he made a mental note of this item of new information.

'Draw for me what he gave you.'

He handed Nicu a sheet of splendid bond paper. He sharpened a pencil with a penknife. Nicu liked to draw, but up until then he had only done so on a blackboard and in the snow. It was the first time he had had the use of a sheet of white paper and a pencil. He flushed and, stopping and starting, as if he were carrying a heavy parcel, he drew the most comical cow of his entire life, accidentally ripping a few holes in the paper as he did so. He gave it a black piratical eye patch, but did not succeed in drawing the legs, which came out as spindly as straws, each ending in a pinhead. He handed the drawing to Costache, after giving it a dissatisfied look, like a painter who had rushed his work.

'She's called Fira. That's what I called her. She hasn't got an udder. The only thing worse would have been a udder with three teats!'

Costache seemed able to view people like the mirrored surface of clear water, but when you looked at him the water grew murky and no longer reflected anything.

He announced his conclusions: 'First of all, you lied about not being left-handed, since you hold the pencil in your left hand, and secondly, you lied about not being hungry, I know that without any proof, and thirdly you lied about not having the toy on your person. This I can prove. Empty your left pocket; don't make me do it myself.'

Nicu very reluctantly obeyed. His eyebrows were at a more acute angle than usual, like upturned letters v. He kissed the toy cow and handed it over, glancing sideways. Costache examined it and then stood up and went to the fireplace. Nicu was convinced that he was about to throw it on the fire and tried not to cry out. Costache dropped it, whether deliberately or not, but the legs of Fira the cow got caught in the grating of the fireguard and there she clung.

'You may take her,' said Costache, without giving any explanation. 'You may also take the pencil and the paper, as a present. But here's the thing! Do you want to help the stranger or not?'

Nicu acknowledged that he did. The cop instructed him for a long while and then released him.

'How's your mother?' he asked in lieu of saying goodbye.

'Well,' replied Nicu, ending his visit to the police station as he had begun it, which is to say, with another lie. How did he know his mother? Costache was a good policeman, so much was true, but that did not mean the police station was a good place. He ought not to push his luck. And so he left at a run.

3.

Dr Margulis looked at his *doublé* watch – he had sold his gold one, what with Jacques's infirmity – and discovered it was only 11:48am. There were another three quarters of an hour until the end of his free consultations for the poor, which he gave every Saturday. His assistant was playing truant, an old habit of his. The doctor showed out the old man, who without a doubt had a liver complaint, caused, also without a doubt, by drink (he reeked of plum brandy and was yellow in the face) and was half-gladdened, half-saddened that there was nobody else in the waiting room. But he knew that the people who had need of him would not have read the . If the news spread, it would be from mouth to mouth. Margulis was a good doctor, but had few patients. The charlatans, feldshers and barbers 'with diplomas,' who provided ground aspirin, hair-restoring creams, and abortion pills for women, had queues at their doors. He earned enough to meet his needs, and sometimes Agatha sold an item of value from her dowry. He recalled the announcement about the stranger found out by the lakes, which he had read that morning in the Gazette, and the other item, from the Police, about the man who had been shot. It was he who had given the wounded man first aid: and because the patient had no form of identification, he had then sent him to Dr Rosenberg's House of Health.

Dr Margulis looked out of the window. It was now snowing nicely. He decided to close his surgery early and rush over to his colleague Rosenberg's establishment, to see how the wounded man was doing. It was his duty. He was one of those physicians who felt a responsibility towards those they consult, even after they left their care. For Dr Margulis, the best school was applied medicine at the patient's bedside, hour-by-hour supervision, in other words – hospital. Unfortunately, he had given up hospital work, after an unfortunate misunderstanding with a colleague, preferring to open his own surgery and to be independent. He would have very much liked to build and organize his own hospital, but that was but a dream, only possible if perhaps he won the grand prize in the New Year lottery. Without his family's knowledge, he had entered the lottery with that sole aim. He took the ticket from his pocket and looked at the numbers yet again: 12, 21, and 42: the ages of little Jacob, Iulia and Agatha. He carefully folded the ticket, put it back in the hidden pocket of his *portefeuille*, and then placed the *portefeuille* in the hidden pocket of his coat. He picked up his large, heavy, brown leather bag, in which his instruments were arranged in separate compartments, and climbed the steps of the alleyway to the cab station in front of the National Theatre. Three cabs rushed over all at once at his signal, but the doctor climbed aboard Yevdoshka's, not because he knew he was poor and needy, but because he knew he was a talker. The doctor himself was rather taciturn, and so he liked to listen.

'To Rosenberg's, at the Hospice of Health!'

*

Yevdoshka cussed blood-curdlingly from time to time, and his reedy eunuch's voice was out of keeping with his words. It was amusing to hear such a childlike voice mention *such things*. Like everybody else, the doctor knew that the cabmen belonged to a Russian sect in which the men willingly castrated themselves, some while still young men, the majority only after they had sired two children. But Yevdoshka had told him many more stories, namely that last century there lived a holy man, Selivanov, from the Tula region, who had a revelation about St Matthew the Apostle's verses about eunuchs, the ones that conclude with: 'He that is able to receive it, let him receive it.' That man, already renowned for the goodness with which he answered evil and for the other cheek that he turned when slapped, had at first not been able to understand a word of it, but afterward his mind was illumined and he understood that he must castrate himself. The heresy he preached spread much farther than you would have thought, and Catherine II, worried that her Russians would gradually end up incapable of multiplying sufficiently, tried to put a stop to it. Selivanov had been captured, bound, and beaten with the knout; molten wax had been poured over his head. Exiled to Siberia, he had remained there until Tsar Alexander pardoned him.

He spent his final years in reclusion, in a monastery. But the persecution had had the expected effect: thenceforth the people regarded him as a martyr and a saint, and they willingly gave themselves up to the *nastavnik*, who rid them of the key to hell. The women too sometimes cut off their nipples, so that they would no longer be able to breastfeed and as a sign that they would bear no more children. After that, the men and the women lived without meat, without wine, without tobacco, without carnal sin, and they worshipped the icon of their saint. Yevdoshka had a little icon of St Selivanov at his house on Strada Birjarilor. But he had not relinquished foul language; he sinned with his tongue worse than those whose bodies held the key to hell. Leon Margulis also knew that fortunately his own key was in very good working order, and Agatha had no reason for complaint.

They were making slow progress; there was a traffic jam and the horses moved at a walk, while the cabmen chatted among themselves, side by side, pulling on the reins without looking ahead. If the snow had not already deteriorated into filth, many passengers would have rather walked. Those who had taken the horse-drawn tram were at an advantage, since it had a separate lane, and Dr Margulis was sorry he had not chosen that mode of transport. But it was almost inappropriate for a doctor to take the tram: what would his patients say?

The whole of Bucharest had come into town today, on Strada Batiştei he espied the young Livezeanu coming in the opposite direction, in his open carriage, despite the snow outside. His hat was white with snow-flakes, but he did not seem to care. He was driving the horse by himself, faster than would have been advisable in such a crowd, and overtaking everything in his path. God forbid there be an accident! More and more young men were causing or falling victims to accidents these days. In the last year, four had been brought to his surgery. But somehow he had arrived safely at Strada Teilor. He took note of the splendid houses at the intersection with Strada Sfântul Spiridon, knowing that they had been renovating them for a long time: now, having been completed, they looked dazzling. Inside there were lit chandeliers and through the windows could be seen a throng of people. At that moment, a young man with a slinky, undulating gait emerged from the courtyard and quickly hopped onto the tram whose horses had stopped at the station.

'Here we are, sir!' announced Yevdoshka, and his customer placed his foot on the small iron rung that served as a step. Margulis remembered that on Saturdays Rosenberg did not come to the Hospice of Health, and so he asked at reception after the unknown young man who had been brought from the Police Station the day before and a nurse wearing a white apron and a white headscarf knotted at the back conducted him to a rather narrow room with four iron beds, of which only two were occu-pied. The air was stale and smelled of sweat and disinfectant. In one of the beds he recognized the young, blond man; his eyes were closed, as they had been when he saw him the previous day. The doctor was downcast to ascertain that the patient's chances were slim. Should he have accompa-nied him yesterday, or perhaps the injection of oil of camphor had been a mistake? Sometimes, alas, medicine is not a science, but more a case of trial and error. Perhaps in a hundred years the sick would no longer suffer and a panacea other than death would be discovered, he pondered.

In the other bed dozed a sturdy, ruddy-cheeked young man with his leg in plaster. As he had been about to enter the room, a corpulent rather uncouth man in uniform had rushed through the door in front of him, and the doctor, although he was the elder one, had politely stepped aside.

'I'm from the Police,' said the man brusquely, 'wait outside!'

The doctor felt the blood rise to his face, but restrained himself and answered in an even voice: 'I don't know what police station you are from, maybe you are a night watchman from Ciorogârla, but in any event I kindly ask that you wait outside until I finish *consulting with my patient.*'

Taken by surprise, the man glared biliously at the intruder and just as he was about to yell, he recognized him. All of a sudden he became ingratiating.

'Forgive me, doctor, sir, I'm sergeant Budacu, Mr Costache from the Prefecture of Police sent me to see how this young man is and ordered me to come back with an answer as quick as I can.' He then added, lowering his voice and with a complicit air: 'My wife is waiting for me to come back and slaughter the pig. I'm more afraid of her than I am of the boss. You know what it's like when you have a bad-tempered wife.'

'Before we do anything else, I have to have a look at the patient's condition,' said the doctor, rather grudgingly. 'I don't think he can talk.'

The young man with the broken leg was listening to them with interest. He was the type of person who respects the winner in a fight, no matter who it might be, and consequently he addressed Margulis: 'After they brought him he kept groaning, until just now, but nobody paid any attention to him. You could be dying and nobody would come. She gave him some water –' here he pointed at the woman with the white headscarf '– but he couldn't drink it, and it spilled down his chin and on the bed.'

The doctor twisted the little wheel to turn up the gas lamp, took the moribund man's left wrist, took the watch out of his waistcoat pocket, and began to count.

'His pulse is irregular. I think we are going to lose him. Tell Mr Costache Boerescu from me that he should come straight away,' he said to the policeman. 'Usually a patient in his death throes will have a moment of lucidity. But let him know that he might come all this way for nothing, because there is no absolute rule. I don't think he will last even until five o'clock this afternoon.'

Then he turned to the nurse and told her to send for a priest.

4.

'Do you believe in God?'

Nicu had entered the so-called painters' house without knocking and without being surprised at the mess inside. His house was no palace either, but in any event, when his mother was well, she tidied up, cleaned and washed, for she was a washerwoman by day. In summer, she went to wash down at the embankment, where all the women bathed, stark naked, alongside the men, without embarrassment. In winter of course, it was harder; and she went only to houses that had running water. The poor woman had 'washerwoman's hands', all red and swollen. On the rare occasions when she caressed him, he could feel the calluses on her palms; it was as if she were applying a cheese grater to his face.

Inside, the stranger, resting his head on some rags and wrapped in a light-brown blanket, was looking towards the window, through which the light was beginning to dissipate, and whenever a gust blew through the broken pane a few snowflakes entered, only to perish. The stranger didn't look as well as he had the evening before; he had sprouted a stubbly beard, making his cheeks look dirty. He no longer looked anything like Iulia. His face seemed more sunken. Nicu very much liked the question about God and it was a sign of great friendship on his part when he asked it; for it was his latest discovery. In any event, his range of conversation was limited, although the teacher used to say that his tongue could never stop wagging and sometimes clipped his ears or caned his hands for it: 'You've got an itchy tongue!' he would say, or: 'You can't sit still, you'd think you've got worms!' Nicu had indeed had worms, but Dr Margulis had treated him with garlic and celery root and sweetmeats. He wanted to befriend the stranger, because it was obvious from a mile off how helpless he was. He was not expecting to receive an answer to his question about God, and so he went on, in his teacher's tone of voice: 'I believe in electricity. But I also believe in God, when I'm in a tight spot. Today I believe.'

'Today you're in a tight spot? What day is today?'

Look how the stranger is talking to him and look how he understands what he means, said Nicu to himself. He isn't stupid, or ill in the head: he'd noticed that all too well yesterday. But Nicu did not feel in his element and so he answered: 'Today is Saturday and I'm out of sorts.'

'So am I,' observed the stranger, drily, still looking at the windowpane, hoping for a ray of sunlight. But the sun was cold and broken.

Nicu would have preferred it if he had asked: 'Why?' Then, he would have told him about the wallet he had been seeking in vain all that morning. He felt he could tell the stranger that. And if the man was a Martian, maybe he would know where it was, without having to look for it, and he would know whether there was a lottery ticket in it and whether the numbers were the winning ones, because otherwise there was no point bothering with it.

'What's your name?' asked Nicu. He knew what it was, but the stranger didn't know he knew.

'Dan Crețu.'

'Mine's Nicu, but at school the teacher calls me Niculae, Stanciu Niculae. Do you know Kretzu the pharmacist, the ginger one? His hair isn't curly at all. Sometimes he sends me to fetch all kinds of ointments, tablets and powders that cure you. I'm an errand boy,' said the lad, trying to sound modest, although he was very proud.

'What are you doing here?'

Nicu didn't know what to say, and so he saw to the fire.

'I'm going to the Stork's Nest to buy a candle. It's a nice name, isn't it?'

'Nicu?'

'No, the Stork's Nest! The cantor told me that a long time ago the storks used to build their nests on the roof. It was a shingle roof. I'd be really glad if they came again, I like *all* birds, even crows, and Jacques, who's my friend, likes seagulls a lot. We look at them because they fly... I'd like to fly. I've even dreamed that I was flying. And Jacques sometimes dreams the same thing, poor thing. Have you ever dreamed you were flying?'

'I've done more than that. I have flown,' said the man, and Nicu could hardly believe that his suspicion was being confirmed: the man was from the planet Mars and had fallen to Earth. Disturbed, he did not dare ask him anything else.

He vanished for a few minutes and came back with a thick, lighted candle, sheltering the flame with his cupped hand. He gathered some sticks from amongst the rubbish lying around the room and lit them with ease. Then he ran back outside. This time he came back with some water in a chipped enamel cup.

'I couldn't find any tea. If you like, I'll heat it up over the fire. I've brought some bread, they were preparing it for the service, because tomorrow's Sunday. They didn't want to give me any wine, because they thought I'd drink it, but I've never drunk win in my life. Aren't you hungry? Eat.'

And he emptied the pockets of his coat.

'Have you ever spoken on the telephone?'

The man nodded, chewing.

'I have too, three times already, at *Universu*'. Mr Cazzavillan the director let me. It's difficult to hear, what with all the crackling and popping, but you'd think the other person was right there, in the horn of the receiver, as small as a doll, except you can't see him. Some look like their voices, but others you can't recognize, you'd think they'd got the wrong voice, like it wasn't tailored to fit them. Would you like us to be brothers?'

Nicu received no answer. He said nothing for a while and then sighed. He took the cow from his pocket and fiddled with its legs.

'Now she's called Fira, you know... Look, I came to help you,' he said, looking from the corner of his eye at the bread that was vanishing into the stranger's mouth. The stranger was now sitting up, on the edge of the bed. 'I'll help you and maybe you can help me, I mean, maybe you'll be just as kind, sometime. But I'll help you anyway, for free.'

Nicu looked as if he had swallowed something and it had stuck half way down his gullet.

'Who sent you?'

The question sounded rather harsh, and the lad pondered for a short moment.

'My gran said that God sends us and He knows everybody's path... They wrote about you in *Universu*', old man Cercel read it to me. I know how to read too, a little, especially when it's in capitals. Capitals are the big letters; that's what we call them at our newspaper. And if you're a newspaperman, as it says there, I'll take you to *Universu*', because Mr Procopiu needs a man who knows his letters and who can write nicely. Mr Procopiu is a kind of boss; Mr Cazzavillan the director is the only boss bigger than him. He's been looking for a man ever since the feast of St Demetrios, when three editors left at the same time, and he still hasn't found anybody. You know how to write, don't you? Are you really a newspaperman?'

The man had either not heard or did not want to answer. Nicu examined his coloured footwear. Now he could see the lilac stripes against the green ones more clearly. The shoes didn't look at all solid and they were still damp from the night before. He had slept with his clothes on, like a tramp.

'Maybe they'll give you a pair of galoshes at *Universu*'. The best ones are the St Petersburg brand; all the young people wear them. They've got a double sole.'

Nicu took him by the hand, as he used to do with his mother when she didn't really know what was going on. He picked his bowler hat out of the bucket and wiped it on the sleeve of his coat, wondering where it had come from. As he had told Jacques, he knew for sure that the man was bareheaded. The Margulis family's cook had told the boys about people who walk in their sleep, when there is a full moon, as if they were wide-awake. They walk along the rooftops and if you call out to them, they fall, but otherwise 'nothing happens to them.' Might there have been a full moon last night? He hadn't noticed. He gave the stranger a critical look. You'll be embarrassed by him on the street dressed like that, he thought, what with that overly large greatcoat and him looking like he's just fallen out of the sky. Obviously, he for one would have liked to be in a roofed carriage, with a gleaming equipage, seated next to a well-dressed, cheerful and healthy man, smelling of patchouli, rather than a Martian who smelled of poverty. But there's no choosing your family. It was just like the lottery: some people win, some lose. Nicu had already adopted him as a member of his not very large family; this man Dan Crețu, who in the light of day looked gentle and ill. But what if, he now thought, what if *it really was like that*, if he had an unknown brother who had grown up far away, as happened in the family of that vendor from the fish market? When the brothers met, they both sensed it, like an electric current that passed through them both and made them burst into tears. It was as if he had felt the same current, when he saw the stranger for the first time, except that there had been no tears. But if you don't feel like crying, does it still mean you're brothers?

5.

They entered *Universul* and old man Cercel, who had lately been having stabbing pains in his belly, stood up with a groan. While the stranger brushed the snow off himself, the doorman, surprise, surprise, communicated to the boy in a low voice that he at last had the lottery ticket: 98, 38 and 51. In other words, the coming year, as Nicu had advised, the year of his birth, and the year of his wife's birth. They looked each other in the eyes, with excitement, the same as they always did when they put fate to the test. Old man Cercel, whose face was a little more congested than usual, conducted the two of them to Peppin Mirto. Nicu was unsurprised to discover that Mr Peppin was inclined to help with regard to the stranger; he was a man who filled any gap anytime and entered anywhere it was difficult. On the other hand, he had not understood very well why Mr Costache wanted to help the stranger, but nor did he trouble his head about it. He decided he must have his reasons.

He found Peppin working on a translation. He had just written: *Second Part. The Genius of Evil...* and was about to dip his nib in the inkwell when the motley group made up of the doorman, Nicu and a strange, mild-looking man, appeared in the doorway. The doorman explained what was what, Mr Mirto put his pen down, pressed a piece of blotting paper to the splendidly handwritten title, and in a booming voice invited Dan to sit down. He was surprised to notice that the man did not remove his bowler hat, which was pulled down rather too far over his ears.

'Has Mr Neculai Procopiu arrived yet?' he asked the doorman.

'Not yet,' said Nicu and old man Cercel both at the same time. 'But he should be here any minute now. I'll tell him to come up...' added the doorman.

'I'll tell him too,' Nicu made a point of saying and then withdrew along with the doorman, but not before giving his adopted brother a wink. It was a habit he had picked up at school from the older boys, who were always finding occasions to encourage each other, just as they were always finding occasions to niggle each other. Nicu they preferred to niggle, but he did not care; he took everything as it came.

Peppin did not know how to tell the stranger that he had forgotten to take his hat off and finally abandoned the subject, so as not to make him feel embarrassed. He sought a subject of conversation suitable for two men who did not know each other and had just said, in his melodious voice: 'The snow has started coming down heavily! But fair weather has been announced for tomorrow, I think it must be the mildest winter since–' when he heard, with relief, faint voices in the corridor. It was indeed Neculai Procopiu, who entered wearing a top hat far too elegant for an ordinary working day. Perhaps he will be going from here straight to the opera, thought Peppin, who was always yearning for music.

'Good day, you must be – ' the editor-in-chief began to say, but then he faltered, his eyes fixed on the hat atop the stranger's head.

'This is Mr Dan Kretzu. Are you by chance a relative of Kretzu the pharmacist?' asked Peppin.

Seeing the editor-in-chief's look, the turn of phrase he had been seeking earlier suddenly came to him, as sometimes happened when he was translating and the right word popped up out of the blue: 'If a man sits in a newspaper office with his hat and coat on, it means he does not belong there. Allow me to share this observation from a long-standing newspaperman, in the hope that we shall soon be colleagues. Perhaps you would like to hang your hat and coat on the rack?'

And he accompanied that wonderfully articulated sentence with a gesture of invitation towards the coat rack, next to which could be seen, just as in every other office, the calendar with the Canadian lady skaters. Unconvinced, the man took off his hat and sat holding it. He held it like a ball of rags. For the moment, Peppin Mirto did not feel any great sympathy towards the stranger, who was neither young nor old, and was pale, with dark rings under his eyes. Mr Costache had asked him as a personal favour to help discreetly. He did not very well understand why. As for the editor-in-chief, he fixed the man with a gaze that might mean anything at all.

'Allow me,' said Procopiu, and hastened to take the hat from his hands.

But instead of taking it to the coat-rack, he looked at the lining and let forth an exclamation that astonished the translator. Surely there must be something that eluded him.

'He has come about a job,' Peppin began, 'he is a newspaperman... where have you worked, probably abroad, am I right? We do not wish to be indiscreet, although indiscretion is part of our trade, albeit not between colleagues, and I am sure you will tell us in your own good time, when you feel like it, and so until then.'

Peppin liked the sound of his own voice. Neculai Procopiu interrupted him: 'If you will be kind enough to provide a sample of your work, Mr Peppin Mirto will give you instructions, and when you are ready, bring it upstairs to me, the last door on the right after you climb the stairs. I shall be waiting. Goodbye!'

Peppin felt rather awkward, without knowing why. He helped the stranger to take off his coat with the bone buttons, hung it to the coatrack, under the hat, and then handed him a bundle of letters: a questionnaire that the newspaper had conducted on the subject *Why Do You Fast?*, which was due to be published on Wednesday, 24 December. But the answers received from various subscribers, one hundred in number, had to be grouped by categories, then recopied, with the addition of an introductory sentence and a few closing words.

'I have already started it, so you won't have much to do,' said Peppin with a trace of regret. You see, I am the proof-reader and translator, not an editor, but given our lack of people I do a bit of everything, rather like a housemaid. I translate from Italian, because my mother was from Arezzo, and from English, when the need arises, but with far greater difficulty. As for orthography, we use the new standard, as you will see here, in the work I have done. Please ask me if anything is unclear.'

Peppin poked his head out of the door to call for some coffee and in a short while Nicu arrived with it. On his own authority, Nicu had also asked for two pies, 'on the *Universu'* slate!' and winking at Dan once again, he placed them on the desk, wrapped up in paper. The stranger greedily ate one pie, almost without chewing, and then even more greedily smoked the cigarette offered by Mr Mirto.

After an hour or so the job was done, during which time Peppin dedicated himself to his translation about the genius of evil and the stranger wrote without stumbling – he preferred a pencil to pen and inkpot. He had worked without saying a word, as if he were dumb, and smoked another two cigarettes from Mirto's tobacco tin, until Mirto secreted them in the drawer of the desk and discreetly locked it. At one point Dan Crețu did lift his head and asked what the verb *merimetisi* meant, with reference to the stomach. Peppin hastened to explain the meaning, although he was rather intrigued by the stranger's unfamiliarity with the word, which he could only explain as being a result of exile. He concluded that the man had lived abroad since he was little and who knows what dubious business he was mixed up in; which was why the Police were interested in him. Peppin cast a glance at the pieces of paper, out of curiosity, and it seemed to him that the handwriting was not at all elegant, although it was easy to decipher and that was the principle behind it. But far be it from him to judge the result.

Mr Procopiu made the exact same comment immediately: 'The handwriting is not elegant, but it is easy to read, and that is the main thing.'

He had lit the lamp on his desk, since the shadows of dusk already enveloped the room. Outside it snowed without surcease, but the wood fire and electric light (electricity had been installed a few years earlier along Strada Brezoianu, as far as number 11, which is to say, as far as the newspaper offices) lent the office a pleasant air. Then he carefully read through the material.

(Margin) TRADITIONS: CHRISTMAS FAST
Our questionnaire (centred)

WHY DO PEOPLE FAST (bold)
(Chapeau) The editors of *Universul* asked this question of 100 respondents. For the benefit of our readers the following are the answers we received. Some serious, some humorous, depending on the person.

21 answered: I for one fast because it is the custom.
13 To keep fit.
13 To gain my neighbours' respect.
1 To keep in with my mother-in-law.
3 To cleanse my stomach
3 Because my grandmother (mother, father) asked me to in her (his) will.
3 Because I like beans.
4 Because a good fast is better than a bad dessert
2 So the grocers can sell their octopuses.
1 Because I am a friend of the Metropolitan Bishop.
4 To get rid of my belly.
3 Because that is how our cook cooks.
1 Because my father is a market gardener.
4 To make fun at our priest, who does not fast.
7 So that there will not be any arguments at home.
2 To please my prospective in-laws, who will not give their daughter away to a heretic.
2 It is the fashion.
9 I have no idea why.
A single respondent answered: 'Because I am a Christian.'
Whether you have fasted or whether you have not,
    our newspaper wishes you a *Happy Christmas*
    in the company of your dear ones.

While he read, Mr Procopiu kept fingering his waxed moustache, as if to make sure it was still there. From the top of the page he struck out the word 'respondents' – 'it doesn't sound good, we avoid radicals' – and replaced it with 'Christians' and at the end, instead of 'a single respondent' he wrote: 'a single subscriber to *Universul*, of those questioned.'

'My congratulations, sir, it is very good, you may consider yourself hired,' said the editor-in-chief. 'Welcome to our newspaper! But allow me to tell you that we are two of a kind. I was born in 1854, like the late George Lahovary.'

The man shuddered. Procopiu interpreted it in his own way.

'To die pierced by a sword at the age of forty-three because you have written a political article is some fate, is it not? Well, here at our newspaper we do not write about politics, or at least not for the time being. It is plain that you have had a good education,' said Procopiu, returning to the subject at hand: 'Everything is neat and concise. Our rule is that we avoid adjectives wherever possible. You will receive a list of the new abbreviations. And... I would like to give you a... a new hat from our storeroom, employees receive a present at Christmas and it seems to me that you could use some new galoshes,' he went on, looking in embarrassment now at the new employee's head, now at his feet. Mention of the word 'hat' abruptly caused a sort of unpleasant complicity between the two men. For very different reasons, neither of them was prepared to get to the bottom of the midnight encounter, Procopiu's flight, and the loss of his hat.

'Tomorrow you should be here at nine o'clock in the morning. As you probably know, we work on Sundays and we take it in turns to come in to the office. As for the remaining matters, a place to sleep, meals, wages, Mr Mirto, whom you already know, the man with the deep voice, Peppin, will make arrangements. We have another man, Mirto – Păvălucă, Pavel that is – who sits at the same table, but he took the day off today, as he has to see to slaughtering his pig, today being the feast of St Ignatius. On Christmas Day, he brings us all kinds of good things. He has an excellent cook, as you will see. Here we are like a family. A few good editors happen to have left us and *Călăuza Bucureştiului* and *Adevărul* take swipes at us for not having staff. Once again, welcome,' he added, rather perplexed that the stranger did not respond or react, and, above all, did not leave. He stood up, opened the door and made a polite bow. At that very moment the telephone rang down the hall and Procopiu rushed to lift the receiver.

'Hello, Mr Boerescu, my respects! Of course, it is on the front page, who wouldn't wish to have exclusivity in such a matter? I will come right away.'

6.

After finding out who the newcomer was, the nurse with the white apron conducted Costache Boerescu to the blond man who had been brought in the evening before. The woman felt sorry for the poor boy and sensed, from experience, that he had neither sufficient vital force, *vis vitalis*, nor sufficient will to live. Which is to say, his vital principle was as murky as the waters of a river after rainfall. He had elegant clothes and highly polished boots, and when they had removed his suit she saw that he had the underclothes of a rich gentleman. On the shirt, covered now with clotted blood, was sewn a handsome monogram: three letters with curlicues like snails' shells spelled *R. O. Z.*

The first thing that Mr Costache did was to hold the gas lamp close to the shirt that hung from the back of the chair and to study those three letters. His journey had been worth it for that alone. He sat down at the wounded man's bedside and lost himself in thought, ignoring the grumblings of the well-fed man whose leg was in plaster. It was too hot, the room was too small, and the stove was too close, and so he opened the window a crack and took a deep breath of the cold outside air. He saw a cab stop at the entrance and shortly thereafter the nurse showed Neculai Procopiu inside. Silently, Procopiu sat down on the other side of the bed. To him, a hospital, a sanatorium, was a kind of church or temple, where it was not fitting to speak. Dr Rosenburg also made an unexpected appearance. He had been informed that he had important guests, and although on the Sabbath he tried not to leave the house, he reckoned that an exception would not go against him in heaven. He was not at all a religious fanatic. He ordered that the second man be moved to a different room, and applied gentle persuasion when the man protested and complained of boredom, and then he called for a chair to be brought. Then he sat down with difficulty, for he suffered from osteoarthritis. Being a physician does not exempt one from diseases, as would be fitting in a just world.

In a low voice they spoke together about the strange aspects of the case.

'Do you think there is any connection between Mr Dan Crețu, whom I have just hired – he is well educated and I think he is from abroad – and this young man?' asked Procopiu with a trace of alarm.

'Probably. Coincidences are rare in our trade, but not out of the question,' replied Costache, in an equally low a voice. 'Usually two or three matches will give you a definite answer. For the time being we have only one, connected to the finding of these two.'

Dr Rosenberg, whose hair was completely white and whose voice was of exceptional gentleness, informed the two men as to the young man's condition.

'Dr Margulis sent word that I should come, if I could, because he expected a brief interval of lucidity before... And I think it would be well, as he also suggested, if I give him an intramuscular injection of caffeine, which helps to revive, so that he will have the strength to speak clearly.'

But he warned them that some dying men passed their moment of lucidity in complete silence, while only their eyes spoke, while others spoke in a deceptively logical manner that was hard to understand, and others still let out heart-rending cries or were gripped by ecstasy. And he recounted a number of cases, the most encouraging of which had been that of a woman a few days previously, who before dying said she could see a powerful light and was flying towards it. When she gave her last breath, she was bathed in a beatitude that could be read in her eyes.

They were silent for a long while. Procopiu stood up and went to the window, Dr Rosenberg looked at the patient, almost dozing off, and Mr Costache took refuge in his own thoughts. From time to time he twirled the points of his auburn moustache, twisting them down from their wonted upright position. He had given up wearing a beard a few years ago, after much hesitation. He now thought he looked younger without it. All three gave a start when the patient opened his eyes. For the first time they saw his eyes and were struck by limpid brown depths. His huge eyes were full of astonishment: the patient was trying to understand where he was.

'Be calm, you are in good hands,' said Dr Rosenberg in a caressing voice. Remembering the advice of his fellow physician Margulis, he left the room almost at a run to fetch a syringe from the pan of water boiling over a low flame on the stove in the next room.

When he came back, the blond man had sat up in bed and was saying something in a slurred voice. Costache took out a visiting card and a pencil, trying to write down what he heard: *light, Popescu, light, stars, Holy Mother.* He also thought he heard something like *dar* ("gift") or *sar* ("I leap"), but then, as if relieved of some unknown burden, the blond young man exhaled and stopped breathing. Dr Rosenberg, holding the syringe in the air, had managed only to squirt a test droplet, like a tear. All he could do now was close the man's eyes, confirm the death – at eleven minutes past six pm, Saturday, 20 December – and record it in the register. Procopiu was clasping his hands together. Costache had fastened his eyes on the words he had written on the visiting card and avoided looking around him.

Dr Rosenberg asked: 'who will take care of the funeral if we know nothing about him? Shall I inform the Town Hall, as usual? Mayor Robescu is away in Vienna until the New Year, but Mr Bursan is on duty and in fact he deals with such matters.'

'Be so good as to wait until tomorrow. As it is winter, I think it will be possible for you to move him into an unheated room. I will let you know, since I hope to discover his family. And you too,' said Costache, turning to the newspaperman. 'Have somebody waiting by the telephone, please: number 297, if I remember correctly?'

As they left, they met the priest from the Icoanei Church, who had come to administer the last rites, but had arrived a few minutes too late. Nonetheless, he went in and performed what was needful, reckoning that it is never too late for important matters. Costache spoke in a low voice to Procopiu. It seems that not everything he had learned should appear on the front page, where some things were best said and others best concealed; in any event, it should be printed no earlier than Monday, because he hoped to have new information the following day. The editor waited for the tram and went home, to recoup the hours of sleep he had missed the night before.

Conu Costache set off on foot. He had given Budacu the day off so that he could go and slaughter his pig. He strove not to give his men cause for smouldering resentment. It had now stopped snowing and the fresh snow sparkled here and there in the glow of the street lamps. Costache's feet left large prints in the white of the pavement, with a line of small, deep points on the right, left by his cane. *Popescu* was a common enough name; it would be difficult to find out anything about it. *Light, stars, Holy Mother*: these were all things that probably pertained to a man's last moments. Although... He had not heard the rest clearly. Was it *gift*? On the other hand, *R. O. Z.* would be an easier clue to follow. At home he had an alphabetical list, which he himself had compiled, of all the monograms of Romania's important families. And the young man had spoken Romanian without any trace of an accent, and so he was not a foreigner.

Although Costache was known for his brisk gait, he now trod slowly, heavily, and felt overwhelmed by melancholy. The friendly face of the young man and his dark eyes blended with the shadows of night. Yet another child who had been fooled by the feeling he was immortal! He thought that without doubt, in that very instant, a mother or a father or sisters or brothers were experiencing dreadful fear, because the boy had not come home for two days. Perhaps they had gone to his friends and with each negative answer another hope had been dashed and the conviction that some disaster had befallen him took ever-firmer hold of their hearts. Such agonizing fear is only the beginning. Worse still is the hope. Why do hope and worry exist if they have to end like this? It is as if despair has need of a prelude full of cruelty. And if in the case of joy many believe that the waiting is the most beautiful part, when it comes to pain, the waiting is the most horrible part; the waiting for great pain. And pain, as he knew all too well, has a multitude of tentacles, like an octopus. You lop them off in vain; there are always enough of them to choke you.

He did not look up the monogram that evening, as he was invited to the Margulis house for dinner, and only had time to change quickly, otherwise he would be late. The dogs barked in people's back yards as he approached, and even more loudly after he passed. He saw that the clouds had broken up and in the gaps there gleamed a few stars. *Stars, light?* The smoke from the chimneys rose in straight lines, a sign that tomorrow, Sunday, the weather would be fine.

7.

'A bath in a tub with a shower, please,' said the man, in a strong Moldavian accent, and handed over two lei. He remained with his hand outstretched, waiting for the change.

It looked rather shabby, but to the Grivița Baths came all varieties of the unwashed. The bath attendant was very proud of the fact that he had been born in Bucharest, although he was short on other merits. On Saturdays in particular, it was crowded, as people came to freshen themselves up, ready for Sunday, and the bath attendant hated Saturdays. And ever since Mayor Robescu started giving out free bath vouchers to the poor, it was dreadful! Not to mention the fact that they were insolent and wrote in the complaints book: 'He gave me a dirty towel!' Or 'Down with the Mayor!' and 'Long live the King!' 'The bath attendant is foul-tempered!' One of them had even copied out an obscene joke from *The Ant*, about a woman who was looking for a watch that had disappeared from her house and just when she thought she had found it in a young man's trousers, her husband turned up.

Outside the baths it was already pitch black, but luckily inside everything was illumined with electricity, and the freshly painted walls were still clean and white. The reason why all kinds of people flocked to the Grivița Baths was thanks to the advertisement in *Universul*, a popular newspaper, read, as its editors said, in both working class districts and in palaces; and also thanks to the efforts of Vasiliu the pharmacist, who ran the establishment. As a leading member of Bucharest's council for hygiene, he had taken his colleagues by surprise when he invested his entire personal fortune in opening a bathhouse with the latest amenities. As the prices were reasonable, it was a place suited to every pocket, and even going second-class, at one leu and ten bani, you could come out looking like new. The bath attendant was happy when, gauging a customer with a single glance, he was able to offer, to those with the means, hydrotherapy, massage and electrotherapy, first-class, of course. Another novelty was the discount for all the members of the City's pharmaceutical and medical societies. In any event, the bathhouse was more successful than Mr Vasiliu had anticipated, and he had raised the attendant's wages without the latter having to make any great effort in that direction and without any effect on his general demeanour.

It took the attendant quite a while before he found the 30 bani change and handed over the towel and soap. In the meantime, the Moldavian examined his face, weighing him up. He had with him a large silver-coloured case, and the attendant told him he would have to leave it at the door. The man took him aside and slipped in his pocket an amount that was around twenty times larger than the cost of a first class ticket, causing the attendant to turn red in the face. It was very hot inside as it was, making it a joy to come inside, out of the cold. The Moldavian was afraid the man in the white gown was going to throw a fit, which would have been the last thing he needed right then, but no, after a few moments things returned to normal, and so he went off to take his bath, not in second-class, but in the luxury section. He lingered for almost an hour, delighting in the hot water, which seemed to melt away all the painful knots in his body, and then he went to take a massage. As he was leaving, the attendant gave him a bow, such as he reserved only for distinguished customers. Nobody noticed that the man had arrived with a case and left without it. As for the attendant, he was at that age at which you quickly forget everything non-essential to your life. When he arrived home, he told his wife, who was a housekeeper, that he had come into a sum of money and that for the first time ever they would be able to spend New Year's Eve in Sinaia at a nice hotel, where they would be treated like boyars.

A GOOD DAY.
WITH SOME EXCEPTIONS...

1.

Today I experienced a great joy. A surprise. It was about time, otherwise I would have said that I was beginning to resemble Amelia from *Vanity Fair*, and heaven knows nowadays kind, weepy creatures are more unfashionable than Grandmother's long nails and her bunches of curls hanging next to her ears!

No sooner did I wake up than I saw rays of light shining through the curtains, dancing on the walls in oblique stripes. They made me smile and then laugh. A breeze was blowing and the rays deftly slid over and beneath each other as if wielded by a master swordsman. It was one of those sunny days that make your soul tingle. I got up, stoked the fire, washed, and chose my blue dress to match the sky. I try to paint the world with the colours of my dresses. Since I was not expecting any visits, I did not put on my corset. When I was little, and our teachers at the Central Girls School forbade us to wear corsets, filling our heads with the reason that they hindered normal bone development, that they caused anaemia, because we would not be able to eat sufficiently, we all used to do exactly the opposite. We wanted to do everything they forbade us to do. If I could not wear a corset in the daytime, lest they caught me, I used to wear one at night and sleep in it, to give myself a slender waist and straight spine. But now, when I am allowed to wear one.

The truth is that Dr Gerota is solely to blame for me not liking them any more. I was at Papa's surgery two months ago and Dr Gerota came in. I knew him by reputation: thirty-years-old, talented, educated in Paris, and only recently having returned, with plans to change the world from its foundations upward, a lecturer on all the latest medical trends. Papa told me that since October he has taught anatomy at the Academy of Fine Arts. (I would dearly like to attend the Academy, but unfortunately I have no talent. But in any event, I am determined to enrol in a university faculty next year.) Papa calls Dr Gerota by his first name, Dimitrie. And this Dimitrie, who almost made me forget Alexandru, when he saw me encased in a corset – I had not eaten, because there was a party that evening – clasped my waist between his large hands, with his handsome fingers, and saw that it fit there snugly. But instead of complimenting me, as I thought would have been polite, and as Safta and the cook had done at home, he scolded me so severely that the tears came to my eyes.

'Miss,' he said, 'how can your mother allow you to strangulate yourself like this? How old are you? You do not even need a corset: you are slim already, thin even. I think that in the evening your skin must be red and sore, if not bruised, am I right? Have you any idea what you are doing to your internal organs?'

Papa blushed and I felt as if I were suffocating. But Dr Gerota, with his noble fighter's mien, with his swept-back hair and wilful chin, calmly delivered his damning verdict, without one pang of his physician's heart: 'Look at how you are panting, your lungs are imprisoned in a vice. You certainly suffer migraines and faintness, and, I suspect, nasal haemorrhages, and insufficient blood reaches your brain. My esteemed Mr Margulis –' having finished with me he now took father to task '– why do you allow her to subject herself to such torture? For the sake of your daughter, I am going to prepare a lecture on the disadvantages of the corset and I shall send you, your lady wife and your daughter an invitation. Try not to faint, there is no cause for tears, but I ask you to go into the other room this very moment and loosen the laces.'

Rarely have I felt such strength in a man. Papa, although almost twenty years older, was almost completely cowed. I think Gerota is destined for great things.

*

And so, without a corset, I went into the salon. I saw from the pendulum clock that it was quite late. I had slept for a long time – but what should one do on a bright morning such as this? I rushed to open the window, then to the piano, my old, worn-out but trusty Bösendorfer. I picked up an armful of scores, which had started to gather dust, so long had it been since I last touched them. Mama often goes to Graeve's shop and buys scores for me. I leafed through them, but nothing tempted me, when all of a sudden, *as if by magic*, I felt drawn to one. It was a transcription for piano of a minuet by Handel. It was as if somebody had guided my hand to pick this one out of the whole sheaf. I had started out with the thought of playing something new, something happy and unpretentious, like the compositions in *Le Journal*, the review to which Mama subscribes, but nonetheless this page caught my eye. It was the first time I had looked at it; I do not even know when it appeared in the pile. I began to decipher it tentatively, it was in G minor, in three-four time and it was not easy. I kept playing wrong notes, and I could not keep to the right time. And so I fumbled along, but gradually I caught the musical theme and it gave me goose-bumps when I realized what I was playing: *it was the music from Jacques' figurine clock!* I had been desperately trying to find out what it was for two years, and nobody, but nobody, had recognized it – no matter whom I had asked – even Mr Wiest! And now, unexpectedly, I had discovered it in my piano pile. Who knows how long it had been there. This is what happens to me: I seek afar and find the desired thing right next to me.

It was only then that I felt the cold. I had left the window open. Like a whirlwind I went to my little brother's room. He was sitting at the table, upon which a real war of lead soldiers was in progress. I think all the lead soldiers he had must have been there. The dear boy, he was fighting the War of Independence. On the table it was a true massacre; few soldiers were still standing. He has not looked well for some time; he is too pale. I said: 'Jacques, I have a present for you. Something you have spent a long time waiting for.'

Curious, he said: 'A r-real sword. An officer-r's uniform. *R-robinson Cr-rusoe*. A r-real Alsatian?'

'No, Jacques, not something tangible, but something spiritual.' And so as not to torture him any longer, I said: 'Come into the salon and you will see, or rather, you will hear.'

I sat down at the piano and began to play the minuet, still making the odd mistake, but Jacques grew even paler and from the very first musical phrase he let out a cry. 'You have found it! You have found it! Who is it? What is it?'

He said it was the most wonderful present he had ever received in his life and almost wept for joy. I brought his flute. We decided to learn it properly, secretly, before Christmas, and to play it then, as a surprise for our family and friends. Maybe Mr Costache will come too, and our neighbour Giuseppe, the guitar teacher, will certainly join us.

Mama and Papa warned us yesterday that they would be going to the countryside very early in the morning, to our uncle's in Giurgiu, and would not be back until afternoon. At Christmas, they always bring good things back from our uncle's place. We have not reared our own pig for a few years. That was because Jacques chanced to see a newly born piglet taken away from the sow to be killed. The servant explained it to him clearly: 'Count the teats and count the piglets. One is condemned to death!' Jacques' sorrow for the *innocent* piglet condemned to death was so great, his suffering was so material and physical, that Mama and Papa gave up rearing animals.

Both Jacques and I rejoice when we are left to our own devices. And so we played undisturbed until we felt hungry. I have not seen Jacques eat with such an appetite for a long time. I have observed that joy is the best medicine, and even Papa agrees. And so too does the irascible Mr Gerota, probably.

2.

After he combed his mother's hair, looking carefully to see whether she had picked up any more lice, and after he had tied the prematurely grey hair as nicely as he could, Nicu prepared breakfast. He was happy that she was at home, especially on winter days such as these, and he catered to her every whim, as if she were a child. Sometimes the woman smiled at him with the gentleness of a mother, sometimes she glared at him fiercely, like a wild animal, but it no longer frightened the boy. Of course, when he was younger he used to take fright and join in the yelling, which did not calm the situation one bit. Now, he treated her as he had seen his grandmother do, up until not long ago, talking to her softly and calming her. How could a daughter so ill, so tormented by demons as his mother have been brought into the world by a woman so good-natured and balanced as his grandmother? He hoped with all his heart that he would grow up to be like his grandmother, rather than his mother. Was it possible for a person's qualities to bypass her children and appear in her grandchildren, like a legacy bequeathed by Nature? Such a legacy would do him much good in future. His grandmother had died at the age of sixty and to him that seemed young. As for his father, he knew only that he was a soldier or adjutant. He told everybody that his father had been an officer. He also said that he was dead, but of that he was not at all sure, and he was fearful lest he turn up and make his life complicated, just as he had made his poor mother's life complicated – according to his grandmother.

Nicu inspected the larder with satisfaction: they had food to eat. When the other children asked him what he would rather be, a cricket or an ant, they made fun of him when he replied gravely: 'An ant!' Almost all the boys wanted to be crickets, but ants were wonderfully organized. The larder was quite tidily arranged: he had kept the boxes and jars in exactly the same order as his grandmother had. True, friends from various houses had given him and his mother food and even clothes as presents. He thanked them and accepted everything, even things for which he had no use. Whenever he went to visit Jacques, they sent him home, to the potters' quarter, in the carriage with a box of good things, which, now that his grandmother was gone, he made last as best he could. His greatest satisfaction was to open the parcels and arrange the treasures they contained on the larder shelves: ground sugar, salt, lard, maize flour, jam, and cheese. The provisions that kept the longest, the flour and the rice, he placed on the highest shelf, climbing on top of a chair to do so.

The things he used every day he kept conveniently to hand. He was always calculating how long the provisions would last and was determined not to throw anything away. In summer, if he received a litre of milk and it was not drunk, he would leave it in a cup to go sour, and then, placing the shank of a wooden spoon in the curdled milk and twisting it back and forth between his palms, he would thin it so that it would be fit to drink. It was harder when it came to bread. He had to be careful lest it turned stale or mouldy, and sometimes he would find they had no bread at all. In other houses, they baked bread in an oven in the yard; you could smell it from the street and the scent entered your nostrils and went straight to your belly. But he had to buy bread and he never had time. He had rusks and sometimes he could trick his mother with them, although she often grimaced and spat them out, making a mess.

That morning, having had her hair combed, she smiled sweetly and calmly, as he had not seen her do for a long time. Maybe it was also because the weather was sunny and he was quietly singing what he had been rehearsing at school: 'The star rises high, / God's sign in the sky, / The star shines bright, / Brings tidings of light...'

She too had started murmuring something, in a cracked voice, more and more delighted. He laid the table: bread for her and some rather old marmalade for him. And then he lit the fire. He reminded her to make sure it did not go out, showing her the firewood he had laid by, and put some balls of coloured wool in her hands, with which she played just like a cat. She was happy to ravel and unravel them all day long, and sometimes when he came home he would find wool unravelled all around the room, filling it with colour. By the door, Nicu put on his boots, carefully tied the laces and left. *At the time* he had promised his grandmother he would go to see her on Sundays whenever he was able. Today he was able. It did him good to chat to her about this and that and to ask her advice. And her voice as it was in life seemed to answer him, albeit now only in his mind, where it had somehow remained, stored alongside other voices, like the provisions in their larder. She always gave him good advice on what to do and how to overcome life's trials. And for the hardest trials, once you had done all in your power, there were also the miracle-working icons, as follows: St Stelian, in Vergului Church, who looks after children's health; Sts Cosmas and Damian the Unmercenary Physicians; and St Minas, who looks after the bodily health of all people; a saint whose name he forgot, who prevents girls from being scarred by the chickenpox; and St Eleutherius from the church in Cotroceni, who was to be visited when he wished to get engaged, said his grandmother. On the other hand, you could pray to the icon of St Nicholas any time at all; he looked after the poor and so deeply did he care for them that once he was late for a meeting with God, because he had stopped on the way to lend a helping hand to a peasant whose cart was stuck in the mud. When he arrived for his meeting with God, his boots were caked with mud. But God was not angry, said his grandmother. Nicu also remembered St Spiridon, whose purpose was 'to prove thieves.' He did not know what proving thieves meant, but if that was what the saint did, then proved they must be.

Naturally, there was also the icon in the Icoanei Church, which was also to cure the sick, above all the sicknesses of the soul. As for the Virgin Mary at Sărindar, the church that Nicu Filipescu decided to demolish when he was mayor, this was the most beautiful, the most famous; she had diamond stars on her shoulders, said Grandmother, but Nicu had not seen it and did not know where it might be now or what it might be good for, because he only had use for icons as salves or medicines. On the other hand, he thought that if the man whose first name, Nicu, he shared was now being punished by God and might even go to prison for killing Bucharest's best journalist, then it was because he had allowed the church to be demolished, rather than repairing it. That was what people said, it was also what old man Cercel said, and in the present case he himself was of the exact same opinion. Every day, he passed the site where the church had stood, on his way to *Universul*, and every day he felt sorry for it. Last year, they had built a fancy fountain there, just because Franz Josef was visiting, and now there was nothing but an empty space.

*

His grandmother's grave was covered with snow, like a mound. With his hand Nicu traced a cross in the snow and wrote in large letters, slightly sloping to the left: 'I AM WELL, NICU.' Then he took the cow out of his pocket, showed it to the white mound, and left. The bells had chimed noon some time ago, and the boy decided, because the weather was fine and he felt his soul to be at peace, to go Cişmigiu Park. It was Sunday, and so it was not fitting to work, which is to say, to look for the wallet with the lottery ticket. If the weather allowed, there would be skating on Cişmigiu Lake. No longer ago than the previous year, from the edge of the lake he had seen Princess Maria skating, holding hands with her husband. She was beautiful and seemed so slender, even though she wearing a thick jacket, and her skirts almost swept the ice. Nicu looked especially at her dark green hat, with bows and feathers that blew back as she skated forward. The prince was in uniform, belted at the waist and with a rigid cap, like Nicu's, but with gold braid. In the middle of the ice, next to the flagpole, stood his adjutants. That was what Nicu would be when he grew up; he would become a skater or a sailor.

Pairs of skaters were beginning to arrive. The military brass band was playing in the bandstand, and the skaters tried to glide to the rhythm of the music: tra-la-la-la-la... tra-la... tra-la... tra-la-la-la-la... tra-la... tra-la. They did pirouettes, and picked up speed. One officer was skating backwards. Nicu laughed and jumped up and down when someone fell; it was too funny to see them hit the ice with their bottoms and fling their legs in the air, like beetles. The women fell more gracefully and gathered their skirts around their legs, and then Nicu did not laugh but looked to see how much leg they exposed. When the music stopped he could hear the metal scratching the hard gleam of the lake. If old man Cercel won the lottery, he would definitely give him something, and maybe he could buy himself a pair of ice skates and learn to glide forwards and backwards over the ice. When he turned his head, he thought he glimpsed Petre, who was Inger the confectioner's coachman, on the other side of the lake. Thinking that he might find out from him something about his new friend, Dan Crețu, he ran around the rink to meet him. But before he could reach him, Petre started to walk away. So Nicu followed him, not having anything better to do. Petre had brought his sleigh, and Nicu sat down comfortably on the plank at the back, leaning against the edge of the sleigh. All the boys knew the trick: some even tied their sledges to the back and let themselves be pulled along.

Petre's sleigh stopped in Filaret Garden. The coachman climbed down from the box and set off towards the trees, which, next to the central lane, formed a miniature forest. Near the entrance to the park there were a few people with children, out for a stroll, but the rest of the garden was deserted. Petre vanished among the trees. When the confectioner's coachman reappeared on the lane, Nicu was still among the trees, following the footprints in the snow. He had just reached the place where the footprints had come to a stop, and was sure he would discover something mysterious. But he found nothing – Petre had merely relieved himself against the trunk of a tree, and Nicu decided to do likewise.

3.

Liza, Costache's little white dog, was curled up next to the fire. She was getting old, her hair was falling out, and her back hurt. She had difficulty standing up, but Costache consoled her, saying aloud: 'Never mind, wee dove, we'll grow old together. You ten-years-old, me five times that.' However, he still felt very fit and healthy. Neatly arranged in the bookcase, all his catalogues were to hand, their spines inscribed with gilt letters applied by the hand of the same bookbinder. Still in his white nightshirt, decorated with convoluted blue embroidery, Mr Costache sat down in a comfortable armchair, upholstered in dark leather, and set to work. His hair, lighter in colour than the leather of the armchairs, with but few white strands, was dishevelled and needed cutting. His moustache was also awry.

Grudgingly resigned to being more of a batman and barber than an adjutant, Zaharia was no longer surprised by his master's caprices, nor by anything in the wider world. But he had become gloomy and rather solitary, although there was a time when he had liked to laugh, sing and drink. He pined for 1877 and the War of Independence, when he and his master were young and carefree. He had forgotten the mounds of corpses and the groans of the wounded; he had forgotten the cold and the booming cannons that had left him hard of hearing ever after. Like all simple folk, he associated his own youth with better times. Drawing the velvet drapes, the sun streamed into the room, its rays hitting one of the shelves of the bookcase, lending the titles an unexpected brilliance. Without asking, Zaharai brought his master his rather modest breakfast and placed it on one of the *gigogne* tables. He then saw to the fire and left the room. Mr Costache paid no attention to him. Impatiently, he opened a thick tome near the end: O... P... R. R? No, the monograms were in order of surname, a idea adopted from the Police files, where it made more sense. He needed to look up O or Z. It depended whether R was a Christian name – probably Radu – or whether O too was a Christian name, but men's first names beginning with O were rare. Oprea? Ovidiu? Oliver? No, the other variant was better, and so he went back to surnames beginning with O. OA, OB, Odebeanu, Odivoianu, Odobescu, Olănescu... OMN, ONN, OR, Otetelişanu, no, that was not it. It had to be Z. But under Z there were only three monograms: Zbârcea, Zătreanu, Zorilă. What then? Probably he had overlooked something.

He leafed through the R's, in the event that R might be a surname. There were fourteen names, from Racottă to Rosetti, but none in combination with O and Z or even one of the two.

He paused and took a sip of coffee. Ugh, weak! He had forgotten to tell Zaharia to put an extra spoonful in the coffee pot and to measure the water by the cup. His adjutant was an old man who was thrifty to the point of avarice and constantly subjected him to unwanted rationing. Although Costache had pointed out to him that the war finished twenty years ago, that he personally could afford it, and indeed had always been able to, Zaharia always scrimped on coffee, sugar and firewood. He made savings at the market, on water and lighting, although the only advantage of living in the centre of town was running water and electricity. It would even be hard now for Costache to live in a place without all these delights and the benefits of modern times. When he visited the Margulis family on Strada Fântânei, he could appreciate the difference; the difference in his favour, obviously. On the other hand, the constant din of the carriages had begun to weary him. He decided to take a shower before continuing his search, and so he called for his old adjutant to heat up the water in the boiler. 'Twenty-three degrees, mind you!' The doctors did not recommend frequent showers and advised him to use hotter water, but he neither accepted nor imparted advice. Here he differed from his friend Margulis, who nagged people as to what was and was not best, although he wagged his tongue for nothing. The hardest thing to bear is to do something stupid not on your own initiative, but on somebody else's advice.

Reinvigorated after his wash, Costache resumed his search, just as the bells chimed noon. He remembered that he had thought of talking in person to Epiharia, the woman from the Icoanei Church, because he did not wish to frighten her by inviting her to come to the Prefecture, but now it was too late to catch her at the service. He would look for her another day, he said to himself, since she attended church more punctually than a clerk at his office. He opened the catalogue again at the letter O and this time found an Oz and an M – probably another member of the family. He studied the monogram, recognized it, read the few lines that accompanied it, and got ready to go out. Firstly, he would go to the police station, to telephone 297. Ilie was on duty and to Costache fell the duty of going to the Filaret Station in time to catch the Giurgiu train.

*

When he discovered with whom he had the honour of talking, the stationmaster at Giurgiu straightened his back and directed him to the manor of Manolache Ochiu-Zănoagă, after placing at his disposal a good, rested, roan horse. Costache had not ridden very much lately, but now he felt the need to expend his energy. He felt young when he rode at a gallop. And he knew he would have to undergo a policeman's hardest test: announcing a violent death to the family. He had chosen to perform this duty for a simple reason: he wished to find out what the young man's last words might mean, the riddle that had been in his mind when he went to bed and again when he woke up. Unfortunately, he would have to take advantage of sudden grief, when people least guard their words. He arrived at half past four, just as the sun was setting.

4.

Young aristocrat slain near Băneasa Forest. The editor-in-chief of *Universul* had got out of the habit of writing. He was the newspaper's clear head, he verified, he rectified, but rarely did he take up his pen to write, and then only in exceptional circumstances. This was why he was pleased to come up with the headline from the very first, although he had wavered between *boyar, nobleman, of good family* and *aristocrat*, the latter word won in the end. That was what happened to him with headlines: either they presented themselves straight away or he could not hit on them at all, and then he would have to ask his colleagues' advice. Păvălucă was the best at them: it was if he pulled them out of his sleeve, like a conjurer or a card sharp. But he had discovered two months ago that the man with whom he shared an office was writing a novel; which explained a lot. All he had managed to wrest from him was that it was set in the future or something of that sort. He suspected that it was an imitation of Jules Verne and he did not have very much faith in his colleague making a success of it.

He looked at the clock: it was barely ten in the morning. He had the whole day ahead of him; he had told his wife that he would be coming home for lunch at two. And so he dipped his nib and wrote. *On 19 December, in our Friday issue, our Gazette published the news of an unknown man who had been found shot, but was alive...* He paused and above the line, he added a *still* after the *but*. He continued the sentence: *...but was still alive, near the Băneasa Forest. The young man was taken, according to an understanding with...* he crossed out the *with* and changed it to *between ...an understanding between the Town Hall and Dr Rosemberg's Hospice of Health...* He crossed out the *m* and changed it to an *n. Dr Rosenberg's...* It did not work. He crossed out the whole sentence and rewrote it, after which he pressed the blotter to it, rolling the wooden holder back and forth. *As there is an understanding between the Town Hall and Dr Rosenberg, with regard to unidentified patients in need of medical treatment, the young man, in his death throes, was taken to the Hospice of h...* he crossed out the *h* and made it a capital letter *...Health, where every effort was made to... to...* hmm, *to help him.* He stopped and reread what he had written. He blotted the ink once more and continued writing. But the throes of creation do not concern us here, they are far too intimate a matter, and so we shall look at the final result, the article on the first page of *Universul*, published on Monday,

22 December, a fair copy having been made and a vignette added the day before, at twenty to two on Sunday:

Young aristocrat slain near Băneasa Forest

On 19 December, in our Friday issue, our Gazette published the news of an unknown man who had been found shot, but was still alive, near the Băneasa Forest. As there is an understanding between the Town Hall and Dr Rosenberg, with regard to unidentified patients in need of medical treatment, the young man, in his death throes, was taken to the Hospice of Health, where every effort was made to help him. Notwithstanding, at eleven minutes past six on Saturday, the young man breathed his last. A special reporter from our newspaper witnessed the sad event. Because some of the young man's items of clothing were embroidered with the monogram R. O. Z., Colonel Costache Boerescu, the eminent Chief of Public Security, managed to discover that the letters referred to the Ochiu-Zănoagă family from Giurgiu. Before breathing his last, the young man uttered a few words and a name. An investigation is in progress, but the Police have a lead, which, we hope, will lead to the murderer. It is possible that it was a duel with pistols, which is why we believe that the law against duelling proposed by Senator Viișoreanu will be adopted as soon as possible. We remind you that the Senator has proposed that the articles regarding duelling be struck from the Penal Code, which means that in the future duellists will be treated as common criminals and tried by jury.

Mr Procopiu spoke in the name of the newspaper, and so he did not sign his name to the article. Satisfied at having finished in time, he took his stovepipe hat, since he no longer had a bowler, and went down to the print shop to have the article replace the current front page. Then he went home with a hearty appetite, for he never fasted.

5.

I dreamed that my soul had separated from my body. So much peace, so much solitude – and with those words I woke up. It is still dark and I can hear a crowing cock shattering the stillness of night. How has so much sadness coagulated within me? Whence all the strangeness from which we are made? Who guides us? It doesn't take a great leap of imagination to see that such thoughts seem to obtrude from outside you rather than to rise from within, as if somebody injected them into you with an unseen needle. Maybe we ought to start from scratch and conceive of everything in a different way, if we are to understand it at all. Maybe we should take a different path, one nobody has ever taken, if we are to get to the core. What would we find, if we stopped couching everything in other people's words and images? What if we thought with the whole of our bodies, rather than just a part of them? What would we remember about our past, our future? What would we make of the independent choices we have made? I keep thinking about the big question and my head strikes against a thick ceiling of silence. There is something that prevents me from talking intelligibly, even in the moments of grace when I understand. It lasts but an instant, no longer. How can anybody live when we all *know*... and when we all *don't know*? Can we even be sure we are alive?

In the room there is a fire and a bed, in which a man is asleep. The hotel is called the Frascati and is unfamiliar to me. A 'colleague' from the newspaper brought me here. What will my real colleagues be doing right now? In a register I wrote my name, profession and the city where I live, as the hotelier requested. Dan Crețu, journalist, Bucharest. It is true but even so it feels more and more a lie when I say that. Maybe I really will lose my mind, lying even as I tell the truth.

I was taken to a room with two beds, I washed using the water a hotel employee poured into a porcelain basin, dried myself with a rough white towel, and went down to the dining room, although I do not know what I ate, since I was drained of strength. Coming back upstairs, I was surprised to find this stranger, with whom I am given to understand I have to share the room. I lay down on the iron bedstead, the berth of my fears. The sheet was clean, white, and the quilt thick, made of cherry-red silk. It smelled nasty, of cockroach powder, I think. Then I fell into a deep sleep, where I dreamt of so much peace and so much solitude. Day is beginning to break.

My room-mate woke up and made all kinds of sounds. I don't know whether he was choking or spitting or giving up the ghost. Then, he stripped stark naked and started washing his whole body thoroughly, without any embarrassment at my presence. I noticed his whitish skin. In the meantime, he started to speak, without turning around to see whether his words had any effect. He is called Otto and he is a Saxon, but he speaks Romanian, albeit with an accent. He was born in *Michelsberg*, that is, Cisnădioara, in Transylvania. They made him an apprentice at the age of twelve, *mit zwölf* – he is a mason – he finished his army service, and now he is twenty-six and has come here in search of work. Only in a big city can you find work in his trade even in winter, he told me. He arrived on the *Zug*. At the border, in Predeal, he says that people change their clothes, putting on the luxury items they have bought in Kronstadt, Budapest or Vienna, so that they will not have to pay customs taxes on them, and putting their ordinary clothes in their suitcases.

He found himself with a new hat on his head and had to put his old one in his suitcase: a lady in his compartment asked him to wear it; she had bought it for her husband. They were worried, because in the train there was a rumour that the Romanians from the Kingdom were demanding a *Pass*. The Turks and the Russians are the only others who demand them. When his turn came, he handed the customs officer all kinds of *Papiere*, but the customs officer was still not satisfied and handed them back. A foreign traveller before him had been turned back, and so Otto was afraid. Luckiy he had his military passbook, which saved him: the customs officer declared himself satisfied and Otto continued his journey. 'I escaped by a hair's breadth!', said Otto, towelling himself and looking in the mirror, in which he could also see me. He admired *die Transsylwanischen Alpen*, impressed by their height and peaks, and sat looking out of the train window the whole way. When he alighted at the station, where the wind was blowing, nobody said anything to him, and he liked that, *rumänische Ordnung*, because in the Empire nothing of the sort would have been allowed. He also liked the train station at Sinaia and the royal platform, but Bucharest's Gara de Nord had not impressed him much, particularly given that the paving was rather broken. On the other hand, he was bowled over by *die Droschken*, the elegant cabs, with the cabmen dressed in velvet, with their velvet caps and sturdy roan horses. On the train, he discovered from another Saxon that in Bucharest Germans stay at the Wilhelm, a hotel near the Elisabeta Boulevard.

Otto had finished towelling himself. He hung the towel on the peg by the sink and started to dress, pulling on long-johns and a flannel undershirt. In the afternoon, he reached the capital of Romania, and at dusk the Wilhelm. He walked down a long but rather narrow street, *Victory Avenue*, passed the Royal Palace, which was like a large hotel – he had done his army service in Vienna and so he could make the comparison – and finally reached a boulevard with electric lighting and trams. He turned right down a short street next to the park. Wilhelm had died, unfortunately, and the current owner said he could stay overnight on a sofa, without charge, but no longer than that. And so he arrived at the Frascati, where he was staying also free of charge, on the condition that he repaint the kitchens and outbuildings in the spring. But he was looking for serious work at some church, because he was hard up. He had met some mural painters and masons and befriended them. Then, he started asking me questions: who I am, how old I am, whether I have a wife and children and a mother, a father and brothers. There are people, such as this Otto, who think that you have to say everything about yourself from the very first moment and you don't know when they might stop asking questions. So I pretended to be asleep. After he went about his business, I got up and tried to adapt to life, like an animal cub. It is not easy, nothing is where it should be, but it is like a game: I have to find out, discover, pretend, and, above all, not say anything. Every word is laden with danger.

A DIFFICULT BEGINNING TO THE WEEK

1.

I have a chubby cheek, the like of which I have not had since I was a child. You would think my mouth were full. It might even suit me, if the other cheek did not look starved. Half of my face is well fed and the other half wasting away. I made the discovery as soon as I opened my eyes. I felt the illness in me. I had a fright and, barefoot, I went to the mirror. There I saw a girl with a ridiculous pink bonnet, from beneath which poked black locks of hair, the bulging cheek, and in the whites of the eyes all kinds of pink capillaries, the likes of which can be found in Papa's anatomy books. They looked like branches and were painful and itchy, like dust in the eye. What could it be? Dust in the eyes and a swollen jaw? I would have liked to study medicine, to study how an illness lurks in concealment and then pops up overnight, becomes visible, strikes the eye, sometimes literally, as in my case. Papa is not at home and he won't be back until evening. It's bad not to have a doctor in the house, and it means I will have to stay like this until this evening. I did not know whether I should take a bath, but in the end I did so anyway. I did not know whether I should brush my teeth, either. In the end I did so, but taking great care to avoid the molar that was pulsing more than aching. I put on my *gris souris* dress.

Six fingernails had already been cut and were lying in a heap on the bathroom table, while the thin white arcs of another four were still attached to the fingers of the right hand that is writing these lines. Naturally, as I write, now, the other four have already gone the way of the first six. But the situation was as I have described it, six to four, swollen cheek, sand in the eyes, grey dress, when Safta entered the room and, with visible excitement, handed me a visiting card on a silver tray. I shivered when I read the name. The house was in a mess, in the middle of being cleaned, and I – well, see above. Of course, who else would have dared to come unannounced on a Monday morning! Safta had always taken his side, even against her mistress (it is of myself I speak!), but as it happens, you should never trust the people in your pay! Sooner or later they betray you: if not from spite or hatred, then from love. I think that Safta is one of the many young women who cannot resist him. True, he treats the servants nicely, which is, I think, one of his major qualities. One of his few major qualities... The other is... it is of no importance.

What did I do? I continued to cut my fingernails with seeming calm, an operation that I perform by myself, unlike others, and then I told the maid: 'I am not acquainted with any Mr Alexandru Livezeanu. I know a Mr Hristea Livezeanu, a Mrs Maria Livezeanu, a Miss Marioara Livezeanu, Vişinescu by marriage and Livezeanu by divorce, a Miss Elena, who is the sister of Mrs Livezeanu *mère*, unmarried and undivorced, I know the gentleman Mr Mihai Livezeanu, known as Mişu, a student of medicine in Paris, who last year was kind enough to invite me to his birthday party, but not any Mr Alexandru Livezeanu. And so I cannot receive him, not now, not ever. Tell him that he has no business in Strada Fântânei, to forget the existence of this house and the Margulis family. And further tell him that a well-bred man knows that this is no day and no hour for visits. And tell him to... to...'

I was about to say something very *rude*, since his nearness, even at a few rooms' distance, induced in me an indescribable state of nerves. But I refrained, by quite simply clenching my fists as hard as I could; it was lucky I had cut my nails. It is not well to show one's weaknesses, especially in front of people who take your enemy's side and particularly in front of women who take his side. After Safta went out, I picked up *Vanity Fair* and tried to read a page. Naturally, I was unable: I was holding the book upside down! When I realized, I blushed. I went to the window. There was no longer the good, spring-like light of yesterday; it was snowing listlessly as I looked out into the street. I did not allow myself a single tear, and that filled me with pride.

I went to Jacques. He was au fait with the unsuccessful attempt at a visit and held my hand in his cold little hand, without saying a word. To cheer ourselves up, I told him that I had arranged to go to our cousin's to collect the gifts and we conferred on what we should get Papa and the others who would be coming to our house for Christmas.

'But would it not be better-r to stay at home? You look very funny. Doesn't it hur-rt?'

Yet it was not my tooth but my soul that was hurting. The infection from my molar and the redness of my eyes overflowed in my soul. And shopping is very good for the soul. I reasoned that as it was winter, I could muffle my cheek with a scarf. In any event, I had to buy presents; there was no more time left. I do not know what I was thinking of to have left it for so many days. (I do not know of *what*, but I know of *whom*.)

*

Alexandru told me, on our second meeting, in that tone of his, tender and impertinent at the same time: 'I would like a little bad to enter you! Beware of me!' Strange how words can haunt you... He looked at me with gentleness, with a somewhat worried smile – he has nice lips and a little chestnut moustache and a face that almost speaks wordlessly – and in that moment time stopped, the ballroom froze, I could no longer hear anything around me, although there was music and noise and much laughter. Then, as if waking from sleep, I saw once more that we were in a ballroom with lots of people and movement. I knew his double-edged reputation and that it was hard to fight him, that I was not the only girl, that many ladies full of choice qualities had lost the battle before me, but I liked the challenge and it thrilled me. I did not care about the dangers or the victims. Life became more colourful, after those words of his. I had allowed him to address me using *toi* not *vous* and it was the first time he had done so, and that in itself was like a caress. He invited me, no, he almost carried me to the dance floor and when we moved closer to each other, he held me slightly away, as if protecting me from himself, but I could feel his breath. He smelled faintly of tobacco. Immediately after his waltz with me, he left the soirée, to the regret of many of the ladies, young and old, who had written him down in their dance cards. But the gentlemen also liked him, because he emanates a kind of energy, and he understands them, defects and all, but does not try to rectify them, as Papa does, for example. I have noticed that he immediately leaps to the defence of those in difficulty, before they themselves realize that they are in a corner. Look at me praising him, still praising him! Once I saw his photograph in *Universul*. '... a little bad to enter you. Beware of me!' The dance ended, he bowed, conducted me to my seat without letting me out of his sight for a second, clinging to me with his eyes, as if I were a child. He was about to touch my hair, but then clenched his fist with a shiver, quickly turned his back and left. It was just the beginning. My impression... No, I do not want to know anything, I do not want to know him, *he* does not exist, he has never existed, get it into your head, Iulia Margolis! It is as if stones were weighing down on my soul.

Couldn't the week have started on Tuesday instead? For, I have noticed that on Mondays everything goes wrong, and things set their face against you.

*

And so I went shopping with Vasilica, something, which, as I was saying, does you good when you are in a bad mood. And I got out of the house, which is very good indeed on a day of household cleaning. I will clean the silver when I get back. My cousin's carriage was waiting for me at the entrance and I looked to see whether Alexandru's coach was nearby, because I have learned to recognize it from a distance, to pinpoint it on the wallpaper of the street. I do not know whether I was hoping to see it or if on the contrary I was terrified at the possibility. No, it was not there, but I did see its tracks in the fresh snow and like a fool I gazed at them. Vasi and I made our plans: our first stop would be on our street, at Marie Rose's, the seamstress, purveyor of lingerie, modes and much more, and then Maison Jobin, on Victory Avenue, for gentlemen's hats and cravats, and then the confectioner's a little farther down the avenue. I am loyal to the gentlemen from Capşa, whereas Vasilica, who has a bigger heart than I, is a loyal customer of old man Fialkowski, especially given that the poor man is ill and his business is being run by somebody else, who has been losing customers. I used to like Fialkowski's when it had the old stove, a kind of oven in the wall, with a *chamotte*, on which a cat lazed. After they changed the stove, the cat died of pneumonia, like Violetta, and ever since our Polish confectioner fell ill, I do not like going into the shop. Anyway, after the confectioner's, we are going to *Universul*, where you can find everything, at reasonable prices, and after that, we shall see, depending on how much time and money we have left. *Time is money*, as my cousin told me recently – I like how it sounds, although I do not think it is true. For, I have a whole heap of time and not one penny. Whereas *he*, the villain, has a heap of money from his family, but does not have time, at least not for me; he expends his time with all and sundry, without keeping a tally. Maybe herein lies the similarity: both can be spent wisely or unwisely. For a moment I thought that maybe we would bump into him on Victory Avenue, but then I tried to put him out of my mind's eye. I will not allow him to ruin yet another holiday: such is my personal judicial decision! And Vasilica and I started laughing so loudly that people were looking at us.

But you never know what surprises a new day has in store for you, a day that began so agitatedly. When I arrived at *Universul*, I espied him through a half-open door, just for an instant, no, not *him*, but the stranger about whom they have been talking so much in the last few days. I am sure it was he, I sensed it was he, I knew it was he, as if I had known in advance. He was downstairs in Mr Peppin Mirto's office. He was thin and I saw that his face was unshaven, darkened by the shadow of a beard, nothing more than that. I slowed my steps as much as I was able, but I caught only a hum of voices, nothing distinct. He too looked at me as I passed, for no more than two seconds, and broke off what he was saying. He seemed astonished – undoubtedly because my scarf had slipped, showing my swollen cheek. We went with the doorman to the director's office, where some of the things advertised in the newspaper are stored. There was a terrible mess. Our headmistress from the Central Girls School would have been scandalized. She has repeated the same rules to us so many times that I know them by heart: 'Without tidiness in things, in thoughts, in feelings and in life, nobody can live properly. Just as you cannot live without oxygen, you cannot live without tidiness. You are dead; you cannot control your life. You are wretched and unhappy; you do not feel comfortable in your own house, among your things, in your kitchen, in your bed. Maintain tidiness in your rooms and in your hearts, girls, and you will be happy!'

The director, Mr Luigi Cazzavillan, was not present. He comes and goes as he pleases, like all directors, and so we were able to choose among the things undisturbed. We laughed so much that I forgot all about my troubles. What did we laugh at? – At how the toys were presented; each with a written explanation. If only you could stock up on laughter for when things go badly for you! If only you could store it on a shelf in the larder or cellar and take it out when you are feeling depressed. But perhaps in the future someone will succeed in doing it, because nothing is impossible for the man of the future. I stocked up on laughter by copying a few of the presentations (even now, as I transcribe them, I burst out laughing). I would also like to read them to Jacques.

'*Mama*! A mysterious little box that pronounces very distinctly the word *Mama*! This child's cry sounding in your pocket will cause astonishment to all, since they will not know where it is coming from.' Vasilica set it aside for herself, because she is expecting another child, probably in May.

'*The Mewler!* This device perfectly imitates the mewling of a cat.' She did not want this one, because she is not expecting any kittens in the near future. On the contrary, she drowns her cat's litters. I bought it, as I have neither children nor cats.

'*The wonderful tobacco tin!* Offer somebody a cigarette from this tobacco tin. But the cigarettes disappear and instead a grimacing face appears.' I liked the 'grimacing face' very much, and so I bought one, for Papa, who will be able to appreciate it. In fact, it is because of him that we do not have a cat or a dog: he says that they shed hair and that you can contract various illnesses from them, particularly intestinal worms.

'*The domino box!* When you open it, a mouse jumps out. A very good trick for ladies who like to play dominos.' It cost only one leu, but ladies such as our aunts do not appreciate jokes like that.

'*The magic awl!* With this awl, you can pretend to bore your jaw, your forehead, your nose, without leaving a trace.' Two lei. I imagined Papa's face if I were to give him such a thing.

After totting and re-totting up the money I had saved, I bought for Jacques, at the huge price of four lei fifty bani, exactly how much a Marie Rose corset costs, a little wonder: *Luminous fountains*. The description was so enticing that I could not resist: 'Those who were at the exhibition in Paris have not forgotten the impression made on them by the *Luminous Fountains*. But why only in Paris? Who on 10 May did not see Bucharest's Luminous Fountains in Cişmigiu? Those who have never seen them, however –' and this is precisely Jacques' case '– or who would like to see them again in miniature –' my own case '– can do so with these, which are just as real and as beautiful as the full-sized fountains. The apparatus comes complete with all the necessary parts and instructions.' A delight! Apart from that, there were also the 'Hellish Globes,' which emanate a nasty smell, to be used against guests who forget to leave, a snake that moved 'by means of an invisible system,' as if it were alive,' a cravat and brooch pin that sprayed perfume, and fake moustaches, beards and sideburns to be worn at masked balls. Vasilica said they were silly. She has become very serious since she started giving birth all the time. I like them all, if only I had the money.

As I was leaving, I met Mr Peppin Mirto, a very gallant gentleman, who sings operatic arias beautifully at soirées and does translations for the newspaper. Muffling my cheek in my scarf, I asked him how he would translate Thackeray's title. He suggested *Târgul Zădărniciei* (The Market of Pointlessness) or *Bâlciul Vanității* (The Fair of Vanity), but I did not like either of them. I invited him to our house. I wanted to ask him about some of the things I have underlined in the novel, because I did not understand them.

The meeting with Mr Mirto, and especially the half-meeting with the stranger and the time I spent choosing presents, made me forget about my infected molar, my stinging eyes and the fact that in the morning I had refused the very visit that for two months I had been waiting for every evening, a visit from a man who has preoccupied me for the last year. A little bad... a lot of bad! And nevertheless, nevertheless, nevertheless, what did he want? I started polishing the silverware with energy, using tooth-cleaning powder – an invention I ought to patent.

Alexandru had been expecting not to be received, although he had
hoped for a miracle. That one does not pay visits on a Monday morning
was as certain, and in the present case more certain, than the fact that
Monday comes after Sunday. But his need to ask her help, hers alone,
had gone beyond all fear of rules, and his faith in his luck and in *her* had
gone beyond all shame. Safta had told him in a regretful voice: 'Milady
asks you to forgive her, she is very sorry, but she cannot receive you
now!' and had looked at him from beneath lowered eyelashes. It was
quite certain that the message had reached him in altered form, and he
would have dearly wished to hear the original message. But as is well
known, servants are often their masters' censors.

He turned his coach in the direction of St Joseph's and set off without
looking where he was going. A mangy cur only just avoided the wheels,
yelping. His first encounter with Iulia had been on four wheels, six years
earlier. Only he himself and the Good Lord knew of that encounter.
Miss Margulis did not. It was on the feast of St George, a day suddenly
mild after a long period of rain. And the ferment in his body and soul
surpassed that of nature herself. He was like a steamship ready to set
off over the open seas. Margareta, with whom he thought he was in
love at the time, a widow of just twenty, with all her senses aroused by
a two-year marriage and full of desire, had just been pointing through
the window of the mail coach at a blossoming tree and letting out little
squeals, when his eyes fell on the two young ladies sitting together on
the bench opposite them. One was a pretty young lady, pregnant, who
was not feeling well and kept dabbing her flushed face with a lace-
trimmed handkerchief, the other an adolescent girl of about fourteen,
asleep. He looked at the flowers blossoming on the tree, which was
now behind the mail coach, and then at the girl once more: there was
something about her that was more delicate than the flowers. Her chin
did loll on her chest in an unseemly fashion, as some people's do, but
pointed slightly towards her shoulder, like the head of a little bird. Her
breathing was not visible, and her lips were soft, as if just having closed.
Her thick black eyelashes hid the colour of her eyes. Like a painter, he
thought of what colour he might give those eyes. Given the girl's dark
hair, both hazel and blue eyes would have suited her. He would have
preferred blue and he made a wager with himself that they were indeed
blue. He could barely tear his eyes away from the sleeping girl's face,

and Margareta, sensing that his thoughts were elsewhere, kept touching him for trifling reasons, kept talking to him, laughing, kept turning him towards her, already alarmed that she was losing him. Poor Margareta! Nevertheless, his eyes kept caressing the girl's face, lest he forget it, and in an attempt to make her open her eyes.

At the first station the coachman reined in the horses with such great artistry that the girl did not wake up and barely shifted the position of her head. He bade the heavily pregnant woman a good day and she smiled painfully but with great politeness, and then he took one last look in the direction of the sleeping girl. Her body was delicate and her breasts were only just beginning to swell. He alighted, assisted Margareta, who hung on his neck with her full weight, and then the coach departed, taking with it the secret of an undiscovered colour. He regretted that he would never see her again. It was strange that two years later he recognized her immediately. He was coming out of the theatre, unaccompanied this time, hurrying to a woman who was waiting for him, a woman other than Margareta. Outside there was a downpour, and in the light of the electric bulbs in Theatre Square could be seen needles of rain. From beneath his umbrella he saw her beneath another umbrella with a gentleman, probably her father. She seemed to have grown, but her head, framed by dark hair covered with a silk and velvet hood, was the same. The only cab – as always in the rain, you can never find one – pulled up next to him, since he was renowned for his tips. With a polite bow, he let them take it and in a trice they boarded. The father thanked him unostentatiously and the girl straight away vanished underneath the tarpaulin. He would have been embarrassed to detain them any longer. Nor was he able to discover the colour of her eyes on this occasion, it was too dark, but he managed to overhear the address. 'Strada Fântânei, by St Joseph's!' Thither went his colour.

The next day the servants were astonished when the young lord wished to find out the names of all those who owned houses on Strada Fântânei, next to St Joseph's Cathedral. They were astonished, but then again they were not overly astonished, since it was obvious that a woman must be behind it. And Toader, the cleverest of them, with his permanently jolly face, as if the world were eternally on holiday, told him directly which were the houses with young girls: the Petrescu family, with five daughters. The poor father: they needed a whole shop to supply all the dresses, a real catastrophe! And of the five, only the youngest was beautiful. Then there was Mr Văleanu, the merchant, with a daughter of seventeen, like a fairy princess, named Elisabeta, like the Queen. Then there was Margulis, the doctor, also with a daughter of seventeen, a spare little thing, whose name Toader did not know, but who, he thought, was not worthy of attention. Toader was sure that his young master's preference was for Elisabeta the fairy princess, endowed with all the plump gifts a girl needed, but Alexandru was equally sure that she was not the sleeping girl in the coach. He did not believe that she could be one of the five sisters; she seemed to be an only child. After driving his gig (he did not yet have a carriage) twice along Strada Fântânei, Alexandru abandoned the whole affair. It seemed to him that he forgot about it and actually did forget. But three years later, when he examined the list of guests invited to the name day of his older brother Mişu, a student in Paris, who returned to Bucharest for family occasions, he saw the names *Dr and Mrs Leon Margulis*. He had not forgotten that name.

'Is Miss Margulis not invited?' asked Alexandru in passing.

Mişu was making connections within the medical world, and for the moment professional interests rather than those of the heart took up most of his time.

'As far as I know, the doctor has two children, a girl, Iulia, and a boy, Jacob, who... why do you ask?'

'Because I once had occasion to do them a small service and I would like to see Miss Margulis again. Iulia,' he then added, aware that it was the first time he had uttered her name.

That was all it took for Mişu to include her on the guest list. Alexandru had selected a simple outfit for his meeting with the sleeping girl: a double-breasted jacket rather than a frock coat and a purple necktie. He gave the impression of being a recent lycée student, which quite suited him. His rather long hair and moustache were a soft auburn, but his cheeks were somewhat harshly chiselled, twitching slightly when he pressed his lips together, as if from a passing shudder. He was a man of the world and it did not take him long to realize that the Margulis family was not very wealthy.

Therefore he did not wish to make a show of his wealth. He still did not know whether dark eyes or blue eyes would come to Mişu's party. He saw her enter and although he was quite far away from the door he crossed the crowded salon. He felt as if he were advancing too slowly, as if he were treading sand. People kept stopping him and he had to waste seconds with them that were as precious as gold. Finally, he reached her. And when Iulia held out her hand and he kissed it, her eyes were lowered. Then, she looked straight at him and he saw her green, child-like eyes. She did not know that she was the heroine of a long search, she did not know that she was his sleeping girl, and that with her eyes open she seemed devoid of mystery. He had thought so intensely about blue eyes that the mismatch irritated him. Hitherto he had not discovered that in such cases every defect plays to the advantage of sentiment. She was indeed a spare little thing. And her curly fringe was quite unusual. He took care of her, that is, he took care of his story. He accompanied her. He fended off the vulgarians, because there is one in every company, and today vulgarity is more common than ever before. He introduced her and her family to people. He noticed only that the young lady's mind was elsewhere. From time to time she smiled at somebody in her mind, not at him. He would have liked to know where she was, but when he asked her: 'Where are you, Miss?' Iulia answered: 'In a carriage, on a long journey. *Comme elle est sage!* There was something so innocently well behaved about her face that Alexandru suddenly wished to see it ravished. When the three left, he conducted them to the front door, and in the play of the lights he saw his and Iulia's shadows stretching over the ground: two grey outlines that kept touching. He again kissed her white hand, deliberately placing his lips far lower than was fitting. And his warm lips felt something like silk.

It is strange that regardless of whether bad or good enters you, the effect is the same. What is more, when good enters you, it can be for the worse. Alexandru did not know whether he was in love with Iulia, and better he did not know. He was seeing Margareta again, after they had been separated for a time, but he felt the need to see once more the girl from his unknown story. And the opportunity came sooner than he expected: the ball thrown by the Lyric Theatre, with a tombola to raise money for orphaned children or war widows, he no longer knew which. It was the ball when he had invited her to dance and then abruptly decided to leave without a word of farewell. Margareta was waiting for him and it did him good to be with her the whole night, so that he might forget the dance with Iulia. But Margareta's laugh was too loud, and he barely restrained himself from telling her that it irritated him. His girl had kept her eyes almost closed, as she had then, with her head to one side, and it reminded him with extraordinary vividness of the coach ride when he had seen her for the first time. One thing he had been able to see: she did not resemble the women who played cunning games with men's minds and with whom he for one was prematurely sated. She was different. She struck him with a kind of inner strength, of which she seemed not to be aware. Or was she?

But in the meantime things had developed badly for them. The Lyric Theatre had burned almost to the ground. Alexandru thought with a kind of horror that the ballroom where he had danced with her, where he had sought her breath, her perfume, had been reduced to ashes. It was as if a part of his story had burned, as if her perfume, her steps, her breath, his love had burned. And he had done nothing to save it. He was now in the cruellest situation of his entire life, a situation so bad that he did not know who could save him. Why had he thought that she was the one? What powers could a physician's daughter, a mere novice in the ways of life, have? He stopped the carriage by a newspaper vendor and asked for *Universul*. He opened it fearfully and there, amid the sparsely falling snowflakes, he read the unsigned front-page article: *Young Aristocrat Slain near Băneasa Forest.* He saw blackness before his eyes: he was dead!

3.

The first headline that caught his eye was *Young Aristocrat Slain near Băneasa Forest*. In other words, the fair-haired man had died! Petre breathed a sigh of relief. Maybe he ought not 'to surrender the burse,' but when he read the announcement in the Gazette and saw the reward, he took fright. He told his wife everything and she advised him to go and hand it in, so that he could lay his hands on the money. But Petre did not have the courage, and after the talk with Mr Costache, he made his decision and told the woman it was final: 'I've got to get rid of it. I don't know where to throw it. In a stream? In a lake? In the forest? In a ditch?'

On Sunday he had quickly scouted some streams and lakes, and if he had had it with him, he would have thrown it in the water. He was afraid it might float. He was afraid he might be seen. That devil of a child had followed him. He took out the wallet and examined it carefully yet again. In the middle there was a circle embossed on the leather, with three interwoven letters within: *R. O. Z.* When you opened it, you found lots of pockets and compartments, some of them visible, some of them hidden; it had taken him a long time to discover them all. That wallet was a real jewel of human ingenuity; in fact it was combination of wallet and *portefeuille*. Unfortunately, all the pockets were empty except one. Disappointed, Petre looked inside the deer-skin 'treasure' once more: a key! It was a rather small key, but heavy and gilded, with elaborately cut bits on both sides of the shank, covering exactly half the shank. Without a doubt it was the key to a safe! Like all genuine treasures, it was a thing that was of use to only a few; to Petre and his wife it was of no use whatever. He had no way of finding out where the key came from, and not being a burglar by trade, but rather a coachman, even if by miracle he found out where the safe was, it would still have been in vain. Petre was reluctant to hand the object in now that the fair-haired man had died, and following the conversation with Mr Costache ("beware, if you are hiding anything, you will be in big trouble"),. He was the only man in Bucharest who, reading *Universul*, had made the connection between the news of the 'young aristocrat's' death and 'a wallet has been lost.' He pieced things together thought by thought, as follows: the fair-haired man's shooting and the wallet's loss had happened on the same morning. Probably the fair-haired man had stolen the wallet and told the people in Strada Teilor (and how strange that he had returned to die in the same place, 'how everything is written by fate!') that he had lost it there. Or maybe they hadn't believed him and had 'shot 'im'? But to be more certain, had they nonetheless taken out the announcement? The people from the new houses, those wonderful new houses, definitely knew that the young man had been taken to Dr Rosenberg. Then why did they not say that they knew him? Obviously, there was a lot of money at stake and great danger. Nobody knew yet that the wallet had not been lost, but stolen, perhaps a second time, and the he, Petre, had become a thief. What had got into him all of a sudden, when up until Friday he had been an honest man? You're honest an entire lifetime, and all of a sudden you become a 'burse snatcher, a bickbocket,' a villain. The more he thought about it, the more frightened Petre became. And now the fair-haired man had died, what if the same fate awaited Petre, the same as in stories about objects under a curse, which bring you misfortune if you steal them? Petre began to pant in terror and felt that he had to make an urgent trip to the backyard privy. He took the copy of *Universul*, tore each sheet into eight pieces and rushed outside. In less than five minutes he had rid himself of both his fear and the wallet. None but the *vidangeurs* would be able to find it now, but it is hard to imagine them rummaging through the not exactly pleasant-smelling raw materials of their labour. Although they do say that where there's muck there's brass.

4.

On this occasion the agitated young man with the lizard-like gait bade good morning in a rather insulting, lofty manner.

'Good morning, young sir,' replied the doorman.

The expression on Nicu's face showed that he was unsure whether the young man warranted a reply. But then, thinking of his teacher ('you, young man, are not well raised!'), he decided to back up the doorman and said as ironically as he could: 'Good morning, *young sir!*'

The lizard looked at him in amazement, but Nicu wasted no more time.

'Has the wallet been found?' asked Nicu, and the extremely acute angle of his eyebrows revealed his alarm, albeit for the opposite reason than would have been appropriate. In that moment the doorman said: 'Will you be repeating the announcement?'

'No... yes... we will repeat it,' said the young man. 'Do not get up, I know the way,' he added, and sidled swiftly in the direction of the office he had visited a few days before, to pay for a whole week's worth of announcements.

'I think it must be something very valuable,' mused the doorman, and then Nicu revealed his secret to him, after begging him in the name of all that was holy not to tell anybody: it was without doubt a ticket for the New Year lottery. Then, they returned to what they had been doing and old man Cercel started to read aloud in that flat way of his: "Important!!' – Two exclamation marks. 'At the offices of *Universul* newspaper, No. 11 Strada Brezoianu, any watch, pendulum clock et-ce-te-ra can be repaired more cheaply than anywhere else. Regular time keeping guaranteed for one year and...' listen to this '...in the contrary case, further repairs will be *free of charge*'! My wife has a pendulum clock from my father-in-law, which doesn't work. I've brought it here twice already, now they tell me not to bring it in any more, because not even Edison himself could repair it. But you're not interested in that, because you don't have a clock.'

Nicu shrugged regretfully, with a look on his face like that of a beaten dog. He sometimes liked to exaggerate misfortunes in order to receive more compassion. He was stocking up on sentiments.

'Look, here's one for you,' said the doorman quickly: 'THINGS FROM ALL OVER THE WORLD: The record for skating. We bring to the attention of amateurs and pro-fe-ssi-on-als that the world record for *patinage* has for the last three years been held by a young English *skater*, Mr Harry Tay, who, putting on his skates at ten in the morning, managed to skate for the whole day and the whole night until the next day at the same time...' they mean ten in the morning, that's twenty-four hours, you understand '...without stopping for a single moment. Not only did Mr Tay not stop for a single minute during his hours of varied ex-er... ex-er-ci-ses on ice, but also he neither ate nor drank...' good grief! don't let anybody ever try to make me do that...'nor drank during this in-ter-val.' It says he's the champion skater and that he went round and round in a circle, for six hundred kilometres.'

'How many kilometres do you think the hour hand on your pendulum went round in a circle for?' asked Nicu. 'Probably its skates broke and it got tired, poor thing, and that's why it won't go any more. I don't understand what time is, do you?'

'No. Let me tell you another one, for when you get married. A LECAR... RECALCITRANT FIANCÉE – they mean a restive mare, say I. 'A few days ago, according to the *United States Courier*, a big wedding was to take place in Ood-la... Voodlavn, one of the most important districts of the city of Chicago.' And look how it ended: 'The marriage of Mr Tho-mas Leo de de Shong and Miss She-perd had been arranged when the girl was just eight-years-old."

'The same as me,' rejoiced Nicu, who was highly sensitive to news about love. 'Do you think I should be looking for a fiancée? My gran always used to talk to me about getting married.'

'Let me finish: 'The engaged couple had lived apart for many years without seeing each other, and when Mr De Shong arrived in Chicago to get marry, Miss Shep-herd, undoubtedly finding that her fiancé did not live up to the ideal she had created for her future husband, ob-sti-nate-ly refused to marry him. And now the ceremony has been postponed until the Greek calendars. The Greek calendars? The Greek *calends*.' Which is to say, forever,' explained the doorman, although he would not have been able to explain what the calends were.

'In other words, never!' explained Nicu, but with regret, as if it had been his own wedding.

And the boy marvelled at how forever can mean the same thing as never and imagined that forever was a mountain peak as high as the Himalayas and never a bottomless pit.

*

'I am somewhat surprised that you have not heard of the Lahovary case, no matter where you lived until now. *L'Indépendance Roumaine* is also published for foreign readers, in Europe's best-known language. Or perhaps you were not interested in news about Romania...?'

In the office of Mr Peppin Mirto, the door was ajar, to allow air to enter. The truth was that Mr Crețu, who, whether he liked it or not, now shared an office with him, had brought in a whiff of perspiration. Peppin looked at Dan, who had become tense, his face had darkened, and so Peppin hastened to explain, in a tone of great amiability: 'George Lahovary was, I am sure, a man of character. You see, this year, in January, just before Unification Day, *L'Indépendance* published a letter from him, worded with the greatest respect, but also with firmness, addressed to the leader of the Conservative Party, the venerable Mr Lascăr Catargiu. Lahovary was also a Conservative, a member of their executive committee in fact, and in his letter he announced his resignation. You will ask me why,' said Peppin, precisely because Dan had not asked. 'Because *monsieur Georges Lahovary* announced, *en français* that he was beginning, 'in good faith and without partiality,' a campaign that he considered to be vital to his country, Romania, one that was above the daily, petty polemics of the gazettes. And here came the thunderbolt...'

Peppin lit a cigarette, offering Dan one from his tin. The aromatic smoke attenuated the reek of sweat.

'The campaign in the Frenchies' newspaper – I think you have seen the firm, it is in that yellow building with the clock that has a cast-iron soldier and its own post box, which is to say, their correspondence is collected from there – the campaign was an unsparing series of essays which formed an analysis of the political parties, of the clubs, which govern political life, and an examination of the press servile to the parties. Oh, the part on the press is awful, on my word! You ought to read it! It rocked the industry to its foundations. Luckily we are not a political paper; we started out as an advertiser, which is how we gained our readership. But above all else, it was a critique of the current Constitution and today's parliamentary system.'

Two young women passed by the half-open door, and Dan's eyes lingered on one of them, who even stopped by the doorway for an instant, before walking away, towards the stairs. It seemed to him that he had seen her somewhere before.

'That was all the newspapermen needed. It was as if somebody had set them ablaze. They blackened the name of Lahovary and his newspaper along with him. Some said he was "in the pay of the French," others that he was in the pay of the Russians, still others that the King had bought him, newspaper and all, so that he could turn Romania into a despotic state. Some even called him "a pathological case." I believe that we, and *Constituționalul* in Jassy were the only ones not to attack him. They reviled him and showed no sign of letting up. And do you know what Lahovary did?'

Mr Mirto stubbed out his cigarette in the ashtray, next to Dan's.

'He immediately published the series of articles in a book, at the newspaper's press, because like we do, they have their own printing press. The title was not quite understood, *Histoire d'une fiction*, and in Romanian it is more unintelligible still, *Povestea unei ficțiuni* (The Story of a Fiction). Some said that it was too abstract, others that it was metaphysical. Some of the opinions from that book would be worth discussing, but nobody discussed them, and hence the tragedy. Upon my word it is a great and very courageous book. Look, let me tell you honestly that I for one would not have dared to write such a book...'

For the first time the translator saw Dan smile and he was left almost speechless. It was something that completely illumined and altered him, it sweetened his features, as if he were emerging from one of the paintings in the Florentine churches Peppin had visited in spring, when he went to seek the southern sun and the traces of his Italian ancestors.

After a long moment he continued: 'And after all that, George Lahovary wrote an article against the director of *Epoca*, Nicu Filipescu, whom he accused of being two-faced in certain unpleasant affairs that took place at the end of last month in Strada Carol, I will not describe them; cases of vandalism, in which some students were suspected of being involved, which is why the Rector of the University, Professor Maiorescu, I do not think you will have heard of him, after paternally urging them to keep out of such villainous tricks, nonetheless resigned, which is a great loss. Mr Filipescu, a rather impulsive, agitated man, as well as being from an opposing newspaper, immediately sent his seconds and challenged him to a duel. I wonder whether this was the drop that caused the cup to overflow...'

Here, Mr Peppin Mirto broke off what he was saying and rushed outside to speak to Miss Iulia Margulis, who was just coming down-stairs. After about five minutes he came back.

'As I was saying, forgive me for the interruption – Miss Margulis asked me for an opinion, she consults me about translations, and I assist her with pleasure. As I was saying, the political adversary sent his seconds. Nicu Filipescu trained regularly for two weeks, although he is a good swordsman to start with, but Lahovary had not laid hands on a sword for *five years*, according to his valet, a Frenchman by the name of Paul, and he was a little lame. He says that on the morning of the duel, 29 November – more than three weeks have passed already – he nevertheless did a few exercises.'

For the first time, Dan interposed a one-syllable question: 'And?'

'And they went to the fencing hall on the Dâmbovița embankment. Before the duel, his seconds said that they ought to abandon the duel, because it was very cold, but Filipescu would have none of it; they would fight as planned. The seconds later recounted what happened. By the end of the very first bout, Lahovary had been backed up against the wall; it was as if his fingers had frozen to the sword hilt. Victor Ionescu, one of Filipescu's seconds, who had drawn the straw to oversee the duel, stopped the bout and allowed the adversaries to resume their starting positions and to stand *en garde*. Immediately after they engaged and their blades locked, Filipescu feinted, and then, with astonishing vigour and speed, he plunged his blade in Lahovary's belly. But with such strength that the tip touched a rib and bent! He felled him on the spot. The rule had been that they would fight until one of them was *visibly* unable to continue. The duel was broken off, and what stirred even greater passion and compassion were Lahovary's last words: 'I die! I die! *They have assassinated me...*'

Peppin had recounted the whole duel with an actor's mastery.

'The Police have still not been able to established whether or not it was intentional, whether the director of *L'Indépendance* died for his ideas, for his principles, which were not to the liking of some, or whether 'merely' for his honour. Costache Boerescu interviewed them all, he invited them to dinner – first one, then another – taking a soft-ly-softly approach. In any event, a great loss... I am greatly saddened. I knew him quite well... he was not a fierce man; he was balanced, honest, and rather jolly. His family is devastated... How are things with you? How do you like your new lodgings?'

Dan was about to say something, but Peppin sat back down at the desk. It seemed he shared that trait of people who talk a lot: he listened but little.

*

Upstairs, in the office of the editor-in-chief, the conversation came less easily. Peppin's brother, Pavel, having been around garrulous people from a young age, had become taciturn, while Procopiu, who had a talkative wife, loved silence above all else. When he was not speaking, Pavel dreamed up all kinds of scenes that he wrote in his mind. You couldn't even imagine what was going on behind his round spectacles. You had the impression that he half opened the door, spoke on the threshold to the people outside, and then abruptly slammed it in their faces, shut the windows and drew the curtains, broke off all possibility of contact with the exterior, and tumbled into himself, as if into a deep pit, crawling with the snakes of ideas. Every day, he woke up at the same time as his wife, at seven in the morning, washed, tied his lavaliere, made himself dapper, as if he were about to get engaged to "The Idea." In the meantime, his wife incessantly nagged him, and so when he left the house it was a blessing. He chose the streets that were full of people, he looked in the shop windows, sometimes he even entered a café on the Boulevard, where he always ordered a cappuccino, which he sipped at leisure, keeping an eye out for public figures.

Today, he had ridden the tram around town for a long time, in search of a good story, from the Bishopric to St George's, then as far as Moșilor Avenue, and thence along the Elisabeta Boulevard as far as the Cișmigiu tram stop. From the tram stop he proceeded on foot, along the edge of the park – in summer it was a joy to see the flowerbeds in all their bright colours and the solar clock – before turning right up Strada Brezoianu, and here he was, in despair at not having found any good event to turn into a front-page story. Everything was going too well and all the people that crossed his path were amiable and settled. But it was disorder and incidents, fires and thefts, that were a newspaper's greatest fortune, the things that increased circulation. Should he write something about the City Hall's ordinance regarding printing presses? That was not much of a novelty. Ever since the invention of the printing press, its toxic disadvantages have been known. Of course, the strictest tidiness and cleanliness reduced the risk of inhaling lead dust, but did not eliminate it altogether. And to speak of such a thing was somehow dangerous, when you were a large gazette with its own printing press and you boasted a rotary that had been brought all the way from Würzberg and which was the only one of its kind in Romania. Better the way other confreres do it;

those that print American-style news items that astound you, but which don't become subjects of debate: for example, a compositor sets twelve thousand letters a day. If you take into account the distance the hand moves when setting each letter is about two paces, then in a year, not including holidays, a compositor's hand moves around six thousand kilometres. Which was about the distance to New York.

'Do you think that Nicu Filipescu will be convicted?' asked Pavel, lifting his head, as if he had sensed the anxieties of his colleague and wished to allay them.

'A former mayor? It is hard to believe, although it is possible, because I have never seen public opinion so heated, not even when he was the one who decided to demolish the Sărindar Church. I can remember the dust I inhaled when I was on my way here, and the people from *Adevĕrul*, although their offices were in the Passage Vilacross, took the opportunity to turn it into a big scandal. But when I think that poor Lahovary was exactly the same age as I am, and when I remember what a decent and jolly man he was, I wish with all my soul that Filipescu be convicted.'

'But why?' said Pavel heatedly, his voice more irritated and louder than usual. 'Don't you have the right to send out your seconds when your name is blackened in a gazette? I'm not defending Filipescu, but in this case his honour was at stake. Lahovary was the one who attacked him. And he knew that he was striking at a man who was quick to anger.'

'But you are forgetting how many attacks that *Epoca*, via its director Filipescu, made against George Lahovary and his newspaper?' said the editor-in-chief, becoming upset. 'So, one can wield a cudgel for a whole year without anything happening to him, but when the other gives him a slap, he challenges him to a duel! You force me to tell you what I believe: it was murder! Because to insist at all costs on duelling with a man who is not accustomed to it, and then, instead of dealing him a scratch, to plunge your sword in his belly, is what I call an assassination! Duelling is a mediaeval practice and I am surprised that a man of your sensitivity, a man with the soul of an artist, can approve of it.'

'Don't tell me, Mr Neculai, that you are one of those who agree with the outlawing of duels. Don't tell me that you want to live in a world where anybody can mock you as he pleases and you will not have any weapon with which to protect your honour,' said Pavel, his voice almost trembling with rage. It is possible that such an absurd situation will exist in the future, if such people get their way, but today at least, whatever other advantages we might lack, at least we have our honour.'

The atmosphere had become very tense, the same as it had been in parliament when the matter had been debated. The editor-in-chief rose from his desk and paced up and down with long strides. Pavel lit another cigarette, which only heightened his interlocutor's annoyance.

'And don't forget what started it all,' added Neculai Procopiu, without looking at him.

In a seemingly calmer tone, although they were still seething, they discussed the incidents on Strada Carol, which ultimately had started the avalanche, and tried to establish what had triggered them. Some gangs of ruffians, the dregs of Bucharest, professional thieves, ne'er-do-wells, had broken the windows of the shops on Strada Carol, most of them owned by Jews. The people of Bucharest had never witnessed the like since the robberies carried out by Melanos Bocceagiu and his vagabonds, whom they named the 'kings of the Old Court.' At Inger's and *Au Bon Goût* they even broke glass partitions that were a centimetre thick, while at Dr Steinhart's they broke only the windows. A few people had also been beaten-up. The newspapers had taken the side of the Jewish shop owners. The gendarmes chased the malefactors and made arrests. But here there was a small problem. Around Caton Lecca, also known as 'the Elder,' there floated the disgraceful suspicion that he closed his eyes to anti-Jewish manifestations. His brother from Buzău had been caught up in scandals of the same kind. But the professional probity of Costache Boerescu was, on the contrary, without visible blemish. People knew that the two got along like cat and dog. And it was said that Nicu Filipescu too was an anti-Semite, although later he had taken the side of the Jews. In his article *Two Policies*, Lahovary said that Nicu Filipescu was two-faced, that he wrote according to how the wind blew, and he recalled the affair involving Metropolitan Ghenadie. At this point, the argument almost erupted once more, and so the editor-in-chief saw fit to change the subject.

'Have you seen that barbers and hairdressers are demanding that they be allowed to work on New Year's Eve and Christmas Eve, because otherwise they will lose a large number of customers? And if they are not allowed to, they threaten to go on strike! Have you ever heard of a strike caused by not having the day off? Do you think that would make a front-page story?'

As he asked, Procopiu regarded Pavel with envy: he did not have such problems, when he was asked for a lead article, he found an up -to -date subject, such as the violin concert at the Palace of the Post Office that was relayed over the telephone. Oh, that interested Procopiu in the highest degree! It was as if you could be in two places at the same time, albeit via a single sense, the hearing. But very soon, so his inquisitive mind told him – the engineer in him, who also possessed the faculty of imagination – very soon we would be able to be in two places at once also via the eyesight, and then via the other senses, and, why not, in a hundred years, in two places at once bodily. It was here, in such news items, that the two men intersected, one arriving with science and hope, the other with fantasy and literature. Procopiu sighed and opened the window. In today's paper, his article on the first page was about the young aristocrat who was slain, and the story about the Romanian torn to pieces by jaguars had been moved to the margin, although it ought to have had a central column, since the story was worthy of a novel. Beneath it, rather incongruously, was the following item: 'DAILY ADVICE: *A swollen cheek*. Take a handful of elderberry flowers, another of camomile, and another of linden flowers, mix them well and place them in a sachet. Heat the sachet well and apply it to the swelling.' He thought of Miss Margulis, whom he had just seen, because she had had the bizarre idea of visiting the newspaper offices, although her cheek was swollen, and he regretted not having had the chance to tell her about the advice in the Gazette. Who knows, maybe it worked? In fact, he did not have much faith in such advice and nor in the advertisements they were obliged to publish, advertisements for miraculous cure-alls, such as Genoa Water or remedies against the microbes that caused baldness.

'Now that most young men wear moustaches rather than full beards, the barbers have had a lot of custom; they can't cope. And nor is long hair the mode any longer,' answered Pavel, in a placatory tone.

Somewhat mollified, since in that respect he could be reckoned a young man, Procopiu stroked his waxed black moustache.

'But I for one preferred Mr Costache Boerescu with a beard rather than a moustache. Who knows for what prima donna he shaved off his beard.'

Pavel Mirto added, as a means of erasing the traces of the earlier argument: 'Ah, but I have some more news for you. In France they have founded an all-female newspaper, *La Fronde*. Santa Maria, Madre di Dio! There's a place I would like to work.'

'As a smoker, I think you would have difficulties,' said the editor-in-chief, with implied reproach. 'What are we doing about tomorrow's article, have you any ideas?'

THE CHANCE OCCURENCE

1.

Yesterday evening, Papa, only just having returned from Giurgiu, took fright when he heard that I had been outside in the cold all day, and so today he forbade me to go out of the house under any circumstances. 'I shall call my friend Steinhart to examine you,' he said. 'As far as I can see, the infected molar is a wisdom tooth, and so it must be extracted. Wisdom teeth are good for nothing and cause only problems.' 'Wisdom likewise,' I said, because I was feeling very gloomy. Let us think about it a little: I had every reason to be gloomy, since I still felt poorly, I still felt as if I had grit in my eyes, my cheek was still swollen, and I had dreamed of Alexandru. He had been duelling with Nicu Filipescu and both were wounded, and I was one of the seconds, the referee. But I could not help him, since I was not allowed. Of course, it could only be the result of the newspapers' obsession with the Lahovary-Filipescu case, in other words the *L'Indépendance* versus *Epoca* case, in other words, a political *querelle* I do not believe that Nicu Filipescu killed him on purpose; as the servants say: he is notorious for his hot temper. But nor did he have any mercy on a man unaccustomed to swordplay. In a way, it was murder in the name of honour. Papa put Collir in my eyes; it did not hurt. Nor am I afraid of having my tooth extracted. Papa told me that nowadays there are methods of putting the tooth to sleep, they numb your jaw, and everything is painless, even if later, when the numbness passes, the pain returns. Papa praised me. He says that women are braver than men in the battle with illness. In the family on festive occasions they tell the story of how a colleague once asked Papa: 'Mr Margulis, what is your opinion of the weaker sex?' And Papa straight away replied: 'I think that the weaker sex is the stronger sex.' This saying then circulated, especially given that Papa is not renowned for *bons mots*. When I am ill, he always explains to me what has gone wrong inside me and after that I am not at all afraid;

it seems to me that we are like mechanisms, which from time to time have to be repaired, oiled and adjusted. He told me that I have *conjunctivitis* and that both problems are probably because of a draught: 'Did you keep the window open?' he asked. He taught me that everything inside our head is connected; ears, nose and throat, and all the canals and nerves are inlets for the bad to enter. He speaks of the body; I speak of the soul. And then, Papa tells me: '*Mens sana in corpore sano*, as Juvenal well put it, although he was a poet.' He does not much like poets. And then: 'A good doctor cures both mind and body.' Let us see, Papa, whether you can cure my mind and body of Alexandru, I thought to myself, downcast.

'I will cure you,' he said, as if he had overheard my thoughts.

I have noticed that sometimes he can read thoughts, exactly like our friend, Mr Costache. The truth is that I have qualms of conscience about how I rebuffed Alexandru yesterday. After my dream of last night I see things completely differently. I think he is in danger and that I have to help him. But what if he is very well, thank you, and I make a fool of myself? Ultimately, I have never refused a visit before, and so why should I start with him? And so I opened the drawer of my writing table and began to search for a special-looking envelope. In the end I selected one which, if you held it up to the light, had a fleur-de-lis in filigree. I pondered for a long time. My mind was not working, probably because I did not have a *corpus sanum* either. In the end I penned the following:

Bucharest, 23 December 1897
Sir,
Your visit of yesterday caught me at an inopportune moment.
I am rather ill, I have conjunctivitis *(an illness due to which my eyes have become a mixture of green and red, rather like the colours of garments in Renaissance paintings), I also have other problems, which I will refrain from mentioning to you. Perhaps, if you had taken a few minutes of your time, which, I am sure, is very precious, to write to me at least a day in advance, I would have been able to make our meeting possible. But concern for rules does not preoccupy you. If you nonetheless wish to see me, having been warned about the way that I look, please come on Saturday the 27th to our house at five o'clock in the afternoon. My parents, unfortunately, have to pay a visit. I impatiently await your reply.*
Iulia Margulis

The curlicue on my signature was quite dented, a sign that I was out of sorts. I refuse to feel sorry for myself: my eyes, the tooth that must be extracted, *les règles*, the house cleaning that seems never to end, and which in fact has barely begun, since now Mama is in command, and the bad dream. But as soon as I finished writing the note, I felt better. And since Nicu had come to visit my little brother, I gave him the envelope to deliver to Alexandru, and even gave him his tram fare. A big clock grows inside my heart whenever I am waiting for an answer from him, a clock that runs twice as slowly as it ought to do and whose seconds tick twice as loudly. And it is as if all my other sorrows are smaller and far away, like when you look through the wrong end of a pair of opera glasses.

2.

From her bed, next to his, she could hear the doctor's even breathing. He was still asleep, weary from the journey of the day before. Rarely did he snore, which was one of his great qualities. There were plenty of wives who took separate bedrooms in order to be able to sleep, because their husbands chugged like trains the whole night through. Agatha thought of the chugging of the train to Giurgiu on Sunday, and the train back, yesterday, which had jolted her every bone. Her back ached more and more frequently, although she wrapped her middle with a woollen girdle, and now she could feel a migraine coming on. That was all she needed, when she had so hard a day ahead and so tiring a day behind. Perhaps next year they ought to rear their own pig. So long a journey was not worth it, although it was good to have everything prepared and ready, admitted Mrs Margulis. She lit the gas lamp by the side of the bed. It was still pitch black, but she lay back down so as not to waken her husband: the floor creaked rather loudly.

It had been a pleasant surprise to meet their friend Costache on the return journey. He was alone, and so they moved from the other end of the carriage into his compartment, bringing with them the small suitcase, which emanated delicious odours. They had had to surrender the larger suitcase at the baggage car. The doctor had gone with the porter to the baggage *cassa*, not a quarter of an hour before the train's departure, as required, but a half an hour earlier. Their baggage was weighed: thirty-two kilos, and they had been relieved of it. It was therefore easy to move to Costache's compartment. Outside it was gloomy, snowflakes stuck to the windowpane, revealed their starry patterns for an instant and then melted, but inside it was warm, there was light, they felt sheltered, and the conversation flowed more easily than ever. It was as if you had guests, but without the attendant burdens of the host. The time melts like snowflakes. You know that you have a few suspended hours, in which you have nothing whatever to do, except to glide across the white fields, as if you were flying. They had hesitated before setting off, because in winter the train sometimes got stuck in snowdrifts. But the newspapers had not forecast any blizzards.

'What is the news about the stranger who was found on Friday, Dan Creţu?' asked Agatha. 'People have started talking all kinds of non-sense, and our children – which is to say Jacques mostly – believe he fell from the sky.'

Costache, who was always highly discreet when it came to the cases he was working on, told them that he had not found out very much, but hoped in time to bring everything to light and, without his realizing it, he found himself telling his old friends the story of Rareş Ochiu-Zănoagă and the awkward moments he had spent at the young man's family estate. The policeman had seen many things in his time, but he was still not accustomed to some. He still felt affected by the grief of the parents, who on learning the news had been ripped from the soil of their lives like trees at the height of a tempest. Such a thing ought not to exist in the plan of the world, he said. The child was an artist and sometimes caused them to worry, and it is true, they used to be on tenterhooks because of his frequent trips to Bucharest, but nothing, except perhaps the presentiments of the blood that bring you tidings before any messenger, could have foretold such an end. With the sister of the young Rareş – he found out from her that the lad was not yet twenty-two, Iulia's age – he had managed to speak for somewhat longer, although the girl's eyes kept turning red and she had been unable to utter a word. She was given smelling salts a number of times, but she was a brave girl, she did not faint, and kept choking back her tears. The boy, Rareş, was talented at painting, and every June, he went to Bucharest, where he worked as a volunteer, restoring church frescos. It was his passion and in recent years there had been frequent restorations in Bucharest. No sooner had he finished in one church than he was sent to another. When he was just ten-years-old, a mural painter from Giurgiu had allowed him to climb the scaffolding in the church he was working on and to paint the eyes and mouth of St Constantine and his mother, St Elena, who had become rather smoke-blackened because of the candles. The lad had taken the brush from the painter and working with his child's hand he had displayed an unusual talent. The priest came in and angry lest the painting be ruined, he shouted at both the painter and the lad. It was then that the first portent occurred, for Rareş took fright and fell off the scaffolding. You should have seen how the priest's hand trembled when he cradled the blond head in his palms and saw the closed eyes. You should have seen how Mama, who had been talking to somebody in the churchyard, ran inside and took him in her arms as if he were an infant. But on that occasion they had merely had a fright, nothing worse.

The policeman lowered his voice and urged them to treat with the utmost confidentiality what he was about to tell them, and both Agatha and the doctor, sitting opposite him, leaned forward to hear. He told them the last words spoken by the young man, the visible relief on his face, and how he seemed to die at peace.

'Perhaps it was a case of mystical aspiration,' said the doctor, and Agatha added: 'A kind of prayer.'

But Costache was certain that the 'syndromes' said otherwise. Once, the policeman and her husband had amused themselves finding similarities between their professions, and they had discovered them in droves. Both professions demanded a spirit of observation, a warm heart and a clear head, generosity and dedication, tact and courage. Both required discretion and stamina. Both entailed investigations, since in today's medicine, explained Leon, questioning is obligatory. The answers had to be interpreted: the sick, the same as malefactors, avoid telling the truth. Both professions examined signs with the greatest attention. In both there was need for strong moral fibre and love of one's fellow man. Both the physician and the policeman had to be educated and intelligent, capable of understanding the subtlest bodily, spiritual and social mechanisms. Both the physician and the policeman had to have money, the first for instruments and hospitals and the second in order not to be corrupted. Here, Costache was better off than Agatha's husband: he was from a wealthy family and to him his remuneration was mostly symbolic. You could not become Chief of Police if you were not from a wealthy family, and the reason for that was not only to prevent you being bought but also to ensure you had the education required for such a difficult profession. But above all else, both the physician and the policeman were afraid of the spread of evil and tried to quash it. Perhaps in the society of the future, after man makes progress in all the areas expected of him, there will be no need for either physicians or policemen. They had often said as much, but they were among the few who did not believe it. For, they knew that man, wherever he might be in space or time, was in essence the same. For Agatha, Leon Margulis and Costache Boerescu also had one more thing in common: both of them had fallen in love with her. And it was not the stronger that won.

Still lingering in bed and somewhat drained of strength, Agatha thought of the words she had learned from Costache: in her mind, *light* and *Holy Mother* could only be connected to the final moment. But *Popescu*? A priest (*popă*) or the descendent of a priest... But why had the boy uttered the name? A Popescu must be found, the Popescu with whom the poor child was acquainted. Thinking of his mother's grief,

Agatha wandered down an evil path, a path she almost never allowed herself to follow. Neither Iulia nor Jacques knew that they had had a little sister, born before them, but younger than them, because she had died of meningitis just a few days before her third birthday. She had been unutterably charming, good and happy, until she fell ill. Never in her life had Agatha fought harder for something than she had then. She felt in the most tangible possible way that she was wrestling with death, as she sat by her little girl's bedside day and night. She had talked to her, although the girl could not hear, she had caressed her, she had called to her, she had smothered her little hands in kisses, she had followed to the letter the instructions as to the doses of medicine and everything she had to do to make her well, and she had prayed unceasingly. She had sensed that the doctor-father no longer believed in the possibility of salvation, but she had believed and fought. But Death had been stronger than the mother; Death is always stronger. And Agatha had wanted to follow her daughter immediately, to help her. How could she leave her alone in the darkness? She had always been protected by her mother, by her father, by a night-light next to her bed. It is impossible to speak of what came next, she was in hell, day after day in hell: of that she was sure. What had she done wrong? Why was the child guilty if she was at fault? Did God exist, if he could permit such a thing? Was not the world itself at fault, from its very foundations? Maybe we are living in an imperfect world, a world abandoned to the whim of fate. The doctor-father had to give her injections, to make her sleep for days on end, because when she awoke, she immediately wanted to follow her little girl, demanding a double dose of morphine to make her sleep forever. Since then, the lamp on her little girl's grave had never gone out, she had made sure of it, during her frequent trips, on which none of the children were allowed to accompany her.

She spoke to her constantly and told her: if you are in heaven, be happy, there, in heaven, however unhappy we are here, and if you are not there yet, then I, with my own hand, will take you up above, hold on tight, I won't let you go. And Agatha would clench her fist, grasping thin air. And if there be no heaven, I will make one for you, and if there be no God, you shall have one, your Mama promises. And Agatha could see God plainly and in His arms rested her little girl. And if you are nothingness, then I will love that nothingness and soak it with my tears and protect it with all my being. Do you hear me, nothingness? I love you! You are my nothingness now, my only nothingness.

And the nothingness had her eyes. If you feel poorly, I will stand in for you, so that I will be poorly, but no, you could not feel poorly, I give you all the good I have. If you need us, call us, we will come, we hear you. I will come straight away, send me word! For me death was like pregnancy, but in reverse. I counted the days, I spoke to the departed child, just as then I had spoken with the child who had not yet arrived, I explained to it, I consoled it, I protected the child that was no longer, just as I had protected the one that had not yet come. Except that one was drawing nearer to life, while the other was moving farther away from it.

Agatha always kept the ears of her soul pricked up, to hear whether her little girl needed help. And never could she be fully happy again, as she had been before. And not a day passed but in her mind she kissed her on her little head, on her cheek, and when she kissed Iulia, who had come into the world soon thereafter, on her dark hair, she hoped the kiss would also reach the blonde hair of the other girl. The children sensed something; they sensed that they could never make their mother fully happy, there was always a little corner of her that remained discontented and sad.

And when the trial with Jacques had come, Agatha was no longer able to experience even that as a normal mother would have experienced it. As ever, she reined in her thoughts, toiling with desperation. That was her salvation and, strangely, she also seemed to find salvation in the chatter of the servants and women's affairs, which shifted her thoughts to more concrete things. And Costache's visits also did her good, and his concern, which had still not flagged after such a bitterly long time. Now Costache sometimes seemed to view Iulia as he had once viewed her. She was not surprised; she knew that he could see the inner person more clearly than Roentgen's miraculous rays. But nevertheless, Agatha did not like to see him too much in Iulia's company.

She would now have to inspect all the cleaning that had been done in her absence, to see to the kitchen, the potted plants, to make ready the lamps and candlesticks, to take out and check the crockery for special occasions, to examine the towels in the toilet cabinets next to the bedroom, to make sure they were fresh, to scrub the basins and the porcelain bowls, to remember to send for a piano tuner, because Iulia had asked for one to come, to arrange the things in the larder, to remove the cobwebs that had caught her eye that very moment, to see to the presents, and tomorrow at the break of day she had a meeting of the Mothers' Association. They were going to visit the Elisabeta Crèche at No. 11 Strada Teilor, which had been inaugurated three weeks previously, at the end of November. In Agatha's mind there remained a darling little girl who resembled her departed daughter, except that she was swarthier and her eyes were sadder, whereas her little Maria had made the whole street and the whole city and the whole world smile when she took her for a walk.

She got up and on the nightstand she saw *The Lady's Planet*, which in Giurgiu a cross-eyed organ grinder's parrot had picked from a basket for her. Only now did she read it, putting on her glasses: 'You like to joke, to spend time with your friends, for which reason many ladies envy you, but your heart belongs only to the man with whom you are married. You will live for eighty years. You will have a good marriage. And you have no reason to be wary of your husband. Your reward will be happiness. Lottery: 13, 21 and 26.'

She would buy a ticket and if she won, she would have money to repair the house, for they needed new wallpaper and above all to modernize their home, which was behind the times.

'Are you awake? It seems to me that I have done la *grasse matinée*,' said Leon Margulis and with the soles of his feet he felt around for his house slippers. 'What time is it? I dreamed of Costache. In the end I forgot to ask him: is he or is he not coming to the Christmas dinner?'

3.

Costache carefully pressed the button of the electric doorbell that General Ion Algiu had lately had installed. He heard a buzz and in the same instant a bark. The footfalls of the adjutant and the quadruped reached the door at the same time, as if it were a race, and when the soldier took Costache's hat, a splendid Borzoi wolfhound leapt up and placed his paws on the trousers of the policeman's uniform. Costache thrust the dog aside, although it was friendly and had something very aristocratic about it, with its lively, elongated head and ruff of fur. He deposited his walking stick with the silver beak in the vase in the hall and entered the library, as usual during one of his working visits. The general was in mourning for his wife, who had died the previous winter. It would soon be the first anniversary of her death, but his grief was as great as it had been from the very first. His son, who lived in Craiova, wrote to him frequently, his two daughters, both married and with their own households, tried to cheer him up, inviting him to visit them, but he preferred to be all by himself, taking tobacco amid his memories, in the place that was still filled with all her little gestures. In the beginning, he had not been able to bear the presence of any other person, visiting cards went unanswered on the tray in the hall, but now he had gradually begun to look at them and deigned to reply: to a quarter he answered *yes*, to three quarters *Forgive me, but another time*. However, Costache's visit made him feel better. He had liked him ever since the time when, seven or eight years ago, as Prefect of Police and rather put out at the thought of working in an office, he had sought a decent subaltern and instead found a friend. They measured each other with their eyes, the same as the first time, when between them had arisen that empathy that seems only to exist between certain people, and were happy to observe that they were both the same and that the same empathy still existed between them even now.

'Misfortunes!' said the policeman by way of a greeting, and the General merely raised his unkempt white eyebrows.

Neither wasted words. Mr Costache accepted a coffee and a brandy and mixed them, pouring a few drops of brandy into the coffee *à la manière de Marghiloman*. He briefly recounted the two cases that had been causing him trouble and seemed to be going nowhere; with each passing day they were becoming more and more bogged down. In the meantime many gazettes had begun to make a fuss, and that was deleterious. The young Rareş Ochiu-Zănoagă, who had been found shot, and a certain Dan Creţu – no relative of our red-headed apothecary – cases connected by all kinds of coincidences. The General read four or five gazettes daily, and so he was up to date with the affair. More importantly, he was familiar with the account in *Universul*, which seemed the best informed.

'Do you think there is any connection between the two?'

'Both men were found on the same morning, by the same man, Petre Inger, the confectioner's coachman. Both were unconscious, one wounded, the other not. I do not suspect Petre, he is from a different, unconnected world, and he would not have brought them in had he had anything on his conscience. Besides, I have interrogated him. As for Dan Creţu – if such be his real name, for he has not documents – we would have been able to find out a great deal from his luggage, a safe-type box, but unfortunately it has vanished without trace. The man was held in the cells for an hour, but the other crooks said that he did not speak to them, and nor did he speak to Fane the Ringster, the number one suspect in the disappearance of the box.'

'But what does your nose tell you?'

'I am inclined to believe that he is a high-class fraudster, an upper-class forger or a jewel thief of great panache, who has come from far away, perhaps from overseas. But...'

With his eyebrows the General urged him to continue.

'But it seems to me that his brain is addled, as they say.'

'Why would the one preclude the other?'

'What surprises me is that the editor-in-chief of *Universul*, the one who wrote the article about the other case – I understand you have read it – whom I asked to employ him, so that we could keep an eye on him at all times, told me that he has definitely worked as a journalist before; his experience is obvious.'

'Why do the three preclude each other?'

'I don't know. It seems to me that they preclude each other, not in theory, but from what I have seen of the man. My nose, as you say. And apropos of noses, at a dinner I once saw a Turk with a cardboard nose, placed not over his nose but in its place. A strange sight, I do declare. Unless my nose is made of cardboard too, the man does not resemble an ordinary journalist: when you compare him with Procopiu, for example, you will immediately see why. Nor does he resemble the thieves and fraudsters that you can smell from a mile off. I will not hide from you the fact that for an instant I even thought of Jack the Ripper and I imagined that in his case there might be a razor and a saw. Ultimately, he resembles a normal person, with interludes of mental alienation, but Dr Margulis has assured me that although he speaks rather strangely, as if he had different reference points than the rest of us, he nonetheless speaks rather like the poets. Whatever path I pursue, there appears something that does not fit, I have never experienced the like...'

'I have a single suggestion, but I do not know how much it will help you. It is a question of things that fit. In Saturday's *Universul* three things attracted my attention: the young man who was shot, the so-called Dan Crețu, and a lost wallet for which the reward was entirely unusual. This is what puzzled me the most. What might it contain? Has the wallet been found?'

Mr Costache did not know.

'You see, Costache? I think that at least two of the three things are connected, and the third is the thing that throws them into confusion. But which of the two things go together is what you will have to find out. Pursue the announcement, if the other leads are dead ends for the time being.'

'And there is another thing upon which I should like you to meditate, if you will allow me,' said Costache, standing at the front door, taking his walking stick with the silver beak. 'The young man uttered a few words before he died, which I wrote down: *light, Popescu, light, Holy Mother* and another word that was unclear, either *dar* or *sar*. If you have any ideas, I am sure you will let me know. I am most glad to have seen you, I missed you, and only now do I realize how much,' he said, turning back beneath the entrance marquee and making a joking military salute. Ion Algiu watched him depart with a smile well concealed by his moustache. He had missed him too.

4.

Nicu took the envelope and placed it inside his coat, taking care not to crumple it. Then he bowed to Jacques's sister, in the way he had seen important men bow (such as Mr Cazzavillan to the editors' wives) but the girl burst out laughing and grasping his chin, lifted it towards her. In that way he was able to see that she did not look at all well that morning: one cheek had risen like sweet bread dough, the other was hollow. But both cheeks were rosy. To Nicu, Miss Iulia was like the lighthouses that *Universul* had written about not long ago: one, in Tuzla, had a red beacon, and the other, in Mangalia, a white one. With her too, now one beacon lit up, now the other, because the white one also shone. Now the Tuzla lighthouse was shining.

'I am waiting for his reply – you will tell him, won't you? And above all, deliver it to him personally. If that is not possible, deliver it to Mr Mihai Livizeanu, a man with a lock of hair that falls over his forehead. He is his brother, a student in Paris. If not, then bring it back to me, but no, don't do that, please wait until he comes, do you promise me?'

Now the red Tuzla beacon had gone out and the Mangalia one was shining. That was women for you! He set off towards the tram stop, preoccupied. Iulia Margulis was not a person he could refuse. You could refuse the doctor, because he was a calm man and an understanding one, the doctor's wife you could refuse because she was a mother, Jacques you could refuse because it was between men, but your heart would not allow you to refuse his sister for any reason. Not even he could understand why. But he had absolutely no inclination, he was 'outside working hours,' proof of which was that he was not wearing his peaked cap, but rather a normal hat. He had come to play soldiers with Jacques, but still he could not get away from work.

'You're busy and ultra-busy, young man,' he said confidingly to a dog on the street, 'you don't get a moment's peace or quiet. A thousand chores...'

The dog wagged its tail and followed him for a while, before abandoning him, as if having reached some invisible boundary. The City Hall had given the order that all house-holders and tenants clear the snow from in front of their buildings and scatter ashes, so that people would not slip and break their legs. But even so, his boots were still slippery and he ran and slid wherever he could. Reaching the tram stop, he waited. Then a girl came up, holding her mother's hand, and he felt an electric spark (although he had never felt an electric spark), which tingled from his cap to the toes of his boots. He moved closer to the two and the scent of lemon balm enveloped him like springtime. It was as if the white of the snow was all of a sudden green and on the verdure he saw white flowers of lemon balm with yellow centres.

'Mama, why is that thin little boy alone? And why is he dressed like that?' he heard the girl say, and her mother jerked her hand and made a sign for her to be quiet.

Whereas before he had felt suffused with love, now the tingles, still streaming from his head to the toes of his boots, were of double offence. Who does that little ninny think she is? Little was one way of putting it; in fact she was tall. Therefore he postponed yet again his much-wished-for encounter with his great love, with his beautiful fiancée. His attention was then drawn to a hole and since lately his imagination had been inflamed by the tunnels of moles and their life beneath the earth, he wounded whether it might lead to the dark houses and streets of the moles. He might have asked the lanky girl, but any conversation with her was out of the question now. He made a point of not boarding the tram so that he would not be forced, God forbid, to sit next to her and start smelling of lemon balm. He would take the next one. But it was obvious that it was one of those unlucky Tuesdays that the old biddies talk about. For, after he had been sent out into the cold, instead of being left to play by the fire, and after he had been insulted by a stupid little girl, albeit a rather tall one, instead of sinking into the arms of love, he saw the one man in the world whom he could not abide come to stand next to him at the tram stop, a man for whom he felt fear, and above all repulsion. He was a thief who skinned him like a rabbit whenever he bumped into him. Any attempt at self-defence was futile, and so were cries for help, and so Nicu, after weighing up the situation, either fled, if he was in a crowded place, or suffered himself to be robbed and humiliated. Sandu, known as the Muzzle, one of the police's regular customers, was always to be found wherever there was disorder in the Capital: in the recent events, the riots on Strada Carol, he had looted a number of shops. As he twisted his arm behind his back, Nicu could smell the stench of his muzzle – his moniker came from the shape of his mouth.

'Hey, it's the lad with the crazy ma, come here and hand over the loot.'

The boy, who usually endured aggression like a bitter taste that would soon pass, remembered in horror that today he was carrying two things that the drunkard must not find at any cost: the cow he had received from Dan (Fira as she had been dubbed) and Miss Margulis' letter. He therefore strategically produced the tram fare that Iulia had given him and made a show of reluctantly surrendering it, with lowered eyes. The thief straight away tucked it in an inside pocket, and then he started mocking the lad, now insulting him verbally, now twisting his arm behind his back, loosening his grip and then twisting again even harder. Nicu knew from the fable of the fox that he had to cry out when it did not hurt at all and to keep dead silent when it did, and so he kept dead silent.

'Want some more, eh, you little tyke, what's this, trying to stand up to Sandu? Standing up to Sandu, are you? To the Muzzle, eh, you little whelp?' He thrust his muzzle close to the boy's face.

Nicu reckoned it was the moment to shout at the top of his lungs that he was hurting him, especially since he was crying real tears. But because the tram had just left, there was nobody at the stop to protect him. The thief started searching him, carelessly, pausing frequently, breathing plum brandy fumes into Nicu's face. Nicu thought that he might get away with it, but no, the thief had found Fira. He looked at her without interest and tossed her into the 'mole's hole,' and then straight away he found the envelope in the left-hand pocket of Nicu's coat. He did not know how to read, and so he tore it in two and tossed it after Nicu's cow, into the hole, like a shroud. After convincing himself that there was nothing else worthy of his attention in the lad's pockets, he pummelled him a couple of times, and then told him to sling his hook. Nicu walked away, dragging his feet, and hid behind the first corner. The thief had not left; he sat down on the bench and took out his bottle. People began to arrive, who cast him suspicious glances, and then the tram stop began to fill up, and so the drunkard left, all of a sudden very humble, with his tail between his legs. Like all bullies, he was very courageous in front of the weak. His victims of choice were children and young maidservants. A flock of crows filled the sky with blackness and croaking, as if rasping against the firmament.

Nicu went to the hole and assessed the extent of the damage. He felt almost the same as he had at his grandmother's funeral, when, aged seven, no matter how much it had pained him, he had bawled and wept. That grim Tuesday was the first time he had ever lost something that had been entrusted to him and he was very ashamed. He pictured himself losing his job and his livelihood. The first rule for errand boys was not to lose or damage anything. Not even a petal, his boss used to say, although with some bunches of roses that was almost impossible. He thought of his mother, who had difficulty finding work in winter, and when she had her fits, nobody wanted her. He was terrified she might end up at Mărcuţa's and he at the orphanage, as a woman from his neighbourhood kept threatening he would. He took the envelope out of the mole's hole; it was torn and wet. He could not take it like that to Mr Alexandru Livezeanu, and not could he take it back to Iulia Margulis, who was waiting for an answer. In fact there was nobody in the world he could tell about what had befallen him. He burst into a flood of tears.

5.

...to get used to *this* world and I have to get used to life again, after not daring to look anybody in the eye, because of the pain... I asked what day it was and the man I share an office with told me, looking at the calendar: 23 December here, 4 January in the rest of Europe, including my mother's country and the director's. 'What is your standpoint on the calendar question?' It was lucky that he did not wait for an answer, the same as usual. But his melodious, radiant voice does me good; it keeps my feet on the ground. We went out together, the doorman saluted us, doffing his cap, and as if from some old habit that I had completely forgotten, I doffed my hat too. I have received a felt hat and a pair of black galoshes as a present. How quickly you get used to novelties, how easily wonders become ordinary. Ultimately, perhaps we were created to accept every evil and every good in order to feel our insignificance. As soon as we forget it, we are punished with blows. Perhaps we eke out our days on a prison planet, except that we have never seen our gaolers, and every time we try to revolt, we are dealt blows, but in subtle forms, invented with great imagination. I feel I am in prison. I'm not brave enough to believe myself free and I don't know how to behave like a free man. My colleague asked me whether I wanted him to conduct me to the hotel and I barely dared to tell him that I would rather go for a walk. Politely, he didn't insist, and bid me goodbye, and then he was gone, like a will-o'-the-wisp.

'Mr Crețu! Mr Crețu!'

I started, took fright. It was a man with a beard like maize silk, and he nimbly leapt out of a carriage. I recognized him: the doctor who had examined me in the police cell and asked whether I had tuberculosis. I would say he is a decent fellow; he invited me to his surgery, to have a chat.

'It's here, close by, next to the Lyric Theatre, the one that burned down, we go straight ahead and then down Strada Sfântul Ionică, behind the National Theatre. Many actors live next door and they come to me with various ailments. You would never imagine how tortured actors how, what sufferings afflict them, when you see them on stage, bathed in lights. Excuse me if I do not shake your hand just yet.'

We both climbed into a cab.

'To my surgery, Yevdoshka,' said the doctor.

'I am returning from a patient with typhoid fever, the epidemic has passed, these are the last cases, isolated ones fortunately. Look, we are just passing the house where Pascaly, the actor, died, perhaps you have heard of him: he was an Armand Duval, who broke your heart. I once visited him in the outbuilding of his house, where youngsters gather to rehearse all kinds of rôles; he was charming. He fell ill with tuberculosis and some joked: you've caught consumption from your lady with the camellias. After taking a cure at Reichenhal, which had not effect whatever, he came back, and one mild autumn day he gently faded away, like a candle burning out. They displayed his coffin in the Sărindar Church – it no longer even exists – and throngs of people came, actors and theatregoers of every generation, they came to see the poor Pascaly, in his final rôle, which is the same part for all of us.'

We went into a building from which hung a small sign: *Dr Leon Margulis M.D. First floor*, and with a shudder I wondered who was the host and who the guest, for somewhere it was my house too. A young lad opened the door for us and took my hat and coat. The doctor put down his large leather bag with the snap fastener.

'Before I do anything else, please allow me to wash my hands and to disinfect myself. It is the first thing I must do. Please sit down.'

I looked around with a great deal of curiosity. A cupboard, a bed covered with oilcloth, a chair, a table and a screen with a floral pattern. Some shelves with coloured bottles and jars, green and blue and transparent, full of all kinds of powders and pills. On the highest shelf sat a bottle with a blue stopper, with a long slender neck, whose label read 'Morphine,' and another bottle, a red one, which read 'Extract of Belladonna.' Next to the cupboard were some anatomical charts, rolled up one next to the other. There was a white stove, with firewood neatly stacked in a niche alongside. Everything seemed very clean to me. I approached the bookshelf. Most of the books were medical. I saw Dr Petrini, *Chest Complaints*, Dr Felix, Dr Istrati, and a rather modest looking book by Charles Darwin, *On the Origin of Species*, with London, 1859 embossed on the spine. My host asked me how I felt and whether I had recovered. It was only then that he came and shook my hand, very firmly and, I thought, warmly. He seemed up to date about what had happened to me in the meantime, for this city is like a village, everybody knows everybody else. Unlike my office colleague, the doctor did not give up until he had obtained some precise answers from me. He offered me a cup of tea with rum and a slice of bread with cheese and olives.

'Doctor, is it possible for a healthy man to have the feeling that he is living in two different worlds at the same time?'

He told me that in sensitive people it was possible for the imagination to play tricks on you, even to become inflamed, like another organ.

'Doctor, I don't think you have understood me: in two real worlds and with the same consistency. And in fact I was wrong when I said at the same time, I meant in succession. One comes to an end where the other begins.'

'There are many stories, especially philosophical ones, about people who no longer know when they are dreaming and when they are awake.'

'But I am not talking about a dream, I know the dreams, separately, in both the first world and the second.'

I saw him frown. Something seemed not to satisfy him. He looked at me suspiciously, the same as so many people do lately.

'Might you be using me as a screen...' and here he pointed at the floral screen in the room '...which is to say, might you be concealing some evil deed under the pretext that you are mentally ill, that you have lapses, that you have two personalities? I read something of the sort ten years ago – my girl Iulia urged me to – a book by Stevenson, about the strange case of Dr Jekyll, who by day healed people and by night killed them. When Stevenson died I remember that the papers said that he had suffered from lung disease his entire life and that he had great courage in fighting the illness.'

I asked his permission to light a cigarette from the tin I had received from Mirto, but he refused, saying that smoking was absolutely forbidden in his surgery. I contented myself with the rum tea, which was extraordinarily good and warmed me up. He told me that his instinct told him that I was not mentally ill, but rather a man who was sound and had his head fixed on his shoulders, although he thought that I should give up smoking, since in the long term so much smoke inside the lungs could not do any good.'

'Nevertheless,' I went on, barely restraining a smile, 'nevertheless, doctor, the world I come from is just as real as this one.'

He pretended not to hear, but he fell to thinking.

'You know,' he said suddenly, 'I would like to invite you to our house tomorrow evening, we will be *en famille*, maybe our neighbour, Mr Giuseppe, will also come, he is a very lonely man, he gives guitar and mandolin lessons, he is very short of money. Would you like to?'

I would like to: a feeling I have felt for the first time in my new world.

CHRISTMAS EVE

1.

It is as if I were being punished. The cleaning yesterday was like a war, waged by Mama and from which Papa made a cowardly desertion: he did not arrive home until the evening and was rather pensive. He told us that he had met Dan Crețu and invited him to our house, but he is not certain whether he will come, and he is a case that preoccupies him. I do not think there is one speck of dust in the house. The carpets were laid on the snow face down, having been beaten thoroughly. When you lift them from the snow, they leave a large black square. Each carpet was subjected to the same treatment a number of times, until the snow beneath it remained clean. Personally, I would like to do this kind of cleaning in my soul, but a beater has yet to be invented for the carpets of the soul. We have not progressed that far, but perhaps next century, a new Bell... I cannot believe (but why should I not?) that he has not replied! Nicu did not come back last night. Poor Jacques and I sat up waiting for him until late. Jacques played the music from the figurine clock on his flute and I kept myself busy by writing a list of presents, after which I listlessly read a few pages of *Vanity Fair*, although my mind was still on the letter. I like Becky less and less. I do not wish to resemble her, although I feel sorry for her more than I do for Amelia. Maybe he felt offended? I do not even have a rough copy to see what I wrote, I remember the ideas vaguely, but I no longer have a precise idea of the tone and the words. Or maybe he did not find him at home and gave the letter to his brother, and his brother has not yet given it to him? It is very bad not to know into whose hands your most intimate thoughts have fallen. Most likely, he did not bother to write to me, he has no inclination to see me, if he was not able to do so when he wanted, or maybe he is punishing me for not receiving him. I have to keep my silence and wait, an utterly insufferable task. Nevertheless, marvellous news: the abscess burst by itself, after which I washed my mouth with camomile tea and the swelling subsided. Papa said that we may delay pulling the tooth. And my eyes are better, and it is my eyes I need, in order to finish reading the novel. But I have been too self-preoccupied; it is not a good sign.

Better I see to the preparations. Decorating the tree takes me the longest; I do it all by myself. I am very happy that the mysterious stranger will be coming, Mr Dan Crețu, which is to say, I hope he will be coming, but we shall send Papa to fetch him, if he does not come, especially given that in the end Mr Costache will be visiting *them*, and will not be coming to see us until tomorrow. I would like to fall in love with him, with the stranger, I mean. I would like to forget Alexandru. No, I would not like to. In fact, yes, I would like to. Yes, I want to. This evening I will write what happened and whether I fell in love. But the swelling in my jaw has not subsided completely, so any chance of love is compromized.

2.

No sooner had Mr Costache lifted the thick knocker held in the muzzle of a gilded lion than the door opened and on the threshold appeared a rather irritated young man, who made to leave, while between his legs a striped tomcat slipped outside with a mouse in its teeth. The young man's chest collided with that of the policeman. After they both apologized, simultaneously, the guest stated the purpose of his visit, and the young man quickly went back inside. He had a very strange walk. In the salon it smelled of hot tiles, from the tall stoves that rose almost to the ceiling. Costache regarded the young man with professional interest: he was a man who could not keep still for one moment, rather like a young child, and kept moving first his hands, then his feet. Then he started opening and closing his fist, as if trying to hold something that kept slipping from his grasp.

'The lawyer is not at home, he is out on business, he...' and lowering his voice, he added: 'he... well, he has a mistress. Since you work for the Police and are tight-lipped by the very nature of your profession, I will not lie to you. He spends a fortune on her. Madam suspects, but does not know for sure. The gentleman is away every day, and madam constantly has headaches and makes the servants' lives a misery. But please sit down, forgive me once again, but I was in a hurry, I am the lawyer's right-hand-man, I want to study the law at university, and I was on my way to settle some urgent business.'

Costache asked him about the announcement and what the wallet contained to warrant such a large reward. At that moment, the door to the salon opened with a creak and the master of the house entered. He was quite an imposing figure, with a potbelly, probably furnished by his wife, and a young smile on his smooth face, probably furnished by his mistress. He walked straight up to Mr Costache and stretched out his hand in a friendly manner, even before discovering who he was. When he found out, he became even more amiable. He dismissed the young man with a gesture and then immediately provided the information required.

'It is a wallet with a key to a safe. It was entrusted to me by a friend.'

'Who is the friend? What is his name?'

But before the lawyer could reply, the mistress of the house entered. She was small and *bien en chair*, scowling, furious even, her face all red. When she saw there was a visitor, her anger seemed to melt away, and she extended to Costache a chubby, dimpled hand, which he raised to his lips without touching it, and then the lady asked the maid for two cups of coffee. But the lawyer probably could not bear her presence, for after two minutes of conversation about street vendors, even now, in December, and after inquiring in a neutral tone about her migraines, he asked her to leave them alone to discuss some matters that did not concern her and would only bore her. The anger once more appeared on the lady's face and Costache was afraid lest there be a scene. Nothing irked him more than to be forced by circumstances to witness conjugal quarrels. Fortunately, the lady withdrew, insulted, without saying another word, not even to the guest.

'And so who is the friend who entrusted you with the key?' said Costache hastily, trying to dispel the awkwardness.

The lawyer was curt: 'You know, Mr Boerescu, by the nature of my profession I come into contact with all kinds of people, whom I do not know well, but whom I must grant my trust and the guarantee that I shall keep the secrets they entrust to me. But for you, sir, I can make an exception,' he hastened to add, on seeing how Costache's velvety eyes became flinty and menacing. He stood up and gasping slightly, said: 'It was Rareş Ochiu-Zănoagă, you know, the young man who was shot, as I read in Monday's newspapers. It seems that the poor man died near here, at the House of Health, but I had no idea.'

The policeman concealed his surprise. He had not been expecting anything so important and could only wonder yet again at the perfect mechanism that guided the reasoning of his former head of department.

'Where did you meet him?'

'He came to our house, he had found out from the newspapers that I am a lawyer, I have an advertisement in *Adevǎrul*, although I do not agree with their orientation and methods, but that is a different story: lawyer Movileanu, Strada Teilor, the new houses. He said it was an affair 'of the greatest importance, perhaps even dangerous,' and told me he was going to reveal everything to me soon, before the New Year. He seemed an honest man, and we lawyers know a thing or two about people, perhaps not as much as yourself, of course. He was to come here this morning, before leaving for Giurgiu, if I recall rightly. I found out from the papers that he would not be coming and that he had not yet reached the age of twenty-two. I do not know what is happening, it is as if the whole world has gone mad, nothing goes smoothly any more and everything is askew. I am afraid that the twentieth century will be very difficult and I think of my children, if I ever have any.'

His face darkened and Costache could see that he was not acting a part, although he did not understand exactly what the lawyer was thinking at that moment.

'But what about the wallet? What did he tell you about it? How did you come to lose it?'

I do not know, I cannot understand how it disappeared. It was here, on the table. He asked me whether it would disturb me if I kept it here for a few days, because he was afraid lest he lose it, and it was a precious item. He told me that it was the key to the safe, but he did not tell me what the safe contained, money or other valuables. I had no reason to ask him any further questions, or to refuse him. I went out to post something urgent, and on my return, wishing to lock the wallet in my own safe, I found it was no longer on the table.'

The lawyer's amazement could be read on his face with surprising clarity. He looked at the lyre-shaped table, dumfounded, shook himself, and then said: 'The young Trajan, who just left, was not at home. My wife was upstairs with the curtains drawn, with a headache. The servants had the afternoon off, and the two who did not were working in the yard; I know them and trust them. I thought perhaps I had taken it without me without realizing – because I am rather distrait – and that maybe I had dropped it on the street, hence the announcement, but between ourselves this explanation was for the want of anything better; it is true that I am distrait, but not irresponsible. It is more likely a thief entered the house after I left...'

'Was the front door unlocked?' asked Costache, merely doing his duty. He knew what the answer would be. When he entered, he had seen that the door had a Yale lock.

As he left, his host wished him a Happy Christmas, and it was only then that Costache remembered that he had accepted the Livezeanu family's invitation to visit them that evening, and that tomorrow, in order not to disappoint his friends, he would be having lunch in Strada Fântânei. Curiously, he too was distrait, but maybe for the same reason as the lawyer, *une jeune femme*, except that when you worked in the Police such a thing had unpredictable consequences. And the young woman was not a suitable choice, that he knew.

3.

The *Universul* questionnaire on fasting had been published that morning, signed by Dan Kretzu, and occupied half of the front page. Most of the newspaper's articles were unsigned, so when a name appeared on the front page it was seen and remembered. Procopoiu had intended it as a surprise, wanting to help Kretzu stand out. And there had been talk of their new employee, he was well known, and so his name could only help sales of the paper. Even now the ladies from the Materna Association, meeting at the crèche on Strada Teilor, were talking about menus for the fast, about the findings of the questionnaire and the mysterious stranger who had written them up.

'Dr Istrati, whom my husband has known since he was a medical student – now he is a chemist – has harshly criticized the way people fast here and the way they then stuff themselves from Christmas until the feast of St John, so that their stomachs, shrunken from the fast, come under attack, bombarded with food,' Agatha attempted to explain, but the ladies did not laugh at her joke, preferring to continue talking about Dan Crețu. Each of them knew from their servants various details worth sharing. Lucia Argintaru, a fidgety and still quite young-looking brunette, replied. 'Everybody knows that Dr Istrate is an atheist, and so don't let him tell me about fasting...'

Agatha looked at her in amazement, because she had thought her more intelligent, but Lucia brought the conversation back to the topic all the women wanted to discuss: 'That stranger shaved off his moustache and beard in order not to be recognized, which is what people do when they want to go unrecognized.'

'He was mixed up in a life and death love affair, it seems that he was being pursued by a cuckolded husband,' added Marioara Livezeanu, Alexandru's sister, 'my children's nurse told me.'

Since her divorce, Marioara had been reading novels and dreamed of stories full of passion. Normally, she had her feet on the ground and had enough common sense not to listen to rumours. She was beautiful, like her brother, her skin was the colour of camellias, inherited from their mother, with a small nose and dimpled cheeks.

Agatha expressed her astonishment. She knew of nothing of the sort and in her opinion the man was a stranger in hardship who did not have any source of income and was looking for a position in our Capital, which was full of opportunities: 'Don't you see how many foreigners come her and start businesses. On the street you hear all the languages of Europe! I think Mr Crețu is a decent man, who has lived abroad. If the Police immediately released him and *Universul* has employed him, it means that he is an honest man.'

'*Pas du tout, ma chère*, the Police are following him, Budacu, a very good coachman, has kept an eye on him the whole time, and so he cannot be an honest man. He is sooner *un voyou* who has not yet been exposed,' interjected the corpulent wife of Caton Lecca, who did not flinch from divulging the secrets of the Prefecture, which was why she was highly prized in ladies' circles. 'Your friend Mr Boerescu is the one who placed him under surveillance.'

Agatha felt a blush begin to colour her cheeks, because the wife of the Prefect of Police wasted no opportunity to wound her and to impute to her the tension between Messrs Lecca and Costache. It was known that the Chief of Public Security had been in love with Agatha and although she could not abide him, the Prefect's wife admired him, and perhaps in different circumstances she might have abided him very well: to her it was not all comprehensible why their friends had preferred to be Mrs Dr Margulis, an ordinary physician who had no fortune and who, unlike Mr Costache Boerescu, did not command respect by his mere presence. Had she been in the place of Agatha Margulis...

'It is true, now I realize that I too saw a police carriage near him,' said a timid young woman with a round face and grave eyes. She had been introduced as 'Miss Epiharia Surdu, the most devout parishioner from the Icoanei Church, who regularly lent a helping hand at the children's crèche and lives on Strada Teilor.'

'I met the stranger,' continued Epiharia, 'in our church. He was like an angel from far away, not a man of our world.'

Lucica Argintaru regarded her with a mixture of surprise, scorn and envy.

'I would be delighted to meet him. What if we invited him, as a journalist, to...'

In that moment an elderly, voluminous (she was not wearing a corset) woman stood up, having thitherto sat withdrawn and not taking any part in the conversation. She was dressed without grace, in a thick skirt and a dark coat of simple cut, but her still chestnut-coloured hair, parted in the middle, was carefully arranged. She wore no jewellery apart from a wedding ring. Her nose was rather aquiline, and her mouth and eyes lent her an expression of boundless sadness, but also a determination that immediately silenced the other women's twittering.

'Let us not forget, if at all possible, why we have come here,' she said in a tone whose harshness came not from its timbre, which was pleasant, but rather from some inner suffering.

Her name was Mrs Elena Turnescu, and she was the wife of an eminent surgeon. The renown preceded her wherever she went. She had inherited a large amount of property, and had had two husbands and four children. After the death of her second husband, the doctor, to whom she had been a wife, nurse and confidante, and after losing two children, a son and a daughter, she had been left with two sons. Accumulating human misfortunes in her eyes and heart, Mrs Turnescu had dedicated herself with all her strength to charitable works. Not only did she make more than generous donations to people who had fallen into misfortune, but also she did everything in her power to found institutions such as this shelter for orphaned children, for example, and to make sure they functioned well. And so people's feelings towards her were of admiration, love, but also a kind of respectful fear. For a long time nobody had heard her laugh. Sometimes, very rarely, she smiled.

Epiharia met her in the only place where she ever met people: at church. She came the next day, as modestly dressed as she was now, but accompanied by two servants, who were carrying large cardboard boxes. The lady opened the boxes and took out some curtains for the icons, which were so beautiful that they took Epiharia's breath away. Mrs. Turnescu explained that they had been embroidered by 'her' girls, from the charitable home. Then, the lady had gone to the deacon and given him a hundred lei, whispering something to him. She had probably discovered that he had many children and scant means of raising them. Seeing Epiharia's interest, she had spoken to her and warmly invited her to help twice a week at the new Elisabeta orphanage on Strada Teilor. As for the fact that the young woman lived on the very same street, both women had agreed that it was one of those coincidences that have a source higher than the level of humanity.

After Mrs. Turnescu's reprimand, the ladies quickly stood up and each went to the dormitory and the children in her care. Agatha found that a little girl who resembled her Maria had a fever and took fright. The girl's cheeks were flushed and her eyes glassy. It was lucky that Agatha knew what to do: like Mrs Turnescu, she was cognisant of the diseases her husband fought. But the little girl seemed delighted to have visitors; she threw her arms around Agatha's neck and told her she had learned to sew. Before she left, Agatha gave the presents for Christmas Eve to the woman who ran the orphanage.

4.

Nicu thought his must be dreaming of her gentle voice, which now woke him from his sleep: 'Nicu, darling, I'm going to work, to earn some money. Christmas is coming and people still need things cleaning. Be good.'

And she kissed him on the forehead. She was neatly dressed, ready to go out. She had laid food on the table for him. He had not seen *this* mother for months, he could not remember since when. He had missed her sorely and he felt like bursting into tears of joy, but then he remembered the misfortune of the day before, at the tram stop, the first envelope he had not been able to deliver, and again he felt his heart weigh heavily in his chest. He knew what a heart looked like, half red, half blue, with some tubes sticking out of it, he had seen one of Dr Margulis' charts, but he was certain that his was completely black and crumpled with grief.

Should he tell his mother? No, why frighten her? Her heart was certainly like a dove's chick; you could not go near it without making it tremble in fear. Should he tell Iulia? He did not have the courage. She had given him it in such great secrecy and begged him repeatedly to place it in Alexandru's hand. Iulia's heart was like a soft cheese. Should he tell old man Cercel? He could tell him, especially since he would be visiting him today. They were to meet at *Universul* in the afternoon and leave together. But what was the use of telling him? Old man Cercel knew how to read well, although he had had only four years of schooling, he was up to date about politics, he was very clever, but he didn't have any great power. He was even a little afraid of him: he had clouted Nicu a few times, without him understanding why. But what if he made Dan rewrite the note, if he was able to read what was left of it? You can confide in brothers, even adoptive ones, and ask them to do certain things. He took out the two halves of the letter and tried to decipher them. Iulia had beautiful handwriting. The signature was very plain: Iulia Margulis, with a curlicue like a shoelace tied in a double bow, but apart from that he could only decipher four words and a number, 'green and red', 'five'. There was nothing to be done, and so he threw the envelope on the fire.

He decided he might go carolling with the other boys that evening, to the Livizeanu house, and see whether anything could be salvaged. The Livizeanu family gave out lots of nice presents. What if he confessed to

Mr Alexandru? He admired him because he was rich and handsome and self-confident. And it was as if he felt the pitch black of his heart had turned as brown as the chestnuts on the kitchen shelf, which he had collected that autumn. Some of them were skewered on long nails in the shape of a man. But the once plump and glossy chestnuts were now shrivelled. That was what his heart must now look like too.

*

At five in the afternoon, Nicu and old man Cercel climbed aboard a coach on whose sides was inscribed *UNIVERSUL* in white letters. The lad did not know how the doorman had managed to arrange it, because the newspaper reserved the coach for people more important than them, but anyway he was proud to sit next to his friend and look down at people.

'Can we pull the hood down so that we can see better?'

They had both been thinking the same thing, since the doorman was already pushing the canopy back as Nicu made his request. It was a mild day. There had not been a milder Christmas Eve in a long time.

'How many days before they announce the result of the lottery?'

'Well, if today is the twenty-fourth, then it's a whole week, on the thirty-first, on New Year's Eve, but at the newspaper we'll know the result on the evening of the thirtieth, so that we can publish it. If I win, you'll get a third, as much as is rightfully yours.'

They entered the boulevard. Old man Cercel looked admiringly at the University building and Nicu at Michael the Brave, astride his bronze horse and waving an axe with his left hand. And for the first time the lad thought that maybe the prince had been left-handed, like he was, and that thenceforth he would know what to say to the other boys at school when they laughed at him, like they did when he was unable to use a pair of scissors, for example. Why didn't they make scissors for left-handed people, with the cutting edge the other way around?

The doorman's cottage was on Strada Vişinelor (Cherries Street), not far from the Traian Covered Marked, in the Popa Nan quarter. And the strange thing was that old man Cercel did not have any cherry trees in his yard, only plum trees and doves. Nicu was on his way there now, as a customer, to buy a dove, which he wanted to give Jacques as a present for Christmas. It was a long journey, along Carol Boulevard, then Pache

Boulevard, both of which had been cleared of snow, then to the right, along Strada Traian, as far as the Communal School, and finally to the left, the third house along. It was dark in the city. Behind the windows lights could be seen and here and there, in the big houses, Christmas trees. There were garlands on the gates and the all the street lamps were lit. Nicu sensed the festive atmosphere in the air as he sat on the bench of the coach beside old man Cercel, flying above the mud, drawn by the grey horses of *Universul*, which ran like racing champions.

The lad had found a game to amuse him and to stave off the boredom: he watched for the sparks that the horseshoes sometimes gave off when they struck a cobblestone. The coachman had a bottle of strong liquor, which he raised to his mouth from time to time, after which he would gasp as if scorched. The doorman had dozed off, and Nicu spent a long time studying his red splayed nose. Strangely, the coachman did not have a red nose, even though he tippled, while the doorman, who never touched a drop, had nose prone to turning red. One of Nicu's latest preoccupations was studying people's ears and noses, all of which seemed very comical to him, and if you looked at old man Cercel, whose ears were like the solid handles of a mug and whose nose had a bristle hairbrush beneath it, you were overcome with amazement. The coachman's nose was like a snowman's, as long and pointed as a carrot.

They had reached the gate of the house, and Nicu found the fence depressing, without the pink, blue and purple trumpets of the morning glories that bloomed until late autumn. They climbed down and invited the coachman inside. He wanted to buy a capon to cook for New Year. Old man Cercel also had a breeding cock, with a broad chest, fiery eyes, a large crest and a fan of a tail, which crowed frequently and scratched the ground and had a harem of hens, and so he was able to sell the capon without a qualm.

His wife was busy in the kitchen, with her hair tied inside a blue headscarf, her hands and apron covered in flour. She had not yet finished baking for Christmas, and from the threshold came a scent of cabbage mingled with sweet bread dough and grated lemon, an aroma that seemed to enter Nicu's nostrils, ears and eyes and made him feel faint with hunger. What if you could smell with your ears? Or what if you had two noses on either side of your head for smelling and an ear in the middle of your face for hearing? The doorman interrupted his reverie and summoned him to the dovecote, to settle business. Disturbed by the lamp carried by their owner, the doves started moving around and complaining in their guttural language, which Nicu found ugly, but he did not want to offend old man Cercel, and so he said in a conciliatory voice: 'They're sulky because we woke them up. I'd like a female dove for Jacques, but I don't know how you can tell with doves, whether they're boys or girls, it's easier with other birds...'

Old man Cercel explained some very curious things to him about how doves mate and that only by their size and behaviour can you tell, although sometimes you could make a mistake, that is, there were female doves that were larger and more aggressive than the males. That was not to Nicu's liking; he was on the boys' side. The doorman presented his possessions by name and colour: Knight, Collar, Beauty, Cinderella, Goitre, Caviller and Drummer...

'I don't understand where his drum is,' interjected Nicu, and the doorman explained that that was the breed.

'And this here is Parisian, I called him that because he has a lorgnette, as you can see... Look, here's one called Nicu, I named him that after you.'

It was the one that had caught the lad's eye from the very start: it had green scales at its throat, a marvel, and, for some reason, perhaps because it had rubbed against a thistle or some wire, the feathers on top of its head were raised, like a tuft.

'Want him?' asked the owner, but Nicu could not take Nicu, it was better he stay there, to remind the doorman of him. He chose a beautiful female, as white as snow, and speckled with black, as if she were wearing a polka dot dress.

'What's her name?'

She was called Speckle. The doorman took her and put her in a large cage, then he gave her some oats – Nicu was a little surprised that horses and doves ate the same thing – kernels of maize, lentils and rapeseed. The doorman explained to him how to feed Speckle and how to build her a large, airy house.

They went back inside old man Cercel's house, which was small and rather dark, but whitewashed and kept clean by his wife. The woman could not stand the doves, because, she said, they had their living room, privy and promenade all in the same place.

'In spring come and buy a pair, doves are sold in pairs,' said the doorman.

'Do you think I could keep doves when I grow up? I haven't decided yet whether I'm going to be a champion skater or raise poultry. I don't want to be an errand boy, because what do you do if you lose what you're supposed to deliver?'

'What else can you do, they'll give you the sack,' interjected the coachman merrily.

The doorman offered his guests syrup and plum jam and water – but the coachman declined the latter, saying he was not thirsty. Neither the stuffed cabbage nor the Christmas sweet bread was ready, unfortunately, and so Nicu has to content himself with the smell. In any event, it was still the fasting period, although the lad would have been ready to pretend he had forgotten. But even so, old man Cercel's wife would not have given him anything; she liked children less than she did doves. In the coach, Nicu started scratching himself.

'I think I've caught a flea,' he said, but after that he became absorbed in looking after Speckle and worrying about the lost envelope, while the coachman was absorbed in his bottle: he had rediscovered his thirst.

5.

Evening. I have at last met Mr Dan Crețu. Papa himself brought him. He went to collect him from the hôtel in our carriage and with the coachman in the employ of our neighbour, Mr Văleanu, Elisabeta's father. Our Nelu is ill. Papa is taking care of him and I take him food, because everybody else is busy. Let me write here at least that I had been expecting the stranger's visit with my heart in my mouth, and my annoyance at Alexandru's silence took second place. As far as I could see looking outside, where it was quite dark, Mr Crețu seemed to have great difficulty alighting from the carriage and his gait was unsteady. He entered the hall and was about to enter the living room still wearing his galoshes, but Mama, who greeted him, told him with the admirable grace of a true mistress of the house: 'If you wish to take off your galoshes, the boy will help you, so that you will not get dirty.' And she showed him the place. Mr Crețu became highly embarrassed and looked at the pairs of footwear by the door: Papa's galoshes, Mama's *chevreau* boots, my boots with the heels, and Jacques' overshoe. Such little things sadden me the most, so much so that sometimes I feel like lying in bed and never getting up again, I feel like telling life that I'm going on strike. For, whenever we buy Jacques overshoes, we have to throw one away.

Dan Crețu did not understand at first, he looked at me questioningly; then he looked at my feet. So I invited him inside and he took off his galoshes by himself, refusing any help. When he entered he saw Jacques on the couch, and our guest, pale already, turned white, then everything drained from his face and he looked as if he were empty inside. Papa invited him to sit in the place of honour, in the armchair by the fire, which was half turned towards the Christmas tree which, I may say, was decorated rather well (with yellow apples, red candles and an angel at the top, nothing more, since I hadn't draped any tinsel). Since the light of the flames was dancing on his face and I was seated to one side, I was able to gaze at him freely, although it is impolite to gaze at a guest so intensely. Fortunately, Mama was not looking in my direction, or else she would have admonished me. And I think he is younger than they say. At first his face said nothing to me; it is hard to read his physiognomy. I was also hindered by the manner in which he was dressed, which was very slovenly, since I for one believe that the garment maketh the man, although my parents have taught me that this is not so and that I should not judge people by their clothes... I was also confused by his face: he did not have a beard properly speaking, but he was unshaven. His hair was glossy and cut short. Later, I calmed down and after that I was able to read the emotions on his face, whenever he was asked a question. At one point, Mama, who seemed to me to have taken to him from the very first, said to him with a gayness out of keeping to her: 'Is it true that you forge banknotes? I ask merely because we ourselves could do with some...'

And then a miracle occurred. Dan Crețu smiled for the first time and I saw his handsome white teeth, but above all else, I saw a face more luminous and sweeter than I could ever remember seeing before. He all but grew a halo, like the moon does on some nights. It was as if there were two people in him: one utterly blank most of the time, a person that did not capture the attention and faded into the background, and the other of a beauty that was, how can I put it? It was a beauty that was like that of a romantic painting, but that appeared only when he smiled.

At eight o'clock Signor Giuseppe, our neighbour, arrived: he does not speak Romanian very well, but he played the guitar for us, he is a good and a jovial man, but the cook always scolds me for thinking that all people are good. (Except one!) Then we sat down at the table, for we were all hungry. Papa was jovial too and he told us a large number of medical stories, to which Mr Crețu listened very carefully and made knowledgeable comments, to the amazement of all. Papa started telling us about the world of the theatre, with which he is familiar as a physician, because otherwise I have to plead with him to come with us to see performances. And he told us a story that we had not heard, about Grigore Manolescu, our first true Hamlet: 'He is from a boyar family, his father was Alexandru Manolescu, who had a house next to the Măgureanu Hermitage, and he did not study hard at the St Sava College, near our house, where he was a pupil, and he had to repeat the year. And when he was growing up, aged fourteen, he went to the Conservatory, without his father's knowledge. He was not at all attractive, his arms were too long, like a monkey's, and his hands were like paddles, lacking in expressivity, and above all he was bandy-legged. Worse still, he had a lisp.'

'*Mio Dio!*' exclaimed Signor Giuseppe, who is sensitive to all that pertains to the stage.

'And so, out of pity, the teacher sat him at the back of the class. One day, he invited him to stand on the dais to recite a poem, and oh how the rest of the class laughed, even though the poem was sad. But the lad had mettle. He rehearsed with stones in his mouth, stubbornly, in front of the mirror at home, and he rectified his diction in every respect. Many miracles happen in the theatre, and also in medicine, if there be a will. And for the second time he mounted the dais and recited Lamartine's *The Lake*, so beautifully that nobody laughed this time. One day, in class, they read a play that moved him more than any other ever had, and so Grigoraş asked the teacher what it was, and the teacher told him: *Hamlet*. Thereafter, the lad had the fixed idea that he had to play Hamlet. But his father read in the newspaper of the fact that his son was at the Conservatory and so, in order to stay the hand that was about to strike him – old man Manolescu had a heavy hand – the son said: 'I went to the Conservatory to correct my diction and to become a lawyer.' He kept the play *Hamlet*, a small book translated into French, with him at all times, it was his visiting card, although in rehearsals he was given only the rôles of comic Pantaloons. When he reached the age of sixteen, his father admonished him for being in danger of having to repeat the school year yet again. One day, during a lesson at the Conservatory, Matei Millo the great actor and director came into the classroom. He told the teacher that he wanted to take a pupil. The teacher showed him a star pupil, a handsome young man who sat at the front of the class, but Millo pointed at Grigore Manolescu, at the back. And so it was that Grigore, now aged sixteen, played the rôle of a Pantaloon on stage alongside Millo and Frosa Sarandy.'

Here, Papa paused and explained to Dan Creţu who Frosa Sarandy was, since he seemed not to have heard of our great actress. In the meantime, our guest was eating pensively, Mama was whispering to the servant, telling her what to fetch, what to take away, although she had coached her beforehand, Jacques and I were making all kinds of discreet signals, and Giuseppe was guzzling heartily and laughing raucously. When dessert arrived, Papa received an urgent call. We are accustomed to it. I do not know how, but on holidays especially, illness always arrives, like an uninvited guest. And so he told us the end of the story in a hurry: 'At the performance, Manolescu *père* was in the audience. The lad's name was not on the bill: next to the part of Tochenbourg in *A High-class Ball* there were some asterisks and his father did not recognize him with his make-up on and with his Pantaloon voice. But at the end of the play, the audience cried out: *Millo, Millo, Frosa, Frosa!* And even more loudly: *Tochenbourg, Tochenbourg!* And when the curtain was raised, Millo took the debuting actor by the hand and in a booming voice introduced him: Grigore Manolescu! In short, since now I have to leave, his father kicked him out of the house. A few years later, Grigore Manolescu triumphed in *Hamlet*. I was thirty-four, and so it was in... in the autumn of 1884, I even remember the day, how could I forget? It was the 2nd of October, your mother's birthday. I have never seen the like: people were falling on their knees in front of him, the audience was thrilled, the ovation lasted for minutes on end, in the wings everybody was in tears. Today's theatre seems pallid, lifeless, compared with what your mother and I used to see in our youth,' and here Papa looked at Mama with a smile.

I asked him whether he knew when and how Grigore Manolescu died.

'Seven years ago,' he said. 'He was only thirty-five! It was from smoking, he lit one cigarette after another –' and here he glanced at Dan Crețu, like an upset father; you would have thought he had some right to scold him, but to Papa we are all like children '– and after his final performance he collapsed in his doctor's arms as soon as he left the stage. They buried him with the pages of *Hamlet* laid on his chest, as he had requested in his will, and with a procession of weeping mourners. I was there too. It was like at the theatre, When I arrived at the cemetery and asked where the grave was, the man at the gate gave me directions and added: 'But the dead man hasn't got here yet, we're expecting him to turn up at any moment!' But anyway, I don't have time to tell the whole story right now...'

Both Jacques and I were left open-mouthed, because Papa is very sparing with his words most of the time. To think what our parents conceal! I would have dearly liked to see Papa aged twenty, in Paris, when he was a student! Papa bid his guest farewell and we were served the Christmas sweet-bread. I did not want to share out the presents without him, and so I postponed it until tomorrow. Mr Crețu was very embarrassed at not having brought us anything, he mumbled apologies, but we knew that he did not have any money and Mama said, laughing: 'The cobbler does not have time to make boots, and the forger does not have a chance to manufacture banknotes. I am joking, please do not take it amiss, but you are as dear to me already as Jacques and Julie, you may count yourself one of the family. The present you have given us is your being here, it has done us the world of good.'

Oh, this coming from my mother!... Dan Crețu does not even know what it means, for if he had known, he would have leapt up and embraced her. Now it is almost midnight, I look back and in my mind I thank Dan Crețu for having made me forget my misfortunes. He has been invited to come tomorrow, for lunch, when Mr Costache and Nicu will also be coming, and this proves that the new guest is dear to all of us. I did not fall in love with him (although his smile is the loveliest I have ever seen), but somehow he is like an older brother to me. It was the most beautiful Christmas Eve in the Margulis family. Dan Crețu gave my little brother a thousand signs of friendship. Jacques was happy too, and before we lit the candles on the Christmas tree, his eyes glittered in the dark like agates. Now I understand: Jacques has inherited Mama's black agate eyes, while I have to put up with the age-old mistrust of green eyes. Papa has not returned yet. Will I receive a reply tomorrow?

6.

Marioara gazed with great concern at her younger, but much taller brother. Alexandru kept going out to smoke, he quickly ate what was served and rose from the table, which was inconceivable at the best of times, but *unforgivable* when you had guests. Each time, the company watched him in amazement, turning their heads as if on a signal, but nobody dared ask him about it. Mişu supposed that it must be connected to a woman, as it always was with his brother.

Conu Costache had arrived laden with sweetmeats from Inger's confectionary shop on Strada Carol, which likewise surprised the family: it was a break with tradition, which demanded sweets from Capşa or Fialkowski, or ever since Fialkowski fell ill, Capşa alone. The Christmas tree reached almost to the ceiling, which was tall. Decorating it had required a ladder. The chandeliers were all lit, and the lights were multiplied in the mirrors of the salon. Nevertheless, Hristea Livizeanu was in a bad mood, as he always was during the holidays, and vented his nerves on his wife: 'Be so kind as to tell your son that when we have guests...'

But his lady wife was never lost for a reply; she took pleasure in such battles with her husband. They were like two generals engaged in a war of attrition, she with her small, wrinkled head, but with a *décolleté* that revealed the splendid camellia flesh colouring of the women in the family, and he with his scarlet face and white side- whiskers.

'Tell *your* son, you mean, I may have borne him, but as for his inheritance, that was provided by none but you. The other two have inherited me,' and here the lady gazed first at Marioara, with her perfect little nose, and then at Mişu, with the lock of hair that tumbled over his forehead, lending him an impish air.

Maria's older sister, Elena, a spinster, always took Hristea's side, and had her reasons. Elena tried to divert Costache's attention from the family scene: 'Mr Boerescu, what is the news concerning the young Ochiu-Zănoagă? I do not expect you to know who shot him yet, but do you at least have a motive?'

'Miss, I must disappoint you. I do not know, we do not know, the Police do not know anything yet.'

Mr Costache was out of his element. The evening promised to be hard, and was presently intolerable, whereas he had been hoping for a little peace. The roast was insipid, although it looked marvellously browned and garnished, or perhaps the atmosphere altered the taste of the food. He sipped the wine, which, on the other hand, was impeccable, since the Livezeanu family had the best wines in the Capital, and he felt slightly heartened. Marioara smiled at him, with her dimpled cheeks, but it was an unconvinced, almost frightened smile. In that moment, from the street they heard a choir singing shrilly and with false notes: the carollers had arrived. Mr Hristea began to sing along, immediately followed by his wife, drowning out the children's voices; he in a baritone of extraordinarily pure timbre, she in a soprano, whose velvety warm voice was unexpected from one so war-like. Their voices interwove tenderly as they looked at each other as if they had not seen each other for a long time: they formed a happy couple, their mouths opening together in harmony as they sang the same words. Costache suspected that music was one of the reasons they had stayed together for so many years and looked pityingly at Elena, who was suffering and had hunched up, with a pained look on her face.

After the carols outside had finished, Alexandru came in, said that he had taken care of the gifts for the carollers and asked Costache to grant him two minutes of his time after dinner. Marioara's fear turned to horror, and Mișu too began to realize that something was wrong, and that his previous suspicions had been off the mark. Their parents, on the other hand, feeling better thanks to the communion of their voices, were oblivious of everything else, as if they were on their second honeymoon. Costache had remarked a visible brightening on Alexandru's part since he had come back in and was intrigued as to what had happened outside.

PRESENTS

1.

Up until last year I wrote my diary in French, but after I attended a lecture at the Athenaeum about the poor Romanian language and how many tempests it had weathered without it being uprooted completely, I made the grand decision to write only in Romanian. But sometimes it is hard, because intimate things are much easier to put down on paper when you write them in French. For example, this evening, I would have very much liked to hide behind a foreign language, like behind a carnival mask, to write how excited I am and for what reasons, *mais puisque j'ai promis d'écrire en roumain, je dois tenir promesse.* And so *courage*, let me take a deep breath and write in the language of my ancestors (which is not entirely true, since some of them were Greek). Today Nicu, Mr Costache and Dan Crețu came for lunch, and also Signor Giuseppe, I almost forgot. I began with Nicu, my brother's official guest, because I kept trying to catch his eye and divine whether my envelope had arrived where it had to arrive and whether he had brought a reply, but as if on purpose, the lad was always looking at somebody else. It was not until he left that I was able to take him aside and ask: 'Did you give him it?' He nodded, but still without looking at me. Then I asked him whether he had brought me a reply and he shook his head. It seemed to me that he felt sorry for me, maybe he suspects something; maybe he saw that the addressee did not care. But then he added: *But I think he is coming at five. Green and red.* I kissed him on the top of the head; for me it was the best of presents. I did not get a chance to ask him anything else, about what green and red might mean – it sounded like a password – and whether Alexandru had told him specifically to say those words, because Mr Costache came up to us to say goodbye. He irritated me, angered me even; it was as if he were following me. He had been moody throughout lunch, annoyed, which is not in his nature, and now he said rather abruptly: 'Who is coming?' But Nicu vanished, and I pretended not to hear. He has no right to interfere in my life and usually he is so tactful that you would not even think he were a policeman. He asked me to come to the Prefecture of Police tomorrow morning, if I can, because he has to talk to me about something privately. He had already spoken to Papa and asked him to accompany me there, on his way to the surgery, and either he or somebody else will bring me back home. I do not understand what it could be or how I could possibly help him, and the invitation to the police station is the most unusual *rendez-vous* a man has ever given me. And the day after Christmas too, when everybody stays at home! But most of all I am preoccupied by Nicu's words: 'But I think he is coming at five. Green and red.' Why does he only *think* so? Why is he not sure? Perhaps he did not have time to write a reply? Or is he playing cat and mouse with me?

After lunch, Jacques and I gave everybody, but especially our neighbour, Signor Giuseppe, a big surprise: we gave a concert rendition of Handel's minuet. I made only three mistakes, Jacques a few more than that, but everybody said it was perfect, although I think we rather grated on their hearing. Mama and Papa were truly surprised at our present and the progress we have made without a music teacher (we gave up lessons a year ago, to save money), and then I brought Jacques' carillon and accompanied the clock, as if we were making the time sing in three different ways, and Giuseppe began to applaud like a madman. He has something of the gondolier about him, with his glossy black curls and his pencil moustache, and he is very gallant with me, but without ever going too far. I like Italian people, they have a warmth that does not suffocate you. He came to stand next to the piano, he took my hand and kissed it in recognition of 'this celestial music' and since my *manina* was cold – as my hands always are – he began to sing from Puccini's latest opera, *La Bohème*: '*Che gelida manina se la lasci riscaldar...*' Papa, who speaks Italian, translated: What a cold little hand, if you will allow, let me warm it... He was a seductive Rodolfo, I a Mimi who could barely contain her laughter. And then Mr Costache continued Rodolfo's aria, how about that! He knew it very well and from time to time he looked at me as I sang, but in vain, since I understood absolutely nothing apart from the word *signorina*. At one point he turned to look at Mr Crețu, however, and Papa told me in a whisper that it was about a theft and a box or something of the sort. Signor Giuseppe was enthusiastic, he embraced us all for joy, it seems that he even attended the premiere in Turin (or did he say Milan?). I discovered that Mr Costache has an enchanting voice and sings very well, and I told him so. And that he speaks Italian, which was a surprise. Things I would never have imagined about him. Maybe he was more carefree in his youth; a pity that he has chosen a profession that ages him. For, rarely have I seen him in a good mood. But what about Papa? Both men are gloomier than anybody else I know.

I gave Jacques the *Luminous Fountains* from *Universul* and Nicu *The Mewler*. When we were about to make the fountains, we discovered that the instructions were missing, and so I shall have to go back to the newspaper offices to get a full set. I shall have to take this one back, and so Jacques was sad. *The Mewler* mewled twice and then refused to mewl any more, but Nicu said it was better that way, because he did not like cats, – he has a dog and he keeps it in the yard, because it is full of fleas. Papa's hat did not fit, although I had measured it against the old one. I sat perched on the crown of his head so comically that we all laughed. An example of how a man can end up with laughter instead of a present. Ah, yes, and for Mama I bought Veronica Micle's *Poesies*. She thanked me from the bottom of her heart. You would have said that it was exactly what she wanted, but Mr Costache later told me that he knew she did not like the work, although I cannot see why. As for me, they gave me a nice white fur muff. I hate muffs, because it is as if my hands were cuffed. And nor are they fashionable any more. Nicu did not bring Jacques anything. Apparently there had been a mix up and he kept explaining something to him in a whisper. And so I proposed that in the next few days we should redistribute our unsuitable presents by means of a tombola draw, but they all thought it an absurd suggestion and looked at me in consternation. It was a complete catastrophe.

Anyway, the most difficult part concerned Mr Dan Crețu. When he saw Mr Costache, he was struck dumb, while Costache kept trying to pry things out of him, as if it were an interrogation. I thought he went too far. After all, they were both guests and the candles on the tree had been lit for reconciliation. But in the end, reluctantly, and more out of embarrassment, Dan Crețu still had to say something and in this way I discovered something new and exciting. Petre, Inger's coachman, who found Mr Crețu and the young boyar from Giurgiu, is supposed to have taken a wallet from the dying man's pocket. Mr Crețu said it *en passant*, I do not think he thought it important, but Costache was troubled, he almost rose from his chair and left, and only good manners prevented him from doing so in the end. And so, unlike yesterday, today was very confused, as if somebody had put spokes in our wheels, or at least in two of the four. And the two wheels still turning like a velocipede relate to Alexandru and me, to our permanently precarious balance.

2.

Having come back from old man Cercel's, Nicu wished with all his heart that his mother would be at home so that he could show her what he had bought her, but he found the house cold and empty. He lit the fire in the tin stove in the kitchen and the one inside the house, whose smoke had already begun to blacken the white-washed walls, and he placed the birdcage on the bed. The speckled creature within was calm, almost asleep.

'Do you want to eat? Do you want to drink?' asked Nicu and in his mind he heard Speckle say she wanted to sleep and that he should leave her in peace.

Nicu did not say anything else to her. He ate quickly and almost without chewing. Dr Margulis had advised him to always eat at the same hours and to chew thoroughly. But Nicu did exactly the opposite: he ate when he got home or whenever other people gave him food and he bolted it down, not wanting to waste time on chewing, like a sheep. The doctor was very good to him and always examined him lest he have some illness, and if he coughed he gave him pills and told him how to look after himself. Once, he made him inhale the steam from a pot of boiling salt water. Another time, he taught him to throw his head back and gargle. He made him practice using plain water first of all, and then gave him one of his syrups. When, after the death of his grandmother, Nicu found his mother in *that* state one hot July day, he ran straight to Strada Fântânei and the doctor, who was resting with the curtains drawn, immediately got up, put on his straw hat, had Nelu ready the carriage and went to the potters' quarter at a gallop. The doctor saw to everything, he took Nicu's mother to Dr Marinescu (Nicu did not even know how much it cost) and he took the lad to stay with Jacques for a while, where he was as if in heaven. But after that the doctor called him to the library one day and asked him man to man whether he wanted to take care of his mother, who would continue to have 'lapses,' and whether he felt capable of living alone with her. Nicu had said that he could manage and wanted to stay with her. Since then, the doctor had kept his eye on them, and not a week passed without him asking about 'our patient' and giving Nicu medical advice without taking the time to repeat it. Why did he do that?

A snowball struck the kitchen window. Nicu obeyed the call and went outside with his tinsel star, leaving Speckle asleep on the kitchen table.

Now, besides having a mother, a collection of shrivelled chestnuts and a cow without an udder, he also had a living pigeon, which he was going to part with the following day. The other boys were waiting for him, and together they went carolling along the street. Apples and walnuts began to fill their cloth bags, and since Nicu did not have a bag of his own, he asked the choir leader, a tall boy with wavy long hair and a voice too hoarse for a chorister, to keep the goodies for him. When they came across Alexandru on the threshold, smoking a cigarette, they immediately surrounded him. He was bareheaded and the wind was ruffling his soft auburn hair. The repertoire of the five-boy choir was unvarying: *Oh, Wonderful Tidings, Three Shepherds* and a closing carol, which Nicu liked more thanks to the words than the tune, which was quite difficult.

Nicu thrilled in particular to the words 'but there are hovels without a hearth' and the rousing finale: 'Romanians, do not forget to be good when thou art merry!' on hearing which people immediately went inside to fetch goodies, and some even gave the boys pennies. It is good to remind people what they have to do; for some quite simply forget. Alexandru gave each of them money and sweets, and he ordered Toader to fetch treats from inside. Strangely, Toader was not in a good mood that evening and he went off grudgingly. The choir leader asked Alexandru for some cigarettes, and Alexandru obliged. Just as he was about to leave, Nicu quickly told him: 'Miss Iulia sends word to you. Five o'clock, green and red! Green and red!' and thereupon made himself scarce, before Alexandru had time to ask him anything, given that he knew absolutely nothing. He hoped that Alexandru would understand what was to be understood better than he did. He was aware that besides 'five o'clock' he ought to have specified a day, but since he had no idea, he left it hanging. On his return home he suffered another misfortune, like the ones that had lately been plaguing him: the choir leader did not want to part with Nicu's share of the booty, and so he was left with only the coins he had managed to put in his pockets. So he crept home along his poorly lit alley, with terror in his heart lest on top of this he meet the Muzzle and be deprived of all the fruits of his labour, as had happened the previous year.

Speckle was asleep in the kitchen and his mother was inside the house, thank God. She had come back, but she was drunk again, and that meant she would have one of her turns. But Nicy went to bed and slept well anyway, because he had resolved a large number of things, Iulia's letter in particular.

And the next day, as he was about to go to the Margulis' house for lunch, taking Speckle, his heart broke at the thought of parting with her, of giving her away as a gift, just when he had found a peaceful companion in life, one bought with his own money. His friend would understand, thought Nicu, when he explained that Speckle did not want to come with him, that he had been unable to persuade the bird in any shape or form, although he had tried, and indeed, Jacques had said: 'My dear-r, ther-re is no need for pr-resents between us. You know, I do not much like doves, I pr-refer-r seagulls! But unfor-rtunately nobody in Bucharrest r-rear-rs seagulls. Maybe I should make a business of it? Will you join me if need be?'

Nicu promised to help him and assured him he would bring him another present, a copy of *Universul Ilustrat*, the issue with the mammoths. And he had made another strange discovery: his cow loved money! When she found a coin in Nicu's pocket she clasped it with her legs and it was hard to tear it away from her. (True, Nicu liked money too and did more or less the same thing.)

3.

There was no trace of festivity in General Algiu's house, where only a single lamp was lit, on the desk. His former colleagues from the Prefecture of Police, who maintained the warmest feelings toward him, had sent him, via a sub-lieutenant with smiling eyes, a small Christmas tree decorated with thick candles. The General surmised that the man who had had the idea for the gift could be none other than Costache. But it was still a bad idea, even if it had come from good friends and with good intentions. And so Ion Algiu forbade his adjutant to bring the tree into the house and it had remained leaning next to the front door, filling the hall with the scent of a mountain forest. At lunchtime, the General mounted his horse and went to the Bellu Cemetery. His adjutant, following behind, struggled with the Christmas tree, placing it, with regret, on the grave of Mrs Algiu, God rest her soul! The adjutant's opinion was that the lady had no need of such things in the place where she now resided, a place of shade and verdure, which they themselves could have done with: the tree would have brightened up the salon, because for the last year they had been living like hermits and he had grown sick of such a life!

When they returned, also at a gallop, the adjutant strained to take off the General's tall boots, which came off with difficulty since they were long and rigid. After he had polished them to a sheen and inserted boot trees, he was given the day off, to go where he pleased and celebrate as he saw fit. As for Algiu, he remained alone, with nothing but the philodendron by the window and his Borzoi dog, Lord, whose age was only a little greater than his master's period of mourning. The General was touched at the thought that Lord had known his wife, as a small puppy, and had once lain on her bed of suffering. Being so young, the hound was playful and gambolled around his master, constantly provoking him. It gave him pleasure to stroke the long, white, silkily undulating hair, with the russet collar around his neck. The dark, elongated eyes regarded him with aristocratic pride and whenever he heard the slightest noise outside he pricked up his ears. However, the electric doorbell quite simply drove him out of his mind. The General almost regretted having had it installed. But the dog stubbornly refused to be trained and Algiu's pride as a general was often affected when Lord was insubordinate, as he was now, for example, and refused to sit. It was a good job there were no witnesses.

He took a pile of old magazines and newspapers and began to flick through them, wetting his finger on his tongue, reading an article here and there in the light of the lamp, aimlessly, although somehow he lingered over all the news items connected to the ex-mayor Filipescu. This was a public figure that had preoccupied him for a long time, and he had remarked that his haughty and determined gaze in a way resembled his Borzoi, but sometimes he had less brains than the hound. After leafing through a few calendars, particularly those that had historical headings, he picked up the 3 September 1893 edition of *Universul*. 'On Monday a tender for the demolition of the Sărindar Church was held at the Ministry of Religions. The demolition was awarded for the price of three thousand, five hundred lei. The work must be completed within a month.' This had certainly not done Filipescu's reputation any good. Although at the end of this century the people of Bucharest thought less and less about things holy, compared with folk from the beginning of the century, and although many, including himself, declared themselves atheists, their heaven was not altogether empty and at a pinch they were capable of remembering that man was as insignificant as a worm. At the time, Nicu Filipescu was thirty-years-old, and had been Mayor of the Capital for around half a year and was determined to do great things. And since Sărindar had been abandoned, rather than seeking to repair it, he decided to demolish it. He was, let us admit, justified in a small way: ever since two spires had been added inappropriately, the building had been a public menace. On top of which, the General remembered that rats and dead cats had been the only adornment of the churchyard, which looked worse than a patch of waste ground. But it was in that church that a large number of Bucharest's leading citizens had been married, and others, less fortunate, had set out thence on their final journeys. And so the demolition wounded many memories.

Nicu Filipescu was one of those young men who believed it was better to demolish what tottered rather than waste time consolidating and salvaging it. He had brought in convicts to do the job, since nobody else wanted to damage a holy place. The effect on the people of Bucharest was worse than could have been foreseen: the elderly came weeping and asking to be given at least a brick to take home, to guard them against evil. Strangely, now that it no longer existed, Sărindar looked better in the eyes of Bucharest's inhabitants than it had when it still stood. But was it not the same for him, the General, now that his beloved wife was no more? Now, she was always there with him. The General moved on to the news items about duels, a subject of great controversy. Yet he felt it to be true that honour had to ben defended, and he did not agree that two men who fought in a duel mutually agreed upon and in the presence of witnesses could be considered 'common criminals': the law proposed by Viişoreanu was intolerable! But nevertheless, he felt sorry for Lahovary, the man had the courage of an entire army. It was a pity that he had not had time to train; the general himself could have taught him, given ten days of serious training...

Even before the electric doorbell shattered the silence, Lord had pricked up his ears. He then sped to the door like a cannonball, barking deafeningly. At the door was an unknown woman of around sixty, modestly dressed, who alighted from a luxurious carriage that had pulled up to the entrance. The General was struck by the woman's aquiline nose and the stony expression on her face such as only his best soldiers could manage. He invited her into the salon, bringing the dog to heel with difficulty. The guest was not intimidated by Lord, however, and seemed not even to notice the poor dog.

'I have sent you countless visiting cards and since you did not reply, I decided to break the rule,' said the lady with the faintest of smiles. 'Look, here is the last one,' said the guest, discovering a visiting card on the tray by the door. The General held it at a distance from his eyes and read: *Mrs Elena Dr Turnescu*. He could not imagine to what he owed the honour of her visit.

'I cannot imagine to what I owe the honour of this visit, Madam Dr Turnescu, or rather the *joy* of this visit. I know you by your reputation.'

'I have an important matter to communicate to you. I know that you were the Prefect of Police, and my husband spoke of you with respect.'

And without further ado, in words sparse and clear, she told him the reason for her coming.

4.

The street was deserted and the air brisk. Fane the Ringster trod softly, with the gait of a wild animal. He suspected that they had not released him for nothing. Of course, they never had any evidence against him, because he worked cleanly, as he himself was in the habit of boasting. The real reason had to be the stranger's safe. They probably hoped that by following him they would find it, whereas if he was locked up it didn't profit them at all, and besides, it only gave them an extra mouth to feed.

'Leave it to me, Jean,' said Fane by way of farewell to the unfortunates who were spending their Christmas in the cells, 'I weren't born yesterday!'

As he walked along the street, he gave a whistle of amazement when he found a barber's shop open. He stepped over the broom shank, which propped open the door, and flung himself down on a wooden chair in front of the mirror. Everything was going like clockwork; he would be dapper when he visited his 'fiancée'.

'What's this, Jean, open on a holiday, you're not a Turk, by any chance, are you?'

'My name's Mitică – Dumitru that is, not Jean, Jean is a barber on Strada Măgureanu, as far as I know,' said the barber and then started talking about politics, unions and the barbers' refusing to have a day off during the holidays. The truth was that the Government had rejected their request and ruled that the barbers' shops should close, but a few of them, including him, had broken the law. What could happen, after all?

The customer chided him: 'Shut your trap, you're sending me to sleep.' And indeed, his eyes, the colour of Quetsch plums, were on the point of closing.

Fane was above social disputes, because he had his own politics, and was his own master. The barber admired his moustache, offering to trim it according to the latest fashion, which dispensed with such long fringes.

'Trim it, and trim that tongue of yours with that there razor while you're at it,' said Fane gently, and the barber gave a rather horsey laugh. Perhaps it wasn't such a good idea to open on a holiday after all; all kinds of dubious characters turned up. He began to hum softly, so as not to be obliged to talk, and dipped the shaving brush in the lather. Then he lathered the customer's cheeks nicely, taking especial care to avoid his moustache. He trimmed his hair and then massaged his scalp with eau de cologne, causing Fane to grunt with pleasure.

After he left Mitică's shop, trimmed, shaved and perfumed, Fane checked to see whether he still had a police tail and then decided it wouldn't look amiss if he went to a public bath, and so he headed in the direction of Grivița Avenue, to Vasiliu the pharmacist's establishment. This time he was going for a reason that nobody else must suspect. But he was out of luck: the establishment was closed and locked. He chewed his moustache and swore so loudly that even his tail must have heard him. But you never know what luck has in store for you and it seems that somebody within had heard him or perhaps seen him, because with his ear finely tuned to certain sounds he heard a key turning in the lock. The door opened and in the crack appeared a tousled young head.

'Good people,' said Fane by way of introduction, 'I want to take a bath!'

The lad said they were closed and that he was there merely to guard the cash box, which had vanished on previous occasions.

'Jean, let me take a bath and I'll put some money in the cash box and in your pocket too,' pleaded Fane in his most civil voice.

The lad would have been willing, but there was hot water only on working days and he wasn't allowed to light the fire for the boilers.

'Then at least let me use the latrine, since you don't have to light that,' said Fane and started hopping from one leg to the other, clenching his buttocks.

Knowing that a tip was obligatory if you did somebody such an urgent favour, the lad allowed him to enter.

'Down there, turn left and then straight ahead!'

'Thank you very much, Jean!'

When he returned two minutes later, Fane had an indecisive air, as if he did not know whether he should give up the bird in his hand for the two in the bush or abandon all thought of feathered creatures. He entered the small room in which the tousled lad was lazing with his elbows on the table and asked after the bath attendant. He was away in Sinaia for the whole of the holidays, said the watchman.

'Did he leave anything here for me – me name's Fane – because I left a large case here with him?'

The lad didn't know anything about any case and started to get annoyed.

'Let's have a quick look, Jean, maybe we'll find it, it's silver-coloured, I'm in great need of it,' said Fane in his holiday voice and gave him his most persuasive facial expression.

Although the lad looked more and more bad-tempered, and it was obvious he couldn't wait to get rid of him, Fane didn't give up. He dominated him until willy-nilly he had opened all the doors. They looked everywhere, behind the cast-iron bathtubs, in the broom closet. Fane was emanating a sort of cold breeze. The lad wouldn't let him enter the room where the cash box was and assured him that there wasn't anything in there. As he said it, Fane gave him a very strange look, and the lad sensed rather than understood that he was in danger and so from the doorway he cast a quick look inside.

'Are you afraid, Jean? You're afraid, aren't you Jean? What if I clout you over the head right now and steal the money from the cash box?'

Then he slapped him on the shoulders in encouragement, laughed, turned on his heel and left.

Behind him he heard the key turn twice in the lock and he laughed again. It was obvious the watchman was a greenhorn: he was one of those innocents who think a sliver of metal could protect him from harm. Fane looked behind him and then headed towards his woman, taking his tail with him. He had sent word that she should wait for him. After they had eaten and drank, and after he penetrated her twice, with all the mad desire that had accumulated during his days in the cell (she yelled so loud that you could hear it outside, and even more loudly the second time, before groaning gutturally like a pigeon) they both fell fast asleep. The next day, Fane interrogated her about everything that had happened in his absence, and she chirped like any bint when the master returns. As for Jean's case: 'To hell with it. There was nothing but some horrible clothes in it, nothing valuable. Not that I examined it closely, which is why I wanted it, but it didn't seem to have anything that would be of interest to Fane the Ringster!'

They both laughed, happy and carefree. Outside the man from the Police shivered as he waited to be relieved.

NEWS

1.

The two street lamps at the entrance to the Prefecture were lit when I arrived, although it was the middle of the day, and under each street lamp stood a sentinel. In the carriage, which Papa drove by himself, because Nelu was still ill, I asked him why he thought Mr Costache had invited me to his office and why he could not have spoken to me at our house, and Papa told me that his friend never mixed business and private life, and that in his youth he had promised him that he would leave his profession at the door alongside his cane. And indeed, I think that he kept his word, at least up until yesterday, with Dan Crețu. Papa added that there would be nobody at the Prefecture today, since it was the day after Christmas. I have known Mr Costache ever since I can remember. When I grew up and we had to start calling each other *vous* instead of *toi*, I was sorry, because it alienated the person closest to me, for sometimes he was closer to me than my own parents and I could speak to him more freely than I could to them. I remember one summer, when I found a beetle in a book and I screamed, he came to me in alarm, saw the insect and gently said: 'Can you really be afraid of this small and book-loving creature?' And he threw it out of the window.

Papa told me that he probably wanted to ask for some information. He was very calm about the whole thing, since he has been Mr Costache's friend since before I was born. And it was true that there was nobody at the Prefecture this morning. Papa took me upstairs to the first floor. A little old man knocked on the door and opened it wide to allow me to enter. Papa said *bonjour* and then left. Mr Costache quickly got up from his desk and came to greet me. He apologized for having smoked before I arrived, but I smelled only a faint waft of fine tobacco. He looked tired and hid his hazel eyes, which to me have always seemed too normal for my idea of what a policeman should be like. He bade me sit down by the fire and he sat at his desk. I think he must not have slept all night. He told me he had two very difficult cases, which he thought I could help him with, and that he had sat up all night thinking about it.

'About *it*?' I asked.

'About you,' he said. 'I often think about you before I go to sleep.'

He said it without looking at me. He spoke softly, as if he were alone, although he had a deep, firm voice. I sensed how hard it must be for him. His words sounded gentle. For the first time I thought of him as a single man. For the first time I thought of him as a man. For the first time I saw that he had a handsome face, a handsomeness that came from within. I tried to make light of it, sensing a kind of danger to my joy in always seeing him at our house:

'You mean to say that thinking of me always sends you to sleep and that is how interesting I seem to you? I ought to feel offended, but I forgive you. You can use me as a medicament. Papa is the doctor, I the medicament.'

He did not smile, not even from politeness. He got up and stood behind my chair, so that I would not be able to see him.

'You, Miss Iulia, are like a little spider which, when it senses some-body near or when you touch it, ever so slightly, immediately retracts its little legs, and curls up in a ball, so that you might mistake it for a little black speck. In that way it thinks itself safe from intruders. Whenever I have come close to you, whenever I have touched you, you have acted like the spider, you have curled yourself into a ball. And you do so now, except that I do not have time to wait until you uncurl yourself.'

I remained silent and stubbornly gazed at my boots. One had a mud stain.

'Yesterday you praised my voice when I sang from *La Bohème*. Do you know how many times you have praised me since you grew up? Three times – I went over them in my mind last night. And yesterday you seemed amazed that I could sing. I have the feeling that you are amazed whenever you see that I am a man like any other. I thought of these hands when I learned the aria. They are always cold,' continued the voice behind me.

'I did not know that you needed praise,' I ventured to murmur, my eyes still fixed on the mud stain on my boot, and I wished him to understand what I meant, not to take it as a criticism, and so I added: 'You are a strong, wonderful man, I admire you as much as I do Mama and Papa.'

I think I must have said exactly what he did not want to hear, but I do not know, because never had I thought very much about such things. And from a kind of pain in my soul I went on: 'But you are even dearer to me.'

He seemed heartened: 'I shall go all the way, Iulia. I have quite a busy life, I do what I do with passion, and to fight against evildoers, against evil, consumes all my spiritual strength and all my time. I am invited everywhere, I go to the theatre, to me, the opera is a kind of opium, I have admirers... including female admirers. But my life is like a musical scale that lacks one note. It is as if I had to sing without using one note, G, let us say. Think of your piano if it lacked one white key, the note G. And you to me are the note G, which would fill my life with joy. I would like...'

'Please, no, you will be angry with me and I do not want that, in no wise do I want that, I cannot bear to see you angry with me, I want everything to remain like this, until the end,' I said in despair, not precisely those words, but something similar, I cannot remember very well which words, and I stood up so that I could see him. He had the most tortured face in the world and indeed it was very hard for me, because I wanted to do what he wished, but I could not, because of the accident that caused there to be somebody else more important to me. But when he saw my frightened eyes, he controlled himself, he took my hand, which was cold (how could it be otherwise?), and in a different voice, one distant and almost malicious, which made me feel as if he had pushed me down a flight of stairs: 'Women like you, *comme toi*, have a custom: they invest their feelings in an insolvent bank. In the most insecure and inauspicious place possible. They cannot even see the men close to them, they ignore them if they know their presence is assured, and they always look at the man who is far away, at the man who tortures them, the man who is with another woman.'

He released my hand and began to pace up and down the room. I did not dare look at him, but I could feel his voice enveloping me.

'Perhaps I was wrong to tell you what I have told you, but have I not the right to a normal life, a good life? I know that I could make you happy, little by little, the same as he would make you unhappy. Alexandru Livezeanu is involved in a nasty affair. I invited you here to warn you! He has no future!'

I felt now that he was wounding me deliberately. Then, he told me what was to be said, but the effect was completely the opposite to the one he desired. My dwindling feelings for Alexandru were suddenly replenished, like rivers after the rain. Mr Costache is right, and that is what breaks my heart: I invest my feelings in the most insecure and inauspicious place, I look at the man who already has everything and nonetheless I am sure that without me he will drown or that I am on this earth solely to save him. In an alien voice, Mr Costache asked me to be discreet and assured me that he had told my parents exactly as much as it was necessary for them to know and there was no need for further explanation. Then he summoned a man to show me out; he did not even go to the door. But from the moment I left his office, I knew that I would never be able to look at him as before.

2.

The velvet curtains were drawn and from outside the house looked dark. Costache had gone to bed already, at four o'clock in the afternoon. He had drunk two glasses of hard liquor and wanted only to plunge his body and mind into sleep; a dreamless sleep. Zaharia, who had only ever seen him in such a state a handful of times, was walking around on tiptoe, somewhat livelier than usual. On other days, when the adjutant was gloomy, Costache used to encourage him and cheer him up. But when his master was ill, gloomier than the adjutant could ever be, since, as Zaharia suspected, the depth of one's depression matched the height of one's intellect, then he tried to keep the house in balance and encourage his master. Liza, who merely wanted her daily portion of affection, after she was rebuffed, had also withdrawn, with her tail between her legs,.

The knocking on the door surprised and disturbed all three. Mr Costache had fallen asleep a few minutes previously, Zaharia was darning some trousers, and Liza was lying with her head resting on her snowy paws, thinking her own thoughts. The first to get up was Zaharia, in haste, the second Liza, without haste, while Mr Costache merely turned over to lie on his other side, determined that nobody and nothing would disturb him until the next morning. But after five minutes of hearing the adjutant's voice at the door, interspersed with the voice of a woman, which was not loud enough for him to identify, Zaharia came in and said peevishly: 'She refuses to leave till you get up.'

'Who?' In the darkness Costache's voice was hoarse and full of hope.

But the answer was unexpected: 'Mrs Movileanu, the lawyer's wife. Has to give you something really important. What should I do?' asked Zaharia, who just as in wartime, was prepared to carry out any order, no matter how perilous.

Costache groaned as if in pain, a thing he did not often do in the presence of others. Without answering, he turned the knob hidden under the mantle of the lamp on the bedside table and a mushroom of light enveloped his groggy face. He asked for his dressing gown and as he was went out of the bedroom, tousled, reeking of liquor and frowning.

It was not until he saw her that he realized who Mrs Movileanu was: the lady full of airs and migraines who lived on Strada Teilor, the one whose husband was having an affair. Just as she had done the first time he met her, she extended him a plump, dimpled hand, but this time

Costache pretended not to notice and unconvincingly apologized for receiving her like this, since he had not been expecting anybody and did not feel well – a catarrh. The lady looked very well, she was wearing exactly the right amount of powder and was attired tastefully, in an elegant dress with an embroidered bodice and long sleeves, closely fitting at the wrists. She looked at Costache in concern, the way only women know how to look at men, knowing their nature and their ways and wishing to help them. Costache needed such a look and noticing how naturally and gently she treated such an unsightly man and how pleasant she was when she was not upset and angry, he thought that something was not as it should be in this world. Mrs Movileanu apologized for having come unexpectedly and said that she had wanted to detain him when he left her house two days previously. Despite what her husband imagined, together with that impertinent Trajan, who always took his side, she knew about his escapades. She also knew who the *person* was. She would divorce him, if she could, but she had no other source of income, and to divorce a lawyer of Movileanu's calibre meant being left without a roof over your head.

'But I did not come here to talk about my own tribulations, forgive me and please do not be too angry with me. If I have done so now, a little, it is because I do not have anybody else to talk to, I am very lonely, as lonely as only a woman married to my husband could be, if you take my meaning. I came here because I heard from the maid – the one who brought you coffee when you visited – what you spoke to my husband about the other day. The servants keep me informed of what is happening in the house, in town and in the world, whether I like it or not, and so I do not have to read the newspapers.'

Costache nodded, he was of the same opinion, and Mrs Movileanu smiled, looking at Liza, who had come up to her and was sniffing the hem of her skirt.

'But it is not true that the wallet disappeared. If I have been bold enough to take advantage of my husband's absence from home – he did not even stay home with me yesterday, on Christmas day – and to come here to you, it is because I have the wallet and I am determined to give it to you. I got your address from the Prefecture, where I went first. Mr Caton Lecca was also there, and he too asked where you were.'

'But that is impossible,' said Costache, leaping to his feet, ignoring her final remark with a shrug. 'Do you have any connection with Petre, the coachman from Inger's confectionary shop?'

'No. Who is Petre? Who is Inger? Forgive me, but I do not see how it could be impossible, and nor is it, as proof of which, let me give the wallet to you.'

And thereupon she handed him an deer-skin wallet. As he took it, Costache kissed her hand, to make up for the kiss he had denied her earlier. Then he opened the wallet and rummaged in its numerous compartments. In it he found nothing but a gilded key with elaborately cut extensions like lacy wings on each side of the shank.

'There was nothing in it except this key. I think it is from a safe. I took the wallet from the table because I believed it had some connection with *her*. When I discovered that it did not, I would have given it back to the young man in person, as I intended, but I did not have the opportunity. I found out what had happened to him before my husband did, also through the servants. You should know that it is not true that I vent my nerves on them, as the young Trajan told you – I found out everything from the maid – on the contrary, they take my side, even if they pity me, and that is very hard for me.'

'Madam, I cannot thank you enough, forgive me for having received you in this state. I thought that Petre had stolen the wallet, but it would seem that the man who gave me the information was lying or mistaken, and in any case he is not a man I trust.'

Costache took her hands and felt their softness and warmth in his. He tensed slightly, as if remembering something, and then he told the lady with the same naturalness as she had spoken to him: 'I would like you to remain. Your presence has done me good, it does me good.'

Mrs Movileanu smiled. It had done her good too. The proposal itself did her good; it was obvious from her smile.

'I have nothing left to lose. I could remain. But I shall not do so: I do not wish you to judge me later... as men do in such... in situations such as this. And there is something else: I sense that I would yet again take second place. I am tired of being second. But who knows? It is possible that we shall meet again... after the divorce, because in this very moment I have decided. Come what may! Do you know a good lawyer, one who is not a friend of my husband?'

Costache spoke for another hour with the woman who was still Mrs Movileanu, he spoke as he had never spoken to a woman before, and afterwards, the blackness having lifted from his soul somewhat, he went to bed, warning his adjutant: 'Until tomorrow I do not exist! Not for anybody. Do not dare to disturb me. And take Liza for a walk!'

3.

The soldier clock at *L'Indépendance Roumaine* showed four o'clock, and Alexandru did not know what to do. He had left home driving the horse by himself, and as always had left sufficient time for any eventuality, but he did not have the courage to go to the Margulis house. Rather, he ought to find the little errand boy, but he had no idea where to look and no red caps were to be seen in the usual places; it was as if they had vanished into thin air. The one who had answers to such questions and knew the addresses was Nicu, but he could not ask Nicu where to find Nicu, and if he found him, he would have no reason to ask him where he was. How stupid! It was as if he were going out of his mind. 'Five o'clock; green and red.' What could it mean? A meeting, of course, but where? He pulled on the reins and slowed the horse to a walk. Was there a place of green and red in the centre of the capital? Perhaps a park, perhaps a shop, or a confectioner's? He looked at the shop signs but none were green and red. And on which day? That damned child had not told him a thing.

Victory Avenue was quiet except for a few coupés, people dressed elegantly and warmly, since it was a cold day: they were going on visits or coming back from long lunches, and they all looked carefree. But the smiling people just made Alexandru feel all the more, unhappy. It was as if somebody had put the evil eye on him, as if somebody had wished him ill. Everything started well and turned out dreadfully, things evolved *du mal en pis*. In front of him on the pavement he saw a comical man in an over-large overcoat, walking along with his gaze in the air, and he remembered the overcoat aria. He had seen *La Bohème* in Italy, and when he thought of Italy he smiled unwittingly; for him it was heaven on earth. The overcoat aria was an aria of poverty, but Alexandru in that moment would have rather been a philosopher forced to sell him an overcoat than a Livezeanu in the mood he was in today. The man was certainly a starving philosopher or poet, all his clothes were too large for him, like cast-offs, and his head was in the clouds as he walked along slowly, looking in wonderment at the long thick icicles that hung from the eaves. It was the way people walk when nobody is waiting for them. Before he overtook him, the man slipped on a patch of ice, for an instant seemed to regain his balance, but then he fell flat on the pavement. Alexandru stopped the horses and jumped down, immediately reaching the man, who was having difficulty getting to his feet. He tried to pull him by his arm, but the man cried out and then bit his lips in pain: 'I think I have sprained my shoulder,' he said with clenched teeth.

Alexandru hesitated: he would have liked to help him, but at the same time he did not want to miss the opportunity, no matter how slight, of meeting Iulia Margulis. But then, seeing the fright on the face of the man lying on the ground, he took hold of his other arm, and almost lifting him off the ground, he helped him climb into his carriage.

'I think it is dislocated, I have seen something similar before. I will take you home, if you agree: my brother is a medical student and he will help you, unless he is out.'

The man said nothing. He was groaning and kept biting his lower lip. Silence signalled assent, and so Alexandru mounted the box.

'I will drive slowly, but please hold the handle with your other hand, lest you come to any more grief!'

In less than half an hour they reached the entrance, beneath the marquise. The house was lit both outside and inside. Toader came out, as cheerful as always, although now was not the time, and with his master he helped the man out of the carriage. Toader said not a word, although he was not surprised, and made no suppositions. He was used to Alexandru getting into all kinds of scrapes.

'Run and fetch my brother, tell him to come to my room, please.'

Mişu arrived immediately and because Toader had delightedly told him that there was a man knocked to pieces, he brought his medical bag with him. The man was sitting in an armchair, beneath the two portraits of Alexandru's great-grandparents. Toader removed his galoshes, and Alexandru helped him off with his coat, which was a highly delicate operation. In the end, Toader fetched some scissors and cut open the coat. The physician immediately saw that it was a dislocated shoulder.

'What have you done' he asked Alexandru severely, but received such a pained look in response that he hastened to add: 'You are lucky, sir...'

He looked at Alexandru, who shrugged at his brother, over the top of the stranger's head – he was unable to make any introductions, since he had forgotten to ask the stranger his name. The man opened his eyes, which he had been keeping clenched, and said faintly: 'Dan Creţu.'

The brothers looked at each other in amazement, and Alexandru felt the sky was crashing down on his head. This was all he needed!

'You have met my brother Alexandru, and I am Mihai Livizeanu.' He continued with the positive disposition and confidence which, as he had learned, were part of a good physician's obligations: 'You are lucky, Mr Crețu. It can be pushed back into the socket, but it will be painful. We give you permission to scream. I learned in Paris how it is done, but I have never had occasion to try it. I am delighted to do so now. There are many methods and I shall employ the simplest... Alexandru, be so kind as to fetch a large glass of cognac for your patient.'

The lock of hair that fell cheekily over his forehead was the only detail about Mișu Livizeanu that contrasted his cold seriousness. He went to wash his hand and returned to find Dan drinking the cognac, grimacing, although it was the finest Courvoisier; Napoleon himself, had he still lived, would not have been so finicky. Then, they laid Dan in Alexandru's bed. Mișu felt the place and without warning, pushed the bone back into the socket, with an abrupt, powerful shove. There was a clicking sound. Dan screamed, then moved his shoulder gently and felt only the trace of an old pain, but no new pain. They tightly bound the shoulder with a bandage and the physician told him that he should try to move it as little as possible. If he were careful, there would be no need for plaster.

4.

Returning to the hôtel late in the evening, Otto discovered that he had nobody to chatter to, although he had been dying to recount how he had passed the day and what he had managed to find out. Otto was garrulous, and at home in Transylvania he had always had a brother or an aunt or a neighbour to listen to him. The few items laid carefully on his room-mate's bed, tied with a bow, were an indication that he had not left the hôtel and that some good person was concerned about the stranger's fate. Otto stripped and washed himself thoroughly, before getting into bed. He was exhausted and it seemed to him that the smell of insect powder seemed to be stronger than the day before.

He had worn out the soles of his boots and lost a seg from the heel while walking from church to church to ask whether there was work and where he could earn some money, but everywhere he had received the same answer: work begins in July, in June at the earliest, and nobody starts renovations in the winter. But even a barnyard hen could have told him that! For the time being, Otto would have to make do with what was on offer at the hôtel. He took a cart to the nunnery at Pasărea. Thence he was sent to the monastery at Cernica, some ten kilometres away. A beautiful gypsy girl, with a sulky mien, who hoped to scrounge some pennies from him, on hearing where the nuns had sent him asked the abbess, her eyes glittering in amazement: 'Why do you live here when your husbands live ten kilometres away?'

He had travelled all that way, sometimes on foot, sometimes in a cart, sometimes on the horse-drawn tram, *alles umsonst*, for nothing. But he had discovered something worth sharing and he felt sorry that the silent man, who had been so happy to listen to his stories these past few days, was not there. In all the places he visited, he had heard a rumour which, it would seem, currently preoccupied all the ecclesiastical authorities: a miracle-working icon had been lost, a priceless treasure, brought some ten years ago from a cathedral in the centre of town, which had been demolished. The icon, if he understood rightly, had been in the care of a bishop for a while, a bishop who had been caught up in a scandal a year previously and dismissed from his post. The bishop had secretly entrusted it to an abbot who had in the meantime passed away, and the icon had then disappeared without trace. It was hugely valuable because it had two large diamonds on the golden shoulders. Closing his eyes, Otto pictured the icon and imagined discovering it hidden in a wall while he was restoring a church. Through his mind, now only half awake, filed a host of archangels with slender legs, wearing gowns and carrying shields, angels with tumbling curly locks, and saints with yellow skullcaps. He had seen them all before, but he could not remember where exactly. Soon, the saints were swept away by the waters of a river, and the valet walking down the corridor in that moment heard a snore from the room that the stranger Dan Crețu shared with the church restorer from Transylvania. But Mr Dan Crețu had not returned to the hôtel that day.

Saturday, 27 December

1.

The day began badly, with a fog so thick that I could not even see the birch tree in front of my window. I thought about what it would be like if it were the other way around: every day fog so thick that you could not see other people, and clear air only on one or two special days a year, as if an unseen hand had wiped clean the milky, opaque window of the sky. What joy people would feel just to be able to see, what a miracle the transparent, colourless air would seem to them. As it is, nobody delights in the air and they do not even realize what an extraordinary thing it is to be able to see far into the distance, all the way to the horizon. Mama helped me to wash my hair, because since we gave up most of our servants, to make savings (we have kept on only the cook, with her mind stuffed full of superstitions, Safta and the frail, constantly ill Nelu), we have both helped one another. But it is not the washing the that is the hardest, but the drying. You cannot sit too close to the hearth. In school they have always told us of cases of girls whose hair has caught fire in that awful way.

I have made progress with *Vanity Fair*. Last night I finished Chapter LIX and I cannot even begin to describe how greatly I was irritated by the way in which Major Williams pleads: 'Only let me stay near you and see you often!' It irritated me because I might have done the same. It was not the awful way in which Amelia treats the poor Major that disgusted me, the way she lets him desire her exactly like a cake he knows he will never have, but his lack of pride, so similar to mine. But I do not act like that prude Amelia, I do not allow for equivocation, and I am glad that things have been cleared up with Mr Costache, although I feel dreadfully sorry that such a simple thing became so complicated and oppressive. I do not know how I will be able to face him again. Mama and Papa asked me nothing, but Mama said something bad about Alexandru and that she did not trust him – she said it so that I would overhear. That made me feel even more guilty at not having told them about inviting him here this afternoon, when they will both be going with Jacques to visit Dr Rizea, who operated on my brother two years ago. The doctor saved him, but it is hard for me to see him, because it reminds me of all the terror I felt at that time. On the other hand, dear Jacques loves him greatly, and he told me just now that he would be taking his flute with him to play Handel's minuet for the doctor.

But perhaps Mr Livizeanu will not come, who knows... I do not understand the words that Nicu told me: 'green and red.' We shall see! Papa has started mentioning money more and more often, although he has never done so hitherto. Are we really in such a difficult situation? I ought to marry an old millionaire and rid the whole Margulis family of their money worries, which, although they do not mar our cheerfulness, are like a rain cloud in a blue sky. How might I find Nicu? An amusing thought occurred to me: only Nicu would know how to tell me where to find Nicu!

I told Mama my observation about her agate eyes having been inherited by Jacques, but she, who is proud of our Greek ancestors, even though they are rather distant, told me that Agatha means 'good' in Greek and has no connection with the black stone, as I believed. That Papa is Leon, which is to say, lion, that Jacques is named after our godfather Jacob, which is a biblical name, and that she called me Iulia because I was born on the twelfth, or according to the new calendar the twenty-fifth, of July, on exactly the same day as Mama's Mama, grandmother Trandafira. She was surprised that I did not know that *agathos* means *good* and I felt like telling her that I do know that *Andros* means *man*, because I remember only what is connected with the soul. The eternal man – Alexandru.

2.

Alexandru knocked discreetly on the door, but there was no answer. His shirt was unbuttoned and he was not wearing a lavaliere; although over his shirt he had a *gris perle* vest. He knocked again, more loudly, and pressed his ear to the well-polished wood, but there was still no sound. He looked at the clock: It was a few minutes past eleven. He decided to enter, at the risk of waking his guest, but no, he found him sitting on the bed, staring at the silk wallpaper, whose gold patterns coiled over a blue background. With Alexandru entered a servant, who drew the two sets of curtains and asked whether he should bring the patient breakfast in his room.

'Yes, bring it,' said Alexandru, since Dan did not seem to feel the question had anything to do with him. The servant went out and when he returned, with a small trolley, two children slipped through the door behind him, a little girl and boy of about six, who held each other by the hand and stared open-mouthed at the guest.

'They are twins, two of my sister Marioara's three children,' said Alexandru, introducing them. 'Say hello to Mr Dan Crețu and then go to your nurse, you little rascals. How did she let you out of her sight? Tell him your name,' he urged the little boy.

'Ciuciu Penciu. Ciuciu Penciu from Silistra is my name,' he said, repeating himself to make sure he had been heard and then burst into laughter at his joke, which seemed to amuse him no end. 'I have been awake for hours!'

'Good day, sir, and I have been awake for hours too,' added the little girl, in a voice very similar to her brother's, politely, but reproaching the guest, who was still in bed. 'My name is Anica.'

Then they let go of each other's hands, went to the door, and taking each other's hand again, as if in a dance, they galloped laughing down the hall.

'They are very mischievous and spoiled. People say they take after me, especially Ștefănel, whom nobody can resist, and today is his name day. They like funny words. At one time, they imitated the noises of different animals. I hope you are feeling well, with your shoulder. Please eat and allow me to keep you company in the meantime.'

For the first time since they had met, Alexandru saw Dan Crețu smile and he remained with his eyes on him, with a face not particularly intelligent at that moment. It seemed as if he had grown ten years younger and you suddenly felt a desire to be his friend. It even seemed as if his smile resembled Iulia's.

'Everybody has been giving me food since I arrived here. It is good. Thank you, Alexandru, that is your name, isn't it? But I would rather have a cigarette.'

Slightly embarrassed, the host took out his tobacco tin. Dan sighed, as if something bothered him about the gesture, and then he forgot to take a cigarette and started eating. He finished quickly, pulled a face at the coffee – it was obvious it was not to his liking, although it was the finest blend from Levon Harutunian's shop. Alexandru went out, leaving him to get dressed – he had given him a set of Mişu's clothes, who was the same size – and when he came back he was accompanied by his mother. Maria Livezeanu had a mobile head with a furrowed face and large mouth set atop a large, clumsy body, which made her somewhat resemble a tortoise.

'Mr Dan Creţu, I am most glad to have you as our guest. How did you sleep?' she said and, hesitating slightly, extended her hand for him to kiss.

'Very well!' said Dan curtly and when Alexandru's mother's hand appeared next to his lips he kissed it without very much elegance.

'I read in the newspaper about you. What is the ultimate truth of the matter? Forgive me, but I am a very direct person, I do not hide behind nicely turned phrases. You may tell us, we shall not betray you, since we have many defects of our own in the family,' added the lady, trying to catch her son's eye, 'but we are not traitors.'

Not one trace of the earlier smile remained on Dan's face. He now looked forty-three, the age given in the newspaper.

'*Laissez-le, Maman, il a besoin de repos, c'est* le médecin *qui l'a dit,*' said Alexandru, alluding to his brother, who was already known in the family as *the doctor*.

Dan listened to them as if we were watching a pantomime. He was livelier and seemed in a better mood than on the previous evening.

'I don't know, madam, I would like to be able to answer you. What day is it today? I could do with a calendar...'

'Saturday.'

'Ah, I was afraid that I ought to be at work. In fact, I do have to be there, I will have to leave you, I don't want to be fired from the newspaper, I need the money to live on and besides, they've treated me well.'

'Do not worry, I will take you. I heard that you are an employee of *Universul*, I recently had dinner with the Chief of Public Security,

Mr Costache Boerescu, and he told me the news. You know each other, do you not?' said Alexandru.

Dan shrugged, as if he were not interested in the subject.

'My daughter Marioara would have been delighted to make your acquaintance, you know, ever since her divorce she has been rather gloomy, but unfortunately she is visiting a lady friend for the day. But we hope that you will call again in the days to come.'

The guest had fallen completely dumb and after a few unsuccessful attempts to make conversation, the lady went out, casting a meaningful glance at her son. And the meaning was: the man is completely mad! How could you have brought him in off the street? Dan caught the exchange of glances and after the door closed he smiled conspiratorially at Alexandru, without saying a word, and yet again one would have thought he were a different man.

'Mr Crețu,' said Alexandru after his mother left, 'we met at a very difficult moment for me and I would be glad if I could help at least you. Please do not regard me as arrogant if I wish to offer you help of every kind, but it would help *me* if you accepted. I have a very personal reason: you resemble somebody who at this moment is very important to me.'

He went to the window and peered into the fog, but all he could see was a milky sea whose waters had flooded the entire city.

3.

I wouldn't have the courage to go outside now, I get lost even when the weather is fine, let alone now, with this mist – it is as if it has poured out of me and flooded the street. Then again, I can't believe that I slept so deeply, a dreamless sleep, that this morning I woke up more clear-headed and haven't been thinking about the questions that are eating away at my soul. When I opened my eyes I looked for the old walls and I saw wallpaper with a gilt pattern. I went to the windows, I drew the curtains, which were like a wall, and I saw the other wall, the mist. But inside me the walls have started to crumble. When Alexandru came, it was as if he came out of the mist, like a boat, an old friend. Right now, Dr Margulis and he are the only people I trust, the others annoy me, make me coil up like a spring. Alexandru made some veiled confessions to me about the nasty business he is mixed up in and about a girl, Iulia, whom he says he probably doesn't love, although it's obvious from a mile off that there is no point to his doubt. She asked him to meet her, but he doesn't know where and she sent him code words that he can't understand: 'green and red'! The lad is stranger than I am. It turns out that that was why we ended up in the same place yesterday; he was looking for her. The truth is that I fell because of him. I heard the horses behind me, I turned to look, because the clatter of hooves always frightens me, and I slipped on the ice. The medical student seems a bit arrogant and serious, while Alexandru has something about him of the child who has always got his own way in life; and something of the rich kid. But even so, it took me by surprise when he told me, with a warmth and understanding that only very intelligent people possess: 'Mr Crețu, you are a subject of discussion at the moment, the same as everybody who appears in the newspaper. I intend to write for a newspaper very soon, it is a profession that tempts me. Even at the meal with Mr Boerescu, which I was telling you about, you were a topic of conversation.'

I told him not to address me formally, to call me by my first name, but he said that it would be over-familiar and so he carried on addressing me with the formal *you*.

'Do not take it amiss,' he went on, 'but everything you have done this morning puzzles me.'

I did not understand why. He hesitated to tell me, and so I had to insist and finally, reluctantly, he told me the following: I addressed him by his first name, although in effect we did not know each other and, although I am older than he, it is not the done thing, unless you state that it is your intention; I did not rise to my feet when his mother entered and left, which was 'unbelievable,' his poor mother had blushed in embarrassment in my stead; I do not know how to kiss a hand ('you placed your lips in the middle of the back of the hand, whereas the hand should be kissed on the knuckle of the middle finger, you should barely touch it with your lips, you should grasp the fingers, without squeezing them, and then place the shadow of a kiss on the glossy skin of the middle knuckle'); the answers I gave to his mother's questions, as well as to his questions, all had a certain abruptness, lacking the essential terms of polite address, *madam, sir, thank you*; and when he thanked me, I never replied 'you are welcome, sir!'; my hair was cut strangely, freshly cut, but as for my completely shaven cheeks, at my age... ; I seem to have a fear of horses; I talk seldom, but when I do there is something strange about it, he cannot say what; and as for how I ate my breakfast, he does not even want to mention it, it would be indelicate to do so, but he has never seen such a messy, sloppy manner of eating. It would not surprise him if he saw me greet somebody without lifting my hat. He concluded in a different tone of voice: 'Who are you in fact, Mr Crețu? Where do you come from? I am merely curious, but if it is hard for you to tell me, I shall not insist.'

The question made me shudder. It was as if the man divined what was happening to me and to win time I asked him: 'What do you think, Alexandru? Or, if you prefer, what, Sir, do you think?'

'No, please continue to call me by my first name, I like it more, it is more direct, I will try to accustom myself to saying it, in time. To be honest, I have thought of a number of theories, but none of them are satisfactory. If you are from a foreign country, for example, why do you not know how to kiss a hand, for example? If you are, as people say – forgive me, but I repeat it only for the sake of the discussion – a malefactor, why do you have such a gentle and absent air? The hypothesis is out of the question: your face is that of an honest man. I thought that you might be – there have been cases, I know of one that occurred last year – a man with a false identity, let us say, a man of the slums who has invented an aristocratic past for himself, but you do not seem to be from the slums, and nor do you claim to be an aristocrat. But then again, nor do you seem to be from the centre of the city or from a foreign country or from the countryside. You seem not to be from anywhere.'

I said calmly: 'I think you are right. I'm not from anywhere,' but he was afraid that he had insulted me.

And then, in an uncontrolled outburst, which I may end up regretting, I told him everything, with more details than I gave the doctor: the fact that I thought I came from another world, although not from another country. Strangely, unlike the doctor, who immediately suspected I had something to hide and was feigning madness, Alexandru almost believed me.

'That is exactly how you behave, indeed, and it is extraordinary, if I were to put together everything I have observed about you, you seem like a man from another time, one not yet known to me. Mr Crețu, I am not regarded as being very intelligent, in the family – Mișu has the sharp mind – and nor have I made much effort to study hard. But ever since I witnessed Dr Gerota's demonstration of X-rays, ever since microscopic creatures were discovered and it has been known what those strange animals look like, which are responsible for epidemics, the influenza microbe, for example, which killed so many people when I was a youth... erm... ever since it has been possible to speak in a whisper and have a man hundreds of kilometres away hear you as if he were standing next to you, ever since we have been able to see the moon with a telescope, ever since they have made so many attempts to fly away from the earth with the Zeppelin and attempts to replace the hippomobile with an automobile, with horses that cannot be seen and do not need shoeing – what will the ironsmiths do?... erm... so many marvels of science have occurred – I do not even try to know them all, our ancestors would die of amazement on the spot – well, I for one think that anything is possible. Given that people are even talking of immortality, then why should this not be possible? Nothing that man will be able to do or achieve henceforth will surprise me.'

He stood up and started pacing up and down the room agitatedly, between the fireplace and the window, while I listened to him insatiably. But then came the blast of cold water.

'But one thing does not fit, no matter how much I would like to believe you. If science had achieved something of the sort, you would have had to know about it, to know that you were the first who... but since you know nothing, it is more likely to be only an aspiration, an ideal, a figment of imagination that you have come to believe to be real. Perhaps what Dr Margulis supposed is the only acceptable explanation. Have patience and I believe that you will find the explanation for yourself in the end.'

And with the selfishness of all people in love, he turned his attention away from me, as if what I had told him were a mere bagatelle, and came back to his own pressing concerns: he asked me, in fact begged me, to go to the Margulis house that afternoon at five o'clock, finding some pretext or other, and if Miss Iulia was in a position to receive him, to send him word. He would wait for me by the St Sava College. And then he surprised me by inviting me to his New Year's Eve party and told me not to worry, because he would place me in the hands of the family tailor. That was the last thing I was expecting, a tailor! True, I had already been tailored with a bandage, and the tailor would have to take account of my shoulder.

Alexandru added, sombrely: 'I invite you even if I will perhaps not be present. My future is uncertain in this moment. I shall inform my sister Marioara, who is taking care of the preparations. It will be a rather formal party, there will also be newspapermen there, since I've told you that profession interests me.'

The hands revolved unseen, because the fog obscured the face of the clock on the façade of the Prefecture of Police. Petre the coachman had as usual left his watch at home and he was afraid he might be late. He had been summoned to come at eleven o'clock. If he had not known the way, he would have got lost, so alien did the white city seem, not even sounds came from where they should have, and the horse took fright when they came face to face with another carriage. He had with him the chocolate cream and almond cream that he had bought from the confectioner, to sweeten the policemen.

For a Saturday, there was a strangely large number of people there; men and women, some standing, some sitting, some walking up and down the broad ground floor lobby aimlessly, some standing at doors. You would have said every form of distress and person in distress had assembled at the police station, now that Christmas was over. Caton Lecca was there too, and from his first-floor office, the one with the three arched windows right above the main entrance, raised voices could be heard, and the soldiers were walking around on tiptoe. The chiefs were arguing among themselves, and what filtered through the door were mutual accusations the likes of which had never been overheard there before. Petre was growing more and more frightened, because the man who was shouting the loudest was Mr Costache Boerescu, who had sent word that he should come. What would happen when he came face to face with him! Obviously, the wallet could no longer turn up, since the men had come to empty the privy on the very same day – blind luck – and so even if they made a search, nothing would be found, but the thought gave him no peace and it was as if it had begun to reek. His horse, Murguțu, had started to limp in that damned fog, and limping was a bad sign, because he was highly skilled at shoeing horses, he knew how to make a horse stand calmly, and sometimes his assistant did not even need to use the bull tongs. His children ran riot, but horses obeyed him, and anyway he was more patient with them, and spoke to them lovingly. And here he was sweating like a horse in fear, although the dampness of the fog chilled him to the bone.

The door flew open and Mr Costache burst forth, without looking at anybody and without seeing him. Petre followed him and before the Head of Security could enter his office, he stopped him with a hoarse

'Mr Costache!' The policeman turned around and it seemed that only then did he remember him.

'Ah, a good job you came and don't make me waste my time with you, otherwise I'll have you put in a cell downstairs, and then you'll see how they ask you questions.'

Petre looked at Mr Costache in terror and the stump of his index finger started to throb.

'What do you want to know?'

'I want to know everything, and tell me everything you concealed the last time. What you took from that boy and why, and whether you shot him!'

'No, not me, sir, I never even had me gun with me that day. I ran away from home, from me wife's tongue, she were nagging me, 'cause she don't want me to be a Jew's servant all me life, she wants me to be a blacksmith and indebendent. I didn't have no gun! First I saw him on the ground, the one that didn't have no moustache, I thought he were drunk, he were trembling and I gave him me father's overcoat, God rest his soul, and ten minutes later I found the blond one, lying there like he were dead, but he weren't dead, and I bicked him ub.'

Mr Costache looked at him unrelentingly. When he wanted to, he could paralyse all those around him with a single glance; he could give orders without opening his mouth. He had never yet raised his hand to anybody, he lowered his voice to a whisper, but he could get his way like that more quickly than by using the old methods. He had a bearing that cowed even criminals, and Petre all the more so, since he was not a criminal.

'I took it, sir.'

'Took what?'

'The burse.'

'And?'

'I threw it in the shi... er, in the brivy, so as nobody would find it. I don't know why I took it, I thought I could oben a smithy and shut me wife ub and I knew very well that the blond lad didn't have long to live, and so he wouldn't need it. But I swear that all it had in it was a key and not one benny, I swear on the holy icon!'

Petre made a sweeping sign of the cross with thumb and one and a half fingers, and Costache dismissed him with his harshest glare. The coachman retreated backwards, – one advantage a man has over a horse, which doesn't know how to walk backwards so easily.

5.

Mama and Papa and Jacques left at half past four, in our carriage. I thought to myself: if I put my corset on and arrange my hair, he will not come. If I do not put it on, he might come, and then I will appear to him in the worst possible light and with the largest possible waist. Nevertheless, if I do not put my corset on, I have two advantages: I will be comfortable and if he does not come, I will not have gone to ridiculous lengths of preparation for nothing. Often I play the lottery with my thoughts in this way and always have the winning ticket. What a win! By the way, my cousin, who always has good initiatives, urged me to enter the New Year's lottery, only she knows that I have bought a ticket, especially given we have financial difficulties. I have hidden it right here in my diary. I placed the numbers 1, 2, 3, 4, 5, 6 together, not being able to think of anything better, arranged as 12, 34 and 56. Vasilica chose hers at random: 65, 43 and 21. I cannot even imagine what we would do with ten thousand lei, but surely we should start with a bigger surgery for Papa, with the latest instruments, since his a very out of date. How much would a Roentgen machine cost? I have not the faintest idea. At a few minutes to five, I started to bustle around, I looked in the mirror, I arranged my hair a little, although whatever I might do, it will not stay in place, I suppose that it does not like what is inside my head, in my 'cranial container,' as Papa so nicely puts it. Oh, is there anybody who is exactly as she wishes to be in every respect, both inside and out? I have had no news from that person. Who knows from what great-great-somebody I inherited this black and unruly head of hair!

At five o'clock on the dot I almost fainted in fright, because I heard the front door and then Safta appeared. But I could immediately tell she was not wearing her Alexandru Livizeanu face. It was Mr Dan Crețu, seemingly in a better mood – who wished to thank us for lunch – how nice of him, he is well-educated after all! But when he heard that I was alone, he did not wish to stay, although I insincerely begged him to. He was in such a hurry that he did not even take his hat off, the man is very absent-minded, but he is very dear to me the way he is! Well, let us see how I shall recount what happened next, since at the Central School they never taught us such a thing...

After Dan left, I was so disappointed, having believed for an instant that the *other* man had arrived, I was so disappointed that I extinguished all the lights and withdrew to my room.

However, not ten minutes after Dan Crețu's departure, Safta appeared, this time wearing her Alexandru face, which is to say a solemn and defiant mien, as if I were a mule for agreeing to see such a man. I did not even have time to regret that I had not arranged my hair, he entered and I cannot remember whether or how he greeted me. I quickly picked up *Vanity Fair pour me donner une contenance.* He sat down next to me on the couch, although I had invited him to take a chair. He looked deeply and steadily into my eyes, and I did likewise. When Jacques and I were younger, we used to play at looking into animals' eyes, and they would never hold out, always quickly turning aside their gaze, especially dogs. I wanted to show Alexandru that I could hold out, that I was not a dog, but I could not understand what his gaze meant. Perhaps it meant nothing.

'What does 'green and red' mean?' he asked.

'I wanted to ask you the very same question.'

It was not the first time that we had thought the same thing in the same moment. He smiled, although, not as luminously as Mr Dan Crețu smiles. See how objective I can be!

'Nicu brought me a coded message, like in charades: 'Five o'clock, green and red.' Without a day, without a place, and the fact that I came today is boldness on my part, especially given that on Monday I had the honour not to be...'

'But what about the letter?' I said, interrupting, since I felt guilty about Monday. 'My letter was clear!'

'What letter?' and as he said it his face took on that innocence it often shows when he is lying, and which so infuriates me. He was up to his usual tricks again – and my heart felt heavy. Nicu is renowned for never having lost any envelope or parcel that has ever been entrusted to him, by me or anybody else, and he told me that he gave him the envelope. Given the choice between Nicu and Alexandru, allow me to believe Nicu. I rose to my feet, but remembering I was not wearing a corset, I quickly sat back down, thus allowing me the better to conceal my lack of that item of attire, and I think I blushed slightly. It was obvious, however, that he had straight away noticed the lack, because his eyes remained on my dress, namely my waist.

'Why did you come here on Monday?' I asked and the question sounded colder than I had intended.

'Iulia... I am in difficulties, I am in a situation that might turn out badly for me. I have told Mr Boerescu, but I got the impression that he

191

did not believe me, just as you do not believe me when I tell you that I did not receive a letter.'

He had an utterly different tone of voice than any I had heard from him thitherto, but his eyes still had his "*home à femmes*" tone, although he panted slightly as he spoke, as if he had been running. And he quickly stood up to leave. My heart quailed, but just as quickly he came back and sat down, right beside me, and cupped my cheek in his palm. And then rather than telling me about his difficulties, he prepared difficulties for me; a host of future difficulties because the sole lamp could be easily extinguished and the flames in the hearth flickered softly, and because my lack of a corset helped things to happen there, on the couch. He aroused my breasts, alarming each in turn, and then there was an all-encompassing yearning, tighter and tighter, and a boundless compassion. Yes, it was something higher than us, higher than me, and he said: 'you little face looked as if you had been born, it was like a child's first scream.' My body did everything it had to without anybody ever having taught it. I think Safta knows, because since then she has looked at me with a kind of annoyance.

6.

In the afternoon, the fog lifted for a few hours and it was possible to see the smoke from the chimneys. The smoke was not as straight as a candle, as it was on fine days, but hunchbacked and humble, trembling, as if hesitating to go on its way and unravelling into slenderer and slenderer threads. At around four o'clock in the afternoon, the fog engulfed the smoke that had lain hidden in it, and in the evening the darkness engulfed both. Beneath the white and black waves, the top of the *L'Indépendance Roumaine* building disappeared. Inside, the editors talked endlessly about their erstwhile director, hoping with all their hearts that Nicu Filipescu would go to prison.

*

The rather ordinary-looking *Adevĕrul* building on Strada Sărindar also disappeared. Inside, a brand new attack against the monarchy was being hatched. The baroque building of the *Universul* popular newspaper also disappeared, a building atop which two almost naked bodies joined their winged shoulders, right above the window of the director's office. Thence, one by one, Mr Peppin Mirto and Mr Dan Crețu emerged into the whitish murk, each heading in the direction of Theatre Square to take a cab. Then, from the last office on the left, as you look at the front of the building, editor-in-chief Neculai Procopiu came out, later followed by Pavel Mirto, after he had finished writing a few more pages of his book. Old man Cercel was the last to leave, after checking that none of the lights in any of the offices had been left burning. Although there was no longer any danger of a fire, the doorman did his duty the same as he had in the old days, in his youth, when any candle could turn Bucharest's buildings into torches. And besides, electricity was expensive, and Mr Cazzvillan has asked him not to leave any of the lights on. The fog enveloped him, as he headed towards his little house on Strada Vișinelor in a carriage whose side was inscribed *UNIVERSUL* in white letters.

PRESS REVIEW

1.

I am writing in bed, propping the diary against my knees, and so my handwriting is bad. I feel sleepy and spoiled and worried, and my thoughts are all in a muddle. I yearn. Last night I dreamed no more no less than I was in the Garden of Eden, it looked a little like the garden of our old house, the one they sold when my Grandfather died. I pass a cherry plum tree, which did not tempt me, and then I came to an apple tree. In the tree I saw a small golden fruit and I gobbled it up without a second thought. Then I saw another, larger, greener apple, and I gobbled that one up too. It was not until I woke up that I thought of Eve. Am I to understand from this that I am guilty for tempting Adam? But what guilt? Perhaps because I was not wearing a corset? What can be bad in good? What can be bad in us? Proof that it is not a bad thing is that the body knows very well what it has to do. 'A little bad in you.' It is true that he guided me with a gentleness I would not have suspected in him. Our bodies are made to understand, while our words are made to separate us, because on leaving he said to me reproachfully: 'Why did I have to see you asleep?' Incomprehensible words that seemed to be brutal, like a blow. Naturally I was not asleep!

It was still well, but then today I picked up *Universul* (after Papa reads it, it arrives in my room, since Mama cannot abide it, she says it lacks style) and the devil knows what prompted me, or the devil himself prompted me, to read the letters of Dr Bastaki to Miss Gorjan, the woman who, after two years of *amour*, shot her lover with a pistol, because of blighted happiness. Those letters are dreadful. It is worth transcribing two of them here, so that I might be warned, having picked the golden apple from the tree of the knowledge of good and evil. In the summer, in August, he wrote to her thus: '*My darling love*, I have read the letter I received from you this morning and I am still under the influence of a pang of the heart. It is certain that your parents seek only to drive you away from me and employ to that end means that are in keeping with them, means dastardly and unscrupulous. What concern about you grips them, when they speak ill of a man who enjoys the esteem of the whole of society?' Look how modest he is! At least it is not the case with Alexandru. And nor with my parents. But what follows is even more *outré*: 'In order to do so, they ought to have qualities of a higher order, whereas with them it is completely the opposite.' I have said that Miss Elena's father is a general. 'What did they wish to do with their daughter? To marry her off for money?! Therefore they wished to invest you like capital. The question of money trumps all others. Little do they care about quality and intelligence, these to them are a negligible quantity. Well, for people who think only of money, they do not judge badly. Of course, they must now be furious seeing their hopes dashed, their investment lost. That noble body, that palpitating flesh has managed to escape their infamous trafficking and they cannot forgive such an act of independence, the rebellion of a sincere and honest nature. I read and reread your letter and I rage with shame and fury at the very idea that you can be their daughter. You do not deserve to stay one minute in the presence of such people, and this is why I beg you to leave at once that horrible place and come to me. I shall arrange things in such a way as to make you happy. I love you and I want you for the rest of my life.' Less than a year later, in June, the married man from Brăila wrote a letter such as I have never read before – and I am widely read: '*Dear friend*, This morning I am on the bank of the Danube that threatens us; I have so many things to do that I do not know where to start. My solutions have gone to hell. You did badly to leave Bucharest. In this moment I want to go to the dykes, which we are struggling to keep in place. I cannot leave here and think of anything but the danger that threatens the Lake. It is impossible for me to come to town. What will you do in Brăila? Am I not to be left in peace? Neither the lady nor any other person in the world concerns me at the moment. I think of nothing except what is happening here. Are you determined whatever the cost to compete with the Danube? It is true: you too burst your banks. I am furious to discover that you are in town. I embrace you etc.'

I particularly liked that 'Am I not to be left in peace?' and even more so the declaration of love: 'Are you determined to compete with the Danube?' And the final 'I embrace you.' Perhaps I would have lost my mind too, who knows? But I find the unanimously reviled Mr Bastaki rather likeable, he has something of a character from *Vanity Fair* and I think his fury was genuine and probably justified to a certain extent. But what would I have done in Miss Gorjan's place and in the same circumstances? Anyway, I do not have a revolver. Although to use his words, now that I have seen what a man is capable of, 'I am under the influence of a pang of the heart.' Outside there is a blizzard, the errand boys are certainly not on duty, and so I cannot hope for any sign. Now my mind keeps coming back to the 'palpitating flesh' of yesterday evening. For decency's sake, I cannot set down in this notebook what I am thinking.

2.

"People are crying out because not all our roads are paved, because three quarters of the streets do not have drains, because we do not have electric lighting except on the main thoroughfares, because we drop like flies when there are outbreaks of disease. And Mayor Robescu has saved up money in his stocking and proposes to erect statues for us: the statue of Independence and the bust of Ioan Brătianu. When we ask for improvements, there is no cash. When there is cash, they erect statues! Bucharest is burning and the mayor is fiddling!"

'The usual untruths from *Adevĕrul!*'

Procopiu and Pavel Mirto had made their way to the newspaper offices through the blizzard and were planning in broad outline the New Year issue. They were plucking up courage with the help of tea laced with rum. Pavel, whose spectacles were steamed up, warmed his hands on the porcelain tea cup, while Neculai Procopiu warmed himself by reciting from the rival gazette. Although the editor-in-chief had quoted the passage to Pavel only to make fun of their counterparts in Strada Sărindar, he was still a little envious when he thought of them. The article was unsigned, but it seemed to be in the style of Constantin Mille: expressive distortions of reality, beautifully turned phrases, well-honed rhetoric, that of a former professor of literature who had become a lawyer. Overlaying it all was his militant socialism, which was the reason he had been expelled from the University of Jassy many years previously and which, rather than subsiding, was all the more aggressive. And of course Alexandru Beldiman, the newspaper's founder, had been the first to lavish streams of inky bile on King Carol and the heir to the throne, Prince Ferdinand, endlessly repeating like a bird of ill omen that the latter would not reign even for a day. But on the subject of the truth, it ought to be known that a large number of streets had been paved, and the money for Brătianu's statue did not come from the pockets or 'stockings' of the Town Hall, but had been raised by means of tombola draws. A large part of the money from the New Year grand lottery, to whose result Procopiu was by no means indifferent, was earmarked for various municipal works. As for Mr Mille, everybody knew that he had bought shares in the newspaper with funds that were suspect to say the least. He now used *Adevĕrul* to thrash the King black and blue, although the King did not care to react, or refrained from doing so, since as everybody knows that press has become the Fourth Estate throughout the world.

'I wouldn't be surprised if years from now, with the collectivists in power and the King banished, there will be people who do not know or do not want to know the truth, and they will name a street after Mille. Perhaps right here, on Strada Sărindar,' said Pavel in a whisper. Thereupon, he lit a cigar.

Procopiu was accustomed to such original and gloomy ideas: one of his colleague's obsessions was the future, and now that he was writing a novel about it, he seemed almost not to live in the present any longer. And Pavel's future was radically different from all the futures of his friends and acquaintances. Procopiu had told him many times, albeit in vain, to get married, and that he would see life and the future in a different light, which was his own experience. Ever since he became a married man, it was as if his thoughts had been tidier, just as his wife's hand made sure the house was tidy, although she did nag him rather a lot. But on the other hand, the most senior newspaperman at *Universul* was afraid of Pavel's predictions. At least when it came to elections, Pavel's predictions were always systematically borne out. He thought for a moment about the future and, for the first time, he was afraid.

3.

Lately old man Cercel's belly had been behaving like an animal, giving him certain signals, and he spoke to it like he spoke to his doves. For example, that morning, when he woke up, his belly immediately began to squeak, and he said to it: 'So you're awake too, are you?' He said it aloud, and so his wife answered drily: 'For ages! I get up before you every morning.' A short while later, Cercel said to his restless belly: 'Come on then, little dove, let's eat!' and his wife thought he was talking to her, much to her amazement. Now, at work, his belly was annoyed, probably at having to brave the blizzard and go to work on a Sunday, and it stabbed him maliciously, as if it had knives inside, and to placate it, he said: 'Behave, this is what it's always like before New Year, but after that we'll have some time off.' Nevertheless, all was not well with his belly. Should he nip over to Dr Margulis' surgery? But then he would have to get somebody to stand in for him. Surely half an hour wouldn't make any difference... Undecided, the doorman picked up a newspaper at random, from the pile that had arrived from other editorial offices, but on seeing that it was *L'Indépendance Roumaine*, he put it back. With his belly in the state it was, he did not feel like deciphering the Gazette of the late Lahovary, and to tell the truth, there was no much he could decipher. Old man Cercel knew a bit of French, but only enough to be able to communicate when a foreigner came through the door of *Universul*, but reading it was a different kettle of fish. He picked up the next newspaper, which happened to be *Lumea Nouă*. He grimaced and put that one back, too. It was one of those papers that had socialist ideas. Up until two years ago, their neighbour Constantin Mille had been in charge of it, and even now they kept attacking Nicu Filipescu, saying he was worse than a common criminal, because he killed openly and in the presence of witnesses! The doorman respected the former mayor and liked the fact that he was an active young man. Nor did he feel like reading *Românul* or *Drapelul*, and *Adevărul* even less so. *Adevărul* was the paper that annoyed him the most. *Timpul* was too dull and didn't have the wit it used to have in the old days, when the men with the biggest brains in Bucharest wrote for it. In fact, without Nicu, whom he kept up to date on what the papers were saying, he didn't much feel like reading any of them.

'Speak of the devil, I was just thinking about you. But what's up with you? What happened?' he asked, taking fright, when he saw the boy, completely white from the blizzard and carrying a bird cage with a very distressed Speckle inside.

Nicu looked as bedraggled as the bird, his eyebrows joined in the middle like an arrowhead, and despite the cold outside his cheeks were chalky white.

'She doesn't like it at my house, she doesn't love me, I love her. I thinks she's sick, she misses her house!'

He rattled off the words one after the other without a pause.

'Sit down and catch your breath.'

The doorman opened the door to the cage, held Speckle beneath her wings, felt her and turned her on every side.

'I think she hasn't been eating,' he said, and the lad confirmed that she had neither eaten nor drunk, but she had left droppings, as was visible. She had left droppings all over the house, because he had let her out of the cage, and then he had struggled for a long time to put her back in.

The doorman decided to take her back and in spring to give him a pair, but only after he built a coop for them. You don't keep a dove in a cage, like a parrot or a canary, because you'll kill it like that. Seeing the state the lad was in, he decided to read to him from *Universul* and looked for a story of love with obstacles, because Nicu listened to those attentively: '*The flight of a young lady from Vaslui*: Love has no boundaries and neither the laws of the world nor of religion can stop its adventurous flight. Proof of this is what happened a few days ago in Vaslui...' As old man Cercel's voice unravelled the tangled plot, the boy's face grew calm and took on colour, and the melted snowflakes caused his cheeks to glow. Finally, when he saw that nothing could stop the two young people 'of different religions' and that the girl's relatives 'will finally be convinced that they can not easily shatter the strong chains of love,' he felt as if he were one of the bird's relatives and he no longer felt sorry for sending her back to her mate.

'What does it mean, 'different religions'?'

'It means one makes the sign of the cross from right to left and the other from left to right or not at all.'

Nicu thought that maybe it depended on whether you were left- or right-handed and asked curiously: 'If you make the sign of the cross with your left hand, are you of a different religion?'

The doorman did not answer, because to tell the truth, he did not much care about such hare-brained twaddle; he left such things to his wife.

'I know a love story, but it's not to do with religions,' said Nicu. 'I met Mr Alexandru Livezeanu, he was in a big hurry, like he always is, and he sent me on an errand, even though Sunday's my day off. He said it was urgent! Do you believe me when I say it's to do with *the strong chains of love*? You know, young man, who I mean,' he said excitedly.

The doorman didn't ask who it was, unfortunately, although Nicu would have been glad to tell him. Old man Cercel wasn't curious by nature. As a doorman for a big newspaper, he had met too many people in his life. He wasn't curious about people. That was why he reared doves.

4.

On by one, the General took the *Calendars* placed in a pile on the table, then the magazines which the hound had sniffed, firstly with interest, then without interest, before raising his muzzle to the much more entertaining fringes on the upholstery of the armchair. The borzoi looked at Algiu reproachfully: for two hours he had not budged from the armchair. The hound's almond-shaped eyes showed a shadow of puzzlement: his master was reading, motionless, without calling his name, without so much as glancing at him. The General, on the other hand, was reliving every day of the year 1893, when his poor wife had still been there beside him, on the other side of the table, working on her embroidery, a time when the hound had not even been born, and Lord's parents, each a borzoi of impressive *pedigree*, had been separated by many kilometres, one in Craiova, the other in Bucharest. Mrs Turnescu's visit, coming soon after Costache's, had reawakened his longing to work. He went back over the news items about the demolition of the Sărindar Church, although he knew them almost by heart. At the time he had already resigned the post of Prefect, but he well remembered the circumstances of the demolition and told himself yet again, that Filipescu was not to blame. In any event, it was not because of Filipescu that he was rereading the article, although somehow it was all connected. He then returned to the recent newspapers. And just as he was about to give up, he came across a news item in tiny letters that he had hitherto missed, although it was below a drawing of the courtroom in Brăila, during the trial of Miss Gorjan, the daughter of General Gorjan, whom he had known as a colonel. He now read the article and within its circumference he saw that the riddle that the young Costache had told him about was beginning to make sense: *light, Popescu, light, Holy Mother, gift...*

'Not now, Lord, be patient!'

The General made some notes in pencil, consulted other calendars of ephemera, and then summoned his adjutant, who arrived with his ears pricked up and with his usual whiff of boot polish.

'Go and find Mr Costache. If you do not find him, leave word that I invite him to come today, tomorrow, whenever he can, no matter the hour.'

Had he not known that orders are to be obeyed not questioned, the adjutant would have had a number of solid objections. But as it was, the man looked at the General with the same expression in his eyes as that of the borzoi earlier, a similarity compounded by the fact that the eyes of both were almond-shaped.

The hound at last received a pat on the head and was taken out into the yard, where he ran madly around in the blizzard. The General felt like doing the same, but he was accustomed not to reveal his feelings. He stood motionless by the door, between the two naked statues that were impervious to the cold. The wind blew through the ivy that clad the wall, but without being able to snap it. Ivy knew how to fight, and the General admired it for that reason.

5.

I have been talking to myself less and less and perhaps soon this voice that keeps me prisoner in its depths will fall silent and I will be the same as I once was. Perhaps this world will completely swallow me up and I will no longer long for the other world. Perhaps the interior and the exterior will merge. I don't know whether this world is real, but I know that my mind is made in such a way that it cannot but seem real to me. I don't know whether I'll ever be able to understand it more, but I know that until my very last moment I will want *to find out*.

After I went back with the answer that Iulia was home alone, Alexandru put me in a cab and told the cabman to take me to his house in the centre of town. He told me that from now on I was his guest, and would continue to be for as long as I did him the pleasure of wanting to be his guest, but that on the way I should stop off at the hôtel and announce that I wasn't staying there any more. He told me what to tell his servant and assured me that he would come later to see how I felt. He was terribly agitated and kept biting one gloved finger. The cabman stopped at the hôtel and told me in a reedy voice that he would wait for me. I climbed down, almost falling again, as it was almost pitch black. I entered, told them I was leaving, and a man who was like an oriental rug, soft and enveloping and convoluted, answered that he was sorry, since everything was paid for a week in advance, that they had been honoured to have a guest such as myself (but why?) and that an errand boy had left some things for me.

'Are you Mr Frascati?' I asked, but he laughed cheerlessly and gave me a very piercing look.

I went upstairs to fetch my things from the room, intending to leave as quickly as possible. I felt out of my element and I was afraid. Otto, who was upstairs, didn't want to let me leave. He planted himself in front of the door and started telling me something about some miracle-working icon. He told me that the churches were in a ferment and that the rumour had spread swiftly from one to the other: a priceless icon has vanished, *wunderschön*, and then he told me some details that I couldn't follow, especially since he was speaking now in Romanian, now in German. And especially since a rich young man, *sehr sehr reich*, Alexandru Livizeanu, was mixed up in the whole affair, and that came as a blow to me. Everybody thinks he has the icon. Is this what Alexandru suggested to me? That he is a thief?

When I went downstairs at last, the man with the oriental air stopped me and showed me something in a newspaper, *Lumea Nouă* or something like that. I sensed it wasn't good and I wanted not to look, but it wasn't possible, given his enveloping manner. The man forced me to read it, with a malicious gleam in his eye. It was my portrait, drawn quite nicely, and beneath it the title in capital letters: A MYSTERIOUS STRANGER. And below it, in smaller letters: *Whence comes Mr Dan Kretzu?* The unsigned article was about 'the stranger who seems to know more than we' and some of the things I had told Dr Marguis, luckily not very many, about 'a world with other rules and a future time, which will be rather grim for us.' But the doctor was not mentioned. He had promised me absolute discretion. Can he have betrayed me? In less than ten minutes the only people who have helped me in my new life, and whom I trusted, each seemed to have a serious flaw. The man with the oriental smile assured me that he would be honoured (again!) for me to remain there, that he was prepared to cover all the costs, accommodation and board, and that I would have a room to myself. He gave me to understand that lots of people would come, knowing that... I thanked him and left without looking back, feeling his eyes on the back of my neck.

6.

It is obvious that his head is full of his patients today too. Or full of shortages of medicines and money problems, or maybe of his assistant at the surgery, a worthless student, whom he wants to dismiss, but is not brave enough. He does not seem to hear what is said to him. He merely nods, as if he has heard and murmurs *yes, yes*, which might just as well mean *no, no* or anything else. Agatha was accustomed to it and did not take it amiss, but sometimes she did have a great need of a listening ear. When she chose between the two men, she knew that by marrying the doctor she would be the fifth wheel on the cart, the spare wheel. But it was not easy, and sometimes, like today, it was very hard. Agatha's eyelids were red with tears and, strangely, this time the doctor's ear immediately 'heard' those inflamed eyes and he became troubled. Mrs Margulis had the impression that her husband's sense of sight was far more developed than ordinary people's, because every small change in her face, in the colour of her skin, every bag under her eye, every signal her body gave he perceived with a hawk eye, from a great distance, and even if she tried to disguise such signals, she never managed to make them go unobserved. And so, upset, she placed a newspaper under his eyes – it was Saturday's – and the doctor read quickly:

Question of the Day
Protection of the Trades
We have had occasion to speak here of a society of ladies that has been formed with the purpose of providing money, clothes, books and dowries to the poor girls who study at the trade schools or even in private workshops. With all our heart we approved this undertaking...

'This was your idea, two or three years ago, or when was it?'
Agatha nodded her head, because she felt a lump in her throat.

A fact that we came across recently caused us to remember this society and to note a great lack. This lack is as follows: our trade schools have produced graduates for a number of years, trained as seamstresses and in the art of making artificial flowers and other trades. What have these professionally trained girls done, what do they do? As chance would have it, we came across one.

With the small capital she received on finishing the school, she opened a modest workshop with another girl. The girls worked industriously, they lived spartanly, and they sought with all their powers to establish a clientele, working hard, tastefully and cheaply. However, for two years they struggled with all their might; the result of these efforts was the closure of the workshop. They could no longer pay the rent. One of them, the one whom we met, tried to work at home: a fresh struggle, without success, since she cannot find enough work to make a living. At the moment she is seeking an occupation, whatever it might be, merely to survive.

This, in short, is the story of a graduate of our trade schools – and it is more or less the same story for all these girls. The ladies from the charitable society did not think of this. We have sought to uncover the causes of this failure.

'And what are the causes?' asked the doctor, who had read the article aloud, tonelessly, but had not had the patience to read to the end.

'At least on that point they are not unjust. They say that the workshop was closed by the big shops on Victory Avenue and that the public is to blame, because people prefer to buy more expensive goods, as long as they are foreign, rather than buy from our girls.'

'And how are you to blame?'

Agatha now began to weep. After her tears abated, she told him in her most woe-begone voice that it was true, that the girls, Ana and Lenuţa, are desperate and that she had tried to help them. But the journalist, who does not even sign his name –'as usual,' interjected the doctor – presented the whole affair as if it were the rule, which it was not. Many of the girls they helped had succeeded, some had got married, but the newspaper presented her endeavours as if it were a game, a charade... But their society genuinely helped. Even if it was not mentioned by name, everybody knew...

The doctor stopped her.

'In this world there are sufferings you cannot even imagine, Agatha. Not a day passes but I see them. There are children who fall ill and die under their parents' very eyes – we two know that – and some, aged before their time because of illness, seeking to help their parents, to make things easier for them, I have seen with my own eyes countless examples of agony -I will not even tell you what the typhus epidemic was like, but even a simple outbreak of influenza, although they have discovered the bacillus, there are still sufferers, who die young and ruddy-cheeked, as if they were healthy, eager for love, because tuberculosis is a kind of aphrodisiac, and the physician's struggle against the disease is hopeless. Could I tell you about syphilis, which eats away the body, without traumatizing you for the rest of your life? Physicians grope like blind men, helping here, damaging there. Do you know that up until twenty or thirty years ago, that is, during our parents' lifetime, medicine damaged more than it helped? It was a series of experiments on the poor patient, kept in a hospital, which more often than not left him in a worse condition than when he had entered. Today, even the dentist, our friend Steinhardt, for example, asks you: 'With or without pain?' But in the past, every operation meant unendurable pain. Do you remember Dr Biondi from the Brâncoveanu Hospital, the one who operated with Glück, when we were young?'

Agatha nodded, in silence.

'I have not told you the truth about him until now. He operated on five patients with pulmonary tuberculosis. He had previously done a number of pulmonary resections on dogs and the results had at least been encouraging. But the five patients died. All five! And then, in despair, Dr Biondi committed suicide. People sometimes died of the pain; their hearts stopped. And you...'

And I, I complain about a newspaper article that does not even name me directly. I concern myself with girls who are healthy and who will marry. Ana is going to marry the very journalist who has written about her as if by accident. And I concern myself with such things, while you struggle against death, I know. But what if I need comfort and solace, even only once, even only for a trifle? And what if today, I care more about my girls and my petty troubles than about all the world's misfortunes? And what if today I cannot suffer for the whole of mankind and I would like at least one member of mankind to suffer for me? The blood that had risen to Agatha's cheeks showed that she was angrier with her husband than with the newspaperman. But she said nothing, and Dr Margulis postponed his consolation, because he had to visit a patient. Unfortunately, as is well known, illness does not take days off.

TIME PASSES

1.

The year has whizzed past me like an arrow. And although there are only two days left of it, what did I do today? I played and played the piano; I took each score in turn. Then I played without sheet music, from memory. I played worse than ever before, wretchedly and carelessly. As for the rest, I have begun to fill my inner staves with notes in the key of Alexandru. I do believe they are concertos in Alexandru major and I would repeat them over and over again, no matter how many wrong notes I might play. I suppose it is as hard not to play wrong notes when the music is inside you as when it is outside you. But if the Great Composer has made mistakes in the concerto, what then? I still have to wait before I will know for sure whether I am also playing on the inside. I know what I mean and I will not go into explanations here. Last night, when we were all in the salon, and Mama and Papa seemed upset, and Jacques cheered them up by reading to them from a book of jokes – Jacques reads very nicely, even jokes – Safta appeared and made a sign to me with her head, pointing at the door, without a trace of respect. Since Saturday she has been taking more and more liberties, *blackmail*, as my friends from *Vanity Fair* would put it. Jacques alone noticed her impertinent gesture, diverting our parents' attention with a joke he pretended not to understand, and Papa gravely began explaining to him what was funny.

What can I say but that my heart stopped when I saw the servant's sign? I thought that it was Alexandru and I was lost. No, it was not he, but Nicu. I asked him why he did not enter. He told me that he was very busy and that he had business with me. I felt his little hand, colder than mine, opening my palm and in my palm I felt something hard and yet tickly. It was a box covered in velvet and tied with a little bow, but I did not open it, lest somebody see me. I took it to my room and hid it inside a clock: this is my hiding place. In the salon I was no longer able to pay attention to anything, although Mama and Papa each told me about their ancestors and about Greece, which I have never visited and probably we shall not go there even this summer, because we do not have the money and Papa does not have the time. And then Jacques and I withdrew. I quickly told him about the box and he was dying of curiosity about what was inside: 'I think it is something imporrtant, I sense it, I even suspect what it might be.'

We went to my room, he sat on the couch – and *that* memory pierced the very heart of my soul, like a bullet – and I went to the clock. I unlocked the door and took out the velvet box. I gave it to Jacques to open, to let him have the pleasure. And his round eyes were like the oily coffee beans purveyed by our Armenian, Levon Harutunian. In his language Levon means the same as Leon, Papa's name: they are both lions.

'There is a note, folded in four. Oh, and beneath the note there is a ring. Shall I read it?'

I sat down, overcome by a kind of faintness, and my little brother read: "You and your family are invited to our New Year's party. We must...' underlined '...begin the year together. Al. L."

'Is that all?'

'That is all.'

I felt like crying, and then Jacques added: 'For us men it means more than for you girrls.'

And he handed me the box, the note and the ring. I tried on the ring. It is mounted with a small ruby surrounded by a few diamonds, and it is indeed very beautiful, but it is too big for me. A pity, I will not be able to wear it. I was filled with sadness.

*

This morning, we resumed our usual routine, as if everything were the same, except that everything is different. Victory Avenue was different, the empty space left by Sărindar Church was different, the people were different, the waters of the Dâmbovița were different, slower, and Jacques' seagulls were flying in a different direction. But I thought: perhaps all these things are the same, perhaps the seagulls are flying the same as usual, the Dâmbovița is flowing as fast as usual, the people were the same, the empty place where Sărindar stood was the same, Victory Avenue was the same, but I am different. And why, pray tell, should I be different? Perhaps it is because the year has almost passed and the last grains of sand in the hourglass are now rushing down. Perhaps the waters of my rivers are approaching a cataract. Perhaps I am adding a circle to the trunk of life, like a tree, and I am growing (although I have not grown since the age of seventeen!); and I am seeing the world from a different perspective. I feel that time has begun to flow more swiftly: yesterday before I knew it night had fallen, and today likewise. Immediately after lunch – which was Spartan, since Papa takes care that we should not overeat at this time of year, when all the people stuff themselves; once he told us how to prepare a meal in accordance with the digestion time of each food and to combine foods with a low digestion time with sauces and broths, so that we would not tire our delicate stomachs and tender livers. Immediately after lunch, rather than resting, I went into town with Nelu, who was pale after his illness and could barely hold onto the reins. As for myself, I feel I cannot sit still! I went to *Universul* to pick up another box of *Luminous Fountains*, one with all the necessary parts, so that Jacques will at least be able to enjoy them at New Year. As I was going in, Mr Crețu was coming out, he greeted me, but without taking his hat off, and then he seemed to remember and quickly took it off, which made me laugh. He is very nice. I care for him, as for a muddleheaded brother. We talked and he mentioned that he was the guest of Alexandru, not in the big house, or rather the Livezeanu palace, but in a smaller residence of his in the centre of town. And so I have discovered some news. I half rejoiced, because it means he has a heart, and I was half aggrieved, because I know what such residences are used for. At least now it is occupied by a man!

2.

Nicu was tired and still had a long way to go in the pitch darkness. He sensed rather than saw the Muzzle behind him. He heard his panting. He broke into a run, but it was as if he had iron balls shackled to his ankles, like the ones old man Cercel had told him convicts wear. He thought that he would be able to escape only if he could rise above the earth and so he flapped his arms, seeing himself as if from the outside as he rose little by little, like a duck. At first, something was dragging him down, then he succeeded, he was now a metre above the Muzzle, then higher and higher, he escaped, it was now light, below him were houses, lots of little houses, he could see roofs and chimneys and church spires, he took care not to bump into them; and fields and forests, he could see the green tree-tops softly rustling, and then it was as if he were being pulled downward again, but he strained, he dug in his heels, and he kept himself aloft and nothing bad could touch him there. He heard a cock crowing, closer and closer, louder and louder. Oh, Lord, what joy, what joy, and what pain, what pain!

'You were flying, you flew by night again!'

It was dark, winter, he was below, on earth, but in his dream it was summer and he was up in the sky. But what if the world in the dream were real and the world, now that he was awake was the dream? He closed his eyes, trying to prolong the flight, but he did not succeed. No, unfortunately, he knew full well that flying was the dream and his bed was the reality. That he could stay as long as he liked in bed, but that the length of the dream did not depend on his will. His mother was already busy in the kitchen, which meant that she felt well. And he felt well now, for he was warm under the quilt, curled up, and he was wonderfully happy after flying, as if he had really been flying, he was happy that he had no cares that day, that his mother was well, that Alexandru's little parcel had been delivered safely to Iulia, that they had not asked him questions, and above all, that the lottery was so near: there was only one day between him and the result. His arms and hands and fingertips and legs and toes and head and hair and ears and nose and mouth, and heart which today was nicely coloured, as on the doctor's chart. All were waiting, not only for the next day, not only for the New Year and the wish you are allowed to make, because it will be fulfilled, but above all for the future, when he and Jacques would be grown up and stroll each with a charming young lady on his arm, who smelled of lavender and wore a colourful dress that rustled and glinted in the light. In the winter the young ladies would skate holding hands with them on Cişmigiu Lake. Strangely, he could also see Jacques skating next to a young lady. He was impatient, he could hardly wait to grow up and he felt that he was destined for great things, that he would be an important man, like Mr Dan Creţu or Mr Cazzavillan.

'Mama?'

She had come up to his bed on tiptoe and seeing that the boy was awake, she lit the gas lamp, kissed his hair and told him to come to the table.

'It's cold in here, there are ice crystals on the windowpane. Dress up warm, mammy's little chick.'

Nicu wondered which was his real mother, the one now or the one of a few days ago, with the cracked voice and insane eyes, the one who couldn't recognize him? Who was it who took his mother's place and tortured her and why did she torture and frighten him too? He hugged his real mother as tightly as he could, so that she wouldn't go outside and run down a mole hole where he wouldn't be able to reach her.

*

When he came home, after work, which had been tiring – five errands to addresses that were quite far away from each other – but which had also provided a few tips to match, his mother was doing the laundry, scrubbing the clothes on a washboard that tickled your palms if you stroked it, but which gave you calluses if you scrubbed properly. The shirts and handkerchiefs were boiling in a cauldron with starch. In the meantime, they ate and then Nicu offered to hang the clothes on the line. He liked the way the soft, steaming clothes stiffened in the frost and stuck together, and when you separated them, they creaked like a rusty door hinge. He was too restless to stay at home and he told his mother that he was going to visit Jacques, to take him the mammoths he had promised him. He showed her the drawing in *Universul Ilustrat*, and she laughed at their saw-tooth backs and their tails as long as a day of fasting. Her laugh reminded him of another laugh, her mother's, as if his grandmother was still there in his mother's laugh, the same as people who are far away can be inside the funnel of a telephone. He was little then, very little, and they were eating stony cherries together. His grandmother tore them in two for him so that he could chew them more easily. He took one and to his amazement he discovered that something nice was wriggling inside, like the horns of a snail. He showed his grandmother and she said: 'Ugh!' and when he started to laugh, they did the same thing with each cherry: when the little worm appeared, she would say: 'Ugh!' and they both laughed till their bellies ached. The cherries without worms weren't funny, they set them aside; only the ones in which there was movement interested them. It was one of the happiest days he remembered, and ever since Nicu had reckoned that only when he laughed was it a good day. And today was a good day. His grandmother had told him that when she died she wanted to turn into a sparrow, that he should be very careful with sparrows, because maybe it would be her, hopping around among them, although it was hard to imagine her hopping, she had had a stiff back and found it difficult to move around the house. It was very hard to recognize her, since all sparrows looked alike, and so far none had seemed to take special delight in meeting him. He was sure that his grandmother would have drawn his attention by signalling him with her wings. On the way to Strada Fântânei, Nicu thought to hear a voice in his head, which said to him: it will be well! it will be well! it will be well! He didn't know whose voice it was, for he could not believe the voice was his.

Jacques was happy too: Dr Rizea had given him a new flute as a present, a real marvel. He played Nicu Handel's minuet, tee-tum-tum, tee-tum-tum, and then, unexpectedly, he stopped in the middle of a phrase and said: 'You are invited to come with me, I mean with us, to Alexandrrru Livizeanu's New Year parrty. Mr Dan Crreṭu will be coming too. Is that not wonderrful? Papa received an invitation for the whole family and I asked that you come too, Iulia said that she would give you my suit for special occasions from two years ago, I have worrn it only twice, it is brrand new.'

He added in a whisper that Iulia and Alexandrru were 'in love,' and Nicu told him, putting on an uninterested air, that he had known that for a long time. Dr Margulis recommended that when you are ill you should always think about getting better and to keep saying to yourself: I'm getting better, getting better, getting better! Even when you're not ill, it's useful to say to yourself: it will be well, it will be well, it will be well! At least you get to wear a new suit at the end of a worn out year.

216

3.

'Will it be well?'

Pavel Mirto's eyes glittered ironically behind his round glasses, while Procopiu, from the other office, inspected his moustache, as was his habit, as if he were afraid it might disappear.

'Yes, I believe that Romania is like an orchestra, except that it has yet to play in a concert. It is still rehearsing. One of the violinists keeps playing wrong notes, the soloist enters in the wrong place, the wind section plays out of time and the conductor loses his temper, stops the music, scolds them all, everything is fragmentary and has to keep starting all over again, but at the concert, the melody will come together flawlessly and Europe's applause...'

'And when will this concert be, Mr Procopiu?' asked Pavel, his whispery voice laden with a sarcasm that was inappropriate given he was the younger of the two.

'Before you get married,' replied Procopiu, with slight irritation, at which point Peppin came in without knocking.

'Who, my Păvăluca? Are you getting married, laddie?' he said in a voice that filled the office with good humour and scattered tension between the other two men. 'I shall be first, let it be well understood. It is in order of birth, so that there won't be a mad rush. The older brother takes priority.'

'No,' said Pavel drily, without raising his voice, 'we were talking about the future of Romania, which Mr Procopiu was comparing with an orchestra endlessly rehearsing.'

'Ah, no, to me it seems exactly like playing billiards at Fialkowski's. You strike a ball in order to set another in motion, every move has a hidden aim, a zigzag of consequences, and everything moves closer and closer, as part of a cosmic mechanism. Maybe that was how God set the worlds in motion, with a cue. In the end, even if we cannot see it yet, we will win our historic billiard game.'

'No,' said Pavel, just as drily, 'it sooner resembles a swarm of locusts.'

'A flock of locusts,' Procopiu corrected him.

'A cloud of locusts,' proposed Peppin, given his experience as a translator.

'Never mind that, swarm, cloud, whatever! Until recently I didn't even know that locusts do not fly, but only jump, they make huge jumps... And they let themselves be carried away on the wind like swift flying ships, they make no effort, put up no resistance, they harness, as I say, all the services nature provides free of charge.'

'What do you mean?' asked Neculai Procopiu rather threateningly, but at the same time interested in the engineering side of the problem. 'That we destroy everything like locusts?'

'Oh, no, not at all, I have not made myself understood! On the contrary, I meant that the tempests blow over us and that we have no way of resisting them, our powers of resistance cannot compare with the power of history, and the same goes for personal life. Whenever the history of the world turns a page, we make a jump, without being able to control it, and our only chance is to let it carry us away, while harnessing the steam of events to the greatest possible extent, lest we be left behind on the ground. Let us be in step with the speed of time, or rather the times. Let us adjust ourselves, rather than put up resistance.'

'Ah, yes, interesting,' admitted the editor-in-chief, now calmer, 'I can subscribe to that, especially if the times are favourable. But now time presses, rather than the times: we need to get down to the New Year issue. What do we have?'

They talked about the case of the missing icon, but they did not have any details. Procopiu offered to investigate the matter first thing in the morning, and if he could find nothing attractive, they would make a plain announcement. There was no further news about the Rareş Ochiu-Zănoagă case and the holidays had passed quietly. There was nothing they could use.

'Have you communicated the results of the lottery?' asked Peppin, calmly, since neither he nor Pavel had bought tickets.

'Yes, they are appearing tomorrow. I did not win, but what can I say? I was hardly expecting to. Not many people bought tickets, because the weather was bad. The draw was not held in Cişmigiu, as planned, but at the Hôtel Boulevard. The issue will be rather flimsy,' fretted the editor-in-chief, at which Pavel shrugged one shoulder and Peppin both.

They paid great attention to the clichés brought in by Marwan for 'Our Illustration' – in the end they had come to an agreement on the price – they were indeed very good, it did not even matter what you might write next to them, and so if nothing came up by tomorrow afternoon, with the photograph and the satirical poems by Marion (their colleague Dumitru-Ion Marinescu) the issue could be saved. Pavel took off his spectacles (for myopia) and looked closely at the images. One was of Victory Avenue viewed from above, from the first floor of the Theatre, and had been taken in the snow; you could pick out the individual snowflakes, and there were people and carriages made small by the perspective. The other had been taken in fair weather, next to the offices of *L'Indépendance Roumaine*, which the staff of *Universul* envied for its technical endowments: all the machinery had been brought from abroad and the newspaper looked like *Le Figaro*.

'Is that not Mr Costache Boerescu?' asked Peppin and began to laugh.

'It is indeed. Marwan pointed him out to me, when he brought it in.'

'He will have a surprise,' even Pavel laughed softly.

'And then some!'

4.

Two of the seagulls that usually wheeled above the Dâmboviţa had today come as far as the window of Costache Boerescu's office at the Prefecture of Police. They were enormous and floated together, their movements in incredible synchrony, as if somebody were simultaneously pulling unseen strings. Costache gazed at them sadly: probably he would never be in such soothing harmony with anybody. About the couples around him he generally knew more than he would have wished. As a rule, he liked one of the two more than the others, but as Peppin Mirto said, you have to take married couples as a single package; there is no other choice. There were some he sincerely envied, because they flapped their wings and changed direction at exactly the same moment as they flew, and such a pair was Agatha and Leon Margulis. Would he have been able to fly in harmony with her? What would have become of her life if she had chosen him? Would she have been happier? And what would have become of his life if Iulia...

'The priest from the Icoanei Church is here,' announced the sergeant at the door.

Costache stood up to greet him.

The previous day, when, truth to tell, few people ventured out in the blizzard to go to church, Epiharia, who knew all the parishioners by name or at least by sight, had been surprised to see a distinguished man holding a cane with a silver knob in the form of a beak, a man who had never been here – of this she was sure! – who had never hung his hat on the peg above the seat at the end of the row and peacefully listened to the service for the Sunday following the Feast of the Nativity. His mind did not seem to be on things holy, however, he kept looking at the walls, stroking the wooden arm of the chair, although the priest, on seeing him, had all of a sudden become livelier and spoke of the Flight to Egypt so beautifully that he himself might have been present when the angel told Joseph to take the young child and his mother and flee: 'And weeping and great mourning, and Rachel weeping for her children, and would not be comforted, because they are not.' Epiharia wiped the tears from her eyes and little did she suspect, seeing the newcomer look at her from time to time, that the reason for his being there was her insignificant person. She left the church last, as usual. Before her, a man and his daughter made the sign of the cross both at the same time, he a broad cross with his broad hand, she a little cross with her little hand, and Epiharia gazed at them with love. But the newcomer was standing by the door. He greeted her and said he wished to speak with her. Luckily, the priest came up to them, with an air of gaiety. It was a good job that he did, because she was flustered and her face had turned scarlet, to the very dimple in her chin. They fell to talking and with mention of the name Dan Crețu, the man with whom she had been alone in the church not long ago, it turned out that the newcomer was the Chief of Public Security. He discovered something that interested him regarding the missing icon. The priest offered to continue the discussion the next day, because now he had to go home to his wife, who was ill.

'Take a seat here, by the fire,' said Costache, inviting the priest to sit in his favourite armchair, the one in which Iulia had sat not long ago. 'May I offer you a cup of tea? I am indeed very curious as to what else you can tell me about the icon, which, if I understand rightly, has put the whole Church in an uproar. What I do not understand is how an icon could disappear without the Police immediately being informed.'

The priest was glad to sit down by the fire. Like all people forced to stand motionless for long periods, he had problems with his back. Speaking quickly and copiously, in a manner you would not have expected from a pious man, but using choice words, as you would have expected, the priest explained to him a number of matters. His host made a note of them on a sheet of paper. In short:

1. *The miracle-working icon from the Sărindar Church. Distinguishing signs: diamonds on the shoulders. After demolition of the church (1893) it was taken by the future (now former) Metropolitan Ghenadie.*

2. *After the scandal broke out the Metropolitan was taken from his house by force, the icon was – apparently – in a safe. But it might equally have been given to somebody else.*

3. *The Metropolitan, now in reclusion at Căldărușani Monastery, accuses those responsible for his arrest of stealing the safe with the icon, but they deny it and accuse him.*

4. *Because of its large diamonds, the icon is of inestimable value. The newspapers and female public were on the side of the Metropolitan, reckoning him to be innocent, although he had been condemned by the Synod.*

'And what does Your Holiness say?' said Costache, trying to find the right form of address. 'Did the Metropolitan steal?'

'Let us not sin in our choice of words, maligning a servant of the Church,' said the priest sternly. And then, in a whisper, looking around him, lest he be overheard: 'I am wholly on the side of His Holiness the Metropolitan, but not even in thought can I cast doubt on a decision of the Synod. The Unclean One has a hand in it all. Sooner it was one of your men, a policeman, who, taking advantage of the confusion a year ago, you remember how sudden it all was, stole the safe, icon and all. I doubt that he is still in the country.'

'The Unclean One... We will find him!'

5.

The twins were eating soft-boiled eggs and their mouths were smeared with yolk.

'When is New Year? I want to see it more quickly!' said Ştefan, with whom his sister agreed, as always, nodding her head vigorously, with her mouth full.

'Call for it and it will come!'

They loved Uncle Alexandru more than Uncle Mişu, because he always encouraged them, rather than him trying to calm them down. Ştefan therefore believed himself entitled to shout at the top of his lungs: 'Year, year, come more quickly!'

His mother gave a start and scolded him, but then seeing her son's puzzled little face, she asked somewhat more gently: 'Who is being naughty?'

'Anica,' the boy promptly answered.

'And what is your name?'

'Anica,' repeated the boy.

Indeed, the way he looked, with his curls and white cheeks, he might very well have passed for his sister. Marioara sent them away with their nurse, since anyway they had finished eating, and she wanted to talk about the preparations for the New Year party.

The three siblings had not sat at breakfast alone together since they were children, when their parents went off on long voyages abroad and left them in the care of their governess. It was obvious that blood was thicker than water, because Mişu and Alexandru and Marioara were cheerful, although they had no great reason to be. Mişu complained that he had only another four days at home and that he had not done any studying during the holidays, apart from some practical work on Mr Dan Creţu's shoulder, for which his fall on the ice had been welcome. Marioara wondered in a slightly theatrical voice, although what she said came from the heart, whether she would ever find a man who would accept her with three children, two of whom, the twins, were very naughty and 'put every suitor to flight'. And Alexandru told them that he was worried and in love.

'No big news there,' said Marioara and Mişu almost in unison.

The sister poured the coffee in the Limoges service, whose coffee pot, sugar bowl and cups had their handles twisted towards each other, as if they were chatting together. The coffee pot and sugar bowl even looked as if they were in an *aparté*, gossiping about some cup, probably.

'With whom?' asked Marioara, without any great curiosity.

She was tired and always befriended the ladies that Alexandru introduced to her, and subsequently, when he left them, she consoled them or avoided them. Better she did not know.

Rather than answering the question, Alexandru frowned and said: 'This time is it different?'

'No big news there,' laughed his elder siblings.

'Now it is *I* whom am afraid. I think that I have lost her already. Iulia Margulis.'

Marioara knit her brows, the name sounded familiar, but not in a good way, and then she remembered a small and ordinary looking creature, dressed rather inexpensively, who had attended a party thrown by Mişu. Indeed, her brother had paid her great attention, which had surprised her; at parties he usually paid attention to the most dazzling and elegant lady.

'Yes, I remember her, she is a –' Marioara groped for the right word '– she is a delicate creature.'

Alexandru looked at the floor and, in surprise, his sister saw him blush.

'It is very hard to talk to people about somebody you care for greatly,' he said. 'To me it is very hard because you expect people to start making observations. One says she is thus, another says she is the opposite, one says she is intelligent, another says she is stupid, that she has curly hair, that she is gauche or that she speaks through her nose, and slowly but surely people extinguish her light. Once, Iancu, who as you know is an expert in rather scabrous matters, in order to 'rescue' me from a married woman, without whom life seemed to me to have no zest, described her as follows, between drinks and between two... two pigs like us, he described her piece by piece: her lips are like a trout's, her nose has a hump, her eyes are like pondweed, her oval face is too small and her circular rump too large, her...'

'I did not teach you to speak like that,' interrupted Mişu, stiffly, and Marioara added: 'And nor is it any of our concern! Shame on you and your mind! Iancu is an ass, as you say. Although he does have charm,' she could not help but add.

'I said he was a pig. But he did me a great service in rescuing me from her! I would not care for anybody to do me such a service in regard to Iulia. If I could, I would take her away from the world and keep her in a safe place, where nobody could find her.'

'Have you ever asked her if she wants that? In any event, kidnappings are no longer the mode. You were born too late.'

'I know.'

TIME STANDS STILL

1.

I had not been expecting this, not in the middle of winter. There was a huge mosquito in the room, the father of all mosquitos – I do believe – the forerunner, the founder of the nation. In the past I would have killed it without stopping to think about it, but now – it is obvious I have aged a year – I left it in peace. Anyway, it looks tired, like a traveller who wishes only to lay his head on a clean pillow and rest his legs. Maybe it is making a New Year voyage. I will provide it with all the comfort and ease it desires. It is evening, it is pleasant here in my room, it smells of nutmeg and cinnamon from the cakes on the table, and everything is colourful, as I wanted it to be: the wallpaper and curtains are soft yellow, with a hint of russet, the flowery carpet is also yellow, between the green garlands, the armchair and couch are olive green, and only the bedspread does not match, I shall have to change it, when I have the money. It is as if there were no *outside*, but only an *inside*.

Today everything was turned upside down by a piece of news that fell like a thunderbolt: poor Safta read in *Universul* (she collects them after we read them and uses them for wiping the windowpanes) that one of her brothers-in-law – her family is from Boheni, in Oltenia – was buried alive, under some rocks. I would ban news like that, if I had the power! And everything was described in gory detail, how it happened, how the unfortunate man went with a pick to the quarry, to fetch materials to build a school in Cetatea. I refuse to write any more. The family's grief is also described at length. What must Safta have felt when she read it! Of course, Papa straight away gave her money for the journey, because tomorrow, on New Year's Eve, she must go there, and he gave her a sedative. She was in a dreadful state, choking on her tears, I thought she would die. She fainted twice. Nobody should ever have to go through such an ordeal! Even when you hear about such things happening to a complete stranger, you feel the blow. Why should such suffering exist in the world? It makes my head reel when

I try to understand it, and today I even had to lie down, I felt unwell. The ironic thing is that a few days ago, in *Universul*, I read an article with almost the same title, but a comical one: *Buried in Dollars*. It was about some functionaries at a mint in Philadelphia, who, they said in the paper, 'almost came a cropper.' They had been sent to check a money warehouse, to see whether it still held two million dollars. I cannot even imagine so much money; it is like an oriental fairy tale. And when they lifted up the sacks, the cloth split and 'it began raining dollars' on the functionaries' feet. In a short while, said the newspaper, they were buried up to the waist in silver coins. The fire brigade arrived and saved them from certain death. And the moral: 'money is very nice,' but not if you drown in it! I liked that story very much. Lovers of money should read it. Papa said the love of money, *argyrophilia*, is a disease and gave the former Metropolitan Ghenadie as an example. Papa certainly does not have the disease, but rather the opposite one. What might one call it? *Argyrophobia* – a fear of money? And by the way, I read the winning lottery numbers in the newspaper: my No. 12 came up, and Vasilica's No. 21, and so neither of us won. But it seems of no importance now.

Last night, for the first time, I forgot to go to Jacques' room to say good night, as I have been doing ever since he was born, when I was ten years old: I used to go barefoot to his cot and Papa would not allow me to touch him. I am afraid I am becoming selfish: this is a defect that I did not have before.

Perhaps also because of Safta, for whom my heart breaks, perhaps also because I have dark rings under the eyes of my soul, I have decided not to go anywhere on New Year's Eve. I feel sorry only for Jacques; I know only that he would be glad if I came too. Why should I not spend New Year's Eve asleep? I value sleep more and more, and I feel sleepy most of the time. Nevertheless, despite everything I have written above, hidden away in my soul is a feeling of wellness. Everything seems very curious to me, most of all the fact that I am alive!

2.

It is obvious that there is a God of journalists, even when they imagine the Creator as a mechanical engineer in white overalls, constantly sabotaged by a devil in black overalls, with a hole in the seat. And the God of journalists made Mr Neculai Procopiu productively fill his morning reading the *Universul* collection from May 1896. It was the collection that happened to be the handiest. Mrs Procopiu wanted to take advantage of this rare occasion when her husband did not leave the conjugal domicile early in the morning, and she embraced his shoulders, chair back and all, full of the tenderness of an intimate winter morning, in a warm house, with wood crackling softly in the stove and the scent of coffee wafting through the room. But her husband was in a mood that did not allow for dreaming. He gently released himself from her embrace, kissing the back of her hand, and plunged into rereading the news about Metropolitan Ghenadie. His wife had of course taken the Metropolitan's side when he was deposed, but she had a heart in her head, not only in her chest. Betimes, her thinking was affected by that heart in her head. As for him, he was mistrustful by nature and did not allow details to lead him astray. The articles had been written by two editors, who no longer worked for the paper. He did not know where to get hold of them now at short notice, probably they were away for the holidays, and time pressed hard. He reviewed the facts.

17 MAY: The members of the Holy Synod gathered, having been invited to do so by the Ministry of Religions. Archbishop Atanasie of Craiova read the Act of Accusation for the sins of *argyrophilia*, *hierosilia*, and simony. From the judges came a murmur of horror, amid the sound of their rustling beards and cassocks as they shifted in their seats. For the benefit of the newspaper's readers, Procopiu added in parenthesis explanations of the words: excessive love of money, sacrilege, and traffic in holy objects, punishable with defrocking and excommunication. It was unanimously decided that he be brought to trial. 'A locum tenens was hereby appointed and a commission of three apostolic nuncios who would convey to him the three canonical invitations.' The newspapers played a decisive part in the decision, through 'the grave accusations levelled at H. H. Ghenadie.'

18 MAY: The decree suspending him was published. On the same day, *Dreptatea* gave the signal for a campaign 'of the greatest violence' against the Government and in support of the Metropolitan. All the opposition newspapers followed suit.

19 May: In the Dacia Auditorium, N. Fleva, the founder of *Dreptatea*, and his friend, Nicu Filipescu, organized the first meeting in support of the Metropolitan. Others, more violent, were to follow. N. Fleva was also the Metropolitan's lawyer.

20 May: H. H. Metropolitan Primate Ghenadie Petrescu presented himself before the Holy Synod (after receiving the three canonical invitations), accompanied by lawyers N. Fleva and C. Dissescu, who were, however, not allowed into the chamber on the grounds that their presence would have been contrary to the Canons, as the judgement of the Synod was 'a private confession more than a public trial.' The Metropolitan rejected the accusations and handed the Synod a written contestation, before withdrawing. The Synod began its deliberations, 'rejected the defence as unfounded,' and sentenced the Metropolitan to 'loss of the gift of the priesthood' and 'defrocked him from the rank of Metropolitan,' demoting him to the rank of an ordinary monk at the Căldărușani Monastery.

24 May: Procopiu underlined the day, reckoning that here lay the key to events. Like in a childhood game, he sensed he was getting closer to the hidden object and that they were shouting from the side: 'Warmer! Warmer!' He sipped his coffee (which was getting colder, colder) and once more read the news from the day of Ghenadie's arrest, at the Palace of the Metropolia at seven in the evening. Two bishops from the Synod were present, namely Silvestru and Gherasim Timuș, along with Mr Sărățeanu, who was General Prosecutor of the Court of Appeal; Lilovici, the Chief Prosecutor of Ilfov Tribunal; Paul Stătescu, the Prefect of Police before Caton Lecca; Ștefan Sihleanu, the Secretary General from the Ministry of Religions; Dragomir Dumitrescu, a director from the Ministry; and 'agents of the forces of public order.' The Metropolitan refused to receive them, saying he was ill. They burst in, read the sentence to him, and invited him to depart *immediately* for Căldărușani Monastery. The Metropolitan contested the 'legality of the Synod's sentence,' in which he was supported by the venerable former Prime Minister Lascăr Catargiu and by Nicu Filipescu. The two had entered, thrusting aside with their canes the policemen at the gate. But 'the prosecutors resorted to the force allowed them by law, gave the order to empty the buildings and then forced the former Metropolitan to leave. They put him inside a carriage, took him from the courtyard of the Metropolia by the gate facing Filaret, and then from Bucharest by the Șerban-Vodă barrier, where the Prefect of the Capital's Police

formally handed him over to Mr Dobrescu, the Prefect of Ilfov, who took him to Căldăruşani, where he arrived without disturbance at one o'clock in the morning.' In the meantime, Fleva had gathered some protesters, but they arrived too late.

After the opposition newspapers and the female public shrieked in a chorus against the brutality of this deposition, and based on this, had wholly taken the Metropolitan's side, despite the Synod's sentence; and after the ministers' wives had dared to contradict their husbands in public, after Fleva and Filipescu organized demonstrations at which the opposing sides "came to fierce blows, with many being struck by canes and chairs, and with windows being broken," before the "combatants were separated by the police," monk Ghenadie from Căldăruşani was seen once more, in a good mood, smiling or perhaps laughing into his beard. A few days later, as if symbolically, Baronzi, the author of the novel *The Mysteries of Bucharest*, died.

Procopiu thought he was dreaming: he had found the answer in that very passage! He underlined it in red pencil: "the prosecutors gave the order to empty the buildings." The buildings (*casele*) or the safes (*cassele*)? He was annoyed that he had not asked the question earlier. His editors were very careless; a good job they had left. No, it could only mean the safes (*cassele*), otherwise they would have said 'the rooms' or 'the Palace of the Metropolia,' not 'the buildings' (*casele*). He called his wife and told her his reasoning. The icon, which the Metropolitan probably kept in a safe, had been taken by one of the prosecutor's men on the evening of the deposition. Therefore matters went up to the highest level. It would make an eminent front-page article! But his wife was unimpressed by his conclusion and said: 'How do you know it did not vanish before that? If the Metropolitan was accused of simony, which I can hardly credit –' she hastened to add '– then perhaps it was the sale of the icon that was behind it all.'

Now she did not have a heart in her head and made a cool judgement, whereas he was aflame. Perhaps it was because she had placed on ice the lemon cream she had made for the last day of the year.

The servant arrived with an invitation.

'Look at this,' said his wife, 'we are invited, together with your friends, the Mirto brothers, to the Livizeanu house on New Year's Eve! Isn't it rather short notice?'

This time old man Cercel's belly woke up before him. The doorman immediately awoke from his light sleep, wondering what it was he could hear, and then, when he realized *it* had woken him and was making a din, the same as when his daughters were babes in arms and bawled for their mother's milk, he was reassured and at the same time not reassured one bit. He promised himself yet again that he would go to Dr Margulis, of whose verdict he was nonetheless afraid. Anything except the surgeon's knife! In any event, he would go after the New Year. Now wasn't the right moment. And then he turned his mind to something more pleasant and said to himself: 'Today we find out the lottery draw numbers! What will we do if we win?'

Ever since she started hearing her husband speaking sweet and soothing words, which she genuinely imagined were addressed to her, his wife had softened and was no longer as quarrelsome as before. She answered in her voice from her youth that she would like to have a carriage with handsome horses, with elegant bridles, like the upper crust, and at least one or two servants to help her around the house, because she ached all over and could no longer do all the work herself: washing, ironing, dusting, tending the vegetable patch, turning the manure over, checking to see whether the hens had laid, cooking, laying the table, making everything spick and span, and then just when you think you've finished, starting all over again as if... Old man Cercel interrupted her: 'I'd like to extend the coop, buy some more pigeons and give Nicu some money to get married or send him to a big school, because he chipped in for a third of our ticket.'

'Don't count your chickens before they're hatched. Go to work, and if you win, then you won't have to stay there, because we won't need you to, but come home quick and tell me the news.'

Old man Cercel felt a stabbing pain inside and gripped his belly with both hands, doubling up with a gasp as if he were drowning.

'Wife!'

'She's not at home,' she quipped, because her thoughts of horses and servants had put her in a good mood.

'I'm not going to work today, I'm going to the doctor's,' he said in a faint voice. 'I think there's something wrong with my belly.'

The woman took fright. Looking in the wardrobe, where all the things were arranged as neatly as soldiers on parade, she gave him his best underclothes. Then she took out his Sunday best and helped him to get dressed. The doorman left, clutching his belly and groaning.

*

'Is it bad, doctor? Will I have to go under the knife?'

Old man Cercel was lying on the oilcloth-covered bed in Dr Margulis' surgery. He had received him immediately, bringing him to the front of the queue, when he saw him clutching his belly. First of all he asked him countless questions, about childhood illnesses, about what he ate and drank, about how often and since when it hurt, and in what way. Then he told him to take off his coat and shirt and vest, to lie down on the bed and with a light hand he began to press, constantly asking: 'Does it hurt?' 'Is it painful here?' Then he lightly rubbed his hand in a circle over Cercel's belly, which was soothed as if by magic.

'Is it bad?' asked Cercel again in a choked voice.

'I cannot say for sure yet, we will find out in a few weeks. It does not seem to be a... anything suspect. You did well to come immediately.'

Then he reeled off a series of explanations, of which Cercel understood not one jot, although the unfamiliar words horrified him, and finally, speaking in Romanian once more, he gently told him what he had to do from then on.

'You are going on a diet. No more of your plum brandy, even if it is very good; no more of your wife's sour soups; no more garlic onions and pepper, nor even raw fruit and vegetables. No more freshly baked bread. The drier the bread, the healthier it is for you. Instead, eat olive oil, boiled meat and steamed vegetables with butter. Boiled eggs. And let us have a look at you in another two weeks. You can go to work now without any worry.'

Reinvigorated, old man Cercel set off on foot towards No. 11 Strada Brezoianu. No sooner had he talked to the doctor than he felt healthy again. He would have to bring the doctor a demijohn of plum brandy, especially now that he wasn't allowed to touch it. But did the doctor touch the stuff?

From joy and worry, he started talking to himself like a madman. The newspaper was off the press, but old man Cercel did not open it. Nicu had to be there so that the two of them could look at the lottery numbers together.

4.

Numbers 98, 38 and 51 – Nicu kept saying to himself as he passed in front of the soldier of *L'Indépendance Roumaine* and the bells, as if to tell him some good news, started to chime. As Nicu went on his way it was as if he were floating and as he entered the door on the left, as ever, the door which said *Editorial and Administrative Offices*, he took a good look at old man Cercel, trying to read whether or not the numbers were good. But the doorman's face was inscrutable, it was as if he were laughing and crying at the same time; you couldn't tell anything from his face.

'Have you... have we won?' asked Nicu, barely able to articulate the words in his excitement.

The doorman calmly picked up the newspaper. All of a sudden his face lit up and he began to laugh, and Nicu could not believe that his dreams had come true so easily: if he was laughing, then they must have won. But instead of the lottery numbers, the doorman showed him a big photograph. It was Victory Avenue, the avenue down which he came every day. In the photograph it was a sunny day, with lots of carriages and cabs and long icicles on the buildings. A short distance from the *L'Indépendance* building was a gentleman, oh, he recognized him: it was Mr Costache, furious, raising his cane threateningly. And on the other side, among the carriages, was a lad running in terror, in danger of being run over by some horses. He could also see a cabman pulling on his reins, open-mouthed. Nicu had never seen himself in a photograph and he was dissatisfied to the point of indignation. He looked small and ragged, and his smart red cap was grey. He could not remember being scared, as he looked in the photograph. He almost felt like crying, whereas old man Cercel was full of merriment. The doorman took the newspaper back from Nicu and looked for the lottery results. He scanned each page carefully, holding the newspaper, with its small, crabbed type, as far away from his eyes as possible, while Nicu read the other side, getting as close as he could, as if he wanted to climb inside and replace the photograph of himself. Finally, old man Cercel found the announcement and read it out loud: '12, 21 and 20. It's not us. Look, out of all them numbers, they've all got a 1 and a 2. I had 98, which is the coming year, and 38, which was the year of my birth, and 51, that of my wife's. But I got it wrong. She told me yesterday she was born in '52, the same year as they built the Theatre.'

'Maybe we shouldn't have chosen just years, because not all years are winners. Should we have chosen house numbers?'

The doorman said that other things were important in life, like a healthy belly.

'How is Speckle?' Nicu felt duty-bound to ask, although since she decided to leave him, he didn't love her any more.

'She's eating, drinking, shitting, and sends her regards.'

But the lad didn't care about her regards or anything else to do with the past. He cared about his New Year's wish. Because those wishes – as every boy knew – came true and you had to be very careful, like in the story of the golden fish, not to squander your luck. Mr Peppin brought him his commissions and Nicu set off, in more of a hurry than ever. There was one day and eleven hours left until the end of the year.

5.

General Algiu was in the yard trying to train the hound. The snow was covered with the quadruped's footprints. Mr Costache saw him from the carriage. The fence was not high; Algiu was not afraid of burglars. The General must have sensed him, although he had his back to him, because he turned around immediately and one might have presumed that beneath his white moustache he was smiling, although it concealed his mouth.

'Forgive me, but I received your invitation only at midnight on Sunday, when I returned from the opera, and yesterday I was in Giurgiu.

'What was the opera?'

'*Rigoletto*, with Miss Olympia Mărculescu in the role of Gilda. I have never seen the like. There was a storm of applause, and flowers like in the month of May, rather than December.'

Remarking in passing that Mr Costache had told him who played Gilda, but not who was cast in the role of Rigoletto, the General invited him inside. The borzoi led the way, turning his head to see whether they followed.

'I have solved the riddle, but I have not solved the mystery,' Costache hastened to say, holding a cup of Marghiloman coffee. 'I have had occasion to discover that logic is like a drill, but you cannot control the outcome of the battle, for only therein is the truth to be found.'

'I do not like to philosophize, Costache, but I do not understand what the truth is, when you yourself know that every truth takes a different form.'

'I am beginning to believe that it is something above us and maybe the poor in spirit are riper, more prepared than those with an iron logic...'

He was unable to develop the thought because the borzoi jumped up and placed his paws on his knees. The General drove it away with difficulty and urged his friend to continue. Costache told him that after he had searched high and low, almost at random, all the mysteries turned out to be connected to an icon with diamonds on its shoulders, which had once been kept in the Sărindar Church. After the church was demolished, it came into the possession of the erstwhile Metropolitan Ghenadie Petrescu. Here things became complicated. Either before or on the day when the Metropolitan had been deposed, during the confusion, somebody had taken the icon. Or else Ghenadie had given it to a bishop who died, after which the trail became tangled once again. Whatever the case, the icon had ended up in an iron safe to which there were at least two keys. The man who was to remove the icon from the safe, as a mere intermediary, was Rareş Ochiu-Zănoagă: he had received two identical keys, placed separately in two deer-skin wallets. One he kept about his person, the other he had entrusted, as a precautionary measure, to the lawyer Movileanu.

Costache paused to drink some coffee laced with cognac, giving a slight smile.

'Do you know a good lawyer, specializing in divorce?'

The General, who was accustomed to listening to everything until the end before asking any questions nodded to signify that he did and made a gesture with his right hand to signify that he would tell him after he finished. Costache therefore continued. It could be presupposed that with the lawyer Movileanu the young Rareş wished to solve some matters connected with money. If everything succeeded, the sum would have been large, and the money was therefore worth investing. He wanted to have an independent income, so that he could become a painter. He had mentioned something along these lines to the lawyer.

'The rest I found out from Alexandru, the son of Hristea Livezeanu.'

The General frowned slightly, and Costache, who had known him in the days when he was Prefect, thought to understand what he meant, as if he had read his thoughts: He has a reputation as a *coureur*, but he is not a bad boy. I am a friend of his family.

'He himself told me the other day, when I was a guest of the Livezeanu family.'

He refrained from sighing and continued in a neutral voice.

'Rareş Ochiu Zănoagă and Alexandru had a common friend, a certain Grigore Cernea – yesterday I went to Giurgiu to confirm it – a man of thirty-five, rather shady, a one-time monk, who subsequently became a dealer in religious items. In most cases he was covered, the pretext was charitable works, but he pocketed half the money. But the icon from Sărindar could not be sold, the same as the rest of the monastery's goods. When Nicu Filipescu decided to demolish it, the monastery's goods, in the keeping of a number of bishops, had to be preserved for a new church, more beautiful than Sărindar, but whose site had not yet been chosen. As you know, the building of the new monastery has been postponed *sine die*. Grigore Cernea asked Livezeanu to meet a young man, namely Rareş, near the Băneasa estate on Friday, 19 December, at ten o'clock in the morning, to take a parcel from him and to deliver it to another man, whose name we do not know. Rareş himself was to tell Alexandru the man's name and where to meet him. As is plain, Alexandru was nothing but another intermediary, who was the link between Rareş and the other man. He did not even do this for money, but from friendship for Grigore, so he assured me. And I believe that between young men of their sort such help is something usual. He is the type who gets mixed up in messes believing he is making a grand and noble gesture.'

Only now did Mr Costache sigh, looking with envy at the hound, which was as restless as a naughty child.

'There is no need for you to tell me the rest, I understand: when he got there, Rareş had been shot, the package was gone, and he fled, realizing that there was something nasty behind it.'

'That is what he told me, in almost exactly the same words. He offered to describe minute by minute what he did after he fled the place (he said that he did not even approach the man, and that he was quite simply afraid, thinking him dead), he said that we could send men to search his house and his apartment in town, he had nothing to hide. The fact that he knew nothing of the key persuaded me that he was not lying, otherwise he, rather than Petre, would have taken the one in the boy's pocket. And he was greatly afraid lest he be accused of murdering him, which is why in the beginning he breathed not a word. Petre found out from the newspapers, firstly that Rareş Ochiu-Zănoagă was not dead, and then, to his despair, that he had died. Because only Rareş Ochiu-Zănoagă could have confirmed his innocence.'

'And how did you solve the riddle?' asked the General in a tone that reminded Costache of the moments when Algiu knew more than his subalterns and put them to the test.

Sensing a trap, Costache pondered well before saying: 'With the exception of the word *Popescu*, unless it was not *Popescu* but *popa* (priest), the others, *stars*, *light*, *Holy Mother* and *sar* (leap) or *dar* (gift) are clear: Rareş had been curious and found out what he had to pass on, hence his death: the icon of the Holy Mother from Sărin*dar*, the one with the stars and light on her shoulders, that is, diamonds.'

'I am afraid that you have not solved the riddle entirely correctly,' said General Algiu cheerfully, and Costache frowned. 'Do you mind if I smoke?'

He lit his pipe and his guest joined him, lighting a cigar.

'True, it was merely by accident that I came across the additional element. For you the words were written as follows,' and he showed him the visiting card on which he had jotted them down: *light, Popescu, light, with stars, Holy Mother, sar* (*dar*?).

The adjutant entered, bringing his usual odour of boot polish, and asked whether the gentlemen would be eating at home, but Algiu waved his hand to signify that he did not have time for such things right now.

'Understood, I'll make something,' said the adjutant, who knew just as well as the Head of Security how to interpret the General's signals.

'I knew about the story of the icon from Mrs Elena Turnescu, the surgeon's widow, who makes large charitable donations. And then more or less by accident I came across a news item about army promotions and I saw that a few months ago Mr Popescu-Lumină had been promoted to sub-lieutenant. He was the one to whom Alexandru was to entrust the package, that is what the boy said, before he died, like a password, exactly what he should have told Alexandru. Therefore *light* (*lumină*) should be written with a capital letter. I went to see him and talked to him, because I know his superiors well: he seems innocent, but you never know. The same Grigore Cernea told him to expect Alexandru Livezeanu – he knew him by sight – at twelve o'clock at the Gara de Nord, by the first column of the portico. He said he waited twelve hours in the station, until midnight, thinking that he had got the wrong hour, but nobody came. *Konets!*'

'You are formidable,' exclaimed Costache. 'Checkmate. Now everything fits. Grigore Cernea is no longer in the country and something leads me to believe that he will not be coming back. I found out from a porter at the Gara de Nord that he left on a train for Vienna. But I am not at all sure that he is the one who has the icon, because everything seems to rely on a chain of people who each know only the next link. It is the best way of planning a heist, if you want to keep it shadowy.'

And what about Mr Dan Crețu?' asked the General. 'I have read in *Lumea Nouă* things which, to put it bluntly, not even my adjutant would credit.'

'Ah, yes, I found out that the man who talked to the journalists from *Lumea* is the assistant of my friend Margulis, from the surgery, an untrustworthy young man, whom I long ago advised him to dismiss. I hope he will do so now. Who knows what he overheard and what he concluded! In any event, I have found out absolutely nothing new about

Dan Crețu. He has contacted nobody; nobody has contacted him. He seems to have burned every bridge with his past. His safe has not been found, but Fane's mistress told us that it contained nothing but clothes. The Ringster swore to her.'

The sat down at the dinner table and changed the subject.

'Are you invited to the Livezeanu family's New Year party? I beg you to come, I would feel more at ease if you did,' said Costache, and the General's eyelids, after blinking indecisively a few times, closed to signify his acceptance. He raised his glass, which was filled with ruby-red wine that left transparent trails down the side.

'To you,' he said in a tone intended to be impassive.

FUTURE AND PAST

1.

There are just a few more hours before the end of the year. What have I done with the year or rather what have I made of it? I discovered the Handel minuet, the melody in Jacques' musical clock. That was good. I met Mr Dan Crețu, who very easily became part of our family and befriended us all. That is likewise very good, if not somehow a miracle, because Papa, who is rather severe and demanding of people, rebuffs people, all the more so a man above whom float all kinds of unusual suspicions. I met a different Alexandru than the one I had known hitherto. That, I think, was bad, although it was good. I have been invited to begin the year 1998 – how silly of me, and how strange it looks! – The year 1898, I meant, at the Livezeanus'. That is neither good nor bad, it is not anything, especially since I shall be staying at home. I have still not finished *Vanity Fair*. That is good and bad: bad because I have not kept my promise, and good, because I always feel sorry when I finish a good book.

I thought of the people around me, on this last morning of the year, of all those whom I know and whom, most of the time, *entre nous*, I do not remember. I thought, for example, of old man Cercel, the doorman from *Universul*, who raises doves and who, Papa tells us, has problems with his health and is afraid of 'going under the knife.' What he must be going through! I thought of Mr Peppin Mirto, of how hard he works and how he does everything, and of how merry and polite he is, and how wonderful it would have been for him to have had a career as an opera singer. And of Signor Giuseppe, who is less talented, but has a bigger heart, although he lives from hand to mouth. I thought of Mama. And of Papa, who is killing himself by looking after *all* the sick people for very little pay or even for no pay, of how he fights disease, day after day, without a Sunday off, without anybody erecting a statue to him, for no other reason that his desire to make the suffering in the world a speck smaller. As if he could make a speck or ten or even a thousand disappear from the sands of the world's suffering. I thought of Jacques, of how courageous he is and I thought of the future that awaits him. I do not know why I have more faith in him than I do in myself. And I thought of poor Safta, who had up until now been very confident in her fate and full of cheer, but who is now travelling home along snowy roads to a grieving family, a house where the grief is fresh, and again I felt like crying. I thought of Mişu, Alexandru's brother, whose forelock I like and I thought of what he will do with his medical degree and immediately after that I thought of Dr Gerota, the man who has impressed me more than any other and who I know for sure will move mountains in Romanian medicine: you can read it in his eyes when he speaks. I thought of how I had not won the lottery and of how nobody I know won anything. I thought of not thinking about Alexandru and me, because I do that all the time. And I asked myself who caused us all to know each other and to live in the same time and the same place? Finally I thought that if and only if I go to the party, I do not have a suitable dress – perhaps only the one that is the colour of Parma violets, which is not exactly new – and so I won't go. And nor do I want to!

2.

Marioara Livezeanu looked at the table through the half-open door and could not take her eyes off it. It was as beautiful as a dream, like a jeweller's shop window, like a festive gown. The white Holland tablecloth had absorbed a little too much starch: the corners did not undulate, but were stiff, like a woman whose corset was too tight. But she could find no other defect with the table. The cut crystal stars of the glasses glinted softly, but once the chandelier was lit they would flare, giving off rays. The delicately clinking champagne glasses had been placed at the ready on the serving table; their turn would not come until midnight. The bottles of champagne already rested in buckets containing large chunks of ice from Lake Cişmigiu. The thought that the best beverage in the world had come all the way from France to nestle among chunks from a frozen lake in Bucharest intrigued Marioara. A few days ago, in *Universul* she had read which lakes the people of Bucharest were allowed to take ice from: Floreasca, Herăstrău, Cişmigiu, Teiu Doamnei, Pasărea, Mogoşoaia, Fundeni. Floreasca would have been closer for them, but a groom had recently drowned there after being sent to collect ice, and so Hristea Livezeanu had preferred to send their servant to Cişmigiu.

Four women and a serving boy had worked up until now on decorating the table. The Rosenthal plates had gilded borders, pink roses and green-gold leaves, and so everything had to match these colours. Marioara had taken care of the arrangements herself. Pink roses, ordered in advance and delivered on time, alternated with white, opening rosebuds, and the napkins, ironed into fans and fastened with silver rings plated in gold, in the form of curled dolphins, were of pale green cloth. The plates for the hors d'oeuvres rested on the dinner plates like porcelain chicks in their mothers' laps. The other plates waited in stacks, twelve for each guest. And then there was the brand new plate-warmer from Vienna. She had tested the chime of the champagne glasses with her fingernail. The sauce dishes, coffee and tea services, port-liqueur, olivière, samovar, cafetière, all were to hand, but placed to one side, without irritating the eye. Each guest's place was set with four silver forks and as many knives, and two spoons, for the early courses, the knives at the same distance as the forks, not one millimetre more, the fish knives in their correct place, and the spoons above the plates. The soup tureens were also of Rosenthal porcelain, with frilly handles and knobs on the lids. The urn had white undulations and gilt borders, but the lid, alas, had a hairline crack: the cook had accidentally knocked it and then burst into tears, but there was nothing that could be done now, it was too late to replace it. Marioara finally tore herself away from her work of art and hurried to dress and arrange her hair for the most important evening of the year and to get her three children ready. For her, the thirty-first was like placing a full stop at the end of a sentence, while the first of January was like writing the capital letter of a new sentence, in large, thick script, like you see at the beginning of a chapter in a novel. She was dying of curiosity to meet Mr Dan Crețu at last. In her life there were not many events, apart from the children's illnesses and her parents' quarrels.

Alexandru Livezeanu barely had time to arrive home, to change for the party for which he had no enthusiasm. He put on his most handsome cufflinks, a present from his father, and regretted that the rules did not allow flowers in the buttonhole of his tailcoat. He felt as if he were blossoming within. Since the twenty-seventh of December, he had been filled with shame and joy and shyness and timidity in front of people, the likes of which he could have sworn he had never felt before. The New Year, at least this one, was nothing but a noisy occasion, which risked drowning out the delicacy of the thoughts and experiences he had acquired in the last few days. Or perhaps the strength of his silence would drown out the din and the unuttered feeling would be heard like the cry of silence in the midst of the commotion. He felt half luminous, half plunged into darkness. The light came from the past; the darkness was for the future. His greatest fear was that *she* might not come, after their last meeting, because since then he had not seen her and she had not sent a reply to his invitation. The doctor and his wife had announced that they were coming; Marioara had told him. As for her, there was not a word. His hand trembled as he adjusted his silk bow tie, but the mirror did not let him down, reflecting a face that regarded him differently.

Hristea and Maria Livezeanu were squabbling through the open door between their rooms as they prepared for the festive evening. For them, New Year was an occasion for constantly renewed accountings. They managed to recapitulate all the accusations of an entire lifetime, beginning with the moment when they met and Hristea had eyes for anyone but Maria, although she had done what she did to lay hands on the young swain. The time-line of their argument had reached the previous evening, when the gentleman had returned late from his club, as usual. He reminded her, she reminded him, in an endless duel, from which both emerged thicker-skinned and more obstinate than ever. As for the boy, Alexandru, he had let him get completely out of hand, said the mother, and felt her tears begin to flow. A teardrop left a furrow through the powder on her wrinkled cheek. Hristea approached and, as usual, fastened the string of pearls at the back of her neck, a silver wedding present, but he did so clumsily, earning fresh reproaches. Madam Maria Livezeanu was full of nerves: too many unfamiliar guests.

3.

One by one the coachmen came to a stop at the platform, which had been swept clear of snow. There was a frost. The first to arrive was Mişka's cab from Theatre Square, the one with the two handsome white horses. From it alighted the four newspapermen from *Universul*, Procopiu and the Mirto brothers, all in festive garb, and then Mrs Procopiu, followed by Dan Creţu, whose clothes fitted him remarkably well, thanks to Alexandru, or more accurately Alexandru's tailor. He was unrecognizable, and Neculai Procopiu had to remark that for the first time since he met him, his editor fitted in with the décor. Mrs Procopiu gazed at him pensively and her husband could not tell whether her heart was now in her eyes. Peppin, who had lately put on weight, had been astonished to find that his tailcoat no longer fitted. He had had to borrow one from his uncle at the last moment, one that was rather short on him, while Păvăluca's best undershirt, for festive occasions, was moth eaten; it was a good job it was not visible. As for the editor-in-chief, he felt ill at ease in the pair of shoes he wore only on the most special occasions, as if his feet had grown in the meantime. Toader, the cheerful groom, leapt forward to assist them and conducted them to the steps of the entrance, above which the light bulbs were lit and fir garlands hung. It was eight o'clock. Another four hours until midnight.

When she saw Dan, Marioara had the biggest surprise of her life, the man of whom they had spoken so much, the man of mystery, the man whom the press had even suggested might be a stranger to these times, Mr Dan Creţu or Kretzu was an absolutely ordinary man. Her disappointment was short-lived, since she liked Mr Creţu's face, and then, having first hesitated, he delicately kissed her hand, Marioara gave him a seductive, dimpled smile, which she had been saving for an awfully long time, ever since the divorce: now she had rediscovered it.

At half past eight the Margulis family carriage arrived, an old conveyance, but with freshly curried horses and harnesses garnished with new red tassels. Nelu, the coachman, had recovered, but his face was still gaunt. With her voluminous skirts, Mrs Margulis barely fit on one of the bench seats, while the doctor was flanked by Jacques and Nicu the urchin, to whose outfit the whole family had contributed: he looked as if he was fresh out of the box. The lad was red in the face, he felt hot, and his eyes squinted sideways beneath eyebrows couched at an acute angle. Jacques struggled to prevent his crutch slipping, but on the steps the groom quite simply picked him up and set him down by the door as if he were as light as a snowflake. Alexandru, who had at that moment made his appearance at the entrance, although it was his parents who received the guests, felt a lump in his throat when he saw that Iulia had not come with them. He refused to believe his eyes. Half the light in him went out and he sensed the emptiness of a long night opening up before him. But before he could ask, Nicu said to him *aparté*: 'She wasn't ready!' Alexandru quickly seized the opportunity and offered in a man-of-the-world voice to go and fetch Miss Margulis, since he was a skilled driver. 'Drive slowly!' the worried doctor barely had time to call out behind him as Alexandru left.

Old General Algiu arrived at nine o'clock, on the box of his carriage next to his inseparable adjutant, but he was oppressed by the great empty space on the other side of him. The General knew he was too old, in soul rather than body, to fill that empty space with another woman. Today was the last day of a year of mourning, which meant that today was the day when he had lost his beloved wife. New Year's Eve would always be a black day for him. But it was better that he should spend it in company.

Costache arrived an hour later, with Mlle Olympia Mărculescu, Gilda. The two arrived at the same time as the carriage driven by Alexandru, from which alighted Miss Margulis. The surprise was mutual: Costache was amazed to see Iulia alone in Alexandru's carriage, and Iulia to see Mr Costache with a companion, when she thought him to be single. Their eyes met. The policeman apologized to his hosts for being late: he had come straight from the Opera, where the female lead had, as ever, earned a standing ovation. After reminiscing about New Year's Eve parties from the recent past, Mr Hristea Livezeanu showed them a French caricature from *Le Figaro*, which depicted a beautifully arranged festive meal and beneath it, in small letters, the words of the host: 'Please, no politics and no Dreyfus Affair!' And at the bottom of the page, there was a drawing of the same table, in disarray, with drunken guests and the caption, in equally small script: '*Ils en ont parlé*' (They talked about it).

Following that delicate apropos, the company was invited to sit at the dinner table. There were fifteen people seated at the large dining room table, which was of solid wood and could be extended or shortened: a convenient number, although sixteen would have been better for symmetry's sake. Five in number, the children sat at a smaller table. Nicu kept going back and forth between the two tables, since he constantly had something to tell Dan, until Agatha saw him and scolded him.

4.

'If the honour falls upon me to open the first window to the future,' said the host, 'then this is what I see: within a year or two, before the turn of the century, the 'iron lady' will be deposed. At least so I hope!'

Before twelve o'clock on the last day of the year '97 or the hour o of the first day of the year '98, Marioara proposed a game: let each make a prediction about the future, instead of the usual pie containing fortunes on slips of paper, of which everybody was sick. (Marioara did not confess that her pie had burned.) Better to have predictions. The predictions could go as far as one liked. The idea of having a small pause before the roast garnered unanimous approval. The fifteen adults were joined by Nicu, the sixteenth, since he felt he belonged to the big table rather than the children's table. Since people took to him, he was accepted as a novelty. And so numbers were inscribed on slips paper, from 1 to 16, and they were dropped inside Peppin Mirto's hats, which would be drawn to establish the order in which each would speak. The hat and chance determined that Mr Hristea Livezeanu was first, and Dan Crețu last. Of the others, many declined to take part, either from bashfulness or other reasons hard to divine.

Procopiu, who was second, had already prepared a vague answer about the next issue of *Universul*, but when he heard that Hristea Livezeanu wanted the 'iron lady,' in other words *La Tour Eiffel* to be demolished, he felt it his duty as a journalist to intervene. Having risen to his feet, following the example of the first speaker, although his shoes forced him to sit for as long as possible, he asked permission to commit the impoliteness of disagreeing with his host: 'The Eiffel Tower will endure for centuries. It will be visited by many people. Paris will be synonymous with the Eiffel Tower, and the Eiffel Tower with Paris.'

'Encouraged by Mrs Livezeanu's smile, since she always ascribed to the view contrary to that of her consort, he went on: 'It will last for at least as long as the Statue of Liberty in New York, which... on whose metal structure Eiffel also worked. M Gustave Eiffel is a genius of steelwork, as everybody knows. It is true that the Panama Canal affair, which the newspapers, even in this country, have exaggerated so much, has tarnished his fame as an engineer somewhat. But it has been a long time since Léon Bloy, a writer who has written no great books, called the tower a 'tragic lamp,' while a better writer, albeit one rather too eccentric for my taste, M Huysmans, described it, may the ladies forgive me, as a suppository full of holes!'

Procopiu's cheeks flushed and his fellow diners sensed that the journalist's Achilles heel had been struck. His colleague Pavel Mirto knew why. The editor-in-chief's childhood dream had been to become an engineer, and Gustave Eiffel and Anghel Saligny were his great role models, in a world in which models were hard to choose, given they were so numerous. He had been to the Paris Exhibition in '89 and he hoped one day to shake the hand of Eiffel in the flesh. He knew Saligny well; they were of the same generation. Procopiu had attended the ceremony to open the Cernavodă Bridge across the Danube in '96, on 14 September, and he remembered with a thrill the thousands of people who had arrived on five special trains, including the most famous journalists. He even remembered the special train on which the entire royal court, diplomatic corps and ministers had arrived. A week later, Neculai Procopiu had accepted an invitation to attend the banquet held by the Ministry of Public Works in honour of Saligny and the other engineers who had worked on the bridge.

Alexandru politely raised his glass to Procopiu and congratulated him. He had courage and passion of which he would not have believed him capable; he had always seemed to him somewhat banal. And in order to pass over the rather embarrassing mention of the suppository, a word that was *osée* on a festive occasion and in the presence of the ladies, although this was the risk one ran when one invited journalists, he said: 'Number 3? Who has number 3?'

Full of the importance of the occasion, Nicu declared himself. He stood next to Iulia's chair. He had taken off his coat and inserted his thumbs behind his braces, as he had seen old man Cercel do: *his* model. He spoke quickly, as he did at school whenever he had to answer a question, with his eyes fixed on Dan: 'Through the window of the future is Mr Dan and farther away is Jacques, who is going for a walk, without his crutch... with you,' he added, moved by the silence that had fallen around him.

'Bravo!' Now it is my turn,' said Alexandru, since the company was even more embarrassed than they had been at the previous speaker, although Jacques was smiling from his seat. He understood that Nicu had sacrificed his own wishes for his sake. Nicu looked curiously at Alexandru, to see whether he would reveal the secret he knew.

'I do not see anything, but I wish to write for *Universul*. At least a society column, since you do not have one,' he said to the three newspapermen, who seemed to approve the idea, at least out of politeness.'

'A welcome idea!' said Madam Livezeanu. 'I shall claim the right not to make any prediction. But I would like to climb to the top of the Eiffel Tower before it is demolished, as my husband predicts. Naturally, using the *ascenseur*. Surely we shall find the five francs in our pockets. *À bon entendeur, salut,'* she added, for her husband's ears.

It was Pavel's turn. He spoke in his usual muted voice, so that only those sitting next to him were able to hear.

'Some of you know that I am writing a novel. I hope that the God of our future is not a novelist, to kill off his protagonists unexpectedly and invent bad things (although He, the Creator, is good, is He not?) merely so that his book will turn out good and so that the devil will not say that He, the Lord, has not created a world without horns and a tail. Or a different version: let us hope that we are not living in the world of Old Nick, who, a fearless plagiarist, has compiled the world of God, but added some original evil on his own account. And from time to time God manages to sabotage him with something good. Let us hope that whoever is the One has written this world –' here Pavel pointed his finger at the ceiling and then at the floor '– loves happy endings, and that all is well that ends well.'

'Is everything well when it ends with death?' interjected Dr Margulis in irritation.

'This is what we ought to believe, is it not?' replied Pavel, barely audibly, but without getting ruffled. 'Here is a good ending to a novel. All is well when it ends with death. And I believe that is what will be once more.'

'What, the good or death?' said Agatha, losing her patience. She herself had encountered both. To her, too, Păvălucă seemed annoying. 'I have not very well understood your predictions, Mr Mirto, but it is true that the Pythian said more or less the same kind of things.'

Hristea Livezeanu was slightly deaf and could not make out anything.

'Well, if you want it to end with a wedding or a baptism, you should know that my brother is of a mind to marry next year, or at least to get engaged,' said Pavel, looking at his brother, who, contrary to the custom, was gloomy, probably because of his tailcoat.

The following predictions were also made: man would go to the Moon, like in the tales of Jules Verne, the reds would, alas come to power, the whole Earth would be lit up by electricity, and, perhaps, a cure for tuberculosis would be found (this was Leon Margulis prediction, or 'prognosis', as he called it. General Algiu had cheered up somewhat. What was bad to him had been left behind or perhaps he had managed to overtake it. His words sounded differently than on ordinary occasions, as if he had lowered his guard when he stood up to speak.

'For me, the window of my own future is closed. But through the country's window I see good things, for the time being. And I would also tell the children to take delight in the present years, because they are more peaceful and happier than any years ever before! I do not know why I say this, how it came to me, but I am fully convinced that it is so. I do not believe in a rosy future; I have seen too many things in my life. I shall leave the young Boerescu to continue, since he is cleverer than I, both in words and in the battle against time.'

The young Costache felt old on New Year's Eve and hoped to leave before the dancing began, although Mlle Mărculescu gazed at him, smiling enchantingly, her hair piled up around her head like a black halo. She did indeed look dazzling, and Iulia sometimes cast her wondering glances. Costache had known from the start of the evening what he would say. Standing, avoiding Iulia's eye, looking only at the General, he smiled and, raising his glass, filled with the vintage of '78, with which he had barely moistened his lips, he said: 'As for the year on which we are just embarking, I have nothing much to say. But I predict that next century, the twentieth, will begin with General Ion Algiu at the helm of the Prefecture of Police. And that the prints of our fingertips will become the best means of identifying malefactors, who are able to alter their appearance with new moustaches.'

All kinds of comments were bandied back and forth. Some looked at Dan and his newly grown moustache, and a few examined their fingertips. Iulia, who was the penultimate speaker, remained seated, and Alexandru tapped his glass with a teaspoon to elicit silence for her. To the astonishment of all, she turned towards Dan: 'Mr Crețu, how would you translate *Vanity Fair*?'

'Well, it's *Bâlciul Deșertăciunilor* (*The Fair of Futilities*), isn't it?'

'*Formidable*,' said Peppin Mirto, 'amazing, you did not pause one instant to think. In fact, that is what it is like when you translate, either you find the right word straight away or you do not find it at all.'

'My prediction for the future world,' said Iulia, 'is that it will be a fair of futilities or a market of vanities. And I also predict that women will no longer wear corsets,' she added and then blushed furiously and gasped.

At which point Alexandru drank from his glass and Nicu whispered to Dan: 'The Tuzla Lighthouse,' and Dan gazed at him in puzzlement.

There was no time left for the rest of the game. Dan Crețu did not get to speak, to Marioara's regret. She had been looking at him fixedly the whole evening, convincing herself that her first impression had not deceived her: there was nothing, absolutely nothing, mysterious about Mr Crețu; he was a man like any other. She gave a dimpled smile.

The hands of the clock neared twelve. The men uncorked the champagne from the buckets full of ice from Cișmigiu Lake, which was now half melted. At the first of the twelve chimes of the clock, the glasses clinked and the servants extinguished the lights for a few seconds, as if the world stood still. There were whoops and titters, the men's shirt fronts shone in the darkness, and the children bumped up against the adults' legs. Anica hid her head in her mother's lap. The General coughed. Alexandru sought to discern Iulia's outline in the darkness, her waist tightly contained within a corset. Hrista Livezeanu was bored and had a headache. Dan Crețu felt Nicu's little hand grasp his. And then the world set in motion once more, the lights came on, enveloping guests and servants alike. It was as if they had met on the other bank of a river. They expected from the New Year all the good that the old one had denied them. The cannons on Metropolia Hill boomed over the city, causing one first to start and then to rejoice. The invisible enemies of the New Year were put to flight. And the words *Happy New Year!* could be heard so many times, spoken by so many voices in so many houses, that if all the years uttered had been placed end to end they would have stretched far into the future, a future which none could for the time being glimpse.

5.

Dan Crețu alone remained to gaze, as the host so poetically put it, through the 'window of the future,' and the curiosity of the other guests could not have been greater. The glasses were once more filled with champagne and the foam dissolved like the worn lacework of the old year. Even if you are a rational and know that the newspapers alone have turned a man into a mysterious figure, into somebody *different* from everybody else, you still feel a slight thrill, like a cold draught in a well-heated room. And if you have been drinking *Dom Perignon* champagne, you might even believe that there is indeed something shady behind it all. Dan began to speak, as if talking to himself, without rising to his feet, without looking at anybody; it was as if he did not see them.

'It isn't good to look too far back into the past, and if your past is in the future, it's even worse. I will forbid myself to think about my past. Perhaps in my mind, no longer ago than a year, my future was somewhere else entirely. Through a sudden reversal, my past blended with the future. Maybe, as someone here well put it, what was really is what will be. Maybe, as nobody has put it yet, but as somebody soon will say, the years stand still, like a landscape seen from a train window, while we are the ones in motion.'

'We are the ones who are passing by now,' interjected Mrs Marioara Livezeanu with a dimpled smile, peeved that Dan Crețu was playing the role of the mysterious stranger for the sake of the journalists. But fortunately, the band of folk musicians in red coats began a well-known waltz and the lady of the house announced: 'Let the dancing begin! The ladies choose.'

6.

The people of Bucharest were having a bad day. It had snowed, there were still twelve days till the end of the year, and twelve hours till the end of the day. On the large boulevards, where wheels advanced more slowly than legs, the festive lights were lit, but few people looked up to see them. Bluish droplets wept into the net of fairy lights hanging above the procession of wheels, which was without beginning and without end. Somewhere in that procession, like a small yellow splotch, was the old automobile of the journalist, Dan Crețu. He was on his way to the airport, having first dropped into the office of the magazine for which he worked. From the vehicle behind him, four ladies had alighted and set off on foot, impatient with the endlessly stopping traffic. Dan found the sullen air of the driver strange. He had a horn, which he kept blowing, not furiously, but methodically, maniacally. He kept changing lanes, gaining a few metres, only to lose them once more. When the cars drew side by side, Dan could see him in profile: he was smoking. He seemed familiar, but Dan could not place the face. He had black hair and was wearing a cap with a childlike tassel.

At the magazine, Dan had celebrated Christmas a few days in advance, as usual. On the big calendar, which had bold numbers, without any photographs, somebody had moved the red square ahead a week. The whole staff lived to a weekly rhythm, as if somebody moved them seven days at a time, from one window on the calendar to another. The red square on the calendar now framed a Monday: 19 December. Dan Crețu had quickly entered the office, shaking the snow off his coloured footwear. As always, he was late.

He looked around him without curiosity: women and men who did not particularly care about each other. The editor-in-chief was leafing through a science magazine with the Eiffel Tower on the cover. Pavel, a young man with round glasses, was speaking softly to a woman and his mind was elsewhere. The administrator entered, whose voice, by contrast, was loud and melodious, as if he were on stage. In any case, there were few of them. Some were playing truant and for a few moments Dan envied them. People were dressed somewhat smarter than on ordinary days, but the slush on the streets did not encourage fanciful outfits. From waist level upward he could see thin, tightly-fitting blouses, cleavages on display, cheap necklaces and long earrings, or depending on the person, shirts and thick jackets, even a necktie, but at floor level everything was the same, for both the men and the women: blue or black trousers without stripes, comfortable boots, which left muddy prints on the parquet, of different sizes and sole patterns. And then there was Dan's footwear, which rather stood out. A few editors, proof-readers and people from the printing press had gathered, without enthusiasm, the same as at every work party. They didn't even have a Christmas tree; they were making economies. The soft transparent plates and cups would later be thrown in the bin. Dan saw a yellowing newspaper, an old *Universul*, bought from some second-hand bookshop, which Pavel had brought to show his colleagues. He cast a glance at the front page, which featured a questionnaire on the topic *Why Do You Fast?* and for a second he was amazed to see that somebody signed it whose name was almost the same as his: Dan Kretzu.

Ever since he had crossed the psychological threshold of the twenty-first century, Dan had ceased to be interested in Christmas trees, New Year and parties. Few things aroused his curiosity any longer. He lived, constantly weary, in a murky present. In any event, it was the worst period of the year for him, in which time had become the single gift of joy that you could give to anyone. Dan was forty-three and life had quite simply passed him by. He had a great need of time.

. . . .

Publisher Socec Fils put the manuscript down, he took off his pince-nez, and in large violet letters wrote: NO. It was the first manuscript he had rejected since his father's death.

EPILOGUE

Today Strada Fântânei (Fountain Street) is called Berthelot and leads to Romanian Radio Broadcasting headquarters.

Strada Sfântul Ionică, which once ran behind the National Theatre, has vanished, likewise Romanian Passage and the Theatre itself. On the site now stands a hotel, which features a replica of the entrance portico of what was once Bucharest's most famous building.

Strada Teilor (Lindens Street) is now called Vasile Lascăr.

Right next to the old *Universul* newspaper building – a two-storey rococo house – a five-storey building with a peaked roof was constructed, into which the newspaper offices moved in the inter-bellum. On the ground floor of the old building there is now a Romanian restaurant, not one of whose customers seems to know about the people who once published a famous gazette here. But on the threshold there still remains the stone inscription in large letters: *UNIVERSUL*.

In Bucharest, Luigi Cazzavillan has a street and a *belle époque* park named after him. In the park he has a statue.

On the site of the Sărindar Monastery was built the magnificent Military Club, before the First World War. There is a fountain on the spot where the altar once stood. The icon of the Mother of God with diamonds on her shoulders was never found and it is supposed to have been taken abroad. Somewhere in the world, unbeknown, the diamonds glitter even today.

Sub-lieutenant N. I. Popescu-Lumină died in Bucharest in 1939. He reached the rank of colonel. In the inter-bellum, he wrote a column for *Universul* titled 'From Days Gone By'.

Strada Sărindar is now called Constantin Mille, after the director of *Adevărul*. After 1898, when Alexandru Beldiman, the Gazette's founder, died, Mille became synonymous with the newspaper whose owner he had long since become. Between the wars, every cinema on the Elisabeta Boulevard had an 'Exit via Sărindar.'

For the slaying in a duel of George Em. Lahovary, the director of the French-language *L'Indépendance Roumaine*, Nicu Filipescu, former mayor of Bucharest and director of the *Epoca* newspaper, was sentenced to six months imprisonment in Văcărești. This did not dent his renown, nor did it affect his seemingly spotless subsequent political career.

General Algiu served as the Prefect of Police one more year, in 1901, the first year of the twentieth century.

Mr Costache took care to erase his name from the documents. He always suspected Dan Crețu of being an undiscovered criminal, but at the same time he was sure he was not a dangerous man.

At the Athenaeum in 1898 Dr Dimitrie Gerota gave his promised lecture on the need to do away with corsets and the Margulis family were among the audience. At the School of Fine Arts one of his students was Constantin Brancusi, who under his guidance made the cast entitled 'Flayed Man.' Gerota is considered to have been the first Romanian radiologist. He founded a hospital and a museum of anatomical casts. Even today, in departments of surgery and urology and in anatomy classes in France, Germany and Tokyo 'Gerota's fascia' and 'Gerota's capsule' are terms still current.

In 1906, Jacques, having reached the age of twenty-one, read to Nicu the following sentence, translating from the Spanish, which was his latest passion: 'In fact they wanted both lives at once, and man wants all worlds and all centuries and to live in the whole of space and the whole of time, infinitely and eternally.' It was the essence of the century in which both had been born and explains the feeling that gripped the folk of Bucharest on the arrival of a stranger, who seemed to know more about time than they did. 'Who's it by?' asked Nicu, and Jacques replied: 'Nobody has heard of him, a Spaniard, Miguel de Unamuno.'

Niculae Stanciu was one of the first young men in Bucharest to obtain a pilot's licence and in the First World War he flew fighter aeroplanes. He was killed in action and was posthumously awarded the Courage and Faith Medal with swords.

The Handel minuet was later transposed for piano by Wilhelm Kempff, and Idil Biret was the pianist who lent it its strangest velvetiness.

Having made a two-year hiatus in the Great War, *Universul* continued to be published until 1953, when the Communists abolished it, along with every other symbol of the old world.

Pavel Mirto's novel *The Future Begins on Monday* was not published. Publisher Socec Fils was irritated by its description of unimaginable ladies' clothing, not to mention the notion of soft plates and cups, to be discarded after use. And all the rest.

APPENDICES.

1897

(FROM CONTEMPORARY PERIODICALS)

The Orthodox calendar for 1897

St Basil the Great	1 January
Epiphany	6 January
St John	7 January
The Triodyon begins	2 February
Meatfare Sunday	16 February
Cheesefare Sunday	23 February
Palm Sunday	6 April
Easter1	3 April
St George	23 April
Forty Martyrs	7 May
Sts Constantine and Elena	21 May
Ascension	22 May
Whitsuntide	1 June
Beginning of the fast Sts Peter and Paul	8 June
Sts Peter and Paul the Apostles	28 June
Dormition of the Theotokos	15 August
Holy Cross	14 September
St Demetrios	26 October
Archangels Michael and Gabriel	8 November
St Nicholas	6 December
Christmas	25 December
St Stephen	27 December

The Catholic Calendar

Septuagesima	2 February (14 February)
Mardi Gras	18 February (2 March)
Ash Wednesday	19 February (3 March)
Easter	6 April (18 April)
Ascension	15 May (27 May)
Whitsun	25 May (6 June)
Holy Trinity	1 June (13 June)
Green Thursday	5 June (17 June)
Advent Sunday	16 November (28 November)
Christmas	25 December (6 January)

Hebrew Calendar

5657			1897
Adar	1		22 January
	14 Little Purim		4 February
Be Adar	1		21 February
	13 Fast of Esther		5 March
	14 *Purim		6 March
	15 Susan Purim		7 March
Nisan	1		22 March
	15 *Passover 1		4 April
	16 *Passover 2		5 April
	21 *Passover 7		11 April
	22 *Passover 8		12 April
Iyar	1		21 April
	18 Lag Ba'omer		3 May
Sivan	1		20 May
	6 Shavuot		25 May
	7 Second holiday		26 May
Thamuz	1		19 June
	18 *Destruction of theTemple fast		6 June
Av	1		17 July
	10 Burning of the Temple fast		27 July
Elul	1		17 August
5658			
Tishrei	1 *New Year		15 September
	2 *Rosh Hashanah		16 September
	4 *Tzom Gedaliah		18 September

	10 *Yom Kippur	22 September
	15 *Sukkot	26 September
	16 *Second day of Sukkot	27 September
	21 *Hoshanah Rabbah	5 October
	22 *Shemini Atzeret	6 October
	28 *Reception of the Law	7 October
Marchesvan	1	15 October
Kislev	1	24 November
	25 *Hanukkah	8 December
Tevet	1	14 December
	10 *Asara be Tevet	23 December
Shevat	1	12 December

*The holidays marked * are to be kept strictly.*

The Muslim Calendar

1314	1 Ramadan	22 January 1897
	1 Shawwâl	21 February
	1 Dhû al-Qaʾdah	22 March
	1 Dhû al-Ḥijjah	21 April
1315	1 Muḥarram	21 May
	1 Ṣafar	20 June
	1 Rabīʿ al-awwal	19 July
	1 Rabīʿ al-thānī	18 August
	1 Jumādá al-ūlá	16 September
	1 Jumādá al-ākhira	16 October
	1 Rajab	14 November
	1 Shaʿbāan	12 December

National and Royal Holidays

11 February, the anniversary of the revolution 1866, which founded Romania's royal dynasty.

14 March, the proclamation of the King of Romania in 1881.

8 April, the birthday of H.M. the King and the proclamation of the plebiscite for the election of His Highness.

24 April, the name day of H.M. Queen Elisabeta.

1, 8 and 10 May, the election, arrival in Romania and enthronement of H.M. the King in 1866.

10 May, the proclamation of Romania's Independence in 1877 and the coronation of the first King of Romania in 1881.

11 June, the anniversary of the 1848 Revolution, when the foundations of Romania's autonomy were laid.

22 July, St Mary Magdalene, name day of H.R.H. Princess Maria.

12 August, the birthday of H.R.H. the Crown Prince Ferdinand.

3 October, the anniversary of H.R.H. Prince Carol of Romania.

17 December, the anniversary of H.M. the Queen.

Chronology

The creation of the world, Julian Calendar	7384 years ago
The creation of the world, Gregorian Calendar	5990
The foundation of Rome	2852
The foundation of Jassy	620
The foundation of Bucharest	613
The fall of Constantinople	444
The death of Stephen the Great, Prince of Moldavia	393
The first printed books in the Romanian language	328
The first confiscation of Bessarabia	85
The Great Fire of Bucharest	50
The 11 June 1848 European and Romanian Revolution	49
The Union of the Principalities	38
The Emancipation of the Serfs	33
The enthronement of H.M. Carol	31
The inauguration of the first Romanian railway line	28
The International Postal Union	22
The Proclamation of Romania's Independence	20
The second confiscation of Bessarabia	19
Romania's annexation of Dobrudja	19
The proclamation of the Kingdom of Romania	16
The introduction of electric lighting to Romania	14

Eclipses

Two full solar eclipses, which will not be visible in Europe. No lunar eclipses.

The first full solar eclipse occurs on 19 February (1 February): darkness begins at 23 minutes past seven in the evening. The eclipse ends at 9 minutes past one in the morning. It is visible in Central America, South America apart from the eastern and southern tip of Cape Horn, the east coast of Argentina and the southern part of the Atlantic Ocean, and also in south-east Australia. *The second full solar eclipse* will occur on 17 (29) July. Darkness begins at two minutes past three in the after-noon. The eclipse ends at 52 minutes past 8 in the evening. It will be visible on the west coast of Africa, in the tropics of the Atlantic Ocean, in the south of North America, in Central America, and in the north of South America.

The year's regent – Mars, god of war, of upheavals, and of human pair-ings. During the course of this year there will be many phenomenal accidents. Children born in the course of the year will be hot-headed and fractious; the boys will be bold, quarrelsome, bellicose, insubor-dinate, and independent; the girls will be beautiful, clever, industrious, dutiful and devoted, but also bad, cantankerous, irascible.

The members of the Holy Synod who sat in judgement over the former Metropolitan of Hungro-Wallachia Ghenadie Petrescu in May 1896.
Bishops: 1. Ghenadie Bishop of Râmnic, 2. Partenie Bishop of the Lower Danube, 3. Iosif Metropolitan of Moldavia, 4. Gherasim Timuş of Bishop Argeş, 5. Silvestru Bishop of Huşi, 6. Archbishop Ioanichie Flor of Bacău, 7. Dionisie Climescu Bihsop of Buzău, 8. Ieronim Bishop of Roman, 9 Archbishop Calistrat Orleanu of Bârlad, 10 Archbishop Valerian of Râmnic, 11. Archbishop Dosoftei of Botoşani, 12. Archbishop Pimen Georgescu of Piteşti, 13. Archbishop Athanasie Miron of Craiova, 14. Archbishop Meletie of Galaţi, 15. Archbishop Nifon of Ploieşti.

The Government

Between 1895 and 1899 Romania had a Liberal Government. In December 1897 the structure of the Government was as follows:
The President of the Council of Ministers: Dimitrie A. Sturdza
The Minister of the Interior: Mihail Pherekyde
The Minister of Foreign Affairs: Dimitrie A. Sturdza
The Minister of Finance: George D. Pallade
The Minister of Justice: Alexandru G. Djuvara
The Minister of Religions and Education: Spiru Haret
The Minister of War: General Anton Berindei
The Minister of Agriculture, Industry, Commerce and Estates: Anastase Stolojan
The Minister of Public Works: Ion I. C. Brătianu

MIRCEA CĂRTĂRESCU

AFTERWORD:
A THING OF
BEAUTY

If the novel *Life Begins on Friday* seems an unusual text to the foreign reader, it will not be because of any cultural differences: Ioana Pârvulescu's book is unusual even in the context of today's Romanian literature. It is a singular book, which with intelligence and talent defies the current directions of Romanian prose. It has nothing to do with the problematics of the communist regime, the Ceaușescu period and the Securitate, or with the violent, pornographic sound and fury of punk anarchism, or with postmodern re-visitation of historicized artistic styles, or with the minimalistic depiction of everyday life. It is not an ideological text, does not fight on any front, and does not claim to hold any indubitable truth.

It is merely what we like to call a *thing of beauty*, far from the cacophonous din of all battles. It is a book of delicate nostalgia for times less brutal than those of today, and also a book consummately skilled in reconstructing, with infinite detail and infinite patience, an epoch from which we are separated by more than a century. Like a children's pop-up book from whose pages spring three-dimensional palaces and people, *Life Begins on Friday* is a multi-dimensional scale model of the city of Bucharest in the closing years of the nineteenth century, with its topoi and typical inhabitants. But it is a scale model that will soon seem to us disturbingly real.

Published in 2009, the novel was a surprise for the majority of Ioana Pârvulescu's readers. Her previous books, which had grown increasingly visible and admired in Romanian culture, were mostly non-fiction. In the last decade, the author, an admired literary critic and historian, professor in the University of Bucharest, published, among numerous studies about the hotspots of Romanian cultural history, two veritable bestsellers.

Both are affective reconstructions of past epochs, which employ the tools of both the historian and the writer. The first is *Return to Inter-bellum Bucharest*, the second *The Private Life of the Nineteenth Century*. Although the author's undoubted literary talent was immediately remarked upon in the cultural press, the books won multiple awards and were admired above all as histories of cultural ideas. Few could have predicted that their author would next take the step towards total fictionalization.

However, this step was implicit in her previous books. In fact, both books were backdrops for a novel that was merely awaiting fictional characters. For, they were already brimming with characters imbued with a real historical existence: writers, journalists, physicians, lawyers, as well as their wives and children, comprising a vast social fabric, the inhabitants of a different century, one unfamiliar to us. They would continue to live in *Life Begins on Friday*, but the same as in Doctorow's *Ragtime* or in certain novels by Pynchon, their lives were here to be intertwined with those of imaginary beings, although no less vivid and interesting for all that.

Having honed her skill at minutely describing period settings, the author moved on to a novel, a true novel, with a serious and complex plot structure. The book tells the story of the last thirteen days of the year 1897 in Bucharest, in thirteen polyphonic chapters, each chapter having multiple narrative voices. In each chapter, the different characters alternate in having their say, each viewing the same events from different perspectives, as we also find in Agatha Christie's *Five Little Pigs*, for example, although this does not necessarily lead to an elucidation of the events in question.

The name of the famous author of detective novels is by no means out of place in the present discussion. The most obvious connexion with Ioana Pârvulescu's novel is that it employs the structure of a detective novel. From the very first pages a double mystery takes shape, which will subsequently lead to two different but always interwoven levels of the book: a coachman finds two bodies lying in the road at the edge of town. One is still alive and will become the central enigma of the book; the other will turn out to have been shot and dies in hospital soon thereafter, but not before uttering a mysterious string of words. According to the typical pattern, we also have a detective, in the person of Costache, the Chief of Public Security. The book's two strands, one fantastical, the other to do with the detective novel, form a counterpoint and pick up speed before racing towards a shared finale.

The fantasy theme follows the Caspar Hauser archetype: the young Dan Krețu wakes up to find himself in an unfamiliar world, in a Bucharest of the past. He is an alien to everybody, dressed strangely and looking unlike ordinary people. He seems to be the inhabitant of a different world and each of the characters has a different theory about him. Throughout the novel he moves like a sleepwalker among the other characters, bewildered by the huge change that has befallen him, but also enchanted by the world in which he now finds himself: a Bucharest that is different and nonetheless the same as the one that he senses, but is not certain he knew in his other life. Like his illustrious literary predecessor, Poor Dionis, who sprang from the magnificent imagination of Mihai Eminescu, Dan Krețu meditates on the mystery of time, on the fact that past and future are simultaneous with the present. The finale has a big surprise in store for the reader attentive to this theme.

The detective plot provides the bones of the novel, whose soul is the fantastical and metaphysical theme. Its backdrop is a series of interconnected historical occurrences, the kind of sensational events that have always been the preserve of the tabloid press. Some of these events were of international renown: Jack the Ripper and the Dreyfus affair. Others relate to Bucharest life: a duel in which a leading journalist is slain by an equally famous politician, as well as various spectacular thefts. Colourful thieves, greedy aristocrats, fraudsters, and policemen who are now solemn, now ridiculous are all caught up in a complicated plot, full of quid pro quos and confusion: objects crop up, are interchanged, and then vanish in highly synchronized order.

In addition to the two interwoven major themes, what fleshes out the novel and anchors it in reality (albeit a poetic and illusory reality) is the sweeping panorama of everyday life in the Bucharest of yester-year. Throughout the novel the author follows a number of narrative threads to do with typical city places: the *Universul* newspaper offices, the family home of the respected Dr Margulis, the Prefecture of Police, the hospital, the public baths, and finally the aristocratic mansion where the characters come together to spend New Year's Eve. In this socially stratified world, perhaps the strongest voice of the novel is that of Iulia, the doctor's daughter, who with grace and maturity records in her diary the astonishing events that turn the peaceful lives of her friends and family upside down. Iulia's diary is the book's sounding box, the place where each theme acquires affective coloratura. Here too there takes shape a delicate love story, on which Iulia meditates with unexpected lucidity. The model of the romantic girl had passed, and something in Iulia's thought and behaviour anticipates the emancipation of women that was to take place two or three decades later.

A number of other characters prove to be priceless narrative aids to the author as her description of Bucharest takes shape, characters sketched with the assurance of a Balzac or a Hugo: Costache, the chief of police, is a middle-aged philanderer haunted by nostalgia. Newspaper boy Nicu, aged just eight, is an extremely likeable little Gavroche, who with his every appearance brings a ray of sunlight to the novel, a *ficelle* character involved in untangling (and tangling) the novel's threads. He has access to the slums and the down-trodden, the poor part of Bucharest, which could not be left out of the novel's landscape.

In the end, *Life Begins on Friday* is a book that can be read in various different ways (as a detective novel, as a fantastic novel about time travel, or as a historical novel), but the reader will gain enormously if he or she forgets about such categories and views it quite simply as a living world, full of poetry and truth, the same as all the books that mean something in literature.

THE AUTHOR

IOANA PÂRVULESCU was born in Braşov, Romania. She attended the Faculty of Letters in Bucharest and after graduation, became a teacher.Her real literary life began after the Revolution of '89. In 1993 she became an editor at *Romania literară*, a literary magazine where she published a weekly column for 18 years. She was also an editor at Humanitas publishing house for 10 years. She is currently a Professor at the Bucharest Faculty of Letters where she teaches modern Romanian litterature. Pârvulescu has translated extensively from French and German (Maurice Nadeau, Antoine de Saint-Exupéry, Angelus Silesius, Rilke etc.) and has authored ten books, among them *Return to the Inter-war Bucharest* (imaginative non-fiction, 2003), *In the Thick of the Nineteenth Century* (2005) and *Life Begins on Friday* (2009), which won her the EU Prize for Literature and has been translated into a number of European languages. Her most recent novel is *The Future Begins on Monday* (2012).

THE TRANSLATOR

ALISTAIR IAN BLYTH is one of the most active translators working from Romanian to English today. A native of Sunderland, England, Blyth attended the universities of Cambridge and Durham, and has resided for many years in Bucharest. His many translations from Romanian include: *Little Fingers* by Filip Florian; *Our Circus Presents* by Lucian Dan Teodorovici; *Occurrence in the Immediate Unreality* by Max Blecher; *Coming from an Off-Key Time* by Bogdan Suceavă and most recently, *The Bulgarian Truck* by Dumitru Tsepeneag, for Dalkey Archive Press.